JOHN LE CARRÉ

By John le Carré

Call for the Dead
A Murder of Quality
The Spy Who Came in from the Cold
The Looking Glass War
A Small Town in Germany
The Naive and Sentimental Lover
Tinker Tailor Soldier Spy
The Honourable Schoolboy
Smiley's People
The Little Drummer Girl
A Perfect Spy
The Russia House
The Secret Pilgrim
The Night Manager

John le Carré

THE SPY WHO CAME IN FROM THE COLD

THE LOOKING GLASS WAR

Hodder & Stoughton
LONDON SYDNEY AUCKLAND

The Spy Who Came in from the Cold
copyright © 1963 Le Carré Productions
The Looking Glass War
copyright © 1965 Le Carré Productions

The Spy Who Came in from the Cold
first published in Great Britain in 1963
by Victor Gollancz Limited
The Looking Glass War
first published in Great Britain in 1965
by William Heinemann Limited

This collected volume first published in Great Britain in 1994
by Hodder and Stoughton Limited
a division of Hodder Headline PLC

10 9 8 7 6 5 4 3 2 1

A CIP catalogue record for this title is available from
the British Library

ISBN 0 340 62322 5

Printed and bound in Great Britain by
Mackays of Chatham PLC, Chatham, Kent

Hodder and Stoughton Ltd
A Division of Hodder Headline PLC
338 Euston Road
London NW1 3BH

Contents

THE SPY WHO CAME IN FROM THE COLD

Chapter 1

CHECKPOINT

The American handed Leamas another cup of coffee and said, 'Why don't you go back and sleep? We can ring you if he shows up.'

Leamas said nothing, just stared through the window of the checkpoint, along the empty street.

'You can't wait for ever, sir. Maybe he'll come some other time. We can have the polizei contact the Agency: you can be back here in twenty minutes.'

'No,' said Leamas, 'it's nearly dark now.'

'But you can't wait for ever; he's nine hours over schedule.'

'If you want to go, go. You've been very good,' Leamas added. 'I'll tell Kramer you've been damn' good.'

'But how long will you wait?'

'Until he comes.' Leamas walked to the observation window and stood between the two motionless policemen. Their binoculars were trained on the Eastern checkpoint.

'He's waiting for the dark,' Leamas muttered. 'I know he is.'

'This morning you said he'd come across with the workmen.'

Leamas turned on him.

'Agents aren't aeroplanes. They don't have schedules. He's blown, he's on the run, he's frightened. Mundt's after him, now, at this moment. He's only got one chance. Let him choose his time.'

The younger man hesitated, wanting to go and not finding the moment.

A bell rang inside the hut. They waited, suddenly alert. A policeman said in German, 'Black Opel Rekord, Federal registration.'

'He can't see that far in the dusk, he's guessing,' the American whispered and then he added: 'How did Mundt know?'

'Shut up,' said Leamas from the window. One of the policemen left the hut and walked to the sandbag emplacement two feet short of the white demarcation which lay across the road like the base line of a tennis court. The other waited until his companion was crouched behind the telescope in the emplacement, then put down his binoculars, took his black helmet from the peg by the door and carefully adjusted it on his head. Somewhere high above the checkpoint the arclights sprang to life, casting theatrical beams on to the road in front of them.

The policeman began his commentary. Leamas knew it by heart.

'Car halts at the first control. Only one occupant, a woman. Escorted to the Vopo hut for document check.' They waited in silence.

'What's he saying?' said the American. Leamas didn't reply. Picking up a spare pair of binoculars, he gazed fixedly towards the East German controls.

'Document check completed. Admitted to the second control.'

'Mr Leamas, is this your man?' the American persisted. 'I ought to ring the Agency.'

'Wait.'

'Where's the car now? What's it doing?'

'Currency check, Customs,' Leamas snapped.

Leamas watched the car. There were two Vopos at the driver's door, one doing the talking, the other standing off, waiting. A third was sauntering round the car. He stopped at the boot, then walked back to the driver. He wanted the key. He opened the boot, looked inside, closed it, returned the key and walked thirty yards up the road to where, midway between the two opposing checkpoints, a solitary East German sentry was standing, a squat silhouette in boots and baggy trousers. The two stood together talking, self-conscious in the glare of the arclight.

With a perfunctory gesture they waved the car on. It reached the two sentries in the middle of the road and stopped again. They walked round the car, stood off and talked again; finally, almost unwillingly, they let it continue across the line to the Western sector.

'It is a man you're waiting for, Mr Leamas?' asked the American.

'Yes, it's a man.'

Pushing up the collar of his jacket, Leamas stepped outside into the icy October wind. He remembered the crowd then. It was something you forgot inside the hut, this group of puzzled faces. The people changed but the expressions were the same. It was like the helpless crowd that gathers round in a traffic accident, no one knowing how it happened, whether you should move the body.

Smoke or dust rose through the beam of the arclamps, a constant shifting pall between the margins of light.

Leamas walked over to the car, and said to the woman, 'Where is he?'

'They came for him and he ran. He took the bicycle. They can't have known about me.'

'Where did he go?'

'We had a room near Brandenburg, over a pub. He kept a few things there, money, papers. I think he'll have gone there. Then he'll come over.'

'Tonight?'

'He said he would come tonight. The others have all been caught – Paul, Viereck, Ländser, Salomon. He hasn't got long.'

Leamas stared at her for a moment in silence.

'Ländser too?'

'Last night.'

A policeman was standing at Leamas' side.

'You'll have to move away from here,' he said. 'It's forbidden to obstruct the crossing point.'

Leamas half turned.

'Go to hell,' he snapped. The German stiffened, but the woman said:

'Get in. We'll drive down to the corner.'

He got in beside her and they moved slowly down the road to a side turning.

'I didn't know you had a car,' he said.

'It's my husband's,' she replied indifferently. 'Karl never told you I was married, did he?' Leamas was silent. 'My husband and I work for an optical firm. They let us over to do business. Karl only told you my maiden name. He didn't want me to be mixed up with . . . you.'

Leamas took a key from his pocket.

'You'll want somewhere to stay,' he said. His voice sounded flat. 'There's an apartment in the Albrecht-Dürer-Strasse, next to the Museum. Number 28A. You'll find everything you want. I'll telephone you when he comes.'

'I'll stay here with you.'

'I'm not staying here. Go to the flat. I'll ring you. There's no point in waiting here now.'

'But he's coming to this crossing point.'

Leamas looked at her in surprise.

'He told you that?'

'Yes. He knows one of the Vopos there, the son of his landlord. It may help. That's why he chose this route.'

'And he told *you* that?'

'He trusts me. He told me everything.'

'Christ.'

He gave her the key and went back to the checkpoint hut, out of the cold. The policemen were muttering to each other as he entered; the larger one ostentatiously turned his back.

'I'm sorry,' said Leamas. 'I'm sorry I bawled you out.' He opened a tattered briefcase and rummaged in it until he found what he was looking for: a half bottle of whisky. With a nod the elder man accepted it, half filled each coffee mug and topped them up with black coffee.

'Where's the American gone?' asked Leamas.

'Who?'

'The CIA boy. The one who was with me.'

'Bed time,' said the elder man and they all laughed.

Leamas put down his mug and said:

'What are your rules for shooting to protect a man coming over? A man on the run.'

'We can only give covering fire if the Vopos shoot into our sector.'

'That means you can't shoot until a man's over the boundary?'

The older man said, 'We can't give covering fire, Mr . . .'

'Thomas,' Leamas replied, 'Thomas.' They shook hands, the two policemen pronouncing their own names as they did so.

'We can't give covering fire. That's the truth. They tell us there'd be war if we did.'

'It's nonsense,' said the younger policeman, emboldened by the whisky. 'If the Allies weren't here the Wall would be gone by now.'

'So would Berlin,' muttered the elder man.

'I've got a man coming over tonight,' said Leamas abruptly.

'Here? At this crossing point?'

'It's worth a lot to get him out. Mundt's men are looking for him.'

'There are still places where you can climb,' said the younger policeman.

'He's not that kind. He'll bluff his way through; he's got papers, if the papers are still good. He's got a bicycle.'

There was only one light in the checkpoint, a reading lamp with a green shade, but the glow of the arclights, like artificial moonlight, filled the cabin. Darkness had fallen, and with it silence.

They spoke as if they were afraid of being overheard. Leamas went to the window and waited, in front of him the road and to either side the Wall, a dirty, ugly thing of breeze blocks and strands of barbed wire, lit with cheap yellow light, like the backdrop for a concentration camp. East and west of the Wall lay the unrestored part of Berlin, a half-world of ruin, drawn in two dimensions, crags of war.

That damned woman, thought Leamas, and that fool Karl who'd lied about her. Lied by omission, as they all do, agents the world over. You teach them to cheat, to cover their tracks, and they cheat you as well. He'd only produced her once, after that dinner in the Schürzstrasse last year. Karl had just had his big scoop and Control had wanted to meet him. Control always came in on success. They'd had dinner together – Leamas, Control and Karl. Karl loved that kind of thing. He turned up looking like a Sunday School boy, scrubbed and shining, doffing his hat and all respectful. Control had shaken his hand for five minutes and said: 'I want you to know how pleased we are, Karl, damn' pleased.' Leamas had watched and thought, 'That'll cost us another couple of hundred a year.' When they'd finished dinner Control pumped their hands again, nodded significantly and, implying that he had to go off and risk his life somewhere else, got back into his chauffeur-driven car. Then Karl had laughed, and Leamas had laughed with him, and they'd finished the champagne, still laughing about Control. Afterwards they'd gone to the 'Alter Fass', Karl had insisted on it and there Elvira was waiting for them, a forty-year-old blonde, tough as nails.

'This is my best kept secret, Alec,' Karl had said, and Leamas was furious. Afterwards they'd had a row.

'How much does she know? Who is she? How did you meet her?' Karl sulked and refused to say. After that things went badly. Leamas tried to alter the routine, change the meeting places and the catch words, but Karl didn't like it. He knew what lay behind it and he didn't like it.

'If you don't trust her it's too late anyway,' he'd said, and Leamas took the hint and shut up. But he went carefully after that, told Karl much less, used more of the hocus-pocus of espionage technique. And there she was, out there in her car, knowing everything, the whole network, the safe house, everything; and Leamas swore, not for the first time, never to trust an agent again.

He went to the telephone and dialled the number of his flat. Frau Martha answered.

'We've got guests at the Dürer-Strasse,' said Leamas, 'a man and a woman.'

'Married?' asked Martha.

'Near enough,' said Leamas, and she laughed that frightful laugh. As he put down the receiver one of the policemen turned to him.

'Herr Thomas! Quick!' Leamas stepped to the observation window.

'A man, Herr Thomas,' the younger policeman whispered, 'with a bicycle.' Leamas picked up the binoculars.

It was Karl, the figure was unmistakable even at that distance, shrouded in an old Wehrmacht macintosh, pushing his bicycle. He's made it, thought Leamas, he must have made it, he's through the document check, only currency and Customs to go. Leamas watched Karl lean his bicycle against the railing, walk casually to the Customs hut. Don't overdo it, he thought. At last Karl came out, waved cheerfully to the man on the barrier, and the red and white pole swung slowly upwards. He was through, he was coming towards them, he had made it. Only the Vopo in the middle of the road, the line and safety.

At that moment Karl seemed to hear some sound, sense some danger; he glanced over his shoulder, began to pedal furiously, bending low over the handlebars. There was still the lonely sentry on the bridge, and he had turned and was watching Karl. Then, totally unexpected, the searchlights went on, white and brilliant, catching Karl and holding him in their beam like a rabbit in the headlights of a car. There came the see-saw wail of a siren, the sound of orders wildly shouted. In front of Leamas the two policemen dropped to their knees, peering through the sandbagged slits, deftly flicking the rapid load on their automatic rifles.

The East German sentry fired, quite carefully, away from them, into his own sector. The first shot seemed to thrust Karl forward, the second to pull him back. Somehow he was still moving, still on the bicycle, passing the sentry, and the sentry was still shooting at him. Then he sagged, rolled to the ground, and they heard quite clearly the clatter of the bike as it fell. Leamas hoped to God he was dead.

Chapter 2

THE CIRCUS

H e watched the Tempelhof runway sink beneath him.
Leamas was not a reflective man and not a particularly
philosophical one. He knew he was written off – it was a fact of
life which he would henceforth live with, as a man must live with
cancer or imprisonment. He knew there was no kind of preparation
which could have bridged the gap between then and now. He met
failure as one day he would probably meet death, with cynical
resentment and the courage of a solitary. He'd lasted longer than
most; now he was beaten. It is said a dog lives as long as its teeth;
metaphorically, Leamas' teeth had been drawn; and it was Mundt
who had drawn them.

Ten years ago he could have taken the other path – there were
desk jobs in that anonymous government building in Cambridge
Circus which Leamas could have taken and kept till he was God
knows how old; but Leamas wasn't made that way. You might as
well have asked a jockey to become a totalisator clerk as expect
Leamas to abandon operational life for the tendentious theorising
and clandestine self-interest of Whitehall. He had stayed on in
Berlin, conscious that Personnel had marked his file for review
at the end of every year – stubborn, wilful, contemptuous of
instruction, telling himself that something would turn up. Intelligence work has one moral law – it is justified by results. Even the
sophistry of Whitehall paid court to that law, and Leamas got
results. Until Mundt came.

It was odd how soon Leamas had realised that Mundt was the
writing on the wall.

Hans-Dieter Mundt, born forty-two years ago in Leipzig.
Leamas knew his dossier, knew the photograph on the inside of
the cover; the blank, hard face beneath the flaxen hair; knew by
heart the story of Mundt's rise to power as second man in the
Abteilung and effective head of operations. Mundt was hated even
within his own department. Leamas knew that from the evidence

of defectors, and from Riemeck, who as a member of the SED Praesidium sat on security committees with Mundt, and dreaded him. Rightly as it turned out, for Mundt had killed him.

Until 1959 Mundt had been a minor functionary of the Abteilung, operating in London under the cover of the East German Steel Mission. He returned to Germany in a hurry after murdering two of his own agents to save his skin and was not heard of for more than a year. Quite suddenly he reappeared at the Abteilung's headquarters in Leipzig as head of the Ways and Means Department, responsible for allocating currency, equipment and personnel for special tasks. At the end of that year came the big struggle for power within the Abteilung. The number and influence of Soviet liaison officers were drastically reduced, several of the old guard were dismissed on ideological grounds and three men emerged: Fiedler as head of counter-intelligence, Jahn took over from Mundt as head of facilities, and Mundt himself got the plum – deputy director of operations – at the age of forty-one. Then the new style began. The first agent Leamas lost was a girl. She was only a small link in the network; she was used for courier jobs. They shot her dead in the street as she left a West Berlin cinema. The police never found the murderer and Leamas was at first inclined to write the incident off as unconnected with her work. A month later a railway porter in Dresden, a discarded agent from Peter Guillam's network, was found dead and mutilated beside a railway track. Leamas knew it wasn't coincidence any longer. Soon after that two members of another network under Leamas' control were arrested and summarily sentenced to death. So it went on: remorseless and unnerving.

And now they had Karl, and Leamas was leaving Berlin as he had come – without a single agent worth a farthing. Mundt had won.

Leamas was a short man with close, iron-grey hair, and the physique of a swimmer. He was very strong. This strength was discernible in his back and shoulders, in his neck, and in the stubby formation of his hands and fingers.

He had a utilitarian approach to clothes, as he did to most other things, and even the spectacles he occasionally wore had steel rims. Most of his suits were of artificial fibre, none of them had waistcoats. He favoured shirts of the American kind with buttons on the points of the collars, and suede shoes with rubber soles.

He had an attractive face, muscular, and a stubborn line to his thin mouth. His eyes were brown and small; Irish, some said. It was hard to place Leamas. If he were to walk into a London club the porter would certainly not mistake him for a member; in a Berlin night club they usually gave him the best table. He looked like a man who could make trouble, a man who looked after his money; a man who was not quite a gentleman.

The air hostess thought he was interesting. She guessed he was North Country, which he might have been, and rich, which he was not. She put his age at fifty, which was about right. She guessed he was single, which was half true. Somewhere long ago there had been a divorce; somewhere there were children, now in their teens, who received their allowance from a rather odd private bank in the City.

'If you want another whisky,' said the air hostess, 'you'd better hurry. We shall be at London airport in twenty minutes.'

'No more.' He didn't look at her; he was looking out of the window at the grey-green fields of Kent.

Fawley met him at the airport and drove him to London.

'Control's pretty cross about Karl,' he said, looking sideways at Leamas. Leamas nodded.

'How did it happen?' asked Fawley.

'He was shot. Mundt got him.'

'Dead?'

'I should think so, by now. He'd better be. He nearly made it. He should never have hurried, they couldn't have been sure. The Abteilung got to the checkpoint just after he'd been let through. They started the siren and a Vopo shot him twenty yards short of the line. He moved on the ground for a moment, then lay still.'

'Poor bastard.'

'Precisely,' said Leamas.

Fawley didn't like Leamas, and if Leamas knew he didn't care. Fawley was a man who belonged to clubs and wore representative ties, pontificated on the skills of sportsmen and assumed a service rank in office correspondence. He thought Leamas suspect, and Leamas thought him a fool.

'What section are you in?' asked Leamas.

'Personnel.'

'Like it?'

'Fascinating.'

'Where do I go now? On ice?'

'Better let Control tell you, old boy.'

'Do you know?'

'Of course.'

'Then why the hell don't you tell me?'

'Sorry, old man,' Fawley replied, and Leamas suddenly very nearly lost his temper. Then he reflected that Fawley was probably lying anyway.

'Well, tell me one thing, do you mind? Have I got to look for a bloody flat in London?'

Fawley scratched at his ear: 'I don't think so, old man, no.'

'No? Thank God for that.'

They parked near Cambridge Circus, at a parking meter, and went together into the hall.

'You haven't got a pass, have you? You'd better fill in a slip, old man.'

'Since when have we had passes? McCall knows me as well as his own mother.'

'Just a new routine. Circus is growing, you know.'

Leamas said nothing, nodded at McCall and got into the lift without a pass.

Control shook his hand rather carefully, like a doctor feeling the bones.

'You must be awfully tired,' he said apologetically, 'do sit down.' That same dreary voice, the donnish bray.

Leamas sat down in a chair facing an olive green electric fire with a bowl of water balanced on the top of it.

'Do you find it cold?' Control asked. He was stooping over the fire rubbing his hands together. He wore a cardigan under his black jacket, a shabby brown one. Leamas remembered Control's wife, a stupid little woman called Mandy who seemed to think her husband was in the Coal Board. He supposed she had knitted it.

'It's so dry, that's the trouble,' Control continued. 'Beat the cold and you parch the atmosphere. Just as dangerous.' He went to the desk and pressed a button. 'We'll try and get some coffee,' he said, 'Ginnie's on leave, that's the trouble. They've given me some new girl. It really is too bad.'

He was shorter than Leamas remembered him; otherwise, just the same. The same affected detachment, the same donnish conceits; the same horror of draughts; courteous according to a formula miles removed from Leamas' experience. The same milk-and-water smile, the same elaborate diffidence, the same apologetic

– 18 –

adherence to a code of behaviour which he pretended to find ridiculous. The same banality.

He brought a packet of cigarettes from the desk and gave one to Leamas.

'You're going to find these more expensive,' he said, and Leamas nodded dutifully. Slipping the cigarettes into his pocket, Control sat down. There was a pause; finally Leamas said:

'Riemeck's dead.'

'Yes, indeed,' Control declared, as if Leamas had made a good point. 'It is very unfortunate. Most . . . I suppose that girl blew him – Elvira?'

'I suppose so.' Leamas wasn't going to ask him how he knew about Elvira.

'And Mundt had him shot,' Control added.

'Yes.'

Control got up and drifted round the room looking for an ash-tray. He found one and put it awkwardly on the floor between their two chairs.

'How did you feel? When Riemeck was shot, I mean? You saw it, didn't you?'

Leamas shrugged. 'I was bloody annoyed,' he said.

Control put his head on one side and half closed his eyes. 'Surely you felt more than that? Surely you were upset? That would be more natural.'

'I was upset. Who wouldn't be?'

'Did you like Riemeck – as a man?'

'I suppose so,' said Leamas helplessly. 'There doesn't seem much point in going into it,' he added.

'How did you spend the night, what was left of it, after Riemeck had been shot?'

'Look, what is this?' Leamas asked hotly; 'what are you getting at?'

'Riemeck was the last,' Control reflected, 'the last of a series of deaths. If my memory is right it began with the girl, the one they shot in Wedding, outside the cinema. Then there was the Dresden man, and the arrests at Jena. Like the ten little niggers. Now Paul, Viereck and Ländser – all dead. And finally Riemeck.' He smiled deprecatingly; 'that is quite a heavy rate of expenditure. I wondered if you'd had enough.'

'What do you mean – enough?'

'I wondered whether you were tired. Burnt out.' There was a long silence.

'That's up to you,' Leamas said at last.

'We have to live without sympathy, don't we? That's impossible of course. We act it to one another, all this hardness; but we aren't like that really. I mean . . . one can't be out in the cold all the time; one has to come in from the cold . . . d'you see what I mean?'

Leamas saw. He saw the long road outside Rotterdam, the long straight road beside the dunes, and the stream of refugees moving along it; saw the little aeroplane miles away, the procession stop and look towards it; and the plane coming in, neatly over the dunes; saw the chaos, the meaningless hell, as the bombs hit the road.

'I can't talk like this, Control,' Leamas said at last. 'What do you want me to do?'

'I want you to stay out in the cold a little longer.' Leamas said nothing, so Control went on: 'The ethic of our work, as I understand it, is based on a single assumption. That is, we are never going to be aggressors. Do you think that's fair?'

Leamas nodded. Anything to avoid talking.

'Thus we do disagreeable things, but we are *defensive*. That, I think, is still fair. We do disagreeable things so that ordinary people here and elsewhere can sleep safely in their beds at night. Is that too romantic? Of course, we occasionally do very wicked things;' he grinned like a schoolboy. 'And in weighing up the moralities, we rather go in for dishonest comparisons; after all, you can't compare the ideals of one side with the methods of the other, can you, now?'

Leamas was lost. He'd heard the man talked a lot of drivel before getting the knife in, but he'd never heard anything like this before.

'I mean, you've got to compare method with method, and ideal with ideal. I would say that since the war, our methods – ours and those of the opposition – have become much the same. I mean you can't be less ruthless than the opposition simply because your government's *policy* is benevolent, can you now?' He laughed quietly to himself: 'That would *never* do,' he said.

For God's sake, thought Leamas, it's like working for a bloody clergyman. What *is* he up to?

'That is why,' Control continued, 'I think we ought to try and get rid of Mundt . . . Oh really,' he said, turning irritably towards the door, 'where is that damned coffee?'

Control crossed to the door, opened it and talked to some unseen girl in the outer room. As he returned he said: 'I really think we *ought* to get rid of him if we can manage it.'

'Why? We've got nothing left in East Germany, nothing at all. You just said so – Riemeck was the last. We've nothing left to protect.'

Control sat down and looked at his hands for a while.

'That is not altogether true,' he said finally; 'but I don't think I need to bore you with the details.'

Leamas shrugged.

'Tell me,' Control continued, 'are you tired of spying? Forgive me if I repeat the question. I mean that is a phenomenon we understand here, you know. Like aircraft designers . . . metal fatigue, I think the term is. Do say if you are.'

Leamas remembered the flight home that morning and wondered.

'If you were,' Control added, 'we would have to find some other way of taking care of Mundt. What I have in mind is a little out of the ordinary.'

The girl came in with the coffee. She put the tray on the desk and poured out two cups. Control waited till she had left the room.

'Such a *silly* girl,' he said, almost to himself. 'It seems extraordinary they can't find good ones any more. I do wish Ginnie wouldn't go on holiday at times like this.' He stirred his coffee disconsolately for a while.

'We really must discredit Mundt,' he said. 'Tell me, do you drink a lot? Whisky and that kind of thing?'

Leamas had thought he was used to Control.

'I drink a bit. More than most I suppose.'

Control nodded understandingly. 'What do you know about Mundt?'

'He's a killer. He was here a year or two back with the East German Steel Mission. We had an Adviser here then: Maston.'

'Quite so.'

'Mundt was running an agent, the wife of an FO man. He killed her.'

'He tried to kill George Smiley. And of course he shot the woman's husband. He is a very distasteful man. Ex Hitler-Youth and all that kind of thing. Not at all the intellectual kind of Communist. A practitioner of the cold war.'

'Like us,' Leamas observed drily. Control didn't smile.

'George Smiley knew the case well. He isn't with us any more, but I think you ought to ferret him out. He's doing things on seventeenth-century Germany. He lives in Chelsea, just behind Sloane Square. Bywater Street, do you know it?'

'Yes.'

'And Guillam was on the case as well. He's in Satellites Four, on the first floor. I'm afraid everything's changed since your day.'

'Yes.'

'Spend a day or two with them. They know what I have in mind. Then I wondered if you'd care to stay with me for the weekend. My wife,' he added hastily, 'is looking after her mother, I'm afraid. It will be just you and I.'

'Thanks. I'd like to.'

'We can talk about things in comfort then. It would be very nice. I think you might make a lot of money out of it. You can have whatever you make.'

'Thanks.'

'That is, of course, if you're *sure you want* to . . . no metal fatigue or anything?'

'If it's a question of killing Mundt, I'm game.'

'Do you really feel that?' Control enquired politely. And then, having looked at Leamas thoughtfully for a moment, he observed: 'Yes, I really think you do. But you mustn't feel you *have* to say it. I mean in our world we pass so quickly out of the register of hate or love – like certain sounds a dog can't hear. All that's left in the end is a kind of nausea; you never want to cause suffering again. Forgive me, but isn't that rather what you felt when Karl Riemeck was shot? Not hate for Mundt, nor love for Karl, but a sickening jolt like a blow on a numb body . . . They tell me you walked all night – just walked through the streets of Berlin. Is that right?'

'It's right that I went for a walk.'

'All night?'

'Yes.'

'What happened to Elvira?'

'God knows . . . I'd like to take a swing at Mundt,' he said.

'Good . . . good. Incidentally, if you should meet any old friends in the meantime, I don't think there's any point in discussing this with them. In fact,' Control added after a moment, 'I should be rather short with them. Let them think we've treated you badly. It's as well to begin as one intends to continue, isn't it?'

Chapter 3

DECLINE

It surprised no one very much when they put Leamas on the shelf. In the main, they said, Berlin had been a failure for years, and someone had to take the rap. Besides, he was old for operational work, where your reflexes often had to be as quick as those of a professional tennis player. Leamas had done good work in the war, everyone knew that. In Norway and Holland he had somehow remained demonstrably alive, and at the end of it they gave him a medal and let him go. Later, of course, they got him to come back. It was bad luck about his pension, decidedly bad luck. Accounts Section had let it out, in the person of Elsie. Elsie said in the canteen that poor Alec Leamas would only have £400 a year to live on because of his interrupted service. Elsie felt it was a rule they really ought to change; after all, Mr Leamas had *done* the service, hadn't he? But there they were with Treasury on their backs, not a bit like the old days, and what could they do? Even in the bad days of Maston they'd managed things better.

Leamas, the new men were told, was the old school; blood, guts and cricket and School Cert. French. In Leamas' case this happened to be unfair, since he was bilingual in German and English and his Dutch was admirable; he also disliked cricket. But it was true that he had no degree.

Leamas' contract had a few months to run, and they put him in Banking to do his time. Banking Section was different from Accounts; it dealt with overseas payments, financing agents and operations. Most of the jobs in Banking could have been done by an office boy were it not for the high degree of secrecy involved, and thus Banking was one of several Sections of the Service which were regarded as laying-out places for officers shortly to be buried.

Leamas went to seed.

The process of going to seed is generally considered to be a protracted one, but in Leamas this was not the case. In the full view of his colleagues he was transformed from a man honourably put aside to a resentful, drunken wreck – and all within a few months. There is a kind of stupidity among drunks, particularly when they are sober, a kind of disconnection which the unobservant interpret as vagueness and which Leamas seemed to acquire with unnatural speed. He developed small dishonesties, borrowed insignificant sums from secretaries and neglected to return them, arrived late or left early under some mumbled pretext. At first his colleagues treated him with indulgence; perhaps his decline scared them in the same way as we are scared by cripples, beggars and invalids because we fear we could ourselves become them; but in the end his neglect, his brutal, unreasoning malice isolated him.

Rather to people's surprise, Leamas didn't seem to mind being put on the shelf. His will seemed suddenly to have collapsed. The débutante secretaries, reluctant to believe that Intelligence Services are peopled by ordinary mortals, were alarmed to notice that Leamas had become definitely seedy. He took less care of his appearance and less notice of his surroundings, he lunched in the canteen which was normally the preserve of junior staff, and it was rumoured that he was drinking. He became a solitary, belonging to that tragic class of active men prematurely deprived of activity; swimmers barred from the water or actors banished from the stage.

Some said he had made a mistake in Berlin, and that was why his network had been rolled up; no one quite knew. All agreed that he had been treated with unusual harshness, even by a personnel department not famed for its philanthropy. They would point to him covertly as he went by, as men will point to an athlete of the past, and say: 'That's Leamas. He put up a black in Berlin. Pathetic the way he's let himself go.'

And then one day he had vanished. He said good-bye to no one, not even, apparently, Control. In itself that was not surprising. The nature of the Service precluded elaborate farewells and the presentation of gold watches, but even by these standards Leamas' departure seemed abrupt. So far as could be judged, his departure occurred before the statutory termination of his contract. Elsie, of Accounts Section, offered one or two crumbs of information: Leamas had drawn the balance of his pay in cash, which, if Elsie knew anything, meant he was having trouble with his bank. His gratuity was to be paid at the turn of the month, she couldn't say how much but it wasn't four figures, poor lamb. His National Insurance card had been sent on. Personnel had an address for him, Elsie added with a sniff, but of course they weren't revealing it, not Personnel.

Then there was the story about the money. It leaked out – no one, as usual, knew where from – that Leamas' sudden departure was connected with irregularities in the accounts of Banking Section. A largish sum was missing (not three figures but four, according to a lady with blue hair who worked in the telephone room) and they'd got it back, nearly all of it, and they'd stuck a lien on his pension. Others said they didn't believe it – if Alec had wanted to rob the till, they said, he'd know better ways of doing it than fiddling with HQ accounts. Not that he wasn't capable of it – he'd just have done it better. But those less impressed by Leamas' criminal potential pointed at his large consumption of alcohol, at the expense of maintaining a separate household, at the fatal disparity between pay at home and allowances abroad, and above all at the temptations put in the way of a man handling large sums of hot money when he knew that his days in the Service were numbered. All agreed that if Alec had dipped his hands in the honey pot he was finished for all time – the Resettlement people wouldn't look at him and Personnel would give him no reference – or one so icy cold that the most enthusiastic employer would shiver at the sight of it. Peculation was the one sin Personnel would never let you forget – and they never forgot it themselves. If it was true that Alec had robbed the Circus, he would take the wrath of Personnel with him to the grave – and Personnel would not so much as pay for the shroud.

For a week or two after his departure, a few people wondered what had become of him. But his former friends had already learnt to keep clear of him. He had become a resentful bore, constantly attacking the Service and its administration, and what he called the 'Cavalry boys' who, he said, managed its affairs as if it were a regimental club. He never missed an opportunity of railing against the Americans and their intelligence agencies. He seemed to hate them more than the Abteilung, to which he seldom, if ever, referred. He would hint that it was they who had compromised his network; this seemed to be an obsession with him, and it was poor reward for attempts to console him, it made him bad company, so that those who had known and even tacitly liked him, wrote him off. Leamas' departure caused only a ripple on the water; with other winds and the changing of the seasons it was soon forgotten.

His flat was small and squalid, done in brown paint with photographs of Clovelly. It looked directly on to the grey backs of three stone warehouses, the windows of which were drawn, for aesthetic reasons, in creosote. Above the warehouse there lived an Italian family, quarrelling at night and beating carpets in the morning. Leamas had few possessions with which to brighten his rooms. He bought some shades to cover the light bulbs, and two pairs of sheets to replace the hessian squares provided by the landlord. The rest Leamas tolerated: the flower pattern curtains, not lined or hemmed, the fraying brown carpets and the clumsy darkwood furniture, like something from a seamen's hostel. From a yellow, crumbling geyser he obtained hot water for a shilling.

He needed a job. He had no money, none at all. So perhaps the stories of embezzlement were true. The offers of resettlement which the Service made had seemed to Leamas lukewarm and peculiarly unsuitable. He tried first to get a job in commerce. A firm of industrial adhesive manufacturers showed interest in his application for the post of assistant manager and personnel officer. Unconcerned by the inadequate reference with which the Service provided him, they demanded no qualifications, and offered him six hundred a year. He stayed for a week, by which time the foul stench of decaying fish oil had permeated his clothes and hair, lingering in his nostrils like the smell of death. No amount of washing would remove it, so that in the end Leamas had his hair cut short to the scalp and threw away two of his best suits. He spent another week trying to sell encyclopaedias to suburban housewives, but he was not a man that housewives liked or understood; they did not want Leamas, let alone his encyclopaedias. Night after night he returned wearily to his flat, his ridiculous sample under his arm. At the end of a week he telephoned the company and told them he had sold nothing. Expressing no surprise, they reminded him of his obligation to return the sample if he discontinued acting on their behalf, and rang off. Leamas stalked out of the telephone booth in a fury, leaving the sample behind him, went to a pub and got very drunk at a cost of twenty-five shillings, which he could not afford. They threw him out for shouting at a woman who tried to pick him up. They told him never to come back, but they'd forgotten all about it a week later. They were beginning to know Leamas there.

They were beginning to know him elsewhere too, the grey, shambling figure from the Mansions. Not a wasted word did he speak, not a friend, neither man, woman nor beast did he have. They guessed he was in trouble, run away from his wife like as not. He never knew the price of anything, never remembered it when he was told. He patted all his pockets whenever he looked for change, he never remembered to bring a basket, always buying carrier bags. They didn't like him in the street, but they were almost sorry for him. They thought he was dirty too, the way he didn't shave weekends, and his shirts all grubby. A Mrs McCaird from Sudbury Avenue cleaned for him for a week, but having never received a civil word from him withdrew her labour. She was an important source of information in the street, where tradesmen told one another what they needed to know in case he asked for credit. Mrs McCaird's advice was against credit. Leamas never had a letter, she said, and they agreed that that was serious. He'd no pictures and only a few books; she thought one of the books was dirty but couldn't be sure because it was in foreign writing. It was her opinion he had a bit to live on, and that that bit was running out. She knew he drew Benefit on Thursdays. Bayswater was warned, and needed no second warning. They heard from Mrs McCaird that he drank like a fish: this was confirmed by the publican. Publicans and charwomen are not in the way of accommodating their clients with credit; but their information is treasured by those who are.

Chapter 4

LIZ

Finally he took the job in the library. The Labour Exchange had put him on to it each Thursday morning as he drew his unemployment benefit, and he'd always turned it down.

'It's not really your cup of tea,' Mr Pitt said, 'but the pay's fair and the work's easy for an educated man.'

'What sort of library?' Leamas asked.

'It's the Bayswater Library for Psychic Research. It's an endowment. They've got thousands of volumes, all sorts, and they've been left a whole lot more. They want another helper.'

He took his dole and the slip of paper. 'They're an odd lot,' Mr Pitt added, 'but then you're not a stayer anyway, are you? I think it's time you gave them a try, don't you?'

It was odd about Pitt. Leamas was certain he'd seen him before somewhere. At the Circus, during the war.

The library was like a church hall, and very cold. The black oil stoves at either end made it smell of paraffin. In the middle of the room was a cubicle like a witness-box and inside it sat Miss Crail, the librarian.

It had never occurred to Leamas that he might have to work for a woman. No one at the Labour Exchange had said anything about that.

'I'm the new help,' he said; 'my name's Leamas.'

Miss Crail looked up sharply from her card index, as if she had heard a rude word. 'Help? What do you mean, help?'

'Assistant. From the Labour Exchange. Mr Pitt.' He pushed across the counter a roneoed form with his particulars entered in a sloping hand. She picked it up and studied it.

'You are Mr Leamas.' This was not a question, but the first stage of a laborious fact-finding investigation.

'And you are from the Labour Exchange.'

'No. I was sent by the Exchange. They told me you needed an assistant.'

'I see.' A wooden smile.

At that moment the telephone rang: she lifted the receiver and began arguing with somebody, fiercely. Leamas guessed they argued all the time; there were no preliminaries. Her voice just rose a key and she began arguing about some tickets for a concert. He listened for a minute or two and then drifted towards the bookshelves. He noticed a girl in one of the alcoves standing on a ladder sorting large volumes.

'I'm the new man,' he said, 'my name's Leamas.'

She came down from the ladder and shook his hand a little formally.

'I'm Liz Gold. How d'you do. Have you met Miss Crail?'

'Yes, but she's on the phone at the moment.'

'Arguing with her mother I expect. What are you going to do?'

'I don't know. Work.'

'We're marking at the moment; Miss Crail's started a new index.'

She was a tall girl, ungainly, with a long waist and long legs. She wore flat, ballet-type shoes to reduce her height. Her face, like her body, had large components which seemed to hesitate between plainness and beauty. Leamas guessed she was twenty-two or three, and Jewish.

'It's just a question of checking that all the books are in the shelves. This is the reference bit, you see. When you've checked you pencil in the new reference and mark it off on the index.'

'What happens then?'

'Only Miss Crail's allowed to ink in the reference. It's the rule.'

'Whose rule?'

'Miss Crail's. Why don't you start on the archaeology?'

Leamas nodded and together they walked to the next alcove where a shoe-box full of cards lay on the floor.

'Have you done this kind of thing before?' she asked.

'No.' He stooped and picked up a handful of cards and shuffled through them. 'Mr Pitt sent me. From the Exchange.' He put the cards back.

'Is Miss Crail the only person who can ink the cards, too?' Leamas enquired.

'Yes.'

She left him there, and after a moment's hesitation he took out a book and looked at the fly-leaf. It was called *Archaeological Discoveries in Asia Minor*, volume four. They only seemed to have volume four.

*   *   *

It was one o'clock and Leamas was very hungry, so he walked over to where Liz Gold was sorting and said:

'What happens about lunch?'

'Oh, I bring sandwiches.' She looked a little embarrassed. 'You can have some of mine if that would help. There's no café for miles.'

Leamas shook his head.

'I'll go out, thanks. Got some shopping to do.' She watched him push his way through the swing doors.

It was half past two when he came back. He smelt of whisky. He had one carrier bag full of vegetables and another containing groceries. He put them down in a corner of the alcove and wearily began again on the archaeology books. He'd been marking for about ten minutes when he became aware that Miss Crail was watching him.

'*Mister* Leamas.' He was half-way up the ladder, so he looked down over his shoulder and said:

'Yes?'

'Do you know where these carrier bags come from?'

'They're mine.'

'I see. They are yours.' Leamas waited. 'I regret,' she continued at last, 'that we do not allow it, bringing shopping in to the library.'

'Where else can I put it? There's nowhere else I *can* put it.'

'Not in the library,' she replied. Leamas ignored her, and returned his attention to the archaeology section.

'If you only took the normal lunch break,' Miss Crail continued, 'you would not have time to go shopping. Neither of *us* does, Miss Gold or myself; *we* do not have time to shop.'

'Why don't you take an extra half-hour?' Leamas asked, 'you'd have time then. If you're pushed you can work another half-hour in the evening. If you're pressed.'

She stayed for some moments, just watching him and obviously thinking of something to say. Finally she announced:

'I shall discuss it with Mr Ironside,' and went away.

At exactly half past five Miss Crail put on her coat and, with a pointed: 'Good night, Miss Gold', left. Leamas guessed she had been brooding on the carrier bags all afternoon. He went in to the next alcove where Liz Gold was sitting on the bottom rung of her ladder reading what looked like a tract. When she saw Leamas she dropped it guiltily into her handbag and stood up.

'Who's Mr Ironside?' Leamas asked.

'I don't think he exists,' she replied. 'He's her big gun when she's stuck for an answer. I asked her once who he was. She went all shifty and mysterious and said "Never mind". I don't think he exists.'

'I'm not sure Miss Crail does,' said Leamas and Liz Gold smiled.

At six o'clock she locked up and gave the keys to the curator, a very old man with First War shellshock who, said Liz, sat awake all night in case the Germans made a counterattack. It was bitterly cold outside.

'Got far to go?' asked Leamas.

'Twenty minutes' walk. I always walk it. Have you?'

'Not far,' said Leamas. 'Good night.'

He walked slowly back to the flat. He let himself in and turned the light switch. Nothing happened. He tried the light in the tiny kitchen and finally the electric fire that plugged in by his bed. On the door mat was a letter. He picked it up and took it out into the pale, yellow light of the staircase. It was the electricity company, regretting that the area manager had no alternative but to cut off the electricity until the outstanding account of nine pounds four shillings and eightpence had been settled.

He had become an enemy of Miss Crail, and enemies were what Miss Crail liked. Either she scowled at him or she ignored him, and when he came close, she began to tremble, looking to left and right, either for something with which to defend herself, or perhaps for a line of escape. Occasionally she would take immense umbrage, such as when he hung his macintosh on *her* peg, and she stood in front of it shaking, for fully five minutes, until Liz spotted her and called Leamas. Leamas went over to her and said:

'What's troubling you, Miss Crail?'

'Nothing,' she replied in a breathy, clipped way, 'nothing at all.'

'Something wrong with my coat?'

'Nothing at all.'

'Fine,' he replied, and went back to his alcove. She quivered all that day, and conducted a telephone call in a stage whisper for half the morning.

'She's telling her mother,' said Liz. 'She always tells her mother. She tells her about me too.'

Miss Crail developed such an intense hatred for Leamas that she found it impossible to communicate with him. On pay days he would come back from lunch and find an envelope on the third rung of his ladder with his name misspelt on the outside. The first time it happened he took the money over to her with the envelope and said, 'It's L-E-A, Miss Crail, and only one S,' whereupon she was seized with a veritable palsy, rolling her eyes and fumbling erratically with her pencil until Leamas went away. She conspired into the telephone for hours after that.

About three weeks after Leamas began work at the library Liz asked him to supper. She pretended it was an idea that had come to her quite suddenly, at five o'clock that evening; she seemed to realise that if she were to ask him for tomorrow or the next day he would forget or just not come, so she asked him at five o'clock. Leamas seemed reluctant to accept, but in the end he did.

They walked to her flat through the rain and they might have been anywhere – Berlin, London, any town where paving stones turn to lakes of light in the evening rain, and the traffic shuffles despondently through wet streets.

It was the first of many meals which Leamas had at her flat. He came when she asked him, and she asked him often. He never spoke much. When she discovered he would come, she took to laying the table in the morning before leaving for the library. She even prepared the vegetables beforehand and had the candles on the table, for she loved candlelight. She always knew that there was something deeply wrong with Leamas, and that one day, for some reason she could not understand, he might break and she would never see him again. She tried to tell him she knew; she said to him one evening:

'You must go when you want. I'll never follow you, Alec,' and his brown eyes rested on her for a moment: 'I'll tell you when,' he replied.

Her flat was just a bed-sitting-room and a kitchen. In the sitting-room were two armchairs, a divan bed, and a bookcase full of paperback books, mainly classics which she had never read.

After supper she would talk to him, and he would lie on the divan, smoking. She never knew how much he heard, she didn't care. She would kneel by the bed holding his hand against her cheek, talking.

Then one evening she said to him:

'Alec, what do you believe in? Don't laugh – tell me.' She waited and at last he said:

'I believe an eleven bus will take me to Hammersmith. I don't believe it's driven by Father Christmas.'

She seemed to consider this and at last she asked again:

'But what do you believe in?'

Leamas shrugged.

'You must believe in something,' she persisted: 'something like God – I know you do, Alec; you've got that look sometimes, as if you'd got something special to do, like a priest. Alec, don't smile, it's true.'

He shook his head.

'Sorry, Liz, you've got it wrong. I don't like Americans and public schools. I don't like military parades and people who play soldiers.' Without smiling he added, 'And I don't like conversations about Life.'

'But, Alec, you might as well say –'

'I should have added,' Leamas interrupted, 'that I don't like people who tell me what I ought to think.' She knew he was getting angry but she couldn't stop herself any more.

'That's because you don't *want* to think, you don't dare! There's some poison in your mind, some hate. You're a fanatic, Alec. I know you are, but I don't know what about. You're a fanatic who doesn't want to convert people, and that's a dangerous thing. You're like a man who's . . . sworn vengeance or something.' The brown eyes rested on her. When he spoke she was frightened by the menace in his voice.

'If I were you,' he said roughly, 'I'd mind my own business.'

And then he smiled, a roguish smile. He hadn't smiled like that before and Liz knew he was putting on the charm.

'What does Liz believe in?' he asked, and she replied:

'I can't be had that easy, Alec.'

Later that night they talked about it again. Leamas brought it up – he asked her whether she was religious.

'You've got me wrong,' she said, 'all wrong. I don't believe in God.'

'Then what do you believe in?'

'History.'

He looked at her in astonishment for a moment, then laughed.

'Oh, Liz . . . oh *no*. You're not a bloody Communist?' She nodded, blushing like a small girl at his laughter, angry and relieved that he didn't care.

She made him stay that night and they became lovers. He left at five in the morning. She couldn't understand it; she was so proud and he seemed ashamed.

★　　★　　★

He left her flat and turned down the empty street towards the park. It was foggy. Some way down the road – not far, twenty yards, perhaps a bit more – stood the figure of a man in a raincoat, short and rather plump. He was leaning against the railings of the park, silhouetted in the shifting mist. As Leamas approached, the mist seemed to thicken, closing in around the figure at the railings, and when it parted the man was gone.

Chapter 5

CREDIT

Then one day about a week later, he didn't come to the library. Miss Crail was delighted; by half past eleven she had told her mother, and on returning from lunch she stood in front of the archaeology shelves where he had been working since he came. She stared with theatrical concentration at the rows of books and Liz knew she was pretending to work out whether Leamas had stolen anything.

Liz entirely ignored her for the rest of the day, failed to reply when she addressed her and worked with assiduous application. When the evening came she walked home and cried herself to sleep.

The next morning she arrived early at the library. She somehow felt that the sooner she got there, the sooner Leamas might come; but as the morning dragged on her hopes faded, and she knew he would never come. She had forgotten to make sandwiches for herself that day so she decided to take a bus to the Bayswater Road and go to the ABC. She felt sick and empty, but not hungry. Should she go and find him? She had promised never to follow him, but he had promised to tell her; should she go and find him?

She hailed a taxi and gave his address.

She made her way up the dingy staircase and pressed the bell of his door. The bell seemed to be broken; she heard nothing. There were three bottles of milk on the mat and a letter from the electricity company. She hesitated a moment, then banged on the door, and she heard the faint groan of a man. She rushed downstairs to the flat below, hammered and rang at the door. There was no reply so she ran down another flight and found herself in the back room of a grocer's shop. An old woman sat in a corner, rocking back and forth in her chair.

'The top flat,' Liz almost shouted, 'somebody's very ill. Who's got a key?'

The old woman looked at her for a moment, then called towards the front room, where the shop was.

'Arthur, come in here, Arthur, there's a girl here!'

A man in a brown overall and grey trilby hat looked round the door and said:

'Girl?'

'There's someone seriously ill in the top flat,' said Liz, 'he can't get to the front door to open it. Have you got a key?'

'No,' replied the grocer, 'but I've got a hammer,' and they hurried up the stairs together, the grocer, still in his trilby, carrying a heavy screwdriver and a hammer. He knocked on the door sharply, and they waited breathless for an answer. There was none.

'I heard a groan before, I promise I did,' Liz whispered.

'Will you pay for this door if I bust it?'

'Yes.'

The hammer made a terrible noise. With three blows he had wrenched out a piece of the frame and the lock came with it. Liz went in first and the grocer followed. It was bitterly cold in the room and dark, but on the bed in the corner they could make out the figure of a man.

'Oh God,' thought Liz, 'if he's dead I don't think I can touch him,' but she went to him and he was alive. Drawing the curtains, she knelt beside the bed.

'I'll call you if I need you, thank you,' she said without looking back, and the grocer nodded and went downstairs.

'Alec, what is it, what's making you ill? What is it, Alec?'

Leamas moved his head on the pillow. His sunken eyes were closed. The dark beard stood out against the pallor of his face.

'Alec, you must tell me, please, Alec.' She was holding one of his hands in hers. The tears were running down her cheeks. Desperately she wondered what to do; then, getting up, she ran to the tiny kitchen and put on a kettle. She wasn't quite clear what she would make, but it comforted her to do something. Leaving the kettle on the gas she picked up her handbag, took Leamas' key from the bedside table and ran downstairs, down the four flights into the street, and crossed the road to Mr Sleaman, the Chemist. She bought some calvesfoot jelly, some essence of beef and a bottle of aspirin. She got to the door; then went back and bought a packet of rusks. Altogether it cost her sixteen shillings, which left four shillings in her handbag and eleven pounds in her post office book, but she couldn't draw any of that till tomorrow. By the time she returned to his flat the kettle was just boiling.

She made the beef tea like her mother used to, in a glass with a teaspoon in to stop it cracking, and all the time she glanced towards him, as if she were afraid he was dead.

She had to prop him up to make him drink the tea. He only had one pillow and there were no cushions in the room, so taking his overcoat down from the back of the door she made a bundle of it and arranged it behind the pillow. It frightened her to touch him, he was drenched in sweat, so that his short grey hair was damp and slippery. Putting the cup beside the bed she held his head with one hand, and fed him the tea with the other. After he had taken a few spoonfuls, she crushed two aspirin and gave them to him in the spoon. She talked to him as if he were a child, sitting on the edge of the bed looking at him, sometimes letting her fingers run over his head and face, whispering his name over and over again, 'Alec, Alec.'

Gradually his breathing became more regular, his body more relaxed as he drifted from the taut pain of fever to the calm of sleep; Liz, watching him, sensed that the worst was over. Suddenly she realised it was almost dark.

Then she felt ashamed, because she knew she should have cleaned and tidied. Jumping up, she fetched the carpet sweeper and a duster from the kitchen, and set to work with feverish energy. She found a clean teacloth and spread it neatly on the bedside table and she washed up the odd cups and saucers which lay around the kitchen. When everything was done she looked at her watch and it was half past eight. She put the kettle on and went back to the bed. Leamas was looking at her.

'Alec, don't be cross, please don't,' she said. 'I'll go. I promise I will, but let me make you a proper meal. You're ill, you can't go on like this, you're . . . oh, Alec,' and she broke down and wept, holding both hands over her face, the tears running between her fingers like the tears of a child. He let her cry, watching her with his brown eyes, his hands holding the sheet.

She helped him wash and shave and she found some clean bedclothes. She gave him some calvesfoot jelly, and some breast of chicken from the jar she'd bought at Mr Sleaman's. Sitting on the bed she watched him eat, and she thought she had never been so happy before.

Soon he fell asleep, and she drew the blanket over his shoulders and went to the window. Parting the threadbare curtains, she raised the sash and looked out. Two other windows in the courtyard were lit. In one she could see the flickering blue shadow of a television screen, the figures round it held motionless in its spell; in the other a woman, quite young, was arranging curlers in her hair. Liz wanted to weep at the crabbed delusion of their dreams.

She fell asleep in the armchair and did not wake until it was nearly light, feeling stiff and cold. She went to the bed: Leamas stirred as she looked at him and she touched his lips with the tip of her finger. He did not open his eyes but gently took her arm and drew her down on to the bed and suddenly she wanted him terribly, and nothing mattered, and she kissed him again and again and when she looked at him he seemed to be smiling.

She came every day for six days. He never spoke to her much and once, when she asked him if he loved her, he said he didn't believe in fairy tales. She would lie on the bed, her head against his chest, and sometimes he would put his thick fingers in her hair, holding it quite tight, and Liz laughed and said it hurt. On the Friday evening she found him dressed but not shaved and she wondered why he hadn't shaved. For some imperceptible reason she was alarmed. Little things were missing from the room – his clock and the cheap portable wireless that had been on the table. She wanted to ask and did not dare. She had bought some eggs and ham and she cooked them for their supper while Leamas sat on the bed and smoked one cigarette after another. When it was ready he went to the kitchen and came back with a bottle of red wine.

He hardly spoke at supper, and she watched him, her fear growing until she could bear it no more and she cried out suddenly:

'Alec . . . oh, Alec . . . what is it? Is it good-bye?'

He got up from the table, took her hands, and kissed her in a way he'd never done before and spoke to her softly for a long time, told her things she only dimly understood, only half heard because all the time she knew it was the end and nothing mattered any more.

'Good-bye, Liz,' he said. 'Good-bye,' and then: 'Don't follow me. Not again.'

Liz nodded and muttered: 'Like we said.' She was thankful for the biting cold of the street and for the dark which hid her tears.

It was the next morning, the Saturday, that Leamas asked at the grocer's for credit. He did it without much artistry, in a way not calculated to ensure him success. He ordered half a dozen items –

they didn't come to more than a pound – and when they had been wrapped and put into the carrier bag he said:

'You'd better send me that account.'

The grocer smiled a difficult smile and said:

'I'm afraid I can't do that'; the 'sir' was definitely missing.

'Why the hell not?' asked Leamas, and the queue behind him stirred uneasily.

'Don't know you,' replied the grocer.

'Don't be bloody silly,' said Leamas, 'I've been coming here for four months.' The grocer coloured.

'We always ask for a banker's reference before giving credit,' he said, and Leamas lost his temper.

'Don't talk bloody cock,' he shouted. 'Half your customers have never seen the inside of a bank and never bloody well will.' This was heresy beyond bearing, since it was true.

'I don't know you,' the grocer repeated thickly, 'and I don't like you. Now get out of my shop.' And he tried to recover the parcel which unfortunately Leamas was already holding. Opinions later differed as to what happened next. Some said the grocer, in trying to recover the bag, pushed Leamas; others say he did not. Whether he did or not, Leamas hit him, most people think twice, without disengaging his right hand, which still held the carrier bag. He seemed to deliver the blow not with the fist but with the side of the left hand, and then, as part of the same phenomenally rapid movement, with the left elbow; and the grocer fell straight over and lay as still as a rock. It was said in court later, and not contested by the defence, that the grocer had two injuries – a fractured cheek bone from the first blow and a dislocated jaw from the second. The coverage in the daily press was adequate, but not over-elaborate.

Chapter 6

CONTACT

At night he lay on his bunk listening to the sounds of the prisoners. There was a boy who sobbed and an old lag who sang 'On Ilkley Moor bar t'at' beating out the time on his food tin. There was a warder who shouted, 'Shut up, George, you miserable sod', after each verse, but no one took any notice. There was an Irishman who sang songs about the IRA, though the others said he was in for rape.

Leamas took as much exercise as he could during the day in the hope that he would sleep at night; but it was no good. At night you knew you were in prison: at night there was nothing, no trick of vision or self-delusion which saved you from the nauseating enclosure of the cell. You could not keep out the taste of prison, the smell of prison uniform, the stench of prison sanitation heavily disinfected, the noises of captive men. It was then, at night, that the indignity of captivity became urgently insufferable, it was then that Leamas longed to walk in the friendly sunshine of a London park. It was then that he hated the grotesque steel cage that held him, had to force back the urge to fall upon the bars with his bare fists, to split the skulls of his gaolers and burst into the free, free space of London. Sometimes he thought of Liz. He would direct his mind towards her briefly like the shutter of a camera, recall for a moment the soft-hard touch of her long body, then put her from his memory. Leamas was not a man accustomed to living on dreams.

He was contemptuous of his cell mates, and they hated him. They hated him because he succeeded in being what each in his heart longed to be: a mystery. He preserved from collectivisation some discernible part of his personality; he could not be drawn at moments of sentiment to talk of his girl, his family or his children. They knew nothing of Leamas; they waited, but he did not come to them. New prisoners are largely of two kinds – there are those who for shame, fear or shock wait in fascinated horror to be initiated into the lore of prison life, and there are those who trade on their wretched novelty in order to endear themselves to the community. Leamas did neither of these things. He seemed pleased to despise them all, and they hated him because, like the world outside, he did not need them. After about ten days they had had enough. The great had had no homage, the small had had no comfort, so they crowded him in the dinner queue. Crowding is a prison ritual akin to the eighteenth-century practice of jostling. It has the virtue of an apparent accident, in which the prisoner's mess tin is upturned, and its contents spilt on his uniform. Leamas was barged from one side, while from the other an obliging hand descended on his forearm, and the thing was done. Leamas said nothing, looked thoughtfully at the two men on either side of him, and accepted in silence the filthy rebuke of a warder who knew quite well what had happened.

Four days later, while working with a hoe on the prison flower-bed, he seemed to stumble. He was holding the hoe with both hands across his body, the end of the handle protruding about six inches from his right fist. As he strove to recover his balance the prisoner to his right doubled up with a grunt of agony, his arms across his stomach. There was no more crowding after that.

Perhaps the strangest thing of all about prison was the brown paper parcel when he left. In a ridiculous way it reminded him of the marriage service – with this ring I thee wed, with this paper parcel I return thee to society. They handed it to him and made him sign for it, and it contained all he had in the world. There was nothing else. Leamas felt it the most dehumanising moment of the three months, and he determined to throw the parcel away as soon as he got outside.

He seemed a quiet prisoner. There had been no complaints against him. The Governor, who was vaguely interested in his case, secretly put the whole thing down to the Irish blood he swore he could detect in Leamas.

'What are you going to do,' he asked, 'when you leave here?' Leamas replied, without a ghost of a smile, that he thought he would make a new start, and the Governor said that was an excellent thing to do.

'What about your family?' he asked. 'Couldn't you make it up with your wife?'

'I'll try,' Leamas had replied indifferently; 'but she's remarried.'

The probation officer wanted Leamas to become a male nurse

at a mental home in Buckinghamshire and Leamas agreed to apply. He even took down the address and noted the train times from Marylebone.

'The rail's electrified as far as Great Missenden, now,' the probation officer added, and Leamas said that would be a help. So they gave him the parcel and he left. He took a bus to Marble Arch and walked. He had a bit of money in his pocket and he intended to give himself a decent meal. He thought he would walk through Hyde Park to Piccadilly, then through Green Park and St James's Park to Parliament Square, then wander down Whitehall to the Strand where he could go to the big café near Charing Cross station and get a reasonable steak for six shillings.

London was beautiful that day. Spring was late and the parks were filled with crocuses and daffodils. A cool, cleaning wind was blowing from the south; he could have walked all day. But he still had the parcel and he had to get rid of it. The litter baskets were too small; he'd look absurd trying to push his parcel into one of those. He supposed there were one or two things he ought to take out – his wretched pieces of paper – insurance card, driving licence and his E.93 (whatever that was) in a buff OHMS envelope, but suddenly he couldn't be bothered. He sat down on a bench and put the parcel beside him, not too close, and moved a little away from it. After a couple of minutes he walked back towards the footpath, leaving the parcel where it lay. He had just reached the footpath when he heard a shout; he turned, a little sharply perhaps, and saw a man in an army macintosh beckoning to him, holding the brown paper parcel in the other hand.

Leamas had his hands in his pockets and he left them there, and stood, looking back over his shoulder at the man in the macintosh. The man hesitated, evidently expecting Leamas to come to him or give some sign of interest, but Leamas gave none. Instead, he shrugged and continued along the footpath. He heard another shout and ignored it, and he knew the man was coming after him. He heard the footsteps on the gravel, half running, approaching rapidly, and then a voice, a little breathless, a little aggrieved:

'Here, you – I say!' and then he had drawn level, so that Leamas stopped, turned and looked at him.

'Yes?'

'This is your parcel, isn't it? You left it on the seat. Why didn't you stop when I called you?'

Tall, with rather curly brown hair; orange tie and pale green shirt; a little bit petulant, a little bit of a pansy, thought Leamas.

Could be a schoolmaster, ex LSE and runs a suburban drama club. Weak-eyed.

'You can put it back,' said Leamas. 'I don't want it.'

The man coloured:

'You can't just leave it there,' he said, 'it's litter.'

'I bloody well can,' Leamas replied. 'Somebody will find a use for it.' He was going to move on, but the stranger was still standing in front of him, holding the parcel in both arms as if it were a baby. 'Get out of the light,' said Leamas. 'Do you mind?'

'Look here,' said the stranger, and his voice had risen a key, 'I was trying to do you a favour; why do you have to be so damned rude?'

'If you're so anxious to do me a favour,' Leamas replied, 'why have you been following me for the last half-hour?'

He's pretty good, thought Leamas. He hasn't flinched, but he must be shaken rigid.

'I thought you were somebody I once knew in Berlin, if you must know.'

'So you followed me for half an hour?'

Leamas' voice was heavy with sarcasm, his brown eyes never left the other's face.

'Nothing like half an hour. I caught sight of you in Marble Arch and I thought you were Alec Leamas, a man I borrowed some money from. I used to be in the BBC in Berlin and there was this man I borrowed some money from. I've had a conscience about it ever since and that's why I followed you. I wanted to be sure.'

Leamas went on looking at him, not speaking, and thought he wasn't all that good but he was good enough. His story was scarcely plausible – that didn't matter. The point was that he'd produced a new one and stuck to it after Leamas had wrecked what promised to be a classic approach.

'I'm Leamas,' he said at last, 'who the hell are you?'

He said his name was Ashe, with an 'E' he added quickly, and Leamas knew he was lying. He pretended not to be quite sure that Leamas really was Leamas, so over lunch they opened the parcel and looked at the National Insurance card like, thought Leamas, a couple of cissies looking at a dirty post card. Ashe ordered lunch with just a fraction too little regard for expense, and they drank some Frankenwein to remind them of the old days. Leamas began by insisting he couldn't remember Ashe, and Ashe said he was surprised. He said it in the sort of tone that suggested he was hurt.

They met at a party, he said, which Derek Williams gave in his flat off the Ku-damm (he got that right) and all the press boys had been there; surely Alec remembered that? No, Leamas did not. Well, surely he remembered Derek Williams from the *Observer*, that *nice* man who gave such lovely pizza parties? Leamas had a lousy memory for names, after all they were talking about fifty-four; a lot of water had flowed under the bridge since then . . . Ashe remembered (his christian name was William, by the bye, most people called him Bill). Ashe remembered *vividly*. They'd been drinking stingers, brandy and crème de menthe, and were all rather tiddly, and Derek had provided some really gorgeous girls, half the cabaret from the Malkasten, *surely* Alec remembered now? Leamas thought it was probably coming back to him, if Bill would go on a bit.

Bill did go on, *ad lib*. no doubt, but he did it well, playing up the sex side a little, how they'd finished up in a night club with three of these girls; Alec, a chap from the political adviser's office and Bill, and Bill had been so embarrassed because he hadn't any money on him and Alec had paid, and Bill had wanted to take a girl home and Alec had lent him another tenner . . .

'Christ,' said Leamas, 'I remember now, of course I do.'

'I *knew* you would,' said Ashe happily, nodding at Leamas over his glass, 'look, do let's have the other half, this is *such* fun.'

Ashe was typical of that stratum of mankind which conducts its human relationships according to a principle of challenge and response. Where there was softness, he would advance; where he found resistance, retreat. Having himself no particular opinions or tastes he relied upon whatever conformed with those of his companion. He was as ready to drink tea at Fortnum's as beer at the Prospect of Whitby; he would listen to military music in St James's Park or jazz in a Compton Street cellar; his voice would tremble with sympathy when he spoke of Sharpeville, or with indignation at the growth of Britain's coloured population. To Leamas this observably passive role was repellent; it brought out the bully in him, so that he would lead the other gently into a position where he was committed, and then himself withdraw, so that Ashe was constantly scampering back from some cul-de-sac into which Leamas had enticed him. There were moments that afternoon when Leamas was so brazenly perverse that Ashe would have been justified in terminating their conversation – not least since he was paying for it; but he did not. The little sad man with spectacles who sat alone at the neighbouring table, deep in a book on the manufacture of ball bearings, might have deduced, had he been listening, that Leamas was indulging a sadistic nature – or perhaps (if he had been a man of particular subtlety) that Leamas was proving to his own satisfaction that only a man with a strong ulterior motive would put up with that kind of treatment.

It was nearly four o'clock before they ordered the bill and Leamas tried to insist on paying his half. Ashe wouldn't hear of it, paid the bill and took out his cheque book in order to settle his debt to Leamas.

'Twenty of the best,' he said, and filled in the date on the cheque form.

Then he looked up at Leamas, all wide-eyed and accommodating.

'I say, a cheque is all right by you, isn't it?'

Colouring a little, Leamas replied:

'I haven't got a bank at the moment – only just back from abroad, something I've got to fix up. Better give me a cheque and I'll cash it at your bank.'

'My dear chap, I wouldn't *dream* of it! You'd have to go to Rotherhithe to cash this one!' Leamas shrugged and Ashe laughed, and they agreed to meet at the same place on the following day, at one o'clock, when Ashe would have the money in cash.

Ashe took a cab at the corner of Compton Street, and Leamas waved at it until it was out of sight. When it was gone, he looked at his watch. It was four o'clock. He guessed he was still being followed, so he walked down to Fleet Street and had a cup of coffee in the Black and White. He looked at bookshops, read the evening papers displayed in the show windows of newspaper offices, and then quite suddenly, as if the thought had occurred to him at the last minute, he jumped on a bus. The bus went to Ludgate Hill, where it was held up in a traffic jam near a tube station; he dismounted and caught a tube. He bought a sixpenny ticket, stood in the end carriage and alighted at the next station. He caught another train to Euston, trekked back to Charing Cross. It was nine o'clock when he reached the station and it had turned rather cold. There was a van waiting in the forecourt; the driver was fast asleep. Leamas glanced at the number, went over and called through the window:

'Are you from Clements?' The driver woke up with a start and asked:

'Mr Thomas?'

'No,' replied Leamas. 'Thomas couldn't come. I'm Amies from Hounslow.'

'Hop in, Mr Amies,' the driver replied, and opened the door. They drove west, towards the King's Road. The driver knew the way.

Control opened the door.

'George Smiley's out,' he said. 'I've borrowed his house. Come in.' Not until Leamas was inside and the front door closed, did Control put on the hall light.

'I was followed till lunchtime,' Leamas said. They went into the little drawing-room. There were books everywhere. It was a pretty room; tall, with eighteenth-century mouldings, long windows and a good fireplace.

'They picked me up this morning. A man called Ashe.' He lit a cigarette. 'A pansy. We're meeting again tomorrow.'

Control listened carefully to Leamas' story, stage by stage, from the day he hit Ford, the grocer, to his encounter that morning with Ashe.

'How did you find prison?' Control enquired. He might have been asking whether Leamas had enjoyed his holiday. 'I am sorry we couldn't improve conditions for you, provide little extra comforts, but that would never have done.'

'Of course not.'

'One must be consistent. At every turn one must be consistent. Besides, it would be wrong to break the spell. I understand you were ill. I am sorry. What was the trouble?'

'Just fever.'

'How long were you in bed?'

'About ten days.'

'How very distressing; and nobody to look after you, of course.'

There was a very long silence.

'You know she's in the Party, don't you?' Control asked quietly.

'Yes,' Leamas replied. Another silence. 'I don't want her brought into this.'

'Why should she be?' Control asked sharply and for a moment, just for a moment, Leamas thought he had penetrated the veneer of academic detachment. 'Who suggested she should be?'

'No one,' Leamas replied, 'I'm just making the point. I know how these things go — all offensive operations. They have by-products, take sudden turns in unexpected directions. You think you've caught one fish and you find you've caught another. I want her kept clear of it.'

'Oh, quite, quite.'

'Who's that man in the Labour Exchange – Pitt? Wasn't he in the Circus during the war?'

'I know no one of that name. Pitt, did you say?'

'Yes.'

'No, not a name to me. In the Labour Exchange?'

'Oh, for God's sake,' Leamas muttered audibly.

'I'm sorry,' said Control, getting up, 'I'm neglecting my duties as deputy host. Would you care for a drink?'

'No. I want to get away tonight, Control. Go down to the country and get some exercise. Is the House open?'

'I've arranged a car,' he said. 'What time do you see Ashe tomorrow – one o'clock?'

'Yes.'

'I'll ring Haldane and tell him you want some squash. You'd better see a doctor, too. About that fever.'

'I don't need a doctor.'

'Just as you like.'

Control gave himself a whisky and began looking idly at the books in Smiley's shelf.

'Why isn't Smiley here?' Leamas asked.

'He doesn't like the operation,' Control replied indifferently. 'He finds it distasteful. He sees the necessity but he wants no part in it. His fever,' Control added with a whimsical smile, 'is recurrent.'

'He didn't exactly receive me with open arms.'

'Quite. He wants no part in it. But he told you about Mundt; gave you the background?'

'Yes.'

'Mundt is a very *hard* man,' Control reflected. 'We should never forget that. And a good intelligence officer.'

'Does Smiley know the reason for the operation? The special interest?'

Control nodded and took a sip of whisky.

'And he still doesn't like it?'

'It isn't a question of moralities. He is like the surgeon who has grown tired of blood. He is content that others should operate.'

'Tell me,' Leamas continued, 'how are you so certain this will get us where we want? How do you know the East Germans are on to it – not the Czechs or the Russians?'

'Rest assured,' Control said a little pompously, 'that that has been taken care of.'

As they got to the door, Control put his hand lightly on Leamas' shoulder.

'This is your last job,' he said. 'Then you can come in from the cold. About that girl – do you want anything done about her, money or anything?'

'When it's over. I'll take care of it myself then.'

'Quite. It would be very insecure to do anything now.'

'I just want her left alone,' Leamas repeated with emphasis. 'I just don't want her to be messed about. I don't want her to have a file or anything. I want her forgotten.'

He nodded to Control and slipped out into the night air. Into the cold.

Chapter 7

KIEVER

O n the following day Leamas arrived twenty minutes late for
his lunch with Ashe, and smelt of whisky. Ashe's pleasure
on catching sight of Leamas was, however, undiminished. He
claimed that he had himself only that moment arrived, he'd been
a little late getting to the bank. He handed Leamas an envelope.

'Singles,' said Ashe. 'I hope that's all right.'

'Thanks,' Leamas replied, 'let's have a drink.' He hadn't shaved
and his collar was filthy. He called the waiter and ordered drinks,
a large whisky for himself and a pink gin for Ashe. When the
drinks came Leamas' hand trembled as he poured the soda into the
glass, almost slopping it over the side.

They lunched well, with a lot of drink, and Ashe made most of
the running. As Leamas had expected he first talked about himself,
an old trick but not a bad one.

'To be quite frank, I've got on to rather a good thing recently,'
said Ashe; 'free-lancing English features for the foreign press. After
Berlin I made rather a mess of things at first – the Corporation
wouldn't renew the contract and I took a job running a dreary
toffee-shop weekly about hobbies for the over-sixties. Can you
imagine anything more frightful? That went under in the first
printing strike – I can't tell you how relieved I was. Then I went
to live with my mama in Cheltenham for a time; she runs an
antique shop, does very nicely thank you, as a matter of fact. Then
I got a letter from an old friend, Sam Kiever his name is actually,
who was starting up a new agency for small features on English
life specially slanted for foreign papers. You know the sort of thing
– six hundred words on Morris dancing. Sam had a new gimmick,
though; he sold the stuff already translated and do you know, it
makes a hell of a difference. One always imagines anyone can pay
a translator or do it themselves, but if you're looking for a half
column in-fill for your foreign features you don't *want* to waste
time and money on translation. Sam's gambit was to get in touch

with the editors direct – he traipsed round Europe like a gypsy, poor thing, but it's paid hands *down*.'

Ashe paused, waiting for Leamas to accept the invitation to speak about himself, but Leamas ignored it. He just nodded dully and said: 'Bloody good'. Ashe had wanted to order wine, but Leamas said he'd stick to whisky and by the time the coffee came he'd had four large ones. He seemed to be in bad shape; he had the drunkard's habit of ducking his mouth towards the rim of his glass just before he drank, as if his hand might fail him and the drink escape.

Ashe fell silent for a moment.

'You don't know Sam, do you?' he asked.

'Sam?'

A note of irritation entered Ashe's voice.

'Sam Kiever, my boss. The chap I was telling you about.'

'Was he in Berlin too?'

'No. He knows Germany well, but he's never lived in Berlin. He did a bit of devilling in Bonn, free-lance stuff. You might have met him. He's a dear.'

'Don't think so.' A pause.

'What do you do these days, old chap?' asked Ashe.

Leamas shrugged.

'I'm on the shelf,' he replied, and grinned a little stupidly. 'Out of the bag and on the shelf.'

'I forget what you were doing in Berlin? Weren't you one of the mysterious cold warriors?' My God, thought Leamas, you're stepping things up a bit.

Leamas hesitated, then coloured and said savagely, 'Office boy for the bloody Yanks, like the rest of us.'

'You know,' said Ashe, as if he had been turning the idea over for some time, 'you ought to meet Sam. You'd like him,' and then, all of a bother, 'I say, Alec – I don't even know where to get hold of you!'

'You can't,' Leamas replied listlessly.

'I don't get you, old chap. Where are you staying?'

'Around the place. Roughing it a bit. I haven't got a job. Bastards wouldn't give me a proper pension.'

Ashe looked horrified.

'But, Alec, that's awful; why didn't you *tell* me? Look, why not come and stay at my place? It's only tiny but there's room for one more if you don't mind a camp bed. You can't just live in the trees, my dear chap!'

'I'm all right for a bit,' Leamas replied, tapping at the pocket which contained the envelope. 'I'm going to get a job,' he nodded with determination; 'get one in a week or so. Then I'll be all right.'

'What sort of job?'

'Oh, I don't know. Anything.'

'But you can't just throw yourself away, Alec! You speak German like a native, I remember you do. There must be all sorts of things you can do!'

'I've done all sorts of things. Selling encyclopaedias for some bloody American firm, sorting books in a psychic library, punching work tickets in a stinking glue factory. What the hell *can* I do?' He wasn't looking at Ashe but at the table before him, his agitated lips moving quickly. Ashe responded to his animation, leaning forward across the table, speaking with emphasis, almost triumph.

'But Alec, you need *contacts*, don't you see? I know what it's like, I've been on the breadline myself. That's when you need to *know* people. I don't know what you were doing in Berlin, I don't want to know, but it wasn't the sort of job where you could meet people who matter, was it? If I hadn't met Sam at Poznan five years ago I'd *still* be on the breadline. Look, Alec, come and stay with me for a week or so. We'll ask Sam round and perhaps one or two of the old press boys from Berlin if any of them are in town.'

'But I can't write,' said Leamas. 'I couldn't write a bloody thing.'

Ashe had his hand on Leamas' arm: 'Now, don't fuss,' he said soothingly; 'let's just take things one at a time. Where are your bits and pieces?'

'My what?'

'Your things: clothes, baggage and what not?'

'I haven't got any. I've sold what I had – except the parcel.'

'What parcel?'

'The brown paper parcel you picked up in the park. The one I was trying to throw away.'

Ashe had a flat in Dolphin Square. It was just what Leamas had expected – small and anonymous with a few hastily assembled curios from Germany: beer mugs, a peasant's pipe and a few pieces of second-rate Nymphenburg.

'I spend the weekends with my mother in Cheltenham,' he said. 'I just use this place mid-week. It's pretty handy,' he added deprecatingly. They fixed the camp bed up in the tiny drawing-room. It was about four-thirty.

'How long have you been here?' asked Leamas.

'Oh – about a year or more.'

'Find it easily?'

'They come and go, you know, these flats. You put your name down and one day they ring you up and tell you you've made it.'

Ashe made tea and they drank it, Leamas sullen, like a man not used to comfort. Even Ashe seemed a little piano. After tea Ashe said: 'I'll go out and do a spot of shopping before the shops close, then we'll decide what to do about everything. I might give Sam a tinkle later this evening – I think the sooner you two get together the better. Why don't you get some sleep – you look all in.'

Leamas nodded. 'It's bloody good of you –' he made an awkward gesture with his hand '– all this.' Ashe gave him a pat on the shoulder, picked up his army macintosh and left.

As soon as Leamas reckoned Ashe was safely out of the building, he put the front door of the flat carefully on the latch and made his way downstairs to the centre hall where there were two telephone cabins. He dialled a Maida Vale number and asked for Mr Thomas' secretary. Immediately a girl's voice said, 'Mr Thomas' secretary speaking.'

'I'm ringing on behalf of Mr Sam Kiever,' Leamas said, 'he has accepted the invitation and hopes to contact Mr Thomas personally this evening.'

'I'll pass that on to Mr Thomas. Does he know where to get in touch with you?'

'Dolphin Square,' Leamas replied, and gave the address. 'Good-bye.'

After making some enquiries at the reception desk he returned to Ashe's flat, and sat on the camp bed looking at his clasped hands. After a while he lay down. He decided to accept Ashe's advice and get some rest. As he closed his eyes he remembered Liz lying beside him in the flat in Bayswater, and he wondered vaguely what had become of her.

He was woken up by Ashe, accompanied by a small, rather plump man with long, greying hair swept back and a double-breasted suit. He spoke with a slight central European accent; German perhaps, it was hard to tell. He said his name was Kiever – Sam Kiever.

They had a gin and tonic, Ashe doing most of the talking. It was just like old times, he said, in Berlin: the boys together and the night their oyster. Kiever said he didn't want to be too late; he had to work tomorrow. They agreed to eat at a Chinese restaurant that Ashe knew of – it was opposite Limehouse police station and you brought your own wine. Oddly enough Ashe had some Burgundy in the kitchen, and they took that with them in the taxi.

Dinner was very good and they drank both bottles of wine. Kiever opened up a little on the second: he'd just come back from a tour of West Germany and France. France was in a hell of a mess, de Gaulle was on the way out and God alone knew what would happen then. With a hundred thousand demoralised *colons* returning from Algeria he reckoned Fascism was on the cards.

'What about Germany?' asked Alec, prompting him.

'It's just a question of whether the Yanks can hold them.' Kiever looked invitingly at Leamas.

'What do you mean?' asked Leamas.

'What I say. Dulles gave them a foreign policy with one hand, Kennedy takes it away with the other. They're getting waspish.'

Leamas nodded abruptly and said, 'Bloody typical Yank.'

'Alec doesn't seem to like our American cousins,' said Ashe, stepping in heavily, and Kiever, with complete disinterest, murmured, 'Oh, really?' Kiever played it, Leamas reflected, very long. Like someone used to horses, he let you come to him. He conveyed to perfection a man who suspected that he was about to be asked a favour, and was not easily won.

After dinner Ashe said, 'I know a place in Wardour Street – you've been there, Sam. They do you all right there. Why don't we summon a barouche and go along?'

'Just a minute,' said Leamas, and there was something in his voice which made Ashe look at him quickly; 'just tell me something will you? Who's paying for this jolly?'

'I am,' said Ashe quickly, 'Sam and I.'

'Have you discussed it?'

'Well – no.'

'Because I haven't got any bloody money; you know that, don't you? None to throw about anyway.'

'Of course, Alec. I've looked after you up till now, haven't I?'

'Yes,' Leamas replied; 'yes, you have.'

He seemed to be going to say something else, and then to change his mind. Ashe looked worried, not offended, and Kiever as inscrutable as before.

Leamas refused to speak in the taxi. Ashe attempted some conciliatory remark and he just shrugged irritably. They arrived at

– 53 –

Wardour Street and dismounted, neither Leamas nor Kiever making any attempt to pay for the cab. Ashe led them past a shop window full of 'girlie' magazines, down a narrow alley, at the far end of which shone a tawdry neon sign: 'Pussywillow Club. Members Only'. On either side of the door were photographs of girls, and pinned across each was a thin, hand-printed strip of paper which read, 'Nature Study. Members only'.

Ashe pressed the bell. The door was at once opened by a very large man in a white shirt and black trousers.

'I'm a member,' Ashe said. 'These two gentlemen are with me.'

'See your card?'

Ashe took a buff card from his wallet and handed it over.

'Your guests pay a quid a head temporary membership. Your recommendation, right?' He held out the card and as he did so, Leamas stretched past Ashe and took it. He looked at it for a moment, then handed it back to Ashe.

Taking two pounds from his hip pocket Leamas put them into the waiting hand of the man at the door.

'Two quid,' said Leamas, 'for the guests,' and ignoring the astonished protests of Ashe he guided them through the curtained doorway into the dim hallway of the club. He turned to the doorman.

'Find us a table,' said Leamas, 'and a bottle of Scotch. And see we're left alone.' The doorman hesitated for a moment, decided not to argue, and escorted them downstairs. As they descended they heard the subdued moan of unintelligible music.

They got a table on their own at the back of the room. A two-piece band was playing and girls sat around in twos and threes. Two got up as they came in but the big doorman shook his head.

Ashe glanced at Leamas uneasily while they waited for the whisky. Kiever seemed slightly bored. The waiter brought a bottle and three tumblers and they watched in silence as he poured a little whisky into each glass. Leamas took the bottle from the waiter and added as much again to each. This done, he leant across the table and said to Ashe, 'Now perhaps you'll tell me what the bloody hell's going on?'

'What do you mean?' Ashe sounded uncertain. 'What *do* you mean, Alec?'

'You followed me from prison the day I was released,' he began quietly, 'with some bloody silly story of meeting me in Berlin.

– 54 –

You gave me money you didn't owe me. You've bought me expensive meals and you're putting me up in your flat.'

Ashe coloured and said, 'If that's the . . .'

'Don't interrupt,' said Leamas fiercely. 'Just damn' well wait till I've finished, do you mind? Your membership card for this place is made out for someone called Murphy. Is that your name?'

'No, it is not.'

'I suppose a friend called Murphy lent you his membership card?'

'No he didn't as a matter of fact. If you must know I come here occasionally to find a girl. I used a phoney name to join the club.'

'Then why,' Leamas persisted ruthlessly, 'is Murphy registered as the tenant of your flat?'

It was Kiever who finally spoke.

'You run along home,' he said to Ashe. 'I'll look after this.'

A girl performed a striptease, a young, drab girl with a dark bruise on her thigh. She had that pitiful, spindly nakedness which is embarrassing because it is not erotic; because it is artless and undesiring. She turned slowly, jerking sporadically with her arms or legs as if she only heard the music in snatches, and all the time she looked at them with the precocious interest of a child in adult company. The tempo of the music increased abruptly, and the girl responded like a dog to the whistle, scampering back and forth. Removing her brassière on the last note, she held it above her head, displaying her meagre body with its three tawdry patches of tinsel hanging from it like old Christmas decorations.

They watched in silence, Leamas and Kiever.

'I suppose you're going to tell me that we've seen better in Berlin,' Leamas suggested at last, and Kiever saw that he was still very angry.

'I expect *you* have,' Kiever replied pleasantly. 'I have often been to Berlin, but I am afraid I dislike night clubs.'

Leamas said nothing.

'I'm no prude, mind, just rational. If I want a woman I know cheaper ways of finding one; if I want to dance I know better places to do it.' Leamas might not have been listening.

'Perhaps you'll tell me why that cissy picked me up,' he suggested. Kiever nodded.

'By all means. I told him to.'

'Why?'

'I am interested in you. I want to make you a proposition, a journalistic proposition.'

There was a pause.

'Journalistic,' Leamas repeated, 'I see.'

'I run an agency, an international feature service. It pays well – very well – for interesting material.'

'Who publishes the material?'

'It pays so well, in fact, that a man with your kind of experience of . . . the international scene, a man with your background, you understand, who provided convincing, factual material, could free himself in a comparatively short time from further financial worry.'

'Who publishes the material, Kiever?' There was a threatening edge to Leamas' voice, and for a moment, just for a moment, a look of apprehension seemed to pass across Kiever's smooth face.

'International clients. I have a correspondent in Paris who disposes of a good deal of my stuff. Often I don't even know who *does* publish. I confess,' he added with a disarming smile, 'that I don't awfully care. They pay and they ask for more. They're the kind of people, you see, Leamas, who don't fuss about awkward details; they pay promptly, and they're happy to pay into foreign banks, for instance, where no one bothers about things like tax.'

Leamas said nothing. He was holding his glass with both hands, staring into it.

Christ, they're rushing their fences, Leamas thought; it's indecent. He remembered some silly music-hall joke – 'This is an offer no respectable girl could accept – and besides, I don't know what it's worth.' Tactically, he reflected, they're right to rush it. I'm on my uppers, prison experience still fresh, social resentment strong. I'm an old horse, I don't need breaking in; I don't have to pretend they've offended my honour as an English gentleman. On the other hand they would expect *practical* objections. They would expect him to be afraid; for his Service pursued traitors as the eye of God followed Cain across the desert.

And finally, they would know it was a gamble. They would know that inconsistency in human decision can make nonsense of the best-planned espionage approach; that cheats, liars and criminals may resist every blandishment while respectable gentlemen have been moved to appalling treasons by watery cabbage in a Departmental canteen.

'They'd have to pay a hell of a lot,' Leamas muttered at last. Kiever gave him some more whisky.

'They are offering a down-payment of fifteen thousand pounds. The money is already lodged at the Banque Cantonale in Bern. On production of a suitable identification, with which my clients will provide you, you can draw the money. My clients reserve the right to put questions to you over the period of one year on payment of another five thousand pounds. They will assist you with any . . . resettlement problems that may arise.'

'How soon do you want an answer?'

'Now. You are not expected to commit all your reminiscences to paper. You will meet my client and he will arrange to have the material . . . ghost written.'

'Where am I supposed to meet him?'

'We felt for everybody's sake it would be simplest to meet outside the United Kingdom. My client suggested Holland.'

'I haven't got my passport,' Leamas said dully.

'I took the liberty of obtaining one for you,' Kiever replied suavely; nothing in his voice or his manner indicated that he had done other than negotiate an adequate business arrangement. 'We're flying to The Hague tomorrow morning at nine forty-five. Shall we go back to my flat and discuss any other details?'

Kiever paid and they took a taxi to a rather good address not far from St James's Park.

Kiever's flat was luxurious and expensive, but its contents some-how gave the impression of having been hastily assembled. It is said that there are shops in London which will sell you bound books by the yard, and interior decorators who will harmonise the colour scheme of the walls with that of a painting. Leamas, who was not particularly receptive to such subtleties, found it hard to remember that he was in a private flat and not an hotel. As Kiever showed him to his room (which looked on to a dingy inner courtyard and not on to the street) Leamas asked him:

'How long have you been here?'

'Oh, not long,' Kiever replied lightly, 'a few months, not more.'

'Must cost a packet. Still, I suppose you're worth it.'

'Thanks.'

There was a bottle of Scotch in his room and a syphon of soda on a silver-plated tray. A curtained doorway at the further end of the room led to a bathroom and lavatory.

'Quite a little love nest. All paid for by the great Worker State?'

'Shut up,' said Kiever savagely, and added, 'If you want me, there's an internal telephone to my room. I shall be awake.'

'I think I can manage my buttons now,' Leamas retorted.

'Then good night,' said Kiever shortly, and left the room. He's on edge, too, thought Leamas.

Leamas was woken by the telephone at his bedside. It was Kiever.

'It's six o'clock,' he said, 'breakfast at half past.'

'All right,' Leamas replied, and rang off. He had a headache.

Kiever must have telephoned for a taxi because at seven o'clock the door bell rang and Kiever asked, 'Got everything?'

'I've no luggage,' Leamas replied, 'except a toothbrush and a razor.'

'That is taken care of. Are you ready otherwise?'

Leamas shrugged. 'I suppose so. Have you got any cigarettes?'

'No,' Kiever replied, 'but you can get some on the plane. You'd better look through this,' he added, and handed Leamas a British passport. It was made out in his name with his own photograph mounted in it, embossed by the deep press Foreign Office seal running across the corner. It was neither old nor new; it described Leamas as a clerk, and gave his status as single. Holding it in his hand for the first time, Leamas was a little nervous. It was like getting married: whatever happened, things would never be the same again.

'What about money?' Leamas asked.

'You won't need any. It's on the firm.'

Chapter 8

LE MIRAGE

It was cold that morning; the light mist was damp and grey, pricking the skin. The airport reminded Leamas of the war: machines, half hidden in the fog, waiting patiently for their masters; the resonant voices and their echoes, the sudden shout and the incongruous clip of a girl's heels on a stone floor; the roar of an engine that might have been at your elbow. Everywhere that air of conspiracy which generates among people who have been up since dawn – of superiority almost, derived from the common experience of having seen the night disappear and the morning come. The staff had that look which is informed by the mystery of dawn and animated by the cold, and they treated the passengers and their baggage with the remoteness of men returned from the front: ordinary mortals had nothing for them that morning.

Kiever had provided Leamas with luggage. It was a nice detail: Leamas admired it. Passengers without luggage attracted attention, and it was not part of Kiever's plan to do that. They checked in at the airline desk and followed the signs to passport control. There was a ludicrous moment when they lost the way and Kiever was rude to a porter. Leamas supposed Kiever was worried about the passport – he needn't be, thought Leamas, there's nothing wrong with it.

The passport officer was a youngish, little man with an Intelligence Corps tie and some mysterious badge in his lapel. He had a ginger moustache, and a North Country accent which was his life's enemy.

'Going to be away for a long time, sir?' he asked Leamas.

'A couple of weeks,' Leamas replied.

'You'll want to watch it, sir. Your passport's due for renewal on the 31st.'

'I know,' said Leamas.

They walked side by side into the passengers' waiting room.

On the way Leamas said: 'You're a suspicious sod, aren't you, Kiever,' and the other laughed quietly.

'Can't have you on the loose, can we! Not part of the contract,' he replied.

They still had twenty minutes to wait. They sat down at a table and ordered coffee. 'And take these things away,' Kiever added to the waiter, indicating the used cups, saucers and ash-trays, on the table. 'There's a trolley coming round,' the waiter replied.

'Take them,' Kiever repeated, angry again. 'It's disgusting, leaving dirty crockery there like that.'

The waiter just turned and walked away. He didn't go near the service counter and he didn't order their coffee. Kiever was white, ill with anger. 'For Christ's sake,' Leamas muttered, 'let it go. Life's too short.'

'Cheeky bastard, that's what he is,' said Kiever.

'All right, all right, make a scene; you've chosen a good moment. They'll never forget us here.'

The formalities at the airport at The Hague provided no problem. Kiever seemed to have recovered from his anxieties. He became jaunty and talkative as they walked the short distance between the plane and the Customs sheds. The young Dutch officer gave a perfunctory glance at their luggage and passports and announced in awkward, throaty English: 'I hope you have a pleasant stay in the Netherlands.'

'Thanks,' said Kiever, almost too gratefully, 'thanks very much.'

They walked from the Customs shed along the corridor to the reception hall on the other side of the airport buildings. Kiever led the way to the main exit, between the little groups of travellers staring vaguely at kiosk displays of scent, cameras and fruit. As they pushed their way through the revolving glass door, Leamas looked back. Standing at the newspaper kiosk, deep in a copy of the *Continental Daily Mail*, stood a small, frog-like figure in glasses, an earnest, worried little man. He looked like a civil servant. Something like that.

A car was waiting for them in the car park, a Volkswagen with a Dutch registration, driven by a woman who ignored them. She drove slowly, always stopping if the lights were amber, and Leamas guessed she had been briefed to drive that way and that they were being followed by another car. He watched the off-side wing mirror, trying to recognise the car, but without success.

Once he saw a black Peugeot with a CD number, but when they turned the corner there was only a furniture van behind them. He knew The Hague quite well from the war, and he tried to work out where they were heading. He guessed they were travelling north-west towards Scheveningen. Soon they had left the suburbs behind them and were approaching a colony of villas bordering the dunes along the sea front.

Here they stopped. The woman got out, leaving them in the car, and rang the front door bell of a small cream-coloured bungalow which stood at the near end of the row. A wrought-iron sign hung on the porch with the words 'Le Mirage' in pale blue Gothic script. There was a notice in the window which proclaimed that all the rooms were taken.

The door was opened by a kindly, plump woman who looked past the driver towards the car. Her eyes still on the car, she came down the drive towards them, smiling with pleasure. She reminded Leamas of an old aunt he once had who beat him for wasting string.

'How nice that you have come,' she declared; 'we are so *pleased* that you have come!' They followed her into the bungalow, Kiever leading the way. The driver got back into the car. Leamas glanced down the road which they had just travelled; three hundred yards away a black car, a Fiat perhaps, or a Peugeot, had parked. A man in a raincoat was getting out.

Once in the hall the woman shook Leamas warmly by the hand. 'Welcome, welcome to Le Mirage. Did you have a good journey?'

'Fine,' Leamas replied.

'Did you fly or come by sea?'

'We flew,' Kiever said; 'a very smooth flight.' He might have owned the airline.

'I'll make your lunch,' she declared; 'a special lunch. I'll make you something specially good. What shall I bring you?'

'Oh, for God's sake,' said Leamas under his breath, and the door bell rang. The woman went quickly into the kitchen; Kiever opened the front door.

He was wearing a macintosh with leather buttons. He was about Leamas' height, but older. Leamas put him at about fifty-five. His face had a hard, grey hue and sharp furrows; he might have been a soldier. He held out his hand.

'My name is Peters,' he said. The fingers were slim and polished. 'Did you have a good journey?'

'Yes,' said Kiever quickly, 'quite uneventful.'

'Mr Leamas and I have a lot to discuss; I do not think we need to keep you, Sam. You could take the Volkswagen back to town.'

Kiever smiled. Leamas saw the relief in his smile.

'Good-bye, Leamas,' said Kiever, his voice jocular; 'good luck, old man.'

Leamas nodded, ignoring Kiever's hand.

'Good-bye,' Kiever repeated and let himself quietly out of the front door.

Leamas followed Peters into a back room. Heavy lace curtains hung on the window, ornately fringed and draped. The window-sill was covered with potted plants: great cacti, a tobacco plant and some curious tree with wide, rubbery leaves. The furniture was heavy, pseudo-antique. In the centre of the room was a table with two carved chairs. The table was covered with a rust-coloured counterpane more like a carpet; on it before each chair was a pad of paper and a pencil. On a sideboard there was whisky and soda. Peters went over to it and mixed them both a drink.

'Look,' said Leamas suddenly, 'from now on I can do without the goodwill; do you follow me? We both know what we're about; both professionals. You've got a paid defector – good luck to you. For Christ's sake don't pretend you've fallen in love with me.' He sounded on edge, uncertain of himself.

Peters nodded. 'Kiever told me you were a proud man,' he observed dispassionately. Then he added without smiling, 'After all, why else does a man attack tradesmen?'

Leamas guessed he was Russian, but he wasn't sure. His English was nearly perfect, he had the ease and habits of a man long used to civilised comforts.

They sat at the table.

'Kiever told you what I am going to pay you?' Peters enquired.

'Yes. Fifteen thousand pounds to be drawn on a Bern bank.'

'Yes.'

'He said you might have follow-up questions during the next year,' said Leamas, 'you would pay another five thousand if I kept myself available.'

Peters nodded.

'I don't accept that condition,' Leamas continued. 'You know as well as I do it wouldn't work. I want to draw the fifteen thousand and get clear. Your people have a rough way with defected agents; so have mine. I'm not going to sit on my fanny in St Moritz while you roll up every network I've given you.

They're not fools; they'd know who to look for. For all you and I know they're on to us now.'

Peters nodded: 'You could, of course, come somewhere . . . safer, couldn't you?'

'Behind the Curtain?'

'Yes.'

Leamas just shook his head and continued: 'I reckon you'll need about three days for a preliminary interrogation. Then you'll want to refer back for a detailed brief.'

'Not necessarily,' Peters replied.

Leamas looked at him with interest:

'I see,' he said, 'they've sent the expert. Or isn't Moscow Centre in on this?'

Peters was silent; he was just looking at Leamas, taking him in. At last he picked up the pencil in front of him and said:

'Shall we begin with your war service?'

Leamas shrugged:

'It's up to you.'

'That's right. We'll begin with your war service. Just talk.'

'I enlisted in the Engineers in 1939. I was finishing my training when a notice came round inviting linguists to apply for specialist service abroad. I had Dutch and German and a good deal of French and I was fed up with soldiering, so I applied. I knew Holland well; my father had a machine tool agency at Leiden; I'd lived there for nine years. I had the usual interviews and went off to a school near Oxford where they taught me the usual monkey tricks.'

'Who was running that set-up?'

'I didn't know till later. Then I met Steed-Asprey, and an Oxford don called Fielding. They were running it. In forty-one they dropped me into Holland and I stayed there nearly two years. We lost agents quicker than we could find them in those days – it was bloody murder. Holland's a wicked country for that kind of work – it's got no real rough country, nowhere out of the way you can keep a headquarters or a radio set. Always on the move, always running away. It made it a very dirty game. I got out in forty-three and had a couple of months in England, then I had a go at Norway – that was a picnic by comparison. In forty-five they paid me off and I came over here again, to Holland, to try and catch up on my father's old business. That was no good, so I joined up with an old friend who was running a travel agency business in Bristol. That lasted eighteen months then we were sold up. Then out of the blue I got a letter from the Department: would I like to go back? But I'd had enough of all that, I thought, so I said I'd think about it and rented a cottage on Lundy Island. I stayed there a year contemplating my stomach, then I got fed up again so I wrote to them. By late forty-nine I was back on the payroll. Broken service of course – reduction of pension rights and the usual crabbing. Am I going too fast?'

'Not for the moment,' Peters replied, pouring him some more whisky; 'we'll discuss it again of course, with names and dates.'

There was a knock at the door and the woman came in with lunch, an enormous meal of cold meats and bread and soup. Peters pushed his notes aside and they ate in silence. The interrogation had begun.

Lunch was cleared away. 'So you went back to the Circus,' said Peters.

'Yes. For a while they gave me a desk job, processing reports, making assessments of military strengths in Iron Curtain countries, tracing units and that kind of thing.'

'Which section?'

'Satellites Four. I was there from February fifty to May fifty-one.'

'Who were your colleagues?'

'Peter Guillam, Brian de Grey and George Smiley. Smiley left us in early fifty-one and went over to Counter-Intelligence. In May fifty-one I was posted to Berlin as DCA – Deputy-Controller of Area. That meant all the operational work.'

'Who did you have under you?' Peters was writing swiftly. Leamas guessed he had some home-made shorthand.

'Hackett, Sarrow and de Jong. De Jong was killed in a traffic accident in fifty-nine. We thought he was murdered but we could never prove it. They all ran networks and I was in charge. Do you want details?' he asked drily.

'Of course, but later. Go on.'

'It was late fifty-four when we landed our first big fish in Berlin: Fritz Feger, second man in the DDR Defence Ministry. Up till then it had been heavy going – but in November fifty-four we got on to Fritz. He lasted almost exactly two years then one day we never heard any more. I hear he died in prison. It was another three years before we found anyone to touch him. Then, in 1959, Karl Riemeck turned up. Karl was on the Praesidium of the East German Communist Party. He was the best agent I ever knew.'

'He is now dead,' Peters observed.

A look of something like shame passed across Leamas' face:

'I was there when he was shot,' he muttered. 'He had a mistress who came over just before he died. He'd told her everything – she knew the whole damned network. No wonder he was blown.'

'We'll return to Berlin later. Tell me this. When Karl died you flew back to London. Did you remain in London for the rest of your service?'

'What there was of it, yes.'

'What job did you have in London?'

'Banking Section; supervision of agents' salaries, overseas payments for clandestine purposes. A child could have managed it. We got our orders and we signed the drafts. Occasionally there was a security headache.'

'Did you deal with agents direct?'

'How could we? The Resident in a particular country would make a requisition. Authority would put a hoofmark on it and pass it to us to make the payment. In most cases we had the money transferred to a convenient foreign bank where the Resident could draw it himself and hand it to the agent.'

'How were agents described? By cover names?'

'By figures. The Circus calls them combinations. Every network was given a combination; every agent was described by a suffix attached to the combination. Karl's combination was eight A stroke one.'

Leamas was sweating. Peters watched him coolly, appraising him like a professional gambler across the table. What was Leamas worth? What would break him, what attract or frighten him? What did he hate, above all, what did he know? Would he keep his best card to the end and sell it dear? Peters didn't think so; Leamas was too much off balance to monkey about. He was a man at odds with himself, a man who knew one life, one confession, and had betrayed them. Peters had seen it before. He had seen it, even in men who had undergone a complete ideological reversal, who in the secret hours of the night had found a new creed, and alone, compelled by the internal power of their convictions, had betrayed their calling, their families, their countries. Even they, filled as they were with new zeal and new hope, had had to struggle against the stigma of treachery; even they wrestled with the almost physical anguish of saying that which they had been trained never, never to reveal. Like apostates who feared to burn the Cross, they hesitated between the instinctive and the material; and Peters,

caught in the same polarity, must give them comfort and destroy
their pride. It was a situation of which they were both aware; thus
Leamas had fiercely rejected a human relationship with Peters, for
his pride precluded it. Peters knew that for those reasons, Leamas
would lie; lie perhaps only by omission, but lie all the same,
for pride, from defiance or through the sheer perversity of his
profession; and he, Peters, would have to nail the lies. He knew,
too, that the very fact that Leamas was a professional could militate
against his interests, for Leamas would select where Peters wanted
no selection; Leamas would anticipate the type of intelligence
which Peters required – and in doing so might pass by some casual
scrap which could be of vital interest to the evaluators. To all that,
Peters added the capricious vanity of an alcoholic wreck.

'I think,' he said, 'we will now take your Berlin service in some
detail. That would be from May 1951 to March 1961. Have another
drink.'

Leamas watched him take a cigarette from the box on the table,
and light it. He noticed two things: that Peters was left-handed,
and that once again he had put the cigarette in his mouth with the
maker's name away from him, so that it burnt first. It was a gesture
Leamas liked: it indicated that Peters, like himself, had been on
the run.

Peters had an odd face, expressionless and grey. The colour
must have left it long ago – perhaps in some prison in the early
days of the Revolution – and now his features were formed and
Peters would look like that till he died. Only the stiff, grey hair
might turn to white, but his face would not change. Leamas
wondered vaguely what Peters' real name was, whether he was
married. There was something very orthodox about him which
Leamas liked. It was the orthodoxy of strength, of confidence. If
Peters lied there would be a reason. The lie would be a calculated,
necessary lie, far removed from the fumbling dishonesty of Ashe.

Ashe, Kiever, Peters; that was a progression in quality, in
authority, which to Leamas was axiomatic of the hierarchy of an
intelligence network. It was also, he suspected, a progression in
ideology. Ashe, the mercenary, Kiever the fellow traveller, and
now Peters, for whom the end and the means were identical.

Leamas began to talk about Berlin. Peters seldom interrupted,
seldom asked a question or made a comment, but when he did, he
displayed a technical curiosity and expertise which entirely
accorded with Leamas' own temperament. Leamas even seemed

to respond to the dispassionate professionalism of his interrogator
– it was something they had in common.

It had taken a long time to build a decent East Zone network
from Berlin, Leamas explained. In the earlier days the city had been
thronging with second-rate agents: intelligence was discredited and
so much a part of the daily life of Berlin that you could recruit a
man at a cocktail party, brief him over dinner and he would be
blown by breakfast. For a professional it was a nightmare: dozens
of agencies, half of them penetrated by the opposition, thousands
of loose ends; too many leads, too few sources, too little space to
operate. They had their break with Feger in 1954, true enough.
But by '56 when every Service department was screaming for
high-grade intelligence, they were becalmed. Feger had spoilt them
for second-rate stuff that was only one jump ahead of the news.
They needed the real thing – and they had to wait another three
years before they got it.

Then one day de Jong went for a picnic in the woods on the
edge of East Berlin. He had a British military number plate on his
car, which he parked, locked, in an unmade road beside the canal.
After the picnic his children ran on ahead, carrying the basket.
When they reached the car they stopped, hesitated, dropped the
basket and ran back. Somebody had forced the car door – the
handle was broken and the door was slightly open. De Jong swore,
remembering that he had left his camera in the glove compartment.
He went and examined the car. The handle had been forced; de
Jong reckoned it had been done with a piece of steel tubing, the
kind of thing you can carry in your sleeve. But the camera was
still there, so was his coat, so were some parcels belonging to his
wife. On the driving seat was a tobacco tin, and in the tin was a
small nickel cartridge. De Jong knew exactly what it contained: it
was the film cartridge of a sub-miniature camera, probably a
Minox.

De Jong drove home and developed the film. It contained the
minutes of the last meeting of the Praesidium of the East German
Communist Party, the SED. By an odd coincidence there was
collateral from another source; the photographs were genuine.

Leamas took the case over then. He was badly in need of a
success. He'd produced virtually nothing since arriving in Berlin,
and he was getting past the usual age limit for full-time operational
work. Exactly a week later he took de Jong's car to the same place
and went for a walk.

It was a desolate spot that de Jong had chosen for his picnic: a strip of canal with a couple of shell-torn pillboxes, some parched, sandy fields and on the Eastern side a sparse pine wood, lying about two hundred yards from the gravel road which bordered the canal. But it had the virtue of solitude – something that was hard to find in Berlin – and surveillance was impossible. Leamas walked in the woods. He made no attempt to watch the car because he did not know from which direction the approach might be made. If he was seen watching the car from the woods, the chances of retaining his informant's confidence were ruined. He need not have worried.

When he returned there was nothing in the car so he drove back to West Berlin, kicking himself for being a damned fool; the Praesidium was not due to meet for another fortnight. Three weeks later he borrowed de Jong's car and took a thousand dollars in twenties in a picnic case. He left the car unlocked for two hours and when he returned there was a tobacco tin in the glove compartment. The picnic case had gone.

The films were packed with first-grade documentary stuff. In the next six weeks he did it twice more, and the same thing happened.

Leamas knew he had hit a gold mine. He gave the source the cover name of 'Mayfair' and sent a pessimistic letter to London. Leamas knew that if he gave London half an opening they would control the case direct, which he was desperately anxious to avoid. This was probably the only kind of operation which could save him from superannuation, and it was just the kind of thing that was big enough for London to want to take over for itself. Even if he kept them at arm's length there was still the danger that the Circus would have theories, make suggestions, urge caution, demand action. They would want him to give only new dollar bills in the hope of tracing them, they would want the film cartridges sent home for examination, they would plan clumsy tailing operations and tell the Departments. Most of all they would want to tell the Departments; and that, said Leamas, would blow the thing skyhigh. He worked like a madman for three weeks. He combed the personality files of each member of the Praesidium. He drew up a list of all the clerical staff who might have had access to the minutes. From the distribution list on the last page of the facsimiles he extended the total of possible informants to thirty-one, including clerks and secretarial staff.

Confronted with the almost impossible task of identifying an informant from the incomplete records of thirty-one candidates,

Leamas returned to the original material, which, he said, was something he should have done earlier. It puzzled him that in none of the photostat minutes he had so far received were the pages numbered, that none was stamped with a security classification, and that in the second and fourth copy words were crossed out in pencil or crayon. He came finally to an important conclusion: that the photocopies related not to the minutes themselves, but to the *draft* minutes. This placed the source in the Secretariat and the Secretariat was very small. The draft minutes had been well and carefully photographed: that suggested that the photographer had had time and a room to himself.

Leamas returned to the personality index. There was a man called Karl Riemeck in the Secretariat, a former corporal in the Medical Corps, who had served three years as a prisoner of war in England. His sister had been living in Pomerania when the Russians overran it, and he had never heard of her since. He was married and had one daughter named Carla.

Leamas decided to take a chance. He found out from London Riemeck's prisoner of war number, which was 29012, and the date of his release which was November 10th, 1945. He bought an East German children's book of science fiction and wrote in the fly-leaf in German in an adolescent hand: 'This book belongs to Carla Riemeck, born November 10th, 1945, in Bideford, North Devon. Signed Moonspacewoman 29012', and underneath he added, 'Applicants wishing to make space flights should present themselves for instruction to C. Riemeck in person. An application form is enclosed. Long live the People's Republic of Democratic Space!'

He ruled some lines on a sheet of writing paper, made columns of name, address and age, and wrote at the bottom of the page:

'Each candidate will be interviewed personally. Write to the usual address stating when and where you wish to be met. Applications will be considered in seven days. C.R.'

He put the sheet of paper inside the book. Leamas drove to the usual place, still in de Jong's car, and left the book on the passenger seat with five used one-hundred-dollar bills inside the cover. When Leamas returned the book had gone, and there was a tobacco tin on the seat instead. It contained three rolls of film. Leamas developed them that night: one film contained as usual the minutes of the Praesidium's last meeting; the second showed a draft revision of the East Germans' relationship to COMECON and the third a breakdown of the East German Intelligence Service, complete with functions of departments and details of personalities.

Peters interrupted: 'Just a minute,' he said. 'Do you mean to say all this intelligence came from Riemeck?'

'Why not? You know how much he saw.'

'It's scarcely possible,' Peters observed, almost to himself; 'he must have had help.'

'He did have later on; I'm coming to that.'

'I know what you are going to tell me. But did you never have the feeling he got assistance from *above* as well as from the agents he afterwards acquired?'

'No. No, I never did. It never occurred to me.'

'Looking back on it now, does it seem likely?'

'Not particularly.'

'When you sent all this material back to the Circus, they never suggested that even for a man in Riemeck's position, the intelligence was phenomenally comprehensive?'

'No.'

'Did they ever ask where Riemeck got his camera from, who instructed him in document photography?'

Leamas hesitated.

'No . . . I'm sure they never asked.'

'Remarkable,' Peters observed drily. 'I'm sorry – do go on. I did not mean to anticipate you.'

Exactly a week later, Leamas continued, he drove to the canal and this time he felt nervous. As he turned into the unmade road he saw three bicycles lying in the grass and two hundred yards down the canal, three men fishing. He got out of the car as usual and began walking towards the line of trees on the other side of the field. He had gone about twenty yards when he heard a shout. He looked round and caught sight of one of the men beckoning to him. The other two had turned and were looking at him too. Leamas was wearing an old macintosh; he had his hands in the pockets, and it was too late to take them out. He knew that the men on either side were covering the man in the middle and that if he took his hands out of his pockets they would probably shoot him; they would think he was holding a revolver in his pocket. Leamas stopped ten yards from the centre man.

'You want something?' Leamas asked.

'Are you Leamas?' He was a small, plump man, very steady. He spoke English.

'Yes.'

'What is your British national identity number?'

'PRT stroke L 58003 stroke one.'

'Where did you spend VJ night?'

'At Leiden in Holland in my father's workshop, with some Dutch friends.'

'Let's go for a walk, Mr Leamas. You won't need your macintosh. Take it off and leave it on the ground where you are standing. My friends will look after it.'

Leamas hesitated, shrugged and took off his macintosh. Then they walked together briskly towards the wood.

'You know as well as I do who he was,' said Leamas wearily, 'third man in the Ministry of the Interior, Secretary to the SED Praesidium, head of the Co-ordinating Committee for the Protection of the People. I suppose that was how he knew about de Jong and me: he'd seen our counter-intelligence files in the Abteilung. He had three strings to his bow: the Praesidium, straightforward internal political and economic reporting and access to the files of the East German Security Service.'

'But only *limited* access. They'd never give an outsider the run of all their files,' Peters insisted.

Leamas shrugged.

'They did,' he said.

'What did he do with his money?'

'After that afternoon I didn't give him any. The Circus took that over straight away. It was paid into a West German bank. He even gave me back what I'd given him. London banked it for him.'

'How much did you tell London?'

'Everything after that. I had to; then the Circus told the Departments. After that,' Leamas added venomously, 'it was only a matter of time before it packed up. With the Departments at their backs, London got greedy. They began pressing us for more, wanted to give him more money. Finally we had to suggest to Karl that he recruited other sources and we took them on to form a network. It was bloody stupid, it put a strain on Karl, endangered him, undermined his confidence in us. It was the beginning of the end.'

'How much did you get out of him?'

Leamas hesitated.

'How much? Christ, I don't know. It lasted an unnaturally long time. I think he was blown long before he was caught. The standard dropped in the last few months; think they'd begun to suspect him by then and kept him away from the good stuff.'

'Altogether, what did he give you?' Peters persisted.

Piece by piece, Leamas recounted the full extent of all Karl Riemeck's work. His memory was, Peters noted approvingly, remarkably precise considering the amount he drank. He could give dates and names, he could remember the reaction from London, the nature of corroboration where it existed. He could remember sums of money demanded and paid, the dates of the conscription of other agents into the network.

'I'm sorry,' said Peters at last, 'but I do not believe that one man, however well placed, however careful, however industrious, could have acquired such a range of detailed knowledge. For that matter, even if he had he would never have been able to photograph it.'

'He *was* able,' Leamas persisted, suddenly angry, 'he bloody well did and that's all there is to it.'

'And the Circus never told you to go into it with him, exactly how and when he saw all this stuff?'

'No,' snapped Leamas, 'Riemeck was touchy about that, and London was content to let it go.'

'Well, well,' Peters mused.

After a moment Peters said: 'You heard about that woman, incidentally?'

'What woman?' Leamas asked sharply.

'Karl Riemeck's mistress, the one who came over to West Berlin the night Riemeck was shot.'

'Well?'

'She was found dead a week ago. Murdered. She was shot from a car as she left her flat.'

'It used to be my flat,' said Leamas mechanically.

'Perhaps,' Peters suggested, 'she knew more about Riemeck's network than you did.'

'What the hell do you mean?' Leamas demanded.

Peters shrugged.

'It's all very strange,' he observed. 'I wonder who killed her.'

When they had exhausted the case of Karl Riemeck, Leamas went on to talk of other less spectacular agents, then of the procedure of his Berlin office, its communications, its staff, its secret ramifications – flats, transport, recording and photographic equipment. They talked long into the night and throughout the next day and when at last Leamas stumbled into bed the following night he knew he had betrayed all that he knew of Allied Intelligence in Berlin, and drunk two bottles of whisky in two days.

One thing puzzled him: Peters' insistence that Karl Riemeck

must have had help – must have had a high-level collaborator. Control had asked him the same question – he remembered now – Control had asked about Riemeck's access. How could they both be so sure Karl hadn't managed alone? He'd had helpers, of course; like the guards by the canal the day Leamas met him. But they were small beer – Karl had told him about them. But Peters – and Peters, after all, would know precisely how much Karl had been able to get his hands on – Peters had refused to believe Karl had managed alone. On this point, Peters and Control were evidently agreed.

Perhaps it was true. Perhaps there was somebody else. Perhaps this was the Special Interest whom Control was so anxious to protect from Mundt. That would mean that Karl Riemeck had collaborated with this special interest and provided what both of them had together obtained. Perhaps that was what Control had spoken to Karl about, alone, that evening in Leamas' flat in Berlin.

Anyway, tomorrow would tell. Tomorrow he would play his hand.

He wondered who had killed Elvira. And he wondered *why* they had killed her. Of course – here was a point, here was a possible explanation – Elvira, knowing the identity of Riemeck's special collaborator, had been murdered *by* that collaborator . . . No, that was too far-fetched. It overlooked the difficulty of crossing from East to West: Elvira had after all been murdered in West Berlin.

He wondered why Control had never told him Elvira had been murdered. So that he would react suitably when Peters told him? It was useless speculating. Control had his reasons; they were usually so bloody tortuous it took you a week to work them out.

As he fell asleep he muttered, 'Karl was a damn' fool. That woman did for him, I'm sure she did.' Elvira was dead now, and serve her right. He remembered Liz.

THE SECOND DAY

Peters arrived at eight o'clock the next morning, and without ceremony they sat down at the table and began.

'So you came back to London. What did you do there?'

'They put me on the shelf. I knew I was finished when that ass in Personnel met me at the airport. I had to go straight to Control and report about Karl. He was dead – what else was there to say?'

'What did they do with you?'

'They said at first I could hang around in London and wait till I was qualified for a proper pension. They were so bloody decent about it I got angry – I told them that if they were so keen to chuck money at me why didn't they do the obvious thing and count in all my time instead of bleating about broken service. Then they got cross when I told them that. They put me in Banking with a lot of women. I can't remember much about that part – I began hitting the bottle a bit. Had rather a bad patch.'

He lit a cigarette. Peters nodded.

'That was why they gave me the push, really. They didn't like me drinking.'

'Tell me what you *do* remember about Banking Section,' Peters suggested.

'It was a dreary set-up. I never was cut out for desk work, I knew that. That's why I hung on in Berlin. I knew when they recalled me I'd be put on the shelf, but, Christ . . . !'

'What did you do?'

Leamas shrugged.

'Sat on my behind in the same room as a couple of women. Thursby and Larrett. I called them Thursday and Friday.' He grinned rather stupidly. Peters looked uncomprehending.

'We just pushed paper. A letter came down from Finance: "the payment of seven hundred dollars to so and so is authorised with

effect from so and so. Kindly get on with it" – that was the gist of
it. Thursday and Friday would kick it about a bit, file it, stamp it
and I'd sign a cheque or get the bank to make a transfer.'

'What bank?'

'Blatt and Rodney, a chichi little bank in the City. There's a sort
of theory in the Circus that Etonians are discreet.'

'In fact, then, you knew the names of agents all over the
world?'

'Not necessarily. That was the cunning thing. I'd sign the
cheque, you see, or the order to the bank, but we'd leave a space
for the name of the payee. The covering letter or what have
you was all signed and then the file would go *back* to Special
Despatch.'

'Who are they?'

'They're the general holders of agents' particulars. They put in
the names and posted the order. Bloody clever, I must say.'

Peters looked disappointed.

'You mean you had no way of knowing the names of the
payees?'

'Not usually, no.'

'But occasionally?'

'We got pretty near the knuckle now and again. All the fiddling
about between Banking, Finance and Special Despatch led to
cock-ups, of course. Too elaborate. Then occasionally we came in
on special stuff which brightened one's life a bit.'

Leamas got up. 'I've made a list,' he said, 'of all the payments I
can remember. It's in my room. I'll get it.'

He walked out of the room, the rather shuffling walk he had
affected since arriving in Holland. When he returned he held in
his hand a couple of sheets of lined paper torn from a cheap notebook.

'I wrote these down last night,' he said; 'I thought it would save
time.'

Peters took the notes and read them slowly and carefully. He
seemed impressed.

'Good,' he said, 'very good.'

'Then I remember best a thing called Rolling Stone. I got a
couple of trips out of it. One to Copenhagen and one to Helsinki.
Just dumping money at banks.'

'How much?'

'Ten thousand dollars in Copenhagen, forty thousand D-Marks
in Helsinki.'

Peters put down his pencil.

'Who for?' he asked.

'God knows. We worked Rolling Stone on a system of deposit accounts. The Service gave me a phoney British passport; I went to the Royal Scandinavian Bank in Copenhagen and the National Bank of Finland in Helsinki, deposited the money and drew a pass book on a joint account – for me in my alias and for someone else – the agent, I suppose, in his alias. I gave the banks a sample of the co-holder's signature. I'd got that from Head Office. Later the agent was given the pass book and a false passport which he showed at the bank when he drew the money. All I knew was the alias.' He heard himself talking and it all sounded so ludicrously improbable.

'Was this procedure common?'

'No. It was a special payment. It had a subscription list.'

'What's that?'

'It had a code name known to very few people.'

'What was the code name?'

'I told you – Rolling Stone. The operation covered irregular payments of ten thousand dollars in different currencies and in different capitals.'

'Always in capital towns?'

'Far as I know. I remember reading in the file that there had been other Rolling Stone payments before I came to the Section, but in those cases Banking Section got the local Resident to do it.'

'These other payments that took place before you came, where were they made?'

'One in Oslo. I can't remember where the other was.'

'Was the alias of the agent always the same?'

'No. That was an added security precaution. I heard later we pinched the whole technique from the Russians. It was the most elaborate payment scheme I'd met. In the same way I used a different alias and of course a different passport for each trip.' That would please him; help him to fill in the gaps.

'These faked passports the agent was given so that he could draw the money: did you know anything about them: how they were made out and despatched?'

'No. Oh, except that they had to have visas in them for the country where the money was deposited. And entry stamps.'

'*Entry stamps?*'

'Yes. I assumed the passports were never used at the border –
only presented at the bank for identification purposes. The agent
must have travelled on his own passport, quite legally entered the
country where the bank was situated, then used the faked passport
at the bank. That was my guess.'

'Do you know of a reason why earlier payments were made by
the Residents, and later payments by someone travelling out from
London?'

'I know the reason. I asked the women in Banking Section,
Thursday and Friday. Control was anxious that –'

'*Control?* Do you mean to say Control himself was running the
case?'

'Yes, he was running it. He was afraid the Resident might be
recognised at the bank. So he used a postman: me.'

'When did you make your journeys?'

'Copenhagen on the fifteenth of June. I flew back the same night.
Helsinki at the end of September. I stayed two nights there, flew
back around the twenty-eighth. I had a bit of fun in Helsinki.' He
grinned but Peters took no notice.

'And the other payments – when were they made?'

'I can't remember. Sorry.'

'But one was definitely in Oslo?'

'Yes, in Oslo.'

'How much time separated the first two payments, the payments
made by the Residents?'

'I don't know. Not long, I think. Maybe a month. A bit more
perhaps.'

'Was it your impression that the agent had been operating for
some time before the first payment was made? Did the file show
that?'

'No idea. The file simply covered actual payments. First payments early '59. There was no other data on it. That is the principle
that operates where you have a limited subscription. Different files
handle different bits of a single case. Only someone with the master
file would be able to put it all together.'

Peters was writing all the time now. Leamas assumed there was
a tape recorder hidden somewhere in the room but the subsequent
transcription would take time. What Peters wrote down now
would provide the background for this evening's telegram to
Moscow, while in the Soviet Embassy in The Hague the girls
would sit up all night telegraphing the verbatim transcript on
hourly schedules.

'Tell me,' said Peters; 'these are large sums of money. The arrangements for paying them were elaborate and very expensive. What did you make of it yourself?'

Leamas shrugged.

'What could I make of it? I thought Control must have a bloody good source, but I never saw the material so I don't know. I didn't like the way it was done – it was too high-powered, too complicated, too clever. Why couldn't they just meet him and give him the money in cash? Did they really let him cross borders on his own passport with a forged one in his pocket? I doubt it,' said Leamas. It was time he clouded the issue, let him chase a hare.

'What do you mean?'

'I mean, that for all I know the money was never drawn from the bank. Supposing he was a highly placed agent behind the Curtain – the money would be on deposit for him when he could get at it. That was what I reckoned anyway. I didn't think about it all that much. Why should I? It's part of our work only to know pieces of the whole set-up. You know that. If you're curious, God help you.'

'If the money wasn't collected, as you suggest, why all the trouble with passports?'

'When I was in Berlin we made an arrangement for Karl Riemeck in case he ever needed to run and couldn't get hold of us. We kept a bogus West German passport for him at an address in Düsseldorf. He could collect it any time by following a pre-arranged procedure. It never expired – Special Travel renewed the passport and the visas as they expired. Control might have followed the same technique with this man. I don't know – it's only a guess.'

'How do you know for certain that passports were issued?'

'There were minutes on the file between Banking Section and Special Travel. Special Travel is the section which arranges false identity papers and visas.'

'I see.' Peters thought for a moment and then he asked: 'What names did you use in Copenhagen and Helsinki?'

'Robert Lang, electrical engineer from Derby. That was in Copenhagen.'

'When exactly were you in Copenhagen?' Peters asked.

'I told you, June the fifteenth. I got there in the morning at about eleven-thirty.'

'Which bank did you use?'

'Oh, for Christ's sake, Peters,' said Leamas, suddenly angry, 'the Royal Scandinavian. You've got it written down.'

'I just wanted to be sure,' the other replied evenly, and continued writing. 'And for Helsinki, what name?'

'Stephen Bennett, marine engineer from Plymouth. I was there,' he added sarcastically, 'at the end of September.'

'You visited the bank on the day you arrived?'

'Yes. It was the 24th or 25th, I can't be sure, as I told you.'

'Did you take the money with you from England?'

'Of course not. We just transferred it to the Resident's account in each case. The Resident drew it, met me at the airport with the money in a suitcase and I took it to the bank.'

'Who's the Resident in Copenhagen?'

'Peter Jensen, a bookseller in the University bookshop.'

'And what were the names which would be used by the agent?'

'Horst Karlsdorf in Copenhagen. I think that was it, yes it was, I remember. Karlsdorf. I kept on wanting to say Karlshorst.'

'Description?'

'Manager, from Klagenfurt in Austria.'

'And the other? The Helsinki name?'

'Fechtmann, Adolf Fechtmann from St Gallen, Switzerland. He had a title – yes, that's right: Doctor Fechtmann, archivist.'

'I see; both German-speaking.'

'Yes, I noticed that. But it can't be a German.'

'Why not?'

'I was head of the Berlin set-up, wasn't I? I'd have been in on it. A high-level agent in East Germany would have to be run from Berlin. I'd have known.' Leamas got up, went to the sideboard and poured himself some whisky. He didn't bother about Peters.

'You said yourself there were special precautions, special procedures in this case. Perhaps they didn't think you needed to know.'

'Don't be bloody silly,' Leamas rejoined shortly; 'of course I'd have known.' This was the point he would stick to through thick and thin; it made them feel they knew better, gave credence to the rest of his information. 'They will want to deduce *in spite of you*,' Control had said. 'We must give them the material and remain sceptical to their conclusions. Rely on their intelligence and conceit, on their suspicion of one another – that's what we must do.'

Peters nodded as if he were confirming a melancholy truth. 'You are a very proud man, Leamas,' he observed once more.

Peters left soon after that. He wished Leamas good day and walked down the road along the sea-front. It was lunch-time.

Chapter 10

THE THIRD DAY

Peters didn't appear that afternoon, nor the next morning. Leamas stayed in, waiting with growing irritation for some message, but none came. He asked the housekeeper but she just smiled and shrugged her heavy shoulders. At about eleven o'clock the next morning he decided to go out for a walk along the front, bought some cigarettes and stared dully at the sea.

There was a girl standing on the beach throwing bread to the seagulls. Her back was turned to him. The sea wind played with her long black hair and pulled at her coat, making an arc of her body, like a bow strung towards the sea. He knew what it was then that Liz had given him; the thing that he would have to go back and find if ever he got home to England: it was the caring about little things – the faith in ordinary life; the simplicity that made you break up a bit of bread into a paper bag, walk down to the beach and throw it to the gulls. It was this respect for triviality which he had never been allowed to possess; whether it was bread for the seagulls or love, whatever it was he would go back and find it; he would make Liz find it for him. A week, two weeks perhaps, and he would be home. Control had said he could keep whatever they paid – and that would be enough. With fifteen thousand pounds, a gratuity and a pension from the Circus, a man – as Control would say – can afford to come in from the cold.

He made a detour and returned to the bungalow at a quarter to twelve. The woman let him in without a word, but when he had gone into the back room he heard her lift the receiver and dial a telephone number. She only spoke for a few seconds. At half past twelve she brought him lunch, and, to his pleasure, some English newspapers, which he read contentedly until three o'clock. Leamas, who normally read nothing, read newspapers slowly and with concentration. He remembered details, like the names and addresses of people who were the subject of small news items. He did it almost unconsciously as a kind of private pelmanism, and it absorbed him entirely.

At three o'clock Peters arrived, and as soon as Leamas saw him he knew that something was up. They did not sit at the table; Peters did not take off his macintosh.

'I've got bad news for you,' he said, 'they're looking for you in England. I heard this morning. They're watching the ports.'

Leamas replied impassively: 'On what charge?'

'Nominally for failing to report to a police station within the statutory period after release from prison.'

'And in fact?'

'The word is going around that you're wanted for an offence under the Official Secrets Act. Your photograph's in all the London evening papers. The captions are very vague.'

Leamas was standing very still.

Control had done it. Control had started the hue and cry. There was no other explanation. If Ashe or Kiever had been pulled in, if they had talked – even then, the responsibility for the hue and cry was still Control's. 'A couple of weeks,' he'd said; 'I expect they'll take you off somewhere for the interrogation – it may even be abroad. A couple of weeks should see you through, though. After that, the thing should run itself. You'll have to lie low over here while the chemistry works itself out; but you won't mind that I'm sure. I've agreed to keep you on operational subsistence until Mundt is eliminated: that seemed the fairest way.'

And now this.

This wasn't part of the bargain; this was different. What the hell was he supposed to do? By pulling out now, by refusing to go along with Peters, he was wrecking the operation. It was just possible that Peters was lying, that this was the test – all the more reason that he should agree to go. But if he went, if he agreed to go east, to Poland, Czechoslovakia or God knows where, there was no good reason why they should ever let him out – there was no good reason (since he was notionally a wanted man in the West) why he should *want* to be let out.

Control had done it – he was sure. The terms had been too generous, he'd known that all along. They didn't throw money about like that for nothing – not unless they thought they might lose you. Money like that was a *douceur* for discomforts and dangers Control would not openly admit to. Money like that was a warning; Leamas had not heeded the warning.

'Now how the devil,' he asked quietly, 'could they get on to that?' A thought seemed to cross his mind and he said, 'Your friend Ashe could have told them, of course, or Kiever . . .'

'It's possible,' Peters replied. 'You know as well as I do that such things are always possible. There is no certainty in our job. The fact is,' he added with something like impatience, 'that by now every country in Western Europe will be looking for you.'

Leamas might not have heard what Peters was saying. 'You've got me on the hook now, haven't you, Peters?' he said. 'Your people must be laughing themselves sick. Or did they give the tip-off themselves?'

'You overrate your own importance,' Peters said sourly.

'Then why do you have me followed, tell me that? I went for a walk this morning. Two little men in brown suits, one twenty yards behind the other, trailed me along the sea-front. When I came back the housekeeper rang you up.'

'Let us stick to what we know,' Peters suggested. 'How your own authorities have got on to you does not at the moment acutely concern us. The fact is, they have.'

'Have you brought the London evening papers with you?'

'Of course not. They are not available here. We received a telegram from London.'

'That's a lie. You know perfectly well your apparatus is only allowed to communicate with Centre.'

'In this case a direct link between two outstations was permitted,' Peters retorted angrily.

'Well, well,' said Leamas with a wry smile, 'you must be quite a big wheel. Or' – a thought seemed to strike him – 'isn't Centre in on this?'

Peters ignored the question.

'You know the alternative. You let us take care of you, let us arrange your safe passage, or you fend for yourself – with the certainty of eventual capture. You've no false papers, no money, nothing. Your British passport will have expired in ten days.'

'There's a third possibility. Give me a Swiss passport and some money and let me run. I can look after myself.'

'I am afraid that is not considered desirable.'

'You mean you haven't finished the interrogation. Until you have I am not expendable?'

'That is roughly the position.'

'When you have completed the interrogation, what will you do with me?'

Peters shrugged. 'What do you suggest?'

'A new identity. Scandinavian passport perhaps. Money.'

'It's very academic,' Peters replied, 'but I will suggest it to my superiors. Are you coming with me?' Leamas hesitated, then he smiled a little uncertainly and asked:

'If I didn't, what would you do? After all I've quite a story to tell, haven't I?'

'Stories of that kind are hard to substantiate. I shall be gone tonight. Ashe and Kiever . . .' he shrugged, 'what do they add up to?'

Leamas went to the window. A storm was gathering over the grey North Sea. He watched the gulls wheeling against the dark clouds. The girl had gone.

'All right,' he said at last, 'fix it up.'

'There's no plane East until tomorrow. There's a flight to Berlin in an hour. We shall take that. It's going to be very close.'

Leamas' passive role that evening enabled him once again to admire the unadorned efficiency of Peters' arrangements. The passport had been put together long ago – Centre must have thought of that. It was made out in the name of Alexander Thwaite, travel agent, and filled with visas and frontier stamps – the old, well-fingered passport of the professional traveller. The Dutch frontier guard at the airport just nodded and stamped it for form's sake – Peters was three or four behind him in the queue and took no interest in the formalities.

As they entered the 'passengers only' enclosure Leamas caught sight of a bookstall. A selection of international newspapers was on show: *Figaro*, *Le Monde*, *Neue Zürcher Zeitung*, *Die Welt* and half a dozen British dailies and weeklies. As he watched, the girl came round to the front of the kiosk and pushed an *Evening Standard* into the rack. Leamas hurried across to the bookstall and took the paper from the rack.

'How much?' he asked. Thrusting his hand into his trouser pocket he suddenly realised that he had no Dutch currency.

'Thirty cents,' the girl replied. She was rather pretty; dark and jolly.

'I've only got two English shillings. That's a guilder. Will you take them?'

'Yes, please,' she replied, and Leamas gave her the florin. He looked back; Peters was still at the passport desk, his back turned to Leamas. Without hesitation he made straight for the men's lavatory. There he glanced rapidly but thoroughly at each page, then shoved the paper in the litter basket and re-emerged. It was true: there was his photograph with the vague little passage underneath. He wondered if Liz had seen it. He made his way thoughtfully to the passengers' lounge. Ten minutes later they boarded the plane for Hamburg and Berlin. For the first time since it all began, Leamas was frightened.

Chapter 11

FRIENDS OF ALEC

The men called on Liz the same evening.

Liz Gold's room was at the northern end of Bayswater. It had two single beds in it, and a gas fire, rather a pretty one in charcoal grey, which made a modern hiss instead of an old fashioned bubble. She used to gaze into it sometimes when Leamas was there, when the gas fire shed the only light in the room. He would lie on the bed, hers, the one furthest from the door, and she would sit beside him and kiss him, or watch the gas fire with her face pressed against his. She was afraid to think of him too much now because then she forgot what he looked like, so she let her mind think of him for brief moments like running her eyes across a faint horizon, and then she would remember some small thing he had said or done, some way he had looked at her, or, more often, ignored her. That was the terrible thing, when her mind dwelled on it: she had nothing to remember him by – no photograph, no souvenir, nothing. Not even a mutual friend – only Miss Crail in the library, whose hatred of him had been vindicated by his spectacular departure. Liz had been round to his room once and seen the landlord. She didn't know why she did it quite, but she plucked up courage and went. The landlord was very kind about Alec; Mr Leamas had paid his rent like a gentleman, right till the end, then there'd been a week or two owing and a chum of Mr Leamas had dropped in and paid up handsome, no queries or nothing. He'd always said it of Mr Leamas, always would, he was a gent. Not public school, mind, nothing arsy-tarsy but a real gent. He liked to scowl a bit occasionally, and of course he drank a drop more than was good for him, though he never acted tight when he came home. But this little bloke who come round, funny little shy chap with specs, *he* said Mr Leamas had particularly requested, quite particularly, that the rent owing should be settled up. And if that wasn't gentlemanly the landlord was damned if he knew what was. Where he got the money from

Heaven knows, but that Mr Leamas was a deep one and no mistake. He only did to Ford the grocer what a good many had been wanting to do ever since the war. The room? Yes, the room had been taken – a gentleman from Korea, two days after they took Mr Leamas away.

That was probably why she went on working at the library – because there, at least, he still existed; the ladders, shelves, the books, the card index, were things he had known and touched, and one day he might come back to them. He had said he would never come back, but she didn't believe it. It was like saying you would never get better, to believe a thing like that. Miss Crail thought he would come back: she had discovered she owed him some money – wages underpaid – and it infuriated her that her monster had been so unmonstrous as not to collect it. After Leamas had gone, Liz had never given up asking herself the same question: why had he hit Mr Ford? She knew he had a terrible temper, but that was different. He had intended to do it right from the start as soon as he had got rid of his fever. Why else had he said good-bye to her the night before? He knew that he would hit Mr Ford on the following day. She refused to accept the only other possible interpretation: that he had grown tired of her and said good-bye, and the next day, still under the emotional strain of their parting, had lost his temper with Mr Ford and struck him. She knew, she had always known, that there was something Alec had got to do. He'd even told her that himself. What it was she could only guess.

First, she thought he had a quarrel with Mr Ford, some deep-rooted hatred going back for years. Something to do with a girl, or Alec's family perhaps. But you only had to look at Mr Ford and it seemed ridiculous. He was the archetypal *petit-bourgeois*, cautious, complacent, mean. And anyway, if Alec had a vendetta on with Mr Ford, why did he go for him in the shop on a Saturday, in the middle of the weekend shopping rush, when everyone could see?

They'd talked about it in the meeting of her Party branch. George Hanby, the branch treasurer, had actually been passing Ford the grocer's as it happened, he hadn't seen much because of the crowd, but he'd talked to a bloke who'd seen the whole thing. Hanby had been so impressed that he'd rung the *Worker*, and they'd sent a man to the trial – that was why the *Worker* had given it a middle-page spread as a matter of fact. It was just a straight case of protest – of sudden social awareness and hatred against the boss class, as the *Worker* said. This bloke that Hanby spoke to (he was just a little ordinary chap with specs, white collar type) said it had been so sudden – spontaneous was what he meant – and it just proved to Hanby once again how incendiary was the fabric of the capitalist system. Liz had kept very quiet while Hanby talked: none of them knew, of course, about her and Leamas. She realised then that she hated George Hanby; he was a pompous, dirty-minded little man, always leering at her and trying to touch her.

Then the men called.

She thought they were a little too smart for policemen: they came in a small black car with an aerial on it. One was short and rather plump. He had glasses and wore odd, expensive clothes; he was a kindly, worried little man and Liz trusted him somehow without knowing why. The other was smoother, but not glossy – rather a boyish figure, although she guessed he wasn't less than forty. They said they came from Special Branch, and they had printed cards with photographs in cellophane cases. The plump one did most of the talking.

'I believe you were friendly with Alec Leamas,' he began. She was prepared to be angry, but the plump man was so earnest that it seemed silly.

'Yes,' Liz answered. 'How did you know?'

'We found out quite by chance the other day. When you go to . . . prison, you have to give next of kin. Leamas said he hadn't any. That was a lie as a matter of fact. They asked him whom they should inform if anything happened to him in prison. He said you.'

'I see.'

'Does anyone else know you were friendly with him?'

'No.'

'Did you go to the trial?'

'No.'

'No press men called, creditors, no one at all?'

'No, I've told you. No one else knew. Not even my parents, no one. We worked together in the library, of course – the Psychical Research Library – but only Miss Crail, the librarian, would know that. I don't think it occurred to her that there was anything between us. She's queer,' Liz added simply.

The little man peered very seriously at her for a moment, then asked:

'Did it surprise you when Leamas beat up Mr Ford?'

'Yes, of course.'

'Why did you think he did it?'

'I don't know. Because Ford wouldn't give him credit, I suppose. But I think he always meant to.' She wondered if she was saying too much, but she longed to talk to somebody about it, she was so alone and there didn't seem any harm.

'But that night, the night before it happened, we talked together. We had supper, a sort of special one; Alec said we should and I knew that it was our last night. He'd got a bottle of red wine from somewhere; I didn't like it much. Alec drank most of it. And then I asked him, "Is this good-bye" – whether it was all over.'

'What did he say?'

'He said there was a job he'd got to do. I didn't really understand it all, not really.'

There was a very long silence and the little man looked more worried than ever. Finally he asked her:

'Do you believe that?'

'I don't know.' She was suddenly terrified for Alec, and she didn't know why. The man asked:

'Leamas has got two children by his marriage, did he tell you?' Liz said nothing. 'In spite of that he gave your name as next of kin. Why do you think he did that?' The little man seemed embarrassed by his own question. He was looking at his hands, which were pudgy and clasped together on his lap. Liz blushed.

'I was in love with him,' she replied.

'Was he in love with you?'

'Perhaps. I don't know.'

'Are you still in love with him?'

'Yes.'

'Did he ever say he would come back?' asked the younger man.

'No.'

'But he did say good-bye to you?' the other asked quickly.

'Did he say good-bye to you?' The little man repeated his question slowly, kindly. 'Nothing more can happen to him, I promise you. But we want to help him, and if you have any idea of why he hit Ford, if you have the slightest notion from something he said, perhaps casually, or something he did, then tell us for Alec's sake.'

Liz shook her head.

'Please go,' she said, 'please don't ask any more questions. Please go now.'

As he got to the door, the elder man hesitated, then took a card from his wallet and put it on the table, gingerly, as if it might make a noise. Liz thought he was a very shy little man.

THE SPY WHO CAME IN FROM THE COLD

'If you ever want any help – if anything happens about Leamas or . . . ring me up,' he said. 'Do you understand?'

'Who are you?'

'I'm a friend of Alec Leamas.' He hesitated. 'Another thing,' he added, 'one last question. Did Alec know you were . . . did Alec know about the Party?'

'Yes,' she replied, hopelessly, 'I told him.'

'Does the Party know about you and Alec?'

'I've told you. No one knew.' Then, white-faced, she cried out suddenly, 'Where is he; tell me where he is. Why won't you tell me where he is? I can help him, don't you see; I'll look after him . . . even if he's gone mad, I don't care, I swear I don't . . . I wrote to him in prison; I shouldn't have done, I know. I just said he could come back any time. I'd wait for him always . . .' She couldn't speak any more, just sobbed and sobbed, standing there in the middle of the room, her broken face buried in her hands; the little man watching her.

'He's gone abroad,' he said gently. 'We don't quite know where he is. He isn't mad, but he shouldn't have said all that to you. It was a pity.'

The younger man said:

'We'll see you're looked after. For money and that kind of thing.'

'Who are you?' Liz asked again.

'Friends of Alec,' the young man repeated; 'good friends.'

She heard them go quietly down the stairs and into the street. From her window she watched them get into the small black car and drive away in the direction of the park.

Then she remembered the card. Going to the table she picked it up and held it to the light. It was expensively done, more than a policeman could afford, she thought. Engraved. No rank in front of the name, no police station or anything. Just the name with 'Mister' – and whoever heard of a policeman living in Chelsea?

'Mr George Smiley. 9 Bywater Street, Chelsea'. Then the telephone number underneath.

It was very strange.

Chapter 12

EAST

L eamas unfastened his seat-belt.

It is said that men condemned to death are subject to sudden moments of elation; as if, like moths in the fire, their destruction were coincidental with attainment. Following directly upon his decision, Leamas was aware of a comparable sensation; relief, short-lived but consoling, sustained him for a time. It was followed by fear and hunger.

He was slowing down. Control was right.

He'd noticed it first during the Riemeck case, early last year. Karl had sent a message: he'd got something special for him and was making one of his rare visits to Western Germany; some legal conference at Karlsruhe. Leamas had managed to get an air passage to Cologne, and picked up a car at the airport. It was still quite early in the morning and he'd hoped to miss most of the autobahn traffic to Karlsruhe but the heavy lorries were already on the move. He drove seventy kilometres in half an hour, weaving between the traffic, taking risks to beat the clock, when a small car, a Fiat probably, nosed its way out into the fast lane forty yards ahead of him. Leamas stamped on the brake, turning his headlights full on and sounding his horn, and by the grace of God he missed it; missed it by a fraction of a second. As he passed the car he saw out of the corner of his eye four children in the back, waving and laughing, and the stupid, frightened face of their father at the wheel. He drove on, cursing, and suddenly it happened; suddenly his hands were shaking feverishly, his face was burning hot, his heart palpitating wildly. He managed to pull off the road into a lay-by, scrambled out of the car and stood breathing heavily, staring at the hurtling stream of giant lorries. He had a vision of the little car caught among them, pounded and smashed, until there was nothing left, nothing but the frenetic whine of klaxons and the blue lights flashing; and the bodies of the children, torn, like the murdered refugees on the road across the dunes.

He drove very slowly the rest of the way and missed his meeting with Karl.

He never drove again without some corner of his memory recalling the tousled children waving to him from the back of that car, and their father grasping the wheel like a farmer at the shafts of a hand plough.

Control would call it fever.

He sat dully in his seat over the wing. There was an American woman next to him wearing high-heeled shoes in polythene wrappers. He had a momentary notion of passing her some note for the people in Berlin, but he discarded it at once. She'd think he was making a pass at her, Peters would see it. Besides, what was the point? Control knew what had happened; Control had made it happen. There was nothing to say.

He wondered what would become of him. Control hadn't talked about that – only about the technique:

'Don't give it to them all at once, make them work for it. Confuse them with detail, leave things out, go back on your tracks. Be testy, be cussed, be difficult. Drink like a fish; don't give way on the ideology, they won't trust that. They want to deal with a man they've bought; they want the clash of opposites, Alec, not some half-cock convert. Above all, they want to *deduce*. The ground's prepared; we did it long ago, little things, difficult clues. You're the last stage in the treasure hunt.'

He'd had to agree to do it; you can't back out of the big fight when all the preliminary ones have been fought for you.

'One thing I can promise you: it's worth it. It's worth it for our special interest, Alec. Keep alive and we've won a great victory.'

He didn't think he could stand torture. He remembered a book by Koestler where the old revolutionary had conditioned himself for torture by holding lighted matches to his fingers. He hadn't read much but he'd read that and he remembered it.

It was nearly dark as they landed at Tempelhof. Leamas watched the lights of Berlin rise to meet them, felt the thud as the plane touched down, saw the Customs and immigration officials move forward out of the half light.

For a moment Leamas was anxious lest some former acquaintance should chance to recognise him at the airport. As they walked side by side, Peters and he, along the interminable corridors, through the cursory Customs and immigration check, and still no familiar face turned to greet him, he realised that his anxiety had in reality been hope; hope that somehow his tacit decision to go on would be revoked by circumstance.

It interested him that Peters no longer bothered to disown him; it was as if Peters regarded West Berlin as safe ground, where vigilance and security could be relaxed; a mere technical staging post to the East.

They were walking through the big reception hall to the main entrance when Peters suddenly seemed to alter his mind, abruptly changed direction and led Leamas to a smaller side entrance which gave on to a car park and taxi rank. There Peters hesitated a second, standing beneath the light over the door, then put his suitcase on the ground beside him, deliberately removed his newspaper from beneath his arm, folded it, pushed it into the left pocket of his raincoat and picked up his suitcase again. Immediately, from the direction of the car park, a pair of headlights sprang to life, were dipped and then extinguished.

'Come on,' said Peters and started to walk briskly across the tarmac, Leamas following more slowly. As they reached the first row of cars the rear door of a black Mercedes was opened from the inside, and the courtesy light went on. Peters, ten yards ahead of Leamas, went quickly to the car, spoke softly to the driver, then called to Leamas.

'Here's the car. Be quick.'

It was an old Mercedes 180 and he got in without a word. Peters sat beside him in the back. As they pulled out they overtook a small DKW with two men sitting in the front. Twenty yards down the road there was a telephone kiosk. A man was talking into the telephone, and he watched them go by, talking all the time. Leamas looked out of the back window and saw the DKW following them. Quite a reception, he thought.

They drove quite slowly. Leamas sat with his hands on his knees, looking straight in front of him. He didn't want to see Berlin that night. This was his last chance, he knew that. The way he was sitting now he could drive the side of his right hand into Peters' throat, smashing the promontory of the thyrax. He could get out and run, weaving to avoid the bullets from the car behind. He would be free – there were people in Berlin who would take care of him – he could get away.

He did nothing.

It was so easy crossing the sector border. Leamas had never expected it to be quite that easy. For about ten minutes they dawdled, and Leamas guessed that they had to cross at a pre-arranged time. As they approached the West German checkpoint, the DKW pulled out and overtook them with the ostentatious roar of a laboured engine, and stopped at the police hut. The Mercedes waited thirty yards behind. Two minutes later the red and white pole lifted to let through the DKW and as it did so both cars drove over together, the Mercedes engine screaming in second gear, the driver pressing himself back against his seat, holding the wheel at arms' length.

As they crossed the fifty yards which separated the two checkpoints, Leamas was dimly aware of the new fortifications on the Eastern side of the wall – dragons' teeth, observation towers and double aprons of barbed wire. Things had tightened up.

The Mercedes didn't stop at the second checkpoint; the booms were already lifted and they drove straight through, the Vopos just watching them through binoculars. The DKW had disappeared, and when Leamas sighted it ten minutes later it was behind them again. They were driving fast now – Leamas had thought they would stop in East Berlin, change cars perhaps, and congratulate one another on a successful operation, but they drove on eastwards through the city.

'Where are we going?' he asked Peters.

'We are there. The German Democratic Republic. They have arranged accommodation for you.'

'I thought we'd be going further east.'

'We are. We are spending a day or two here first. We thought the Germans ought to have a talk with you.'

'I see.'

'After all, most of your work has been on the German side. I sent them details from your statement.'

'And they asked to see me?'

'They've never had anything quite like you, nothing quite so . . . near the source. My people agreed that they should have the chance to meet you.'

'And from there? Where do we go from Germany?'

'East again.'

'Who will I see on the German side?'

'Does it matter?'

'Not particularly. I know most of the Abteilung people by name, that's all. I just wondered.'

'Who would you expect to meet?'

'Fiedler,' Leamas replied promptly, 'deputy head of security. Mundt's man. He does all the big interrogations. He's a bastard.'

'Why?'

'A savage little bastard. I've heard about him. He caught an agent of Peter Guillam's and bloody nearly killed him.'

'Espionage is not a cricket game,' Peters observed sourly and after that they sat in silence. So it is Fiedler, Leamas thought.

Leamas knew Fiedler all right. He knew him from the photographs on the file and the accounts of his former subordinates. A slim, neat man, quite young, smooth-faced. Dark hair, bright brown eyes; intelligent and savage, as Leamas had said. A lithe, quick body containing a patient, retentive mind; a man seemingly without ambition for himself but remorseless in the destruction of others. Fiedler was a rarity in the Abteilung – he took no part in its intrigues, seemed content to live in Mundt's shadow without prospect of promotion. He could not be labelled as a member of this or that clique; even those who had worked close to him in the Abteilung could not say where he stood in its power complex. Fiedler was a solitary; feared, disliked and mistrusted. Whatever motives he had were concealed beneath a cloak of destructive sarcasm.

'Fiedler is our best bet,' Control had explained. They'd been sitting together over dinner – Leamas, Control and Peter Guillam – in the dreary little seven-dwarfs house in Surrey where Control lived with his beady wife, surrounded by carved Indian tables with brass tops. 'Fiedler is the acolyte who one day will stab the high priest in the back. He's the only man who's a match for Mundt' – here Guillam had nodded – 'and he hates his guts. Fiedler's a Jew of course, and Mundt is quite the other thing. Not at all a good mixture. It has been our job,' he declared, indicating Guillam and himself, 'to give Fiedler the weapon with which to destroy Mundt. It will be yours, my dear Leamas, to encourage him to use it. Indirectly, of course, because you'll never meet him. At least I certainly hope you won't.'

They'd all laughed then, Guillam too. It had seemed a good joke at the time; good by Control's standards anyway.

It must have been after midnight.

For some time they had been travelling an unmade road, partly through a wood and partly across open country. Now they stopped and a moment later the DKW drew up beside them. As he and Peters got out Leamas noticed that there were now three people in the second car. Two were already getting out. The third was sitting in the back seat looking at some papers by the light from the car roof, a slight figure half in shadow.

They had parked by some disused stables; the building lay thirty yards back. In the headlights of the car Leamas had glimpsed a low farmhouse with walls of timber and whitewashed brick. They got out. The moon was up, and shone so brightly that the wooded hills behind were sharply defined against the pale night sky. They walked to the house, Peters and Leamas leading and the two men behind. The other man in the second car had still made no attempt to move; he remained there, reading.

As they reached the door Peters stopped, waiting for the other two to catch them up. One of them carried a bunch of keys in his left hand, and while he fiddled with them the other stood off, his hands in his pockets, covering him.

'They're taking no chances,' Leamas observed to Peters, 'what do they think I am?'

'They are not paid to think,' Peters replied, and turning to one of them he asked in German:

'Is he coming?'

The German shrugged and looked back towards the car.

'He'll come,' he said; 'he likes to come alone.'

They went into the house, the man leading the way. It was got up like a hunting lodge, part old, part new. It was badly lit with pale overhead lights. The place had a neglected, musty air as if it had been opened for the occasion. There were little touches of officialdom here and there – a notice of what to do in case of fire, institutional green paint on the door and heavy spring-cartridge locks; and in the drawing-room, which was quite comfortably done, dark, heavy furniture, badly scratched, and the inevitable photographs of Soviet leaders. To Leamas these lapses from anonymity signified the involuntary identification of the Abteilung with bureaucracy. That was something he was familiar with in the Circus.

Peters sat down, and Leamas did the same. For ten minutes, perhaps longer, they waited, then Peters spoke to one of the two men standing awkwardly at the other end of the room.

'Go and tell him we're waiting. And find us some food, we're hungry.' As the man moved towards the door Peters called, 'And whisky – tell them to bring whisky and some glasses.' The man gave an uncooperative shrug of his heavy shoulders and went out, leaving the door open behind him.

'Have you been here before?' asked Leamas.

'Yes,' Peters replied, 'several times.'

'What for?'

'This kind of thing. Not the same, but our kind of work.'

'With Fiedler?'

'Yes.'

'Is he good?'

Peters shrugged. 'For a Jew, he's not bad,' he replied, and Leamas, hearing a sound from the other end of the room, turned and saw Fiedler standing in the doorway. In one hand he held a bottle of whisky, and in the other, glasses and some mineral water. He couldn't have been more than five foot six. He wore a dark blue single-breasted suit; the jacket was cut too long. He was sleek and slightly animal; his eyes were brown and bright. He was not looking at them but at the guard beside the door.

'Go away,' he said. He had a slight Saxonian twang: 'go away and tell the other one to bring us food.'

'I've told him,' Peters called; 'they know already. But they've brought nothing.'

'They are great snobs,' Fiedler observed drily in English. 'They think we should have servants for the food.'

Fiedler had spent the war in Canada. Leamas remembered that, now that he detected the accent. His parents had been German Jewish refugees, Marxists, and it was not until 1946 that the family returned home, anxious to take part, whatever the personal cost, in the construction of Stalin's Germany.

'Hello,' he added to Leamas, almost by the way, 'glad to see you.'

'Hello, Fiedler.'

'You've reached the end of the road.'

'What the hell d'you mean?' asked Leamas quickly.

'I mean that contrary to anything Peters told you, you are not going further east. Sorry.' He sounded amused.

Leamas turned to Peters.

'Is this true?' His voice was shaking with rage. 'Is it true? Tell me!'

Peters nodded: 'Yes. I am the go-between. We had to do it that way. I'm sorry,' he added.

'Why?'

'Force majeure,' Fiedler put in. 'Your initial interrogation took place in the West, where only an embassy could provide the kind of link we needed. The German Democratic Republic has no embassies in the West. Not yet. Our liaison section therefore

.arranged for us to enjoy facilities and communications and immunities which are at present denied to us.'

'You bastard,' hissed Leamas, 'you lousy bastard! You knew I wouldn't trust myself to your rotten Service; that was the reason, wasn't it? That was why you used a Russian.'

'We used the Soviet Embassy at The Hague. What else could we do? Up till then it was our operation. That's perfectly reasonable. Neither we nor anyone else could have known that your own people in England would get on to you so quickly.'

'No? Not even when you put them on to me yourselves? Isn't that what happened, Fiedler? Well, isn't it?' Always remember to dislike them, Control had said. Then they will treasure what they get out of you.

'That is an absurd suggestion,' Fiedler replied shortly. Glancing towards Peters he added something in Russian. Peters nodded and stood up.

'Good-bye,' he said to Leamas. 'Good luck.'

He smiled wearily, nodded to Fiedler, then walked to the door. He put his hand on the door handle, then turned and called to Leamas again:

'Good luck.' He seemed to want Leamas to say something, but Leamas might not have heard. He had turned very pale, he held his hands loosely across his body, the thumbs upwards as if he were going to fight. Peters remained standing at the door.

'I should have known,' said Leamas, and his voice had the odd, faulty note of a very angry man. 'I should have guessed you'd never have the guts to do your own dirty work, Fiedler. It's typical of your rotten little half-country and your squalid little Service that you get big uncle to do your pimping for you. You're not a country at all, you're not a government, you're a fifth-rate dictatorship of political neurotics.' Jabbing his finger in Fiedler's direction, he shouted:

'I know you, you sadistic bastard; it's typical of you. You were in Canada in the war, weren't you; a bloody good place to be then, wasn't it? I'll bet you stuck your fat head into Mummy's apron any time an aeroplane flew over. What are you now? A creeping little acolyte to Mundt and twenty-two Russian divisions sitting on your mother's doorstep. Well, I pity you, Fiedler, the day you wake up and find them gone. There'll be a killing then, and not Mummy or big uncle will save you from getting what you deserve.'

Fiedler shrugged.

'Regard it as a visit to the dentist, Leamas. The sooner it's all done, the sooner you can go home. Have some food and go to bed.'

'You know perfectly well I can't go home,' Leamas retorted. 'You've seen to that. You blew me sky high in England, you had to, both of you. You knew damn' well I'd never come here unless I had to.'

Fiedler looked at his thin, strong fingers.

'This is hardly the time to philosophise,' he said, 'but you can't really complain, you know. All our work – yours and mine – is rooted in the theory that the whole is more important than the individual. That is why a Communist sees his secret service as the natural extension of his arm, and that is why in your own country intelligence is shrouded in a kind of *pudeur anglaise*. The exploitation of individuals can only be justified by the collective need, can't it? I find it slightly ridiculous that you should be so indignant. We are not here to observe the ethical laws of English country life. After all,' he added silkily, 'your own behaviour has not, from the purist's point of view, been irreproachable.'

Leamas was watching Fiedler with an expression of disgust.

'I know your set-up. You're Mundt's poodle, aren't you? They say you want his job. I suppose you'll get it now. It's time the Mundt dynasty ended; perhaps this is it.'

'I don't understand,' Fiedler replied.

'I'm your big success, aren't I?' Leamas sneered. Fiedler seemed to reflect for a moment, then he shrugged and said, 'The operation was successful. Whether you were worth it is questionable. We shall see. But it was a good operation. It satisfied the only requirement of our profession: it worked.'

'I suppose you take the credit?' Leamas persisted, with a glance in the direction of Peters.

'There is no question of credit,' Fiedler replied crisply, 'none at all.' He sat down on the arm of a sofa, looked at Leamas thoughtfully for a moment and then said:

'Nevertheless you are right to be indignant about one thing. Who told your people we had picked you up? We didn't. You may not believe me, but it happens to be true. We didn't tell them. We didn't even want them to know. We had ideas then of getting you to work for us later – ideas which I now realise to be ridiculous. So who told them? You were lost, drifting around, you had no address, no ties, no friends. Then how the devil did they know you'd gone? Someone told them – scarcely Ashe or Kiever, since they are both now under arrest.'

'Under arrest?'

'So it appears. Not specifically for their work on your case, but there were other things . . .'

'Well, well.'

'It is true, what I said just now. We would have been content with Peters' report from Holland. You could have had your money and gone. But you hadn't told us everything; and I want to know everything. After all, your presence here provides us with problems too, you know.'

'Well, you've boobed. I know damn' all – and you're welcome to it.'

There was a silence, during which Peters, with an abrupt and by no means friendly nod in Fiedler's direction, quietly let himself out of the room.

Fiedler picked up the bottle of whisky and poured a little into each glass.

'We have no soda, I'm afraid,' he said. 'Do you like water? I ordered soda, but they brought some wretched lemonade.'

'Oh, go to hell,' said Leamas. He suddenly felt very tired.

Fiedler shook his head.

'You are a very proud man,' he observed, 'but never mind. Eat your supper and go to bed.'

One of the guards came in with a tray of food – black bread, sausage and cold, green salad.

'It is a little crude,' said Fiedler, 'but quite satisfying. No potato, I'm afraid. There is a temporary shortage of potato.'

They began eating in silence, Fiedler very carefully, like a man who counted his calories.

The guards showed Leamas to his bedroom. They let him carry his own luggage – the same luggage that Kiever had given him before he left England – and he walked between them along the wide central corridor which led through the house from the front door. They came to a large double door, painted dark green, and one of the guards unlocked it; they beckoned to Leamas to go first. He pushed open the door and found himself in a small barrack bedroom with two bunk beds, a chair and a rudimentary desk. It was like something in prison camp. There were pictures of girls on the walls and the windows were shuttered. At the far end of the room was another door. They signalled him forward again.

Putting down his baggage he went and opened the door. The second room was identical to the first, but there was one bed and the walls were bare.

'You bring those cases,' he said; 'I'm tired.' He lay on the bed, fully dressed, and within a few minutes he was fast asleep.

A sentry woke him with breakfast: black bread and *ersatz* coffee. He got out of bed and went to the window.

The house stood on a high hill. The ground fell steeply away from beneath his window, the crowns of pine trees visible above the crest. Beyond them, spectacular in their symmetry, unending hills, heavy with trees, stretched into the distance. Here and there a timber gully or fire-break formed a thin brown divide between the pines, seeming like Aaron's rod miraculously to hold apart massive seas of encroaching forest. There was no sign of man; not a house or church, not even the ruin of some previous habitation – only the road, the yellow unmade road, a crayon line across the basin of the valley. There was no sound. It seemed incredible that anything so vast could be so still. The day was cold but clear. It must have rained in the night; the ground was moist, and the whole landscape so sharply defined against the white sky that Leamas could distinguish even single trees on the furthest hills.

He dressed slowly, drinking the sour coffee meanwhile. He had nearly finished dressing and was about to start eating the bread when Fiedler came into the room.

'Good morning,' he said cheerfully. 'Don't let me keep you from your breakfast.' He sat down on the bed. Leamas had to hand it to Fiedler; he had guts. Not that there was anything brave about coming to see him – the sentries, Leamas supposed, were still in the adjoining room. But there was an endurance, a defined purpose in his manner which Leamas could sense and admire.

'You have presented us with an intriguing problem,' he observed.

'I've told you all I know.'

'Oh no.' He smiled. 'Oh no, you haven't. You have told us all you are *conscious* of knowing.'

'Bloody clever,' Leamas muttered, pushing his food aside and lighting a cigarette – his last.

'Let me ask *you* a question,' Fiedler suggested with the exaggerated bonhomie of a man proposing a party game. 'As an experienced intelligence officer, what would *you* do with the information you have given us?'

'What information?'

'My dear Leamas, you have only given us one piece of intelligence. You have told us about Riemeck: we knew about Riemeck. You have told us about the dispositions of your Berlin organisation, about its personalities and its agents. That, if I may say so, is old hat. Accurate – yes. Good background, fascinating reading, here and there good collateral, here and there a little fish which we shall take out of the pool. But not – if I may be crude – not fifteen thousand pounds' worth of intelligence. Not,' he smiled again, 'at current rates.'

'Listen,' said Leamas, 'I didn't propose this deal – you did. You, Kiever and Peters. I didn't come crawling to your cissy friends, peddling old intelligence. You people made the running, Fiedler; you named the price and took the risk. Apart from that, I haven't had a bloody penny. So don't blame me if the operation's a flop.' Make them come to you, Leamas thought.

'It isn't a flop,' Fiedler replied, 'it isn't finished. It can't be. You haven't told us what you *know*. I said you had given us one piece of intelligence. I'm talking about Rolling Stone. Let me ask you again – what would *you* do if I, if Peters or someone like us, had told *you* a similar story?'

Leamas shrugged:

'I'd feel uneasy,' he said; 'it's happened before. You get an indication, several perhaps, that there's a spy in some department or at a certain level. So what? You can't arrest the whole government service. You can't lay traps for a whole department. You just sit tight and hope for more. You bear it in mind. In Rolling Stone you can't even tell what country he's working in.'

'You are an operator, Leamas,' Fiedler observed with a laugh, 'not an evaluator. That is clear. Let me ask you some elementary questions.'

Leamas said nothing.

'The file – the actual file on operation Rolling Stone. What colour was it?'

'Grey with a red cross on it – that means limited subscription.'

'Was anything attached to the outside?'

'Yes, the Caveat. That's the subscription label. With a legend saying that any unauthorised person not named on this label finding the file in his possession must at once return it unopened to Banking Section.'

'Who was on the subscription list?'

'For Rolling Stone?'

'Yes.'

'PA to Control, Control, Control's secretary; Banking Section, Miss Bream of Special Registry and Satellites Four. That's all, I think. And Special Despatch, I suppose – I'm not sure about them.'

'Satellites Four? What do they do?'

'Iron Curtain countries excluding the Soviet Union and China. The Zone.'

'You mean the GDR?'

'I mean the Zone.'

'Isn't it unusual for a whole section to be on a subscription list?'

'Yes, it probably is. I wouldn't know – I've never handled limited subscription stuff before. Except in Berlin, of course; it was all different there.'

'Who was in Satellites Four at that time?'

'Oh, God. Guillam, Haverlake, de Jong, I think. De Jong was just back from Berlin.'

'Were they *all* allowed to see this file?'

'I don't know, Fiedler,' Leamas retorted irritably; 'and if I were you . . .'

'Then isn't it odd that a whole section was on the subscription list while all the rest of the subscribers are individuals?'

'I tell you I don't know – how could I know? I was just a clerk in all this.'

'Who carried the file from one subscriber to another?'

'Secretaries, I suppose – I can't remember. It's bloody months since . . .'

'Then why weren't the secretaries on the list? Control's secretary was.' There was a moment's silence.

'No, you're right; I remember now,' Leamas said, a note of surprise in his voice; 'we passed it by hand.'

'Who else in Banking dealt with that file?'

'No one. It was my pigeon when I joined the section. One of the women had done it before, but when I came I took it over and they were taken off the list.'

'Then you alone passed the file by hand to the next reader?'

'Yes . . . yes, I suppose I did.'

'To whom did you pass it?'

'I . . . I can't remember.'

'*Think!*' Fiedler had not raised his voice, but it contained a sudden urgency which took Leamas by surprise.

'To Control's PA, I think, to show what action we had taken or recommended.'

'Who brought the file?'

'What do you mean?' Leamas sounded off balance.

'Who brought you the file to read? Somebody on the list must have brought it to you.'

Leamas' fingers touched his cheek for a moment in an involuntary nervous gesture.

'Yes, they must. It's difficult, you see, Fiedler; I was putting back a lot of drink in those days'; his tone was oddly conciliatory. 'You don't realise how hard it is to . . .'

'I ask you again. Think. Who brought you the file?'

Leamas sat down at the table and shook his head.

'I can't remember. It may come back to me. At the moment I just can't remember, really I can't. It's no good chasing it.'

'It can't have been Control's girl, can it? You always handed the file *back* to Control's PA. You said so. So those on the list must all have seen it *before* Control.'

'Yes, that's it, I suppose.'

'Then there is Special Registry, Miss Bream.'

'She was just the woman who ran the strong room for subscription list files. That's where the file was kept when it wasn't in action.'

'Then,' said Fiedler silkily, 'it must have been Satellites Four who brought it, mustn't it?'

'Yes, I suppose it must,' said Leamas helplessly, as if he were not quite up to Fiedler's brilliance.

'Which floor did Satellites Four work on?'

'The second.'

'And Banking?'

'The fourth. Next to Special Registry.'

'Do you remember *who* brought it up? Or do you remember, for instance, going downstairs ever to collect the file from them?'

In despair, Leamas shook his head; then suddenly he turned to Fiedler and cried:

'Yes, yes I do! Of course I do! I got it from Peter!' Leamas seemed to have woken up, his face was flushed, excited. 'That's it: I once collected the file from Peter in his room. We chatted together about Norway. We'd served there together, you see.'

'Peter Guillam?'

'Yes, Peter – I'd forgotten about him. He'd come back from Ankara a few months before. He was on the list! Peter was – of course! That's it. It was Satellite Four and PG in brackets, Peter's initials. Someone else had done it before and Special Registry had glued a bit of white paper over the old name and put Peter's initials.'

'What territory did Guillam cover?'

'The Zone. East Germany. Economic stuff; ran a small section, sort of backwater. He was the chap. He brought the file up to me once too, I remember that now. He didn't run agents though: I don't quite know how he came into it – Peter and a couple of others were doing some research job on food shortages. Evaluation really.'

'Did you not discuss it with him?'

'No, that's taboo. It isn't done with subscription files. I got a homily from the woman in Special Registry about it – Bream – no discussion, no questions.'

'But taking into account the elaborate security precautions sur-rounding Rolling Stone, it is possible, is it not, that Guillam's so-called research job might have involved the partial running of this agent, Rolling Stone?'

'I've told Peters,' Leamas almost shouted, banging his fist on the desk, 'it's just bloody silly to imagine that any operation could have been run against East Germany without my knowledge – without the knowledge of the Berlin organisation. I would have known, d'you see? How many times do I have to say that? I would have known!'

'Quite so,' said Fiedler softly, 'of course you would.' He stood up and went to the window.

'You should see it in the autumn,' he said, looking out; 'it's magnificent when the beeches are on the turn.'

Chapter 13

PINS OR
PAPER CLIPS

Fiedler loved to ask questions. Sometimes, because he was a lawyer, he asked them for his own pleasure alone, to demonstrate the discrepancy between evidence and perfective truth. He possessed, however, that persistent inquisitiveness which for journalists and lawyers is an end in itself.

They went for a walk that afternoon, following the gravel road down into the valley, then branching into the forest along a broad, pitted track lined with felled timber. All the time, Fiedler probed, giving nothing. About the building in Cambridge Circus, and the people who worked there. What social class did they come from, what parts of London did they inhabit, did husbands and wives work in the same Departments? He asked about the pay, the leave, the morale, the canteen; he asked about their love-life, their gossip, their philosophy. Most of all he asked about their philosophy.

To Leamas that was the most difficult question of all.

'What do you mean, a philosophy?' he replied; 'we're not Marxists, we're nothing. Just people.'

'Are you Christians, then?'

'Not many, I shouldn't think. I don't know many.'

'What makes them do it, then?' Fiedler persisted; 'they must have a philosophy.'

'Why must they? Perhaps they don't know; don't even care. Not everyone has a philosophy,' Leamas answered, a little helplessly.

'Then tell me what is your philosophy?'

'Oh for Christ's sake,' Leamas snapped, and they walked on in silence for a while. But Fiedler was not to be put off.

'If they do not know what they want, how can they be so certain they are right?'

'Who the hell said they were?' Leamas replied irritably.

'But what is the justification then? What is it? For us it is easy, as I said to you last night. The Abteilung and organisations like it are the natural extension of the Party's arm. They are in the vanguard of the fight for Peace and Progress. They are to the Party what the Party is to socialism: they *are* the vanguard. Stalin said so –' he smiled drily, 'it is not fashionable to quote Stalin – but he said once "half a million liquidated is a statistic, and one man killed in a traffic accident is a national tragedy." He was laughing, you see, at the bourgeois sensitivities of the mass. He was a great cynic. But what he meant is still true: a movement which protects itself against counter-revolution can hardly stop at the exploitation – or the elimination, Leamas – of a few individuals. It is all one, we have never pretended to be wholly just in the process of rationalising society. Some Roman said it, didn't he, in the Christian Bible – it is expedient that one man should die for the benefit of many.'

'I expect so,' Leamas replied wearily.

'Then what do you think? What is your philosophy?'

'I just think the whole lot of you are bastards,' said Leamas savagely.

Fiedler nodded. 'That is a viewpoint I understand. It is primitive, negative and very stupid – but it is a viewpoint, it exists. But what about the rest of the Circus?'

'I don't know. How should I know?'

'Have you never discussed philosophy with them?'

'No. We're not Germans.' He hesitated, then added vaguely: 'I suppose they don't like Communism.'

'And that justifies, for instance, the taking of human life? That justifies the bomb in the crowded restaurant; that justifies your write-off rate of agents – all that?'

Leamas shrugged. 'I suppose so.'

'You see, for us it does,' Fiedler continued. 'I myself would have put a bomb in a restaurant if it brought us further along the road. Afterwards I would draw the balance – so many women, so many children; and so far along the road. But Christians – and yours is a Christian society – Christians may not draw the balance.'

'Why not? They've got to defend themselves, haven't they?'

'But they believe in the sanctity of human life. They believe every man has a soul which can be saved. They believe in sacrifice.'

'I don't know. I don't much care,' Leamas added. 'Stalin didn't either, did he?'

Fiedler smiled; 'I like the English,' he said, almost to himself; 'my father did too. He was very fond of the English.'

'That gives me a nice, warm feeling,' Leamas retorted, and relapsed into silence.

– 107 –

They stopped while Fiedler gave Leamas a cigarette and lit it for him.

They were climbing steeply now. Leamas liked the exercise, walking ahead with long strides, his shoulders thrust forward. Fiedler followed, slight and agile, like a terrier behind his master. They must have been walking for an hour, perhaps more, when suddenly the trees broke above them and the sky appeared. They had reached the top of a small hill, and could look down on the solid mass of pine broken only here and there by grey clusters of beech. Across the valley Leamas could glimpse the hunting lodge, perched below the crest of the opposite hill, low and dark against the trees. In the middle of the clearing was a rough bench beside a pile of logs and the damp remnants of a charcoal fire.

'We'll sit down for a moment,' said Fiedler, 'then we must go back.' He paused. 'Tell me: this money, these large sums in foreign banks – what did you think they were for?'

'What do you mean? I've told you, they were payments to an agent.'

'An agent from behind the Iron Curtain?'

'Yes, I thought so,' Leamas replied wearily.

'Why did you think so?'

'First, it was a hell of a lot of money. Then the complications of paying him; the special security. And of course, Control being mixed up in it.'

'What did you think the agent did with the money?'

'Look, I've told you – I don't know. I don't even know if he collected it. I didn't know anything – I was just the bloody office boy.'

'What did you do with the pass books for the accounts?'

'I handed them in as soon as I got back to London – together with my phoney passport.'

'Did the Copenhagen or Helsinki banks ever write to you in London – to your alias, I mean?'

'I don't know. I suppose any letters would have been passed straight to Control anyway.'

'The false signatures you used to open the accounts – Control had a sample of them?'

'Yes. I practised them a lot and they had samples.'

'More than one?'

'Yes. Whole pages.'

'I see. Then letters could have gone to the banks after you had opened the accounts. You need not have known. The signatures could have been forged and the letters sent without your knowledge.'

'Yes. That's right. I suppose that's what happened. I signed a lot of blank sheets too. I always assumed someone else took care of the correspondence.'

'But you never did actually *know* of such correspondence?'

Leamas shook his head: 'You've got it all wrong,' he said; 'you've got it all out of proportion. There was a lot of paper going around – this was just part of the day's work. It wasn't something I gave much thought to. Why should I? It was hush-hush, but I've been in on things all my life where you only know a little and someone else knows the rest. Besides, paper bores me stiff. I didn't lose any sleep on it. I liked the trips of course – I drew operational subsistence which helped. But I didn't sit at my desk all day, wondering about Rolling Stone. Besides,' he added a little shame-facedly, 'I was hitting the bottle a bit.'

'So you said,' Fiedler commented, 'and of course, I believe you.'

'I don't give a damn whether you believe me or not,' Leamas rejoined hotly.

Fiedler smiled.

'I am glad. That is your virtue,' he said, 'that is your great virtue. It is the virtue of indifference. A little resentment here, a little pride there, but that is nothing: the distortions of a tape recorder. You are objective. It occurred to me,' Fiedler continued after a slight pause, 'that you could still help us to establish whether any of that money was ever drawn. There is nothing to stop you writing to each bank and asking for a current statement. We could say you were staying in Switzerland; use an accommodation address. Do you see any objection to that?'

'It might work. It depends on whether Control has been corresponding with the bank independently, over my forged signature. It might not fit in.'

'I do not see that we have much to lose.'

'What have you got to win?'

'If the money has been drawn, which I agree is doubtful, we shall know where the agent was on a certain day. That seems to be a useful thing to know.'

'You're dreaming. You'll never find him, Fiedler, not on that kind of information. Once he's in the West he can go to any consulate, even in a small town, and get a visa for another country. How are you any the wiser? You don't even know whether the man is East German. What are you after?'

Fiedler did not answer at once. He was gazing distractedly across the valley.

'You said you are accustomed to knowing only a little, and I cannot answer your question without telling you what you should not know.' He hesitated. 'But Rolling Stone was an operation against us, I can assure you.'

'Us?'

'The GDR.' He smiled. 'The Zone if you prefer. I am not really so sensitive.'

He was watching Leamas now, his brown eyes resting on him reflectively.

'But what about me?' Leamas asked. 'Suppose I don't write the letters?' His voice was rising. 'Isn't it time to talk about me, Fiedler?'

Fiedler nodded.

'Why not?' he replied, agreeably. There was a moment's silence, then Leamas said:

'I've done my bit, Fiedler. You and Peters between you have got all I know. I never agreed to write letters to banks – it could be bloody dangerous, a thing like that. That doesn't worry you, I know. As far as you're concerned I'm expendable.'

'Now let me be frank,' Fiedler replied. 'There are, as you know, two stages in the interrogation of a defector. The first stage in your case is nearly complete: you have told us all we can reasonably record. You have not told us whether your Service favours pins or paper clips because we haven't asked you, and because you did not consider the answer worth volunteering. There is a process on both sides of unconscious selection. Now it is always possible – and this is the worrying thing, Leamas – it is always entirely possible that in a month or two we shall unexpectedly and quite desperately need to know about the pins and paper clips. That is normally accounted for in the second stage – that part of the bargain which you refused to accept in Holland.'

'You mean you're going to keep me on ice?'

'The profession of defector,' Fiedler observed with a smile, 'demands great patience. Very few are suitably qualified.'

'How long?' Leamas insisted.

Fiedler was silent.

'Well?'

Fiedler spoke with sudden urgency. 'I give you my word that as soon as I possibly can, I will tell you the answer to your question. Look – I could lie to you, couldn't I? I could say one month or less, just to keep you sweet. But I am telling you I don't know because that is the truth. You have given us some indications: until we have run them to earth I cannot listen to talk of letting you go. But afterwards if things are as I think they are, you will need a friend and that friend will be me. I give you my word as a German.'

Leamas was so taken aback that for a moment he was silent.

'All right,' he said finally, 'I'll play, Fiedler, but if you are stringing me along, somehow I'll break your neck.'

'That may not be necessary,' Fiedler replied evenly.

A man who lives a part, not to others but alone, is exposed to obvious psychological dangers. In itself, the practice of deception is not particularly exacting; it is a matter of experience, of professional expertise, it is a facility most of us can acquire. But while a confidence trickster, a play-actor or a gambler can return from his performance to the ranks of his admirers, the secret agent enjoys no such relief. For him, deception is first a matter of self-defence. He must protect himself not only from without but from within, and against the most natural of impulses; though he earn a fortune, his role may forbid him the purchase of a razor; though he be erudite, it can befall him to mumble nothing but banalities; though he be an affectionate husband and father, he must under all circumstances withhold himself from those in whom he should naturally confide.

Aware of the overwhelming temptations which assail a man permanently isolated in his deceit, Leamas resorted to the course which armed him best; even when he was alone, he compelled himself to live with the personality he had assumed. It is said that Balzac on his deathbed enquired anxiously after the health and prosperity of characters he had created. Similarly Leamas, without relinquishing the power of invention, identified himself with what he had invented. The qualities he exhibited to Fiedler, the restless uncertainty, the protective arrogance concealing shame, were not approximations but extensions of qualities he actually possessed; hence also the slight dragging of the feet, the aspect of personal neglect, the indifference to food, and an increasing reliance on alcohol and tobacco. When alone, he remained faithful to these habits. He would even exaggerate them a little, mumbling to himself about the iniquities of his Service.

Only very rarely, as now, going to bed that evening, did he allow himself the dangerous luxury of admitting the great lie he lived.

Control had been phenomenally right. Fiedler was walking like
a man led in his sleep, into the net which Control had spread for
him. It was uncanny to observe the growing identity of interest
between Fiedler and Control: it was as if they had agreed on the
same plan, and Leamas had been despatched to fulfil it.

Perhaps that was the answer. Perhaps Fiedler was the special
interest Control was fighting so desperately to preserve. Leamas
didn't dwell on that possibility. He did not want to know. In
matters of that kind he was wholly uninquisitive: he knew that no
conceivable good could come of his deductions. Nevertheless, he
hoped to God it was true. It was possible, just possible in that case,
that he would get home.

Chapter 14

LETTER TO A CLIENT

L eamas was still in bed the next morning when Fiedler brought him the letters to sign. One was on the thin, blue writing paper of the Seiler Hotel Alpenblick, Lake Spiez, Switzerland, the other from the Palace Hotel, Gstaad.

Leamas read the first letter:

To the Manager,
The Royal Scandinavian Bank Ltd.,
Copenhagen.

Dear Sir,
   I have been travelling for some weeks and have not received any mail from England. Accordingly I have not had your reply to my letter of March 3rd requesting a current statement of the deposit account of which I am a joint signatory with Herr Karlsdorf. To avoid further delay, would you be good enough to forward a duplicate statement to me at the following address, where I shall be staying for two weeks beginning April 21st:
c/o Madame Y. de Sanglot,
13 Avenue des Colombes,
Paris XII,
France.
   I apologise for this confusion,
                              Yours faithfully,
                              (Robert Lang)

'What's all this about a letter of March 3rd?' he asked. 'I didn't write them any letter.'
'No, you didn't. As far as we know, no one did. That will worry the bank. If there is any inconsistency between the letter we are sending them now and letters they have had from Control, they will assume the solution is to be found in the *missing* letter of March 3rd. Their reaction will be to send you the statement as you

ask, with a covering note regretting that they have not received your letter of the third.'

The second letter was the same as the first; only the names were different. The address in Paris was the same. Leamas took a blank piece of paper and his fountain pen and wrote half a dozen times in a fluent hand 'Robert Lang', then signed the first letter. Sloping his pen backwards he practised the second signature until he was satisfied with it, then wrote 'Stephen Bennett' under the second letter.

'Admirable,' Fiedler observed, 'quite admirable.'

'What do we do now?'

'They will be posted in Switzerland tomorrow, in Interlaken and Gstaad. Our people in Paris will telegraph the replies to me as soon as they arrive. We shall have the answer in a week.'

'And until then?'

'We shall be constantly in one another's company. I know that is distasteful to you, and I apologise. I thought we could go for walks, drive round in the hills a bit, kill time. I want you to relax and talk; talk about London, about Cambridge Circus and working in the Department; tell me the gossip, talk about the pay, the leave, the rooms, the paper and the people. The pins and the paper clips. I want to know all the little things that don't matter. Incidentally . . .' A change of tone.

'Yes?'

'We have facilities here for people, who . . . for people who are spending some time with us. Facilities for diversion and so on.'

'Are you offering me a woman?' he asked.

'Yes.'

'No, thank you. Unlike you, I haven't reached the stage where I need a pimp.'

Fiedler seemed indifferent to his reply. He went on quickly.

'But you had a woman in England, didn't you – the girl in the library?'

Leamas turned on him, his hands open at his sides.

'One thing!' he shouted. 'Just that one thing – don't ever mention that again, not as a joke, not as a threat, not even to turn the screws, Fiedler, because it won't work, not ever; I'd dry up, d'you see, you'd never get another bloody word from me as long as I lived. Tell that to them, Fiedler, to Mundt and Stammberger or whichever little alley-cat told you to say it – tell them what I said.'

'I'll tell them,' Fiedler replied; 'I'll tell them. It may be too late.'

★　　★　　★

In the afternoon they went walking again. The sky was dark and heavy, and the air warm.

'I've only been to England once,' Fiedler observed casually, 'that was on my way to Canada, with my parents before the war. I was a child then of course. We were there for two days.'

Leamas nodded.

'I can tell you this now,' Fiedler continued. 'I nearly went there a few years back. I was going to replace Mundt on the Steel Mission – did you know he was once in London?'

'I knew,' Leamas replied cryptically.

'I always wondered what it would have been like, that job.'

'Usual game of mixing with the other Bloc Missions I suppose. Certain amount of contact with British business – not much of that.' Leamas sounded bored.

'But Mundt got about all right: he found it quite easy.'

'So I hear,' said Leamas; 'he even managed to kill a couple of people.'

'So you heard about that too?'

'From Peter Guillam. He was in on it with George Smiley. Mundt bloody nearly killed George as well.'

'The Fennan case,' Fiedler mused. 'It was amazing that Mundt managed to escape at all, wasn't it?'

'I suppose it was.'

'You wouldn't think that a man whose photograph and personal particulars were filed at the Foreign Office as a member of a Foreign Mission would have a chance against the whole of British Security.'

'From what I hear,' Leamas said, 'they weren't too keen to catch him anyway.'

Fiedler stopped abruptly.

'What did you say?'

'Peter Guillam told me he didn't reckon they wanted to catch Mundt, that's all I said. We had a different set-up then – an Adviser instead of an Operational Control – a man called Maston. Maston had made a bloody awful mess of the Fennan case from the start, that's what Guillam said. Peter reckoned that if they'd caught Mundt it would have made a hell of a stink – they'd have tried him and probably hanged him. The dirt that came out in the process would have finished Maston's career. Peter never knew quite what happened, but he was bloody sure there was no full-scale search for Mundt.'

'You are sure of that, you are sure Guillam told you that in as many words? No full-scale search?'

'Of course I am sure.'

'Guillam never suggested any other reason why they might have let Mundt go?'

'What do you mean?'

Fiedler shook his head and they walked on along the path.

'The Steel Mission was closed down after the Fennan case,' Fiedler observed a moment later, 'that's why I didn't go.'

'Mundt must have been mad. You may be able to get away with assassination in the Balkans – or here – but not London.'

'He did get away with it though, didn't he?' Fiedler put in quickly. 'And he did good work.'

'Like recruiting Kiever and Ashe? God help him.'

'They ran the Fennan woman for long enough.'

Leamas shrugged.

'Tell me something else about Karl Riemeck,' Fiedler began again. 'He met Control once, didn't he?'

'Yes, in Berlin about a year ago, maybe a bit more.'

'Where did they meet?'

'We all met together in my flat.'

'Why?'

'Control loved to come in on success. We'd got a hell of a lot of good stuff from Karl – I suppose it had gone down well with London. He came out on a short trip to Berlin and asked me to fix up for them to meet.'

'Did you mind?'

'Why should I?'

'He was your agent. You might not have liked him to meet other operators.'

'Control isn't an operator; he's head of Department. Karl knew that and it tickled his vanity.'

'Were you all three together, all the time?'

'Yes. Well, not quite. I left them alone for a quarter of an hour or so – not more. Control wanted that – he wanted a few minutes alone with Karl, God knows why, so I left the flat on some excuse, I forget what. Oh – I know, I pretended we'd run out of Scotch. I actually went and collected a bottle from de Jong in fact.'

'Do you know what passed between them while you were out?'

'How could I? I wasn't that interested, anyway.'

'Didn't Karl tell you afterwards?'

'I didn't ask him. Karl was a cheeky sod in some ways, always pretending he had something over me. I didn't like the way he sniggered about Control. Mind you, he had every right to snigger – it was a pretty ridiculous performance. We laughed about it together a bit, as a matter of fact. There wouldn't have been any point in pricking Karl's vanity; the whole meeting was supposed to give him a shot in the arm.'

'Was Karl depressed then?'

'No, far from it. He was spoilt already. He was paid too much, loved too much, trusted too much. It was partly my fault, partly London's. If we hadn't spoilt him he wouldn't have told that bloody woman of his about his network.'

'Elvira?'

'Yes.' They walked on in silence for a while, until Fiedler interrupted his own reverie to observe:

'I'm beginning to like you. But there's one thing that puzzles me. It's odd – it didn't worry me before I met you.'

'What's that?'

'Why you ever came. Why you defected.' Leamas was going to say something when Fiedler laughed. 'I'm afraid that wasn't very tactful, was it?' he said.

They spent that week walking in the hills. In the evenings they would return to the lodge, eat a bad meal washed down with a bottle of rank white wine, sit endlessly over their Steinläger in front of the fire. The fire seemed to be Fiedler's idea – they didn't have it to begin with, then one day Leamas overheard him telling a guard to bring logs. Leamas didn't mind the evenings then; after the fresh air all day, the fire and the rough spirit, he would talk unprompted, rambling on about his service. Leamas supposed it was recorded. He didn't care.

As each day passed in this way Leamas was aware of an increasing tension in his companion. Once they went out in the DKW – it was late in the evening – and stopped at a call-box. Fiedler left him in the car with the keys and made a long phone call. When he came back Leamas said:

'Why didn't you ring from the house?' But Fiedler just shook his head.

'We must take care,' he replied; 'you too, you must take care.'

'Why? What's going on?'

'The money you paid into the Copenhagen bank – we wrote, you remember?'

'Of course I remember.'

Fiedler wouldn't say any more, but drove on in silence into the hills. There they stopped. Beneath them, half screened by the ghostly patchwork of tall pine trees, lay the meeting point of two great valleys. The steep wooded hills on either side gradually yielded their colours to the gathering dusk until they stood grey and lifeless in the twilight.

'Whatever happens,' Fiedler said, 'don't worry. It will be all right, do you understand?' His voice was heavy with emphasis, his slim hand rested on Leamas' arm. 'You may have to look after yourself a little, but it won't last long, do you understand?' he asked again.

'No. And since you won't tell me I shall have to wait and see. Don't worry too much for my skin, Fiedler.' He moved his arm, but Fiedler's hand still held him. Leamas hated being touched.

'Do you know Mundt?' asked Fiedler, 'do you know about him?'

'We've talked about Mundt.'

'Yes,' Fiedler repeated, 'we've talked about him. He shoots first and asks questions afterwards. The deterrent principle. It's an odd system in a profession where the questions are always supposed to be more important than the shooting.' Leamas knew what Fiedler wanted to tell him. 'It's an odd system unless you're frightened of the answers,' Fiedler continued under his breath.

Leamas waited. After a moment Fiedler said:

'He's never taken on an interrogation before. He's left it to me before, always. He used to say to me – "You interrogate them, Jens, no one can do it like you. I'll catch them and you make them sing." He used to say that people who do counter-espionage are like painters – they need a man with a hammer standing behind them to strike when they have finished their work, otherwise they forget what they're trying to achieve. "I'll be your hammer," he used to say to me. It was a joke between us, at first, then it began to matter; when he began to kill, kill them before they sang, just as you said: one here, another there, shot or murdered. I asked him, I begged him, "Why not arrest them? Why not let me have them for a month or two? What good to you are they when they are dead?" He just shook his head at me and said there was a law that thistles must be cut down before they flower. I had the feeling that he'd prepared the answer before I ever asked the question. He's a good operator, very good. He's done wonders with the

Abteilung – you know that. He's got theories about it; I've talked to him late at night. Coffee he drinks – nothing else – just coffee all the time. He says Germans are too introspective to make good agents, and it all comes out in counter-intelligence. He says counter-intelligence people are like wolves chewing dry bones – you have to take away the bones and make them find new quarry – I see all that, I know what he means. But he's gone too far. Why did he kill Viereck? Why did he take him away from me? Viereck was fresh quarry, we hadn't even taken the meat from the bone, you see. So why did he take him? Why, Leamas, why?' The hand on Leamas' arm was clasping it tightly; in the total darkness of the car Leamas was aware of the frightening intensity of Fiedler's emotion.

'I've thought about it night and day. Ever since Viereck was shot, I've asked for a reason. At first it seemed fantastic. I told myself I was jealous, that the work was going to my head, that I was seeing treachery behind every tree; we get like that, people in our world. But I couldn't help myself, Leamas, I had to work it out. There'd been other things before. He was afraid – he was afraid that we would catch one who would talk too much!'

'What are you saying? You're out of your mind,' said Leamas, and his voice held the trace of fear.

'It all held together, you see. Mundt escaped so easily from England; you told me yourself he did. And what did Guillam say to you? He said they didn't *want* to catch him! Why not? I'll tell you why – he was their man; they turned him, they caught him, don't you see, and that was the price of his freedom – that and the money he was paid.'

'I tell you you're out of your mind!' Leamas hissed. 'He'll kill you if he ever thinks you make up this kind of stuff. It's sugar candy, Fiedler. Shut up and drive us home.' At last the hot grip on Leamas' arm relaxed.

'That's where you're wrong. You provided the answer, you yourself, Leamas. That's why we need one another.'

'It's not true!' Leamas shouted. 'I've told you again and again, they couldn't have done it. The Circus couldn't have run him against the Zone without my knowing! It just wasn't an administrative possibility. You're trying to tell me Control was personally directing the deputy head of the Abteilung without the knowledge of the Berlin station. You're mad, Fiedler, you're just bloody well off your head!' Suddenly he began to laugh quietly. 'You may want his job, you poor bastard; that's not unheard of, you know.

– 119 –

But this kind of thing went out with bustles.' For a moment neither spoke.

'That money,' Fiedler said, 'in Copenhagen. The bank replied to your letter. The manager is very worried lest there has been a mistake. The money was drawn by your co-signatory exactly one week after you paid it in. The date it was drawn coincides with a two-day visit which Mundt paid to Denmark on 15th June. He went there under an alias to meet an American agent we have who was attending a world scientists' conference.' Fiedler hesitated, then added, 'I suppose you ought to write to the bank and tell them everything is quite in order?'

Chapter 15

COME TO
THE BALL

L iz looked at the letter from Party Centre and wondered what
it was about. She found it a little puzzling. She had to admit
she was pleased, but why hadn't they consulted her first? Had the
District Committee put up her name, or was it Centre's own
choice? But no one in Centre knew her, so far as she was aware.
She'd met odd speakers of course, and at District Congress she'd
shaken hands with the Party Organiser. Perhaps that man from
Cultural Relations had remembered her – that fair, rather effeminate man who was so ingratiating. Ashe, that was his name. He'd
taken a bit of interest in her and she supposed he might have
handed her name on, or remembered her when the Scholarship
came up. An odd man, he was; took her to the Black and White
for coffee after the meeting and asked her about her boy-friends.
He hadn't been amorous or anything – she'd thought he was a bit
queer to be honest – but he asked her masses of questions about
herself. How long had she been in the Party, did she get homesick
living away from her parents? Had she lots of boy-friends or was
there a special one she carried a torch for? She hadn't cared for him
much but his talk had gone down quite well – the worker-state in
the German Democratic Republic, the concept of the worker-poet
and all that stuff. He certainly knew all about Eastern Europe, he
must have travelled a lot. She'd guessed he was a schoolmaster,
he had that rather didactic, fluent way with him. They'd had a
collection for the Fighting Fund afterwards, and Ashe had put a
pound in; she'd been absolutely amazed. That was it, she was sure
now: it was Ashe who'd remembered her. He'd told someone at
London District, and District had told Centre or something like
that. It still seemed a funny way to go about things, but then the
Party always was secretive – it was part of being a revolutionary
party, she supposed. It didn't appeal to Liz much, the secrecy, it
seemed dishonest. But she supposed it was necessary, and Heaven
knows, there were plenty who got a kick out of it.

She read the letter again. It was on Centre's writing paper, with the thick red print at the top, and it began 'Dear Comrade'; it sounded so military to Liz, and she hated that; she'd never quite got used to 'Comrade'.

Dear Comrade,

We have recently had discussions with our comrades in the Socialist Unity Party of the German Democratic Republic on the possibility of effecting exchanges between Party members over here and our comrades in democratic Germany. The idea is to create a basis of exchange at the rank and file level between our two parties. The SUP is aware that the existing discriminatory measures by the British Home Office make it unlikely that their own delegates will be able to come to the United Kingdom in the immediate future, but they feel that an exchange of experiences is all the more important for this reason. They have generously invited us to select five Branch Secretaries with good experience and a good record of stimulating mass action at street level. Each selected comrade will spend three weeks attending Branch discussions, studying progress in industry and social welfare and seeing at first hand the evidence of fascist provocation by the West. This is a grand opportunity for our comrades to profit from the experience of a young socialist system.

We therefore asked District to put forward the names of young Cadre workers from your areas who might get the biggest advantage from the trip, and your name has been put forward. We want you to go if you possibly can, and carry out the second part of the scheme – which is to establish contact with a Party Branch in the GDR whose members are from similar industrial backgrounds and have the same kind of problems as your own. The Bayswater South Branch has been paired with Neuenhagen, a suburb of Leipzig. Freda Lüman, Secretary of the Neuenhagen branch, is preparing a big welcome. We are sure you are just the comrade for the job, and that it will be a terrific success. All expenses will be paid by the GDR Cultural Office.

We are sure you realise what a big honour this is, and are confident you will not allow personal considerations to prevent you from accepting. The visits are due to take place at the end of next month, about the 23rd, but the selected comrades will travel separately as their invitations are not all concurrent. Will you please let us know as soon as possible whether you can accept, and we will let you know further details.

The more she read it, the odder it seemed. Such short notice for a start – how could they know she could get away from the library? Then to her surprise she recalled that Ashe had asked her what she did for her holidays, whether she had taken her leave this year, and whether she had to give a lot of notice if she wanted to claim free time. Why hadn't they told her who the other nominees were? There was no particular reason why they should, perhaps, but it somehow looked odd when they didn't. It was such a *long* letter, too. They were so hard up for secretarial help at Centre they usually kept their letters short, or asked comrades to ring up. This was so efficient, so well typed it might not have been done at Centre at all. But it *was* signed by the Cultural Organiser; it was his signature all right, no doubt of that. She'd seen it at the bottom of roneoed notices masses of times. And the letter had that awkward, semi-bureaucratic, semi-Messianic style she had grown accustomed to without ever liking. It was stupid to say she had a good record of stimulating mass action at street level. She hadn't. As a matter of fact she hated that side of Party work – the loudspeakers at the factory gates, selling the *Daily Worker* at the street corner, going from door to door at the local elections. Peace work she didn't mind so much, it meant something to her, it made sense. You could look at the kids in the street as you went by, at the mothers pushing their prams and the old people standing in doorways, and you could say, 'I'm doing it for them.' That really *was* fighting for peace.

But she never quite saw the fighting for votes and the fighting for sales in the same way. Perhaps that was because it cut them down to size, she thought. It was easy when there were a dozen or so together at a Branch meeting to rebuild the world, march at the vanguard of socialism and talk of the inevitability of history. But afterwards she'd go out into the streets with an armful of *Daily Workers*, often waiting an hour, two hours, to sell a copy. Sometimes she'd cheat, as the others cheated, and pay for a dozen herself just to get out of it and go home. At the next meeting they'd boast about it – forgetting they'd bought them themselves – 'Comrade Gold sold eighteen copies on Saturday night – eighteen!' It would go in the Minutes then, and the Branch bulletin as well. District would rub their hands, and perhaps she'd get a mention in that little panel on the front page about the Fighting Fund. It was such a little world, and she wished they could be more honest. But she lied to herself about it all, too. Perhaps they all did. Or perhaps the others understood more *why* you had to lie so much. It seemed so odd they'd made her Branch Secretary. It was Mulligan who'd proposed it – 'Our young, vigorous *and* attractive comrade –' He'd thought she'd sleep with him if he got her made secretary. The others had voted for her because they liked her, and because she could type. Because she'd do the work and not try and make them go canvassing at weekends. Not too often anyway. They'd voted for her because they wanted a decent little club, nice and revolutionary and no fuss. It was all such a fraud. Alec had seemed to understand that; he just hadn't taken it seriously. 'Some people keep canaries, some people join the Party,' he'd said once, and it was true. In Bayswater South it was true anyway, and District knew that perfectly well. That's why it was so peculiar that she had been nominated; that was why she was extremely reluctant to believe that District had even had a hand in it. The explanation, she was sure, was Ashe. Perhaps he had a crush on her; perhaps he wasn't queer but just looked it.

Liz made a rather exaggerated shrug, the kind of overstressed gesture people do make when they are excited and alone. It was abroad anyway, it was free and it sounded interesting. She had never been abroad, and she certainly couldn't afford the fare herself. It would be rather fun. She had reservations about Germans, that was true. She knew, she had been told, that West Germany was militarist and revanchist, and that East Germany was democratic and peace-loving. But she doubted whether all the good Germans were on one side and all the bad ones on the other. And it was the bad ones who had killed her father. Perhaps that was why the Party had chosen her – as a generous act of reconciliation. Perhaps that was what Ashe had had in mind when he asked her all those questions. Of course – that was the explanation. She was suddenly filled with a feeling of warmth and gratitude towards the Party. They really were decent people and she was proud and thankful to belong. She went to the desk and opened the drawer where, in an old school satchel, she kept the Branch stationery and the dues stamps. Putting a sheet of paper into her old Underwood typewriter – they'd sent it down from District when they heard she could type: it jumped a bit but otherwise was fine – she typed a neat, grateful letter of acceptance. Centre was such a wonderful thing – stern, benevolent, impersonal, perpetual. They were good, good people. People who fought for peace. As she closed the drawer she caught sight of Smiley's card.

She remembered that little man with the earnest, puckered face, standing at the doorway of her room and saying: 'Did the Party know about you and Alec?' How silly she was. Well, this would take her mind off it.

Chapter 16

<u>ARREST</u>

Fiedler and Leamas drove back the rest of the way in silence. In the dusk the hills were black and cavernous, the pinpoint lights struggling against the gathering darkness like the lights of distant ships at sea.

Fiedler parked the car in a shed at the side of the house and they walked together to the front door. They were about to enter the lodge when they heard a shout from the direction of the trees, followed by someone calling Fiedler's name. They turned, and Leamas distinguished in the twilight twenty yards away three men standing, apparently waiting for Fiedler to come.

'What do you want?' Fiedler called.

'We want to talk to you. We're from Berlin.'

Fiedler hesitated. 'Where's that damn' guard?' he asked Leamas; 'there should be a guard on the front door.'

Leamas shrugged.

'Why aren't the lights on in the hall?' he asked: then, still unconvinced, he began walking slowly towards the men.

Leamas waited a moment, then, hearing nothing, made his way through the unlit house to the annexe behind it. This was a shoddy barrack hut attached to the back of the building and hidden from all sides by close plantations of young pine trees. The hut was divided into three adjoining bedrooms; there was no corridor. The centre room had been given to Leamas, and the room nearest to the main building was occupied by two guards. Leamas never knew who occupied the third. He had once tried to open the connecting door between it and his own room, but it was locked. He had only discovered it was a bedroom by peering through a narrow gap in the lace curtains early one morning as he went for a walk. The two guards, who followed him everywhere at fifty yards' distance, had not rounded the corner of the hut, and he looked in at the window. The room contained a single bed, made, and a small writing-desk with papers on it. He supposed that someone, with what passes for German thoroughness, watched him from that bedroom. But Leamas was too old a dog to allow himself to be bothered by surveillance. In Berlin it had been a fact of life – if you couldn't spot it so much the worse: it only meant they were taking greater care, or you were losing your grip. Usually, because he was good at that kind of thing, because he was observant and had an accurate memory – because, in short, he was good at his job – he spotted them anyway. He knew the formations favoured by a shadowing team, he knew the tricks, the weaknesses, the momentary lapses that could give them away. It meant nothing to Leamas that he was watched, but as he walked through the improvised doorway from the lodge to the hut, and stood in the guards' bedroom, he had the distinct feeling that something was wrong.

The lights in the annexe were controlled from some central point. They were put on and off by an unseen hand. In the mornings he was often woken by the sudden blaze of the single overhead light in his room. At night he would be hastened to bed by perfunctory darkness. It was only nine o'clock as he entered the annexe, and the lights were already out. Usually they stayed on till eleven, but now they were out and the shutters had been lowered. He had left the connecting door from the house open, so that the pale twilight from the hallway reached, but scarcely penetrated, the guards' bedroom, and by it he could just see the two empty beds. As he stood there peering into the room, surprised to find it empty, the door behind him closed. Perhaps by itself, but Leamas made no attempt to open it. It was pitch dark. No sound accompanied the closing of the door, no click nor footstep. To Leamas, his instinct suddenly alert, it was as if the sound-track had stopped. Then he smelt the cigar smoke. It must have been hanging in the air but he had not noticed it till now. Like a blind man, his senses of touch and smell were sharpened by the darkness.

There were matches in his pocket but he did not use them. He took one pace sideways, pressed his back against the wall and remained motionless. To Leamas there could only be one explanation – they were waiting for him to pass from the guards' room to his own and therefore he determined to remain where he was. Then from the direction of the main building whence he had come he heard clearly the sound of a footstep. The door which had just closed was tested, the lock turned and made fast. Still Leamas did not move. Not yet. There was no pretence: he was a prisoner in the hut. Very slowly, Leamas now lowered himself into a crouch, putting his hand in the side pocket of his jacket as he did so. He was quite calm, almost relieved at the prospect of action, but memories were racing through his mind. 'You've nearly always got a weapon: an ash-tray, a couple of coins, a fountain pen – anything that will gouge or cut.' It was the favourite dictum of the mild little Welsh sergeant at that house near Oxford in the war; 'Never use both hands at once, not with a knife, a stick or a pistol; keep your left arm free, and hold it across the belly. If you can't find anything to hit with, keep the hands open and the thumbs stiff.' Taking the box of matches in his right hand he clasped it longways, and deliberately crushed it, so that the small, jagged edges of boxwood protruded from between his fingers. This done, he edged his way along the wall until he came to a chair which he knew was in the corner of the room. Indifferent now to the noise he made, he shoved the chair into the centre of the floor. Counting his footsteps as he moved back from the chair, he positioned himself in the angle of the two walls. As he did so, he heard the door of his own bedroom flung open. Vainly he tried to discern the figure who must be standing in the doorway, but there was no light from his own room either. The darkness was impenetrable. He dared not move forward to attack, for the chair was now in the middle of the room; it was his tactical advantage, for he knew where it was, and they did not. They must come for him, they must; he could not let them wait until their helper outside had reached the master switch and put on the lights.

'Come on, you windy bastards,' he hissed in German; 'I'm here, in the corner. Come and get me, can't you?' Not a move, not a sound.

'I'm here, can't you see me? What's the matter then? What's the matter, children, come on, can't you?' And then he heard one stepping forward, and another following; and then the oath of a man as he stumbled on the chair, and that was the sign that Leamas was waiting for. Tossing away the box of matches he slowly, cautiously crept forward, pace by pace, his left arm extended in the attitude of a man warding off twigs in a wood until, quite gently, he had touched an arm and felt the warm prickly cloth of a military uniform. Still with his left hand Leamas deliberately tapped the arm twice – two distinct taps – and heard a frightened voice whisper close to his ear in German:

'Hans, is it you?'

'Shut up, you fool,' Leamas whispered in reply, and in that same moment reached out and grasped the man's hair, pulling his head forward and down, then in a terrible cutting blow drove the side of his right hand on to the nape of the neck, pulled him up again by the arm, hit him in the throat with an upward thrust of his open fist, then released him to fall where the force of gravity took him. As the man's body hit the ground, the lights went on.

In the doorway stood a young captain of the People's Police smoking a cigar, and behind him two men. One was in civilian clothes, quite young. He held a pistol in his hand. Leamas thought it was the Czech kind with a loading lever on the spine of the butt. They were all looking at the man on the floor. Somebody unlocked the outer door and Leamas turned to see who it was. As he turned, there was a shout – Leamas thought it was the captain – telling him to stand still. Slowly he turned back and faced the three men.

His hands were still at his side as the blow came. It seemed to crush his skull. As he fell, drifting warmly into unconsciousness, he wondered whether he had been hit with a revolver, the old kind with a swivel on the butt where you fastened the lanyard.

He was woken by the lag singing and the warder yelling at him to shut up. He opened his eyes and like a brilliant light the pain burst upon his brain. He lay quite still, refusing to close them, watching the sharp, coloured fragments racing across his vision. He tried to take stock of himself: his feet were icy cold and he was aware of the sour stench of prison denims. The singing had stopped and suddenly Leamas longed for it to start again, although he knew it never would. He tried to raise his hand and touch the blood that was caked on his cheek, but his hands were behind him, locked together. His feet too must be bound: the blood had left them, that was why they were cold. Painfully he looked about him, trying to lift his head an inch or two from the floor. To his surprise he saw his own knees in front of him. Instinctively he tried to stretch his legs and as he did so his whole body was seized with a pain so sudden and terrible that he screamed out a sobbing agonised cry of self-pity, like the last cry of a man upon the rack. He lay there panting, attempting to master the pain, then through the sheer perversity of his nature, he tried again, quite slowly, to straighten his legs. At once the agony returned, but Leamas had found the cause: his hands and feet were chained together behind his back. As soon as he attempted to stretch his legs the chain tightened, forcing his shoulders down and his damaged head on to the stone floor. They must have beaten him up while he was unconscious, his whole body was stiff and bruised and his groin ached. He wondered if he'd killed the guard. He hoped so.

Above him shone the light, large, clinical and fierce. No furniture, just whitewashed walls, quite close all round, and the grey steel door, a smart charcoal grey, the colour you see on clever London houses. There was nothing else. Nothing at all. Nothing to think about, just the savage pain.

He must have lain there hours before they came. It grew hot from the light, he was thirsty but he refused to call out. At last the door opened and Mundt stood there. He knew it was Mundt from the eyes. Smiley had told him about them.

Chapter 17

MUNDT

They untied him and let him try to stand. For a moment he almost succeeded, then, as the circulation returned to his hands and feet, and as the joints of his body were released from the contraction to which they had been subject, he fell. They let him lie there, watching him with the detachment of children looking at an insect. One of the guards pushed past Mundt and yelled at Leamas to get up. Leamas crawled to the wall and put the palms of his throbbing hands against the white brick. He was half-way up when the guard kicked him and he fell again. He tried once more and this time the guard let him stand with his back against the wall. He saw the guard move his weight on to his left leg and he knew he would kick him again. With all his remaining strength Leamas thrust himself forward, driving his lowered head into the guard's face. They fell together, Leamas on top. The guard got up and Leamas lay there waiting for the pay-off. But Mundt said something to the guard and Leamas felt himself being picked up by the shoulders and feet and heard the door of his cell close as they carried him down the corridor. He was terribly thirsty.

They took him to a small comfortable room, decently furnished with a desk and armchairs. Swedish blinds half covered the barred windows. Mundt sat at the desk and Leamas in an armchair, his eyes half closed. The guards stood at the door.

'Give me a drink,' said Leamas.

'Whisky?'

'Water.'

Mundt filled a carafe from a basin in the corner, and put it on the table beside him with a glass.

'Bring him something to eat,' he ordered, and one of the guards left the room, returning with a mug of soup and some sliced sausage. He drank and ate, and they watched him in silence.

'Where's Fiedler?' Leamas asked finally.

'Under arrest,' Mundt replied curtly.

'What for?'

'Conspiring to sabotage the security of the people.'

Leamas nodded slowly. 'So you won,' he said. 'When did you arrest him?'

'Last night.'

Leamas waited a moment, trying to focus again on Mundt.

'What about me?' he asked.

'You're a material witness. You will of course stand trial yourself later.'

'So I'm part of a put-up job by London to frame Mundt, am I?'

Mundt nodded, lit a cigarette and gave it to one of the sentries to pass to Leamas. 'That's right,' he said. The sentry came over, and with a gesture of grudging solicitude, put the cigarette between Leamas' lips.

'A pretty elaborate operation,' Leamas observed, and added stupidly, 'Clever chaps these Chinese.'

Mundt said nothing. Leamas became used to his silences as the interview progressed. Mundt had rather a pleasant voice, that was something Leamas hadn't expected, but he seldom spoke. It was part of Mundt's extraordinary self-confidence perhaps, that he did not speak unless he specifically wished to, that he was prepared to allow long silences to intervene rather than exchange pointless words. In this he differed from professional interrogators who set store by initiative, by the evocation of atmosphere and the exploitation of that psychological dependency of a prisoner upon his inquisitor. Mundt despised technique: he was a man of fact and action. Leamas preferred that.

Mundt's appearance was fully consistent with his temperament. He looked an athlete. His fair hair was cut short. It lay matt and neat. His young face had a hard, clean line, and a frightening directness; it was barren of humour or fantasy. He looked young but not youthful; older men would take him seriously. He was well built. His clothes fitted him because he was an easy man to fit. Leamas found no difficulty in recalling that Mundt was a killer. There was a coldness about him, a rigorous self-sufficiency which perfectly equipped him for the business of murder. Mundt was a very hard man.

'The other charge on which you will stand trial, if necessary,' Mundt added quietly, 'is murder.'

'So the sentry died, did he?' Leamas replied.

A wave of intense pain passed through his head.

Mundt nodded: 'That being so,' he said, 'your trial for espionage

– 132 –

is somewhat academic. I propose that the case against Fiedler should be publicly heard. That is also the wish of the Praesidium.'

'And you want my confession?'

'Yes.'

'In other words you haven't any proof.'

'We shall have proof. We shall have your confession.' There was no menace in Mundt's voice. There was no style, no theatrical twist.

'On the other hand, there could be mitigation in your case. You were blackmailed by British Intelligence; they accused you of stealing money and then coerced you into preparing a revanchist trap against myself. The court would have sympathy for such a plea.'

Leamas seemed to be taken off his guard.

'How did you know they accused me of stealing money?' But Mundt made no reply.

'Fiedler has been very stupid,' Mundt observed. 'As soon as I read the report of our friend Peters I knew why you had been sent, and I knew that Fiedler would fall into the trap. Fiedler hates me so much.' Mundt nodded, as if to emphasise the truth of his observation. 'Your people knew that of course. It was a very clever operation. Who prepared it, tell me. Was it Smiley? Did he do it?' Leamas said nothing.

'I wanted to see Fiedler's report of his own interrogation of you, you see. I told him to send it to me. He procrastinated and I knew I was right. Then yesterday he circulated it among the Praesidium, and did not send me a copy. Someone in London has been very clever.'

Leamas said nothing.

'When did you last see Smiley?' Mundt asked casually. Leamas hesitated, uncertain of himself. His head was aching terribly.

'When did you last see him?' Mundt repeated.

'I don't remember,' Leamas said at last, 'he wasn't really in the outfit any more. He'd drop in from time to time.'

'He is a great friend of Peter Guillam, is he not?'

'I think so, yes.'

'Guillam, you thought, studied the economic situation in the GDR. Some odd little section in your Service, you weren't quite sure what it did.'

'Yes.' Sound and sight were becoming confused in the mad throbbing of his brain. His eyes were hot and painful. He felt sick.

'Well, when did you last see Smiley?'

'I don't remember . . . I don't remember.'

Mundt shook his head.

'You have a very good memory – for anything that incriminates me. We can all remember when we *last* saw somebody. Did you for instance see him after you returned from Berlin?'

'Yes, I think so. I bumped into him . . . in the Circus once, in London.' Leamas had closed his eyes and he was sweating. 'I can't go on, Mundt . . . not much longer, Mundt; I'm sick,' he said.

'After Ashe had picked you up, after he had walked into the trap that had been set for him, you had lunch together, didn't you?'

'Yes. Lunch together.'

'Lunch ended at about four o'clock. Where did you go then?'

'I went down to the City, I think. I don't remember for sure . . . for Christ's sake, Mundt,' he said holding his head with his hand, 'I can't go on. My bloody head's . . .'

'And after that where did you go? Why did you shake off your followers, why were you so keen to shake them off?'

Leamas said nothing: he was breathing in sharp gasps, his head buried in his hands.

'Answer this one question, then you can go. You shall have a bed. You can sleep if you want. Otherwise you must go back to your cell, do you understand? You will be tied up again and fed on the floor like an animal, do you understand? Tell me where you went.'

The wild pulsation of his brain suddenly increased, the room was dancing; he heard voices around him and the sound of footsteps; spectral shapes passed and re-passed, detached from sound and gravity; someone was shouting, but not at him; the door was open, he was sure someone had opened the door. The room was full of people, all shouting now, and then they were going, some of them had gone, he heard them marching away, the stamping of their feet was like the throbbing of his head; the echo died and there was silence. Then like the touch of mercy itself, a cool cloth was laid across his forehead, and kindly hands carried him away.

He woke on a hospital bed, and standing at the foot of it was Fiedler, smoking a cigarette.

Chapter 18

FIEDLER

Leamas took stock. A bed with sheets. A single ward with
no bars in the windows, just curtains and frosted glass. Pale
green walls, dark green linoleum; and Fiedler watching him,
smoking.

A nurse brought him food: an egg, some thin soup and fruit.
He felt like death, but he supposed he'd better eat it. So he did and
Fiedler watched.

'How do you feel?' he asked.

'Bloody awful,' Leamas replied.

'But better?'

'I suppose so.' He hesitated, 'Those sods beat me up.'

'You killed a sentry, you know that?'

'I guessed I had . . . What do they expect if they mount such a
damn' stupid operation. Why didn't they pull us both in at once?
Why put all the lights out? If anything was over-organised, that
was.'

'I am afraid that as a nation we tend to over-organise. Abroad
that passes for efficiency.'

Again there was a pause.

'What happened to you?' Leamas asked.

'Oh, I too was softened for interrogation.'

'By Mundt's men?'

'By Mundt's men *and* Mundt. It was a very peculiar sensation!'

'That's one way of putting it.'

'No, no; not physically. Physically it was a nightmare, but you
see Mundt had a special interest in beating me up. Apart from the
confession.'

'Because you dreamed up that story about –'

'Because I am a Jew.'

'Oh Christ,' said Leamas softly.

'That is why I got special treatment. All the time he whispered
to me. It was very strange.'

'What did he say?'

Fiedler didn't reply. At last he muttered:

'That's all over.'

'Why? What's happened?'

'The day we were arrested I had applied to the Praesidium for a civil warrant to arrest Mundt as an enemy of the people.'

'But you're mad – I told you, you're raving mad, Fiedler! He'll never –'

'There was other evidence against him apart from yours. Evidence I have been accumulating over the last three years, piece by piece. Yours provided the proof we need; that's all. As soon as that was clear I prepared a report and sent it to every member of the Praesidium except Mundt. They received it on the same day that I made my application for a warrant.'

'The day we were pulled in.'

'Yes. I knew Mundt would fight. I knew he had friends on the Praesidium, or yes-men at least, people who were sufficiently frightened to go running to him as soon as they got my report. And in the end, I knew he would lose. The Praesidium had the weapon it needed to destroy him; they had the report, and for those few days while you and I were being questioned they read it and re-read it until they knew it was true and each knew the others knew. In the end they acted. Herded together by their common fear, their common weakness and their common knowledge they turned against him and ordered a Tribunal.'

'Tribunal?'

'A secret one, of course. It meets tomorrow. Mundt is under arrest.'

'What is this other evidence? The evidence you've collected.'

'Wait and see,' Fiedler replied with a smile. 'Tomorrow you will see.'

Fiedler was silent for a time, watching Leamas eat.

'This Tribunal,' Leamas asked, 'how is it conducted?'

'That is up to the President. It is not a People's Court – it is important to remember that. It is more in the nature of an enquiry – a committee of enquiry, that's it, appointed by the Praesidium to investigate and report upon a certain . . . subject. Its report contains a recommendation. In a case like this the recommendation is tantamount to a verdict, but remains secret, as part of the proceedings of the Praesidium.'

'How does it work? Are there counsel and judges?'

'There are three judges,' Fiedler said; 'and in effect, there are

counsel. Tomorrow I myself shall put the case against Mundt.
Karden will defend him.'

'Who's Karden?'

Fiedler hesitated.

'A very tough man,' he said. 'Looks like a country doctor, small
and benevolent. He was at Buchenwald.'

'Why can't Mundt defend himself?'

'It was Mundt's wish. It is said that Karden will call a witness.'

Leamas shrugged.

'That's your affair,' he said. Again there was silence. At last
Fiedler said reflectively:

'I wouldn't have minded – I don't think I would have minded,
not so much anyway – if he had hurt me for myself, for hate or
jealousy. Do you understand that? That long, long pain and all the
time you say to yourself, "Either I shall faint or I shall grow to
bear the pain, nature will see to that" and the pain just increases
like a violinist going up the E string. You think it can't get any
higher and it does – the pain's like that, it rises and rises, and all
that nature does is bring you on from note to note like a deaf child
being taught to hear. And all the time he was whispering Jew . . .
Jew. I could understand, I'm sure I could, if he had done it for the
idea, for the Party, if you like, or if he had hated *me*. But it wasn't
that; he hated –'

'All right,' said Leamas shortly, 'you should know. He's a
bastard.'

'Yes,' said Fiedler, 'he is a bastard.' He seemed excited; he wants
to boast to somebody, thought Leamas.

'I thought a lot about you,' Fiedler added. 'I thought about that
talk we had – you remember – about the motor.'

'What motor?'

Fiedler smiled. 'I'm sorry, that is a direct translation. I
mean "*Motor*", the engine, spirit, urge; whatever Christians call
it.'

'I'm not a Christian.'

Fiedler shrugged. 'You know what I mean.' He smiled again.
'The thing that embarrasses you . . . I'll put it another way. Suppose
Mundt is right. He asked me to confess, you know; I was to
confess that I was in league with British spies who were plotting
to murder him. You see the argument – that the whole operation
was mounted by British Intelligence in order to entice us – me, if
you like – into liquidating the best man in the Abteilung. To turn
our own weapon against us.'

'He tried that on me,' said Leamas indifferently. And he added, 'As if I'd cooked up the whole bloody story.'

'But what I mean is this: suppose you had done that, suppose it were true – I am taking an example, you understand, a hypothesis, would you kill a man, an innocent man –'

'Mundt's a killer himself.'

'Suppose he wasn't. Suppose it were me they wanted to kill: would London do it?'

'It depends . . . it depends on the need . . .'

'Ah,' said Fiedler contentedly, 'it depends on the need. Like Stalin, in fact. The traffic accident and the statistics. That is a great relief.'

'Why?'

'You must get some sleep,' said Fiedler. 'Order what food you want. They will bring you whatever you want. Tomorrow you can talk.' As he reached the door he looked back and said, 'We're all the same, you know, that's the joke.'

Soon Leamas was asleep, content in the knowledge that Fiedler was his ally and that they would shortly send Mundt to his death. That was something which he had looked forward to for a very long time.

Chapter 19

BRANCH MEETING

Liz was happy in Leipzig. Austerity pleased her – it gave her the comfort of sacrifice. The little house she stayed in was dark and meagre, the food was poor and most of it had to go to the children. They talked politics at every meal, she and Frau Ebert, Branch Secretary for the Ward Branch of Leipzig-Hohengrün, a small, grey woman whose husband managed a gravel quarry on the outskirts of the city. It was like living in a religious community, Liz thought; a convent or a kibbutz or something. You felt the world was better for your empty stomach. Liz had some German which she had learnt from her aunt, and she was surprised how quickly she was able to use it. She tried it on the children first and they grinned and helped her. The children treated her oddly to begin with, as if she were a person of great quality or rarity value, and on the third day one of them plucked up courage and asked her if she had brought any chocolate from *'drüben'* – from 'over there'. She'd never thought of that and she felt ashamed. After that they seemed to forget about her.

In the evenings there was Party Work. They distributed literature, visited Branch members who had defaulted on their dues or lagged behind in their attendance at meetings, called in at District for a discussion on 'Problems connected with the centralised distribution of agricultural produce' at which all local Branch Secretaries were present, and attended a meeting of the Workers' Consultative Council of a machine tool factory on the outskirts of the town.

At last, on the fourth day, the Thursday, came their own Branch Meeting. This was to be, for Liz at least, the most exhilarating experience of all; it would be an example of all that her own Branch in Bayswater could one day be. They had chosen a wonderful title for the evening's discussions – 'Coexistence after two wars' – and they expected a record attendance. The whole ward had been circularised, they had taken care to see that there was no rival meeting in the neighbourhood that evening; it was not a late shopping day.

Seven people came.

Seven people and Liz and the Branch Secretary and the man from District. Liz put a brave face on it but she was terribly upset. She could scarcely concentrate on the speaker, and when she tried he used long German compounds that she couldn't work out anyway. It was like the meetings in Bayswater, it was like midweek evensong when she used to go to church – the same dutiful little group of lost faces, the same fussy self-consciousness, the same feeling of a great idea in the hands of little people. She always felt the same thing – it was awful, really, but she did – she wished no one would turn up, because that was absolute and it suggested persecution, humiliation – it was something you could react to.

But seven people were nothing: they were worse than nothing, because they were evidence of the inertia of the uncapturable mass. They broke your heart.

The room was better than the schoolroom in Bayswater, but even that was no comfort. In Bayswater it had been fun trying to *find* a room. In the early days they had pretended they were something else, not the Party at all. They'd taken back rooms in pubs, a committee room at the Ardena Café, or met secretly in one another's houses. Then Bill Hazel had joined from the Secondary School and they'd used his classroom. Even that was a risk – the headmaster thought Bill ran a drama group, so theoretically at least they might still be chucked out. Somehow that fitted better than this Peace Hall in pre-cast concrete with the cracks in the corners and the picture of Lenin. Why did they have that silly frame thing all round the picture? Bundles of organ pipes sprouting from the corners and the bunting all dusty. It looked like something from a fascist funeral. Sometimes she thought Alec was right – you believed in things because you needed to; what you believed in had no value of its own, no function. What did he say: 'A dog scratches where it itches. Different dogs itch in different places.' No, it was wrong, Alec was wrong – it was a wicked thing to say. Peace and freedom and equality – they were facts, of course they were. And what about history – all those laws the Party proved. No, Alec was wrong: truth existed outside people, it was demonstrated in history, individuals must bow to it, be crushed by it if necessary. The Party was the vanguard of history, the spearpoint in the fight for Peace . . . she went over the rubric a little uncertainly. She wished more people had come. Seven was so few. They looked so cross; cross and hungry.

The meeting over, Liz waited for Frau Ebert to collect the unsold literature from the heavy table by the door, fill in her attendance book and put on her coat, for it was cold that evening. The speaker had left – rather rudely, Liz thought – before the general discussion. Frau Ebert was standing at the door with her hand on the light switch when a man appeared out of the darkness, framed in the doorway. Just for a moment Liz thought it was Ashe. He was tall and fair and wore one of those raincoats with leather buttons.

'Comrade Ebert?' he enquired.

'Yes?'

'I am looking for an English comrade, Gold. She is staying with you?'

'I'm Elizabeth Gold,' Liz put in, and the man came into the hall, closing the door behind him, so that the light shone full upon his face.

'I am Holten from District.' He showed some paper to Frau Ebert who was still standing at the door, and she nodded and glanced a little anxiously towards Liz.

'I have been asked to give a message to Comrade Gold from the Praesidium,' he said. 'It concerns an alteration in your programme; an invitation to attend a special meeting.'

'Oh,' said Liz rather stupidly. It seemed fantastic that the Praesidium should even have heard of her.

'It is a gesture,' Holten said. 'A gesture of goodwill.'

'But I – but Frau Ebert . . .' Liz began helplessly.

'Comrade Ebert, I am sure, will forgive you under the circumstances.'

'Of course,' said Frau Ebert quickly.

'Where is the meeting to be held?'

'It will necessitate your leaving tonight,' Holten replied. 'We have a long way to go. Nearly to Görlitz.'

'To Görlitz . . . Where's that?'

'East,' said Frau Ebert quickly. 'On the Polish border.'

'We can drive you home now. You can collect your things and we will continue the journey at once.'

'Tonight? Now?'

'Yes.' Holten didn't seem to consider Liz had much choice.

A large black car was waiting for them. There was a driver in the front and a flagpost on the bonnet. It looked rather a military car.

Chapter 20

TRIBUNAL

The court was no larger than a schoolroom. At one end, on the mere five or six benches which were provided, sat guards and warders and here and there among them spectators – members of the Praesidium and selected officials. At the other end of the room sat the three members of the Tribunal on tall-backed chairs at an unpolished oak table. Above them, suspended from the ceiling by three loops of wire, was a large red star made of plywood. The walls of the courtroom were white like the walls of Leamas' cell.

On either side, their chairs a little forward of the table, and turned inwards to face one another, sat two men; one was middle-aged, sixty perhaps, in a black suit and a grey tie, the kind of suit they wear in church in German country districts. The other was Fiedler.

Leamas sat at the back, a guard on either side of him. Between the heads of the spectators he could see Mundt, himself surrounded by police, his fair hair cut very short, his broad shoulders covered in the familiar grey of prison uniform. It seemed to Leamas a curious commentary on the mood of the court – or the influence of Fiedler – that he himself should be wearing his own clothes, while Mundt was in prison uniform.

Leamas had not long been in his place when the President of the Tribunal, sitting at the centre of the table, rang the bell. The sound directed his attention towards it, and a shiver passed over him as he realised that the President was a woman. He could scarcely be blamed for not noting it before. She was fiftyish, small-eyed and dark. Her hair was cut short like a man's, and she wore the kind of functional dark tunic favoured by Soviet wives. She looked sharply round the room, nodded to a sentry to close the door, and began at once without ceremony to address the court.

'You all know why we are here. The proceedings are secret, remember that. This is a Tribunal convened expressly by the Praesidium. It is to the Praesidium alone that we are responsible.

We shall hear evidence as we think fit.' She pointed perfunctorily towards Fiedler. 'Comrade Fiedler, you had better begin.'

Fiedler stood up. Nodding briefly towards the table he drew from the briefcase beside him a sheaf of papers held together in one corner by a piece of black cord.

He talked quietly and easily, with a diffidence which Leamas had never seen in him before. Leamas considered it a good performance, well adjusted to the role of a man regretfully hanging his superior.

'You should know first, if you do not know already,' Fiedler began, 'that on the day that the Praesidium received my report on the activities of Comrade Mundt I was arrested, together with the defector Leamas. Both of us were imprisoned and both of us . . . invited, under extreme duress, to confess that this whole terrible charge was a fascist plot against a loyal comrade.

'You can see from the report I have already given you how it was that Leamas came to our notice: we ourselves sought him out, induced him to defect and finally brought him to Democratic Germany. Nothing could more clearly demonstrate the impartiality of Leamas than this: that he still refuses, for reasons I will explain, to believe that Mundt was a British agent. It is therefore grotesque to suggest that Leamas is a plant: the initiative was ours, and the fragmentary but vital evidence of Leamas provides only the final proof in a long chain of indications reaching back over the last three years.

'You have before you the written record of this case. I need do no more than interpret for you facts of which you are already aware.

'The charge against Comrade Mundt is that he is the agent of an imperialist power. I could have made other charges – that he passed information to the British Secret Service, that he turned his Department into the unconscious lackey of a bourgeois state, that he deliberately shielded revanchist anti-Party groups and accepted sums of foreign currency in reward. These other charges would derive from the first: that Hans-Dieter Mundt is the agent of an imperialist power. The penalty for this crime is death. There is no crime more serious in our penal code, none which exposes our state to greater danger, nor demands more vigilance of our Party organs.' Here he put the papers down.

'Comrade Mundt is forty-two years old. He is deputy head of the Department for the Protection of the People. He is unmarried. He has always been regarded as a man of exceptional capabilities, tireless in serving the Party's interests, ruthless in protecting them.

'Let me tell you some details of his career. He was recruited into the Department at the age of twenty-eight and underwent the customary instruction. Having completed his probationary period he undertook special tasks in Scandinavian countries -- notably Norway, Sweden and Finland – where he succeeded in establishing an intelligence network which carried the battle against fascist agitators into the enemy's camp. He performed this task well, and there is no reason to suppose that at that time he was other than a diligent member of his Department. But, Comrades, you should not forget this early connection with Scandinavia. The networks established by Comrade Mundt soon after the war provided the excuse, many years later, for him to travel to Finland and Norway, where his commitments became a cover enabling him to draw thousands of dollars from foreign banks in return for his treacherous conduct. Make no mistake: Comrade Mundt has not fallen victim to those who try to disprove the arguments of history. First cowardice, then weakness, then greed were his motives; the acquirement of great wealth his dream. Ironically, it was the elaborate system by which his lust for money was satisfied that brought the forces of justice on his trail.'

Fiedler paused, and looked round the room, his eyes suddenly alight with fervour. Leamas watched, fascinated.

'Let that be a lesson,' Fiedler shouted, 'to those other enemies of the state, whose crime is so foul that they must plot in the secret hours of the night!' A dutiful murmur rose from the tiny group of spectators at the back of the room.

'They will not escape the vigilance of the people whose blood they seek to sell!' Fiedler might have been addressing a large crowd rather than the handful of officials and guards assembled in the tiny, white-walled room.

Leamas realised at that moment that Fiedler was taking no chances: the deportment of the Tribunal, prosecutors and witnesses must be politically impeccable. Fiedler, knowing no doubt that the danger of a subsequent counter-charge was inherent in such cases, was protecting his own back: the polemic would go down in the record and it would be a brave man who set himself to refute it.

Fiedler now opened the file that lay on the desk before him.

'At the end of 1956 Mundt was posted to London as a member of the East German Steel Mission. He had the additional special task of undertaking counter-subversionary measures against *émigré* groups. In the course of his work he exposed himself to great dangers – of that there is no doubt – and he obtained valuable results.'

Leamas' attention was again drawn to the three figures at the centre table. To the President's left a youngish man, dark. His eyes seemed to be half closed. He had lank, unruly hair and the grey, meagre complexion of an ascetic. His hands were slim, restlessly toying with the corner of a bundle of papers which lay before him. Leamas guessed he was Mundt's man; he found it hard to say why. On the other side of the table sat a slightly older man, balding, with an open agreeable face. Leamas thought he looked rather an ass. He guessed that if Mundt's fate hung in the balance the young man would defend him and the woman condemn. He thought the second man would be embarrassed by the difference of opinion and side with the President.

Fiedler was speaking again.

'It was at the end of his service in London that recruitment took place. I have said that he exposed himself to great dangers; in doing so he fell foul of the British secret police, and they issued a warrant for his arrest. Mundt, who had no diplomatic immunity (NATO Britain does not recognise our sovereignty), went into hiding. Ports were watched, his photograph and description were distributed throughout the British Isles. Yet, after two days in hiding, Comrade Mundt took a taxi to London airport and flew to Berlin. "Brilliant," you will say, and so it was. With the whole of Britain's police force alerted, her roads, railways, shipping and air routes under constant surveillance, Comrade Mundt takes a plane from London Airport. Brilliant indeed. Or perhaps you may feel, Comrades, with the advantage of hindsight, that Mundt's escape from England was a little *too* brilliant, a little *too* easy, that without the connivance of the British authorities it would never have been possible at all!' Another murmur, more spontaneous than the first, rose from the back of the room.

'The truth is this: Mundt *was* taken prisoner by the British; in a short historic interview they offered him the classic alternative. Was it to be years in an imperialist prison, the end of a brilliant career, or was Mundt to make a dramatic return to his home country, against all expectation, and fulfil the promise he had shown? The British, of course, made it a condition of his return that he should provide them with information, and they would pay him large sums of money. With the carrot in front and the stick behind, Mundt was recruited.

'It was now in the British interest to promote Mundt's career. We cannot yet prove that Mundt's success in liquidating minor Western intelligence agents was the work of his imperialist masters betraying their own collaborators – those who were expendable – in order that Mundt's prestige should be enhanced. We cannot prove it, but it is an assumption which the evidence permits.

'Ever since 1960 – the year Comrade Mundt became head of the Counter-Espionage section of the Abteilung – indications have reached us from all over the world that there was a highly placed spy in our ranks. You all know Karl Riemeck was a spy; we thought when he was eliminated that the evil had been stamped out. But the rumours persisted.

'In late 1960 a former collaborator of ours approached an Englishman in the Lebanon known to be in contact with their Intelligence Service. He offered him – we found out soon afterwards – a complete breakdown of the two sections of the Abteilung for which he had formerly worked. His offer, after it had been transmitted to London, was rejected. That was a very curious thing. It could only mean that the British already possessed the intelligence they were being offered, *and that it was up to date.*

'From mid-1960 onwards we were losing collaborators abroad at an alarming rate. Often they were arrested within a few weeks of their despatch. Sometimes the enemy attempted to turn our own agents back on us, but not often. It was as if they could scarcely be bothered.

'And then – it was early 1961 if my memory is correct – we had a stroke of luck. We obtained, by means I will not describe, a summary of the information which British Intelligence held about the Abteilung. It was complete, it was accurate, and it was astonishingly up to date. I showed it to Mundt, of course – he was my superior. He told me it came as no surprise to him: he had certain enquiries in hand and I should take no action for fear of prejudicing them. And I confess that at that moment the thought crossed my mind, remote and fantastic as it was, that Mundt himself could have provided the information. There were other indications too . . .

'I need hardly tell you that the last, the very last person to be suspected of espionage is the head of the Counter-Espionage section. The notion is so appalling, so melodramatic that few would entertain it, let alone give expression to it! I confess that I myself have been guilty of excessive reluctance in reaching such a seemingly fantastic deduction. That was erroneous.

'But, Comrades, the final evidence has been delivered into our hands. I propose to call that evidence now.' He turned, glancing towards the back of the room. 'Bring Leamas forward.'

The guards on either side of him stood up and Leamas edged his way along the row to the rough gangway which ran, not more than two feet wide, down the middle of the room. A guard indicated to him that he should stand facing the table. Fiedler stood a bare six feet away from him. First the President addressed him.

'Witness, what is your name?' she asked.

'Alec Leamas.'

'What is your age?'

'Fifty.'

'Are you married?'

'No.'

'But you were.'

'I'm not married now.'

'What is your profession?'

'Assistant librarian.'

Fiedler angrily intervened. 'You were formerly employed by British Intelligence, were you not?' he snapped.

'That's right. Till a year ago.'

'The Tribunal has read the reports of your interrogation,' Fiedler continued. 'I want you to tell them again about the conversation you had with Peter Guillam some time in May last year.'

'You mean when we talked about Mundt?'

'Yes.'

'I've told you. I was at the Circus, the office in London, our headquarters in Cambridge Circus. I bumped into Peter in the corridor. I knew he was mixed up with the Fennan case and I asked him what had become of George Smiley. Then we got talking about Dieter Frey, who died, and Mundt, who was mixed up in the thing. Peter said he thought that Maston – Maston was effectively in charge of the case then – had not wanted Mundt to be caught.'

'How did you interpret that?' asked Fiedler.

'I knew Maston had made a mess of the Fennan case. I supposed he didn't want any mud raked up by Mundt appearing at the Old Bailey.'

'If Mundt had been caught, would he have been legally charged?' the President put in.

'It depends who caught him. If the police got him they'd report it to the Home Office. After that no power on earth could stop him being charged.'

'And what if your Service had caught him?' Fiedler enquired.

'Oh, that's a different matter. I suppose they would either have interrogated him and then tried to exchange him for one of our own people in prison over here; or else they'd have given him a ticket.'

'What does that mean?'

'Got rid of him.'

'Liquidate him?' Fiedler was asking all the questions now, and the members of the Tribunal were writing diligently in the files before them.

'I don't know what they do. I've never been mixed up in that game.'

'Might they not have tried to recruit him as their agent?'

'Yes, but they didn't succeed.'

'How do you know that?'

'Oh, for God's sake, I've told you over and over again. I'm not a bloody performing seal . . . I was head of the Berlin Command for four years. If Mundt had been one of our people, I would have known. I couldn't help knowing.'

'Quite.'

Fiedler seemed content with that answer, confident perhaps that the remainder of the Tribunal was not. He now turned his attention to Operation Rolling Stone; took Leamas once again through the special security complexities governing the circulation of the file, the letters to the Copenhagen and Helsinki banks and the one reply which Leamas had received. Addressing himself to the Tribunal, Fiedler commented:

'We had no reply from Helsinki. I do not know why. But let me recapitulate for you. Leamas deposited money at Copenhagen on June 15th. Among the papers before you there is the facsimile of a letter from the Royal Scandinavian Bank addressed to Robert Lang. Robert Lang was the name Leamas used to open the Copenhagen deposit account. From that letter (it is the twelfth serial in your files) you will see that the entire sum – ten thousand dollars – was drawn by the co-signatory to the account one week later. I imagine,' Fiedler continued, indicating with his head the motionless figure of Mundt in the front row, 'that it is not disputed by the Defendant that he was in Copenhagen on June 21st, nominally engaged on secret work on behalf of the Abteilung.' He paused and then continued:

'Leamas' visit to Helsinki – the second visit he made to deposit money – took place on about September 24th.' Raising his voice he turned and looked directly at Mundt. 'On the third of October Comrade Mundt made a clandestine journey to Finland – once more allegedly in the interests of the Abteilung.' There was silence. Fiedler turned slowly and addressed himself once more to the Tribunal. In a voice at once subdued and threatening he asked:

'Are you complaining that the evidence is circumstantial? Let me remind you of something more.' He turned to Leamas.

'Witness, during your activities in Berlin you became associated with Karl Riemeck, formerly Secretary to the Praesidium of the Socialist Unity Party. What was the nature of that association?'

'He was my agent, until he was shot by Mundt's men.'

'Quite so. He was shot by Mundt's men. One of several spies who were summarily liquidated by Comrade Mundt before they could be questioned. But before he was shot by Mundt's men he was an agent of the British Secret Service?'

Leamas nodded.

'Will you describe Riemeck's meeting with the man you call Control.'

'Control came over to Berlin from London to see Karl. Karl was one of the most productive agents we had, I think, and Control wanted to meet him.'

Fiedler put in: 'He was also one of the most trusted?'

'Yes, oh yes. London loved Karl; he could do no wrong. When Control came out I fixed up for Karl to come to my flat and the three of us dined together. I didn't like Karl coming there really, but I couldn't tell Control that. It's hard to explain but they get ideas in London, they're so cut off from it and I was frightened stiff they'd find some excuse for taking over Karl themselves – they're quite capable of it.'

'So you arranged for the three of you to meet,' Fiedler put in curtly. 'What happened?'

'Control asked me beforehand to see that he had a quarter of an hour alone with Karl, so during the evening I pretended to have run out of Scotch. I left the flat and went over to de Jong's place. I had a couple of drinks there, borrowed a bottle and came back.'

'How did you find them?'

'What do you mean?'

'Were Control and Riemeck talking still? If so, what were they talking about?'

'They weren't talking at all when I came back.'

'Thank you. You may sit down.'

Leamas returned to his seat at the back of the room. Fiedler turned to the three members of the Tribunal and began:

'I want to talk first about the spy Riemeck, who was shot: Karl Riemeck. You have before you a list of all the information which Riemeck passed to Alec Leamas in Berlin, so far as Leamas can recall it. It is a formidable record of treachery. Let me summarise it for you. Riemeck gave to his masters a detailed breakdown of the work and personalities of the whole Abteilung. He was able, if Leamas is to be believed, to describe the workings of our most secret sessions. As secretary to the Praesidium he gave minutes of its most secret proceedings.

'That was easy for him; he himself compiled the record of every meeting. But Riemeck's *access* to the secret affairs of the Abteilung is a different matter. Who at the end of 1959 co-opted Riemeck on to the Committee for the Protection of the People, that vital sub-committee of the Praesidium which co-ordinates and discusses the affairs of our security organs? Who proposed that Riemeck should have the privilege of access to the files of the Abteilung? Who at every stage in Riemeck's career *since* 1959 (the year Mundt returned from England, you remember) singled him out for posts of exceptional responsibility? I will tell you,' Fiedler proclaimed. 'The same man who was uniquely placed to shield him in his espionage activities: Hans-Dieter Mundt. Let us recall how Riemeck contacted the Western Intelligence Agencies in Berlin – how he sought out de Jong's car on a picnic and put the film inside it. Are you not amazed at Riemeck's foreknowledge? How could he have known where to find that car, and on that very day? Riemeck had no car himself, he could not have followed de Jong from his house in West Berlin. There was only one way he could have known – through the agency of our own Security police, who reported de Jong's presence as a matter of routine as soon as the car passed the Inter Sector checkpoint. That knowledge was available to Mundt, and Mundt made it available to Riemeck. *That* is the case against Hans-Dieter Mundt – I tell you, Riemeck was his creature, the link between Mundt and his imperialist masters!'

Fiedler paused, then added quietly:

'Mundt – Riemeck – Leamas: that was the chain of command, and it is axiomatic of intelligence technique the whole world over that each link of the chain be kept, as far as possible, in ignorance of the others. Thus it is *right* that Leamas should maintain he knows nothing to the detriment of Mundt: that is no more than the proof of good security by his masters in London.

'You have also been told how the whole case known as Rolling Stone was conducted under conditions of special secrecy, how Leamas knew in vague terms of an intelligence section under Peter Guillam which was supposedly concerned with economic conditions in our Republic – a section which surprisingly was on the distribution list of Rolling Stone. Let me remind you that that same Peter Guillam was one of several British security officers who were involved in the investigation of Mundt's activities while he was in England.'

The youngish man at the table lifted his pencil, and looking at Fiedler with his hard, cold eyes wide open he asked:

'Then why did Mundt liquidate Riemeck, if Riemeck was his agent?'

'He had no alternative. Riemeck was under suspicion. His mistress had betrayed him by boastful indiscretion. Mundt gave the order that he be shot on sight, got word to Riemeck to run, and the danger of betrayal was eliminated. Later, Mundt assassinated the woman.

'I want to speculate for a moment on Mundt's technique. After his return to Germany in 1959 British Intelligence played a waiting game. Mundt's willingness to co-operate with them had yet to be demonstrated, so they gave him instructions and waited, content to pay their money and hope for the best. At that time Mundt was not a senior functionary of our Service – nor of our party – but he saw a good deal, and what he saw he began to report. He was, of course, communicating with his masters unaided. We must suppose that he was met in West Berlin, that on his short journeys abroad to Scandinavia and elsewhere he was contacted and interrogated. The British must have been wary to begin with – who would not be? – they weighed what he gave them with painful care against what they already knew, they feared that he would play a double game. But gradually they realised they had hit a gold mine. Mundt took to his treacherous work with the systematic efficiency for which he is renowned. At first – this is my guess, but it is based, Comrades, on long experience of this work and on the evidence of Leamas – for the first few months they did not dare to establish any kind of network which included Mundt. They let him be a lone wolf, they serviced him, paid and instructed him independently of their Berlin organisation. They established in London, under Guillam (for it was he who recruited Mundt in

England), a tiny undercover section whose function was not known even within the Service save to a select circle. They paid Mundt by a special system which they called Rolling Stone, and no doubt they treated the information he gave them with prodigious caution. Thus, you see, it is consistent with Leamas' protestations that the existence of Mundt was unknown to him although – as you will see – he not only paid him, but in the end *actually received from Riemeck and passed to London the intelligence which Mundt obtained.*

'Towards the end of 1959 Mundt informed his London masters that he had found within the Praesidium a man who would act as intermediary between them and Mundt. That man was Karl Riemeck.

'How did Mundt find Riemeck? How did he dare to establish Riemeck's willingness to co-operate? You must remember Mundt's exceptional position: he had access to all the security files, could tap telephones, open letters, employ watchers; he could interrogate anyone with undisputed right, and had before him the most detailed picture of their private life. Above all he could silence suspicion in a moment by turning against the people the very weapon' – Fiedler's voice was trembling with fury – 'which was designed for their protection.' Returning effortlessly to his former rational style, he continued:

'You can see now what London did. Still keeping Mundt's identity a close secret, they connived at Riemeck's enlistment and enabled indirect contact to be established between Mundt and the Berlin Command. That is the significance of Riemeck's contact with de Jong and Leamas. *That* is how you should interpret Leamas' evidence, *that* is how you should measure Mundt's treachery.' He turned and, looking Mundt full in the face, he shouted:

'There is your saboteur, terrorist! There is the man who has sold the people's right!

'I have nearly finished. Only one more thing needs to be said. Mundt gained a reputation as a loyal and astute protector of the people, and he silenced for ever those tongues that could betray his secret. Thus he killed in the name of the people to protect his fascist treachery and advance his own career within our Service. It is not possible to imagine a crime more terrible than this. That is why – in the end – having done what he could to protect Karl Riemeck from the suspicion which was gradually surrounding him he gave the order that Riemeck be shot on sight. That is why he arranged for the assassination of Riemeck's mistress. When you come to give your judgement to the Praesidium, do not shrink from recognising the full bestiality of this man's crime. For Hans-Dieter Mundt, death is a judgement of mercy.'

Chapter 21

THE WITNESS

The President turned to the little man in the black suit sitting directly opposite Fiedler.

'Comrade Karden, you are speaking for Comrade Mundt. Do you wish to examine the witness Leamas?'

'Yes, yes, I should like to in one moment,' he replied, getting laboriously to his feet and pulling the end of his gold-rimmed spectacles over his ears. He was a benign figure, a little rustic, and his hair was white.

'The contention of Comrade Mundt,' he began – his mild voice was rather pleasantly modulated – 'is that Leamas is lying; that Comrade Fiedler either by design or ill chance has been drawn into a plot to disrupt the Abteilung, and thus bring into disrepute the organs for the defence of our socialist state. We do not dispute that Karl Riemeck was a British spy – there is evidence for that. But we dispute that Mundt was in league with him, or accepted money for betraying our Party. We say there is no objective evidence for this charge, that Comrade Fiedler is intoxicated by dreams of power and blinded to rational thought. We maintain that from the moment Leamas returned from Berlin to London he lived a part; that he simulated a swift decline into degeneracy, drunkenness and debt, that he assaulted a tradesman in full public view and affected anti-American sentiment – all solely in order to attract the attention of the Abteilung. We believe that British Intelligence has deliberately spun around Comrade Mundt a mesh of circumstantial evidence – the payment of money to foreign banks, its withdrawal to coincide with Mundt's presence in this or that country, the casual hearsay evidence from Peter Guillam, the secret meeting between Control and Riemeck at which matters were discussed that Leamas could not hear: these all provided a spurious chain of evidence and Comrade Fiedler, on whose ambitions the British so accurately counted, accepted it; and thus he became party to a monstrous plot to destroy – to murder in fact, for Mundt now stands to lose his life – one of the most vigilant defenders of our Republic.

'Is it not consistent with their record of sabotage, subversion and human trafficking that the British should devise this desperate plot? What other course lies open to them now that the rampart has been built across Berlin and the flow of Western spies has been checked? We have fallen victim to their plot; at best Comrade Fiedler is guilty of a most serious error; at worst of conniving with imperialist spies to undermine the security of the worker state, and shed innocent blood.

'We also have a witness.' He nodded benignly at the court. 'Yes. We too have a witness. For do you really suppose that all this time Comrade Mundt has been in ignorance of Fiedler's fevered plotting? Do you really suppose that? For months he has been aware of the sickness in Fiedler's mind. It was Comrade Mundt himself who authorised the approach that was made to Leamas in England: do you think he would have taken such an insane risk if he were himself to be implicated?

'And when the reports of Leamas' first interrogation in The Hague reached the Praesidium, do you suppose Comrade Mundt threw his away unread? And when, after Leamas had arrived in our country and Fiedler embarked on his own interrogation, no further reports were forthcoming, do you suppose Comrade Mundt was then so obtuse that he did not know what Fiedler was hatching? When the first reports came in from Peters in The Hague, Mundt had only to look at the dates of Leamas' visits to Copenhagen and Helsinki to realise that the whole thing was a plant – a plant to discredit Mundt himself. Those dates did indeed coincide with Mundt's visits to Denmark and Finland: they were chosen by London for that very reason. Mundt had known of those "earlier indications" as well as Fiedler – remember that. Mundt too was looking for a spy within the ranks of the Abteilung . . .

'And so by the time Leamas arrived in Democratic Germany, Mundt was watching with fascination how Leamas nourished Fiedler's suspicions with hints and oblique indications – never overdone, you understand, never emphasised, but dropped here and there with perfidious subtlety. And by then the ground had been prepared . . . the man in the Lebanon, the miraculous scoop to which Fiedler referred, both seeming to confirm the presence of a highly placed spy within the Abteilung . . .

'It was wonderfully well done. It could have turned – it could still turn – the defeat which the British suffered through the loss of Karl Riemeck into a remarkable victory.

'Comrade Mundt took one precaution while the British, with Fiedler's aid, planned his murder.

'He caused scrupulous enquiries to be made in London. He examined every tiny detail of that double life which Leamas led in Bayswater. He was looking, you see, for some human error in a scheme of almost superhuman subtlety. Somewhere, he thought, in Leamas' long sojourn in the wilderness, he would have to break faith with his oath of poverty, drunkenness, degeneracy, above all of solitude. He would need a companion, a mistress perhaps; he would long for the warmth of human contact, long to reveal a part of the other soul within his breast. Comrade Mundt was right, you see. Leamas, that skilled, experienced operator, made a mistake so elementary, so human that . . .' He smiled. 'You shall hear the witness, but not yet. The witness is here; procured by Comrade Mundt. It was an admirable precaution. Later I shall call – that witness.' He looked a trifle arch, as if to say he must be allowed his little joke. 'Meanwhile I should like, if I may, to put one or two questions to this reluctant incriminator, Mr Alec Leamas.'

'Tell me,' he began, 'are you a man of means?'

'Don't be bloody silly,' said Leamas shortly; 'you know how I was picked up.'

'Yes, indeed,' Karden declared, 'it was masterly. I may take it, then, that you have no money at all?'

'You may.'

'Have you friends who would lend you money, give it to you perhaps? Pay your debts?'

'If I had I wouldn't be here now.'

'You have none? You cannot imagine that some kindly benefactor, someone perhaps you have almost forgotten about, would ever concern himself with putting you on your feet . . . settling with creditors and that kind of thing?'

'No.'

'Thank you. Another question: do you know George Smiley?'

'Of course I do. He was in the Circus.'

'He has now left British Intelligence?'

'He packed it up after the Fennan case.'

'Ah – the case in which Mundt was involved. Have you ever seen him since?'

'Once or twice.'

'Have you seen him since you left the Circus?'
Leamas hesitated.
'No,' he said.
'He didn't visit you in prison?'
'No. No one did.'
'And before you went to prison?'
'No.'
'After you left prison – the day of your release in fact – you were picked up, weren't you, by a man called Ashe?'
'Yes.'
'You had lunch with him in Soho. After the two of you had parted, where did you go?'
'I don't remember. Probably I went to a pub. No idea.'
'Let me help you. You went to Fleet Street eventually and caught a bus. From there you seem to have zigzagged by bus, tube and private car, rather inexpertly for a man of your experience, to Chelsea. Do you remember that? I can show you the report if you like, I have it here.'
'You're probably right. So what?'
'George Smiley lives in Bywater Street, just off the King's Road, that is my point. Your car turned into Bywater Street and our agent reported that you were dropped at number nine. That happens to be Smiley's house.'
'That's drivel,' Leamas declared. 'I should think I went to the Eight Bells; it's a favourite pub of mine.'
'By private car?'
'That's nonsense too. I went by taxi, I expect. If I have money I spend it.'
'But why all the running about beforehand?'
'That's just cock. They were probably following the wrong man. That would be bloody typical.'
'Going back to my original question, you cannot imagine that Smiley would have taken any interest in you after you left the Circus?'
'God, no.'
'Nor in your welfare after you went to prison, nor spent money on your dependants, nor wanted to see you after you had met Ashe?'
'No. I haven't the least idea what you're trying to say, Karden, but the answer's no. If you'd ever met Smiley you wouldn't ask. We're about as different as we could be.'
Karden seemed rather pleased with this, smiling and nodding to

himself as he adjusted his spectacles and referred elaborately to his file.

'Oh yes,' he said, as if he had forgotten something; 'when you asked the grocer for credit, how much money had you?'

'Nothing,' said Leamas carelessly. 'I'd been broke for a week. Longer, I should think.'

'What had you lived on?'

'Bits and pieces. I'd been ill; some fever. I'd hardly eaten anything for a week. I suppose that made me nervous too – tipped the scales.'

'You were, of course, still owed money at the library, weren't you?'

'How did you know that?' asked Leamas sharply. 'Have you been –'

'Why didn't you go and collect it? Then you wouldn't have had to ask for credit, would you, Leamas?'

He shrugged.

'I forget. Probably because the library was closed on Saturday mornings.'

'I see. Are you sure it was closed on Saturday mornings?'

'No, it's just a guess.'

'Quite. Thank you, that is all I have to ask.' Leamas was sitting down as the door opened, and a woman came in. She was large and ugly, wearing a grey overall with chevrons on the sleeve. Behind her stood Liz.

Chapter 22

THE PRESIDENT

She entered the court slowly, looking around her, wide-eyed, like a half-woken child entering a brightly lit room. Leamas had forgotten how young she was. When she saw him sitting between two guards she stopped.

'Alec.'

The guard beside her put his hand on her arm and guided her forward to the spot where Leamas had stood. It was very quiet in the courtroom.

'What is your name, child?' the President asked abruptly. Liz's long hands hung at her sides, the fingers straight.

'What is your name?' she repeated, loudly this time.

'Elizabeth Gold.'

'You are a member of the British Communist Party?'

'Yes.'

'And you have been staying in Leipzig?'

'Yes.'

'When did you join the Party?'

'1955. No – fifty-four, I think it was –'

She was interrupted by the sound of movement; the screech of furniture forced aside, and Leamas' voice, hoarse, high-pitched, ugly, filling the room.

'You bastards! Leave her alone!'

Liz turned in terror and saw him standing, his white face bleeding and his clothes awry, saw a guard hit him with his fist, so that he half fell; then they were both upon him, had lifted him up, thrusting his arms high behind his back. His head fell forward on his chest, then jerked sideways in pain.

'If he moves again, take him out,' the President ordered, and she nodded to Leamas in warning, adding: 'You can speak again later if you want. Wait.' Turning to Liz she said sharply, 'Surely you know when you joined the Party?'

Liz said nothing, and after waiting a moment the President

– 159 –

shrugged. Then leaning forward and staring at Liz intently she asked:

'Elizabeth, have you ever been told in your Party about the need for secrecy?'

Liz nodded.

'And you have been told never, never to ask questions of another comrade on the organisation and dispositions of the Party?'

Liz nodded again. 'Yes,' she said, 'of course.'

'Today you will be severely tested in that rule. It is better for you, far better, that you should know nothing. Nothing,' she added with sudden emphasis. 'Let this be enough: we three at this table hold very high rank in the Party. We are acting with the knowledge of our Praesidium, in the interests of Party security. We have to ask you some questions, and your answers are of the greatest importance. By replying truthfully, and bravely, you will help the cause of Socialism.'

'But *who*,' she whispered, '*who* is on trial? What's Alec done?'

The President looked past her at Mundt and said, 'Perhaps no one is on trial. That is the point. Perhaps only the accusers. It can make no difference *who* is accused,' she added, 'it is a guarantee of your impartiality that you cannot know.'

Silence descended for a moment on the little room; and then, in a voice so quiet that the President instinctively turned her head to catch her words, she asked:

'Is it Alec? Is it Leamas?'

'I tell you,' the President insisted, 'it is better for you – far better – you should not know. You must tell the truth and go. That is the wisest thing you can do.'

Liz must have made some sign or whispered some words the others could not catch, for the President again leant forward and said, with great intensity:

'Listen, child, do you want to go home? Do as I tell you and you shall. But if you . . .' She broke off, indicated Karden with her hand and added cryptically, 'This comrade wants to ask you some questions, not many. Then you shall go. Tell the truth.'

Karden stood again, and smiled his kindly, churchwarden smile.

'Elizabeth,' he enquired, 'Alec Leamas was your lover, wasn't he?'

She nodded.

'You met at the library in Bayswater, where you work.'

'Yes.'

'You had not met him before?'

She shook her head: 'We met at the library,' she said.

'Have you had many lovers, Elizabeth?'

Whatever she said was lost as Leamas shouted again: 'Karden, you swine,' but as she heard him she turned and said, quite loud:

'Alec, don't. They'll take you away.'

'Yes,' observed the President drily; 'they will.'

'Tell me,' Karden resumed smoothly, 'was Alec a Communist?'

'No.'

'Did he know you were a Communist?'

'Yes. I told him.'

'What did he say when you told him then, Elizabeth?'

She didn't know whether to lie, that was the terrible thing. The questions came so quickly she had no chance to think. All the time they were listening, watching, waiting for a word, a gesture, perhaps, that could do terrible harm to Alec. She couldn't lie unless she knew what was at stake; she would fumble on and Alec would die – for there was no doubt in her mind that Leamas was in danger.

'What did he say then?' Karden repeated.

'He laughed. He was above all that kind of thing.'

'Do you believe he was above it?'

'Of course.'

The young man at the Judges' table spoke for the second time. His eyes were half closed:

'Do you regard that as a valid judgement of a human being? That he is *above* the course of history and the compulsions of dialectic?'

'I don't know. It's what I believed, that's all.'

'Never mind,' said Karden; 'tell me, was he a *happy* person, always laughing and that kind of thing?'

'No. He didn't often laugh.'

'But he laughed when you told him you were in the Party. Do you know why?'

'I think he despised the Party.'

'Do you think he *hated* it?' Karden asked casually.

'I don't know,' Liz replied pathetically.

'Was he a man of strong likes and dislikes?'

'No . . . no; he wasn't.'

'But he assaulted a grocer. Now why did he do that?'

Liz suddenly didn't trust Karden any more. She didn't trust the caressing voice and the good-fairy face.

'I don't know.'

– 161 –

'But you thought about it?'

'Yes.'

'Well, what conclusion did you come to?'

'None,' said Liz flatly.

Karden looked at her thoughtfully, a little disappointed perhaps, as if she had forgotten her catechism.

'Did you,' he asked – it might have been the most obvious of questions – 'did you *know* that Leamas was going to hit the grocer?'

'No,' Liz replied, perhaps too quickly, so that in the pause that followed Karden's smile gave way to a look of amused curiosity.

'Until now, until today,' he asked finally, 'when had you last seen Leamas?'

'I didn't see him again after he went to prison,' Liz replied.

'When did you see him last, then?' – the voice was kind but persistent. Liz hated having her back to the court; she wished she could turn and see Leamas, see his face perhaps; read in it some guidance, some sign telling how to answer. She was becoming frightened for herself; these questions which proceeded from charges and suspicions of which she knew nothing. They must know she wanted to help Alec, that she was afraid, but no one helped her – why would no one help her?

'Elizabeth, when was your last meeting with Leamas until today?' Oh that voice, how she hated it, that silken voice.

'The night before it happened,' she replied, 'the night before he had the fight with Mr Ford.'

'The fight? It wasn't a fight, Elizabeth. The grocer never hit back, did he – he never had a chance. Very unsporting!' Karden laughed, and it was all the more terrible because no one laughed with him.

'Tell me, where did you meet Leamas that last night?'

'At his flat. He'd been ill, not working. He'd been in bed and I'd been coming in and cooking for him.'

'And buying the food? Shopping for him?'

'Yes.'

'How kind. It must have cost you a lot of money,' Karden observed sympathetically; 'could you afford to keep him?'

'I didn't keep him. I got it from Alec. He . . .'

'Oh,' said Karden sharply, 'so he *did* have some money?'

Oh God, thought Liz, oh God, oh dear God, what have I said?

'Not much,' she said quickly, 'not much, I know. A pound, two pounds, not more. He didn't have more than that. He couldn't

pay his bills – his electric light and his rent – they were all paid
afterwards, you see, after he'd gone, by a friend. A friend had to
pay, not Alec.'

'Of course,' said Karden quietly, 'a friend paid. Came specially
and paid all his bills. Some old friend of Leamas, someone he knew
before he came to Bayswater perhaps. Did you ever meet this
friend, Elizabeth?'

She shook her head.

'I see. What other bills did this good friend pay, do you know?'

'No . . . no.'

'Why do you hesitate?'

'I said I don't know,' Liz retorted fiercely.

'But you hesitated,' Karden explained, 'I wondered if you had
second thoughts.'

'No.'

'Did Leamas ever speak of this friend? A friend with money
who knew where Leamas lived?'

'He never mentioned a friend at all. I didn't think he had any
friends.'

'Ah.'

There was a terrible silence in the courtroom, more terrible to
Liz because like a blind child among the seeing she was cut off
from all those around her; they could measure her answers against
some secret standard, and she could not know from the dreadful
silence what they had found.

'How much money do you earn, Elizabeth?'

'Six pounds a week.'

'Have you any savings?'

'A little. A few pounds.'

'How much is the rent of your flat?'

'Fifty shillings a week.'

'That's quite a lot, isn't it, Elizabeth? Have you paid your rent
recently?'

She shook her head helplessly.

'Why not?' Karden continued. 'Have you no money?'

In a whisper she replied: 'I've got a lease. Someone bought the
lease and sent it to me.'

'Who?'

'I don't know.' Tears were running down her face. 'I don't
know . . . Please don't ask any more questions. I don't know who
it was . . . six weeks ago they sent it, a bank in the City . . . some
charity had done it . . . a thousand pounds. I swear I don't know

– 163 –

who . . . a gift from a charity they said. You know everything –
you tell me who . . .'

Burying her face in her hands she wept, her back still turned to
the court, her shoulders moving as the sobs shook her body. No
one moved, and at length she lowered her hands but did not look
up.

'Why didn't you enquire?' Karden asked simply, 'or are you
used to receiving anonymous gifts of a thousand pounds?'

She said nothing and Karden continued: 'You didn't enquire
because you guessed. Isn't that right?'

Raising her hand to her face again, she nodded.

'You guessed it came from Leamas, or from Leamas' friend,
didn't you?'

'Yes,' she managed to say. 'I heard in the street that the grocer
had got some money, a lot of money from somewhere after the
trial. There was a lot of talk about it, and I knew it must be Alec's
friend . . .'

'How very strange,' said Karden almost to himself. 'How odd.'
And then: 'Tell me, Elizabeth, did anyone get in touch with you
after Leamas went to prison?'

'No,' she lied. She knew now, she was sure they wanted to
prove something against Alec, something about the money or his
friends; something about the grocer.

'Are you sure?' Karden asked, his eyebrows raised above the
gold rims of his spectacles.

'Yes.'

'But your neighbour, Elizabeth,' Karden objected patiently,
'says that men called – two men – quite soon after Leamas had
been sentenced; or were they just lovers, Elizabeth? Casual lovers,
like Leamas, who gave you money?'

'Alec *wasn't* a casual lover,' she cried, 'how can you . . .'

'But he gave you money. Did the men give you money, too?'

'Oh God,' she sobbed, 'don't ask . . .'

'Who were they?' She did not reply, then Karden shouted, quite
suddenly; it was the first time he had raised his voice.

'*Who?*'

'I don't know. They came in a car. Friends of Alec.'

'*More* friends? What did they want?'

'I don't know. They kept asking me what he had told me . . .
they told me to get in touch with them if . . .'

'*How? How* get in touch with them?'

At last she replied:

'He lived in Chelsea . . . his name was Smiley . . . George Smiley . . . I was to ring him.'

'And did you?'

'No!'

Karden had put down his file. A deathly silence had descended on the court. Pointing towards Leamas Karden said, in a voice more impressive because it was perfectly under control:

'Smiley wanted to know whether Leamas had told her too much. Leamas had done the one thing British Intelligence had never expected him to do: he had taken a girl and wept on her shoulder.' Then Karden laughed quietly, as if it were all such a neat joke:

'Just as Karl Riemeck did. He's made the same mistake.'

'Did Leamas ever talk about himself?' Karden continued.

'No.'

'You know nothing about his past?'

'No. I knew he'd done something in Berlin. Something for the government.'

'Then he did talk about his past, didn't he? Did he tell you he had been married?'

There was a long silence. Liz nodded.

'Why didn't you see him after he went to prison? You could have visited him.'

'I didn't think he'd want me to.'

'I see. Did you write to him?'

'No. Yes, once . . . just to tell him I'd wait. I didn't think he'd mind.'

'You didn't think he would want that either?'

'No.'

'And when he had served his time in prison, you didn't try and get in touch with him?'

'No.'

'Did he have anywhere to go, did he have a job waiting for him – friends who would take him in?'

'I don't know . . . I don't know.'

'In fact you were finished with him, were you?' Karden asked with a sneer. 'Had you found another lover?'

'No! I waited for him . . . I'll always wait for him.' She checked herself. 'I wanted him to come back.'

'Then why had you not written? Why didn't you try and find out where he was?'

'He didn't want me to, don't you see? He made me promise . . .
never to follow him . . . never to . . .'

'*So he expected to go to prison, did he?*' Karden demanded
triumphantly.

'No . . . I don't know. How can I tell you what I don't
know . . .'

'And on that last evening,' Karden persisted, his voice harsh and
bullying, 'on the evening before he hit the grocer, did he make
you renew your promise? . . . Well, did he?'

With infinite weariness, she nodded in a pathetic gesture of
capitulation. 'Yes.'

'And you said good-bye?'

'We said good-bye.'

'After supper, of course. It was quite late. Or did you spend the
night with him?'

'After supper. I went home . . . not straight home . . . I went
for a walk first, I don't know where. Just walking.'

'What reason did he give for breaking off your relationship?'

'He didn't break it off,' she said. 'Never. He just said there
was something he had to do; someone he had to get even
with, whatever it cost, and afterwards, one day perhaps, when
it was all over . . . he would . . . come back, if I was still there
and . . .'

'And you said,' Karden suggested with irony, 'that you would
always wait for him, no doubt? That you would always love him?'

'Yes,' Liz replied simply.

'Did he say he would send you money?'

'He said . . . he said things weren't as bad as they seemed . . .
that I would be . . . looked after.'

'And that was why you didn't enquire, wasn't it, afterwards,
when some charity in the City casually gave you a thousand
pounds?'

'Yes! Yes, that's right. Now you know everything – you knew
it all already . . . Why did you send for me if you knew?'

Imperturbably Karden waited for her sobbing to stop.

'That,' he observed finally to the Tribunal before him, 'is the
evidence of the defence. I am sorry that a girl whose perception is
clouded by sentiment, and whose alertness is blunted by money,
should be considered by our British comrades a suitable person for
Party office.'

Looking first at Leamas and then at Fiedler he added brutally:
'She is a fool. It is fortunate, nevertheless, that Leamas met her.

This is not the first time that a revanchist plot has been uncovered through the decadence of its architects.'

With a little precise bow towards the Tribunal, Karden sat down.

As he did so, Leamas rose to his feet, and this time the guards left him alone.

London must have gone raving mad. He'd told them – that was the joke – he'd told them to leave her alone. And now it was clear that from the moment, the very moment he left England – before that, even, as soon as he went to prison – some bloody fool had gone round tidying up – paying the bills, settling the grocer, the landlord; above all, Liz. It was insane, fantastic. What were they trying to do – kill Fiedler, kill their agent? Sabotage their own operation? Was it just Smiley – had his wretched little conscience driven him to this? There was only one thing to do – get Liz and Fiedler out of it and carry the can. He was probably written off anyway. If he could save Fiedler's skin – if he could do that – perhaps there was a chance that Liz would get away.

How the hell did they know so much? He was sure, he was absolutely sure, he hadn't been followed to Smiley's house that afternoon. And the money – how did they pick up the story about him stealing money from the Circus? That was designed for internal consumption only . . . then how? For God's sake, how?

Bewildered, angry and bitterly ashamed he walked slowly up the gangway, stiffly, like a man going to the scaffold.

Chapter 23

CONFESSION

'All right, Karden.' His face was white and hard as stone, his head tilted back, a little to one side, in the attitude of a man listening to some distant sound. There was a frightful stillness about him, not of resignation but of self-control, so that his whole body seemed to be in the iron grip of his will.

'All right, Karden, let her go.'

Liz was staring at him, her face crumpled and ugly, her dark eyes filled with tears.

'No, Alec . . . no,' she said. There was no one else in the room – just Leamas tall and straight like a soldier.

'Don't tell them,' she said, her voice rising, 'whatever it is, don't tell them just because of me . . . I don't mind any more, Alec; I promise I don't.'

'Shut up, Liz,' said Leamas awkwardly. 'It's too late now.' His eyes turned to the President.

'She knows nothing. Nothing at all. Get her out of here and send her home. I'll tell you the rest.'

The President glanced briefly at the men on either side of her. She deliberated, then said:

'She can leave the court; but she cannot go home until the hearing is finished. Then we shall see.'

'She knows nothing, I tell you,' Leamas shouted. 'Karden's right, don't you see? It was an operation, a planned operation. How could she know that? She's just a frustrated little girl from a crackpot library – she's no good to you!'

'She is a witness,' replied the President shortly. 'Fiedler may want to question her.' It wasn't Comrade Fiedler any more.

At the mention of his name, Fiedler seemed to wake from the reverie into which he had sunk, and Liz looked at him consciously for the first time. His deep brown eyes rested on her for a moment, and he smiled very slightly, as if in recognition of her race. He was a small, forlorn figure, oddly relaxed she thought.

'She knows nothing,' Fiedler said. 'Leamas is right, let her go.' His voice was tired.

'You realise what you are saying?' the President asked. 'You realise what this means? Have *you* no questions to put to her?'

'She has said what she had to say.' Fiedler's hands were folded on his knees and he was studying them as if they interested him more than the proceedings of the court. 'It was all most cleverly done.' He nodded. 'Let her go. She cannot tell us what she does not know.' With a certain mock formality he added, 'I have no questions for the witness.'

A guard unlocked the door and called into the passage outside. In the total silence of the court they heard a woman's answering voice, and her ponderous footsteps slowly approaching. Fiedler abruptly stood up and taking Liz by the arm, he guided her to the door. As she reached the door she turned and looked back towards Leamas, but he was staring away from her like a man who cannot bear the sight of blood.

'Go back to England,' Fiedler said to her. 'You go back to England.' Suddenly Liz began to sob uncontrollably. The wardress put an arm round her shoulder, more for support than comfort, and led her from the room. The guard closed the door. The sound of her crying faded gradually to nothing.

'There isn't much to say,' Leamas began. 'Karden's right. It was a put-up job. When we lost Karl Riemeck we lost our only decent agent in the Zone. All the rest had gone already. We couldn't understand it – Mundt seemed to pick them up almost before we'd recruited them. I came back to London and saw Control. Peter Guillam was there and George Smiley. George was in retirement really, doing something clever. Philology or something.

'Anyway, they'd dreamed up this idea. Set a man to trap himself, that's what Control said. Go through the motions and see if they bite. Then we worked it out – backwards so to speak. "Inductive" Smiley called it. If Mundt *were* our agent how would we have paid him, how would the files look, and so on. Peter remembered that some Arab had tried to sell us a breakdown of the Abteilung a year or two back and we'd sent him packing. Afterwards we found out we'd made a mistake. Peter had the idea of fitting that in – as if we'd turned it down because we already knew. That was clever.

'You can imagine the rest. The pretence of going to pieces; drink, money troubles, the rumours that Leamas had robbed the till. It all hung together. We got Elsie in Accounts to help with the gossip, and one or two others. They did it bloody well,' he added with a touch of pride. 'Then I chose a morning – a Saturday morning, lots of people about – and broke out. It made the local press – it even made the *Worker* I think – and by that time you people had picked it up. From then on,' he added with contempt, 'you dug your own graves.'

'Your grave,' said Mundt quietly. He was looking thoughtfully at Leamas with his pale, pale eyes. 'And perhaps Comrade Fiedler's.'

'You can hardly blame Fiedler,' said Leamas indifferently, 'he happened to be the man on the spot; he's not the only man in the Abteilung who'd willingly hang you, Mundt.'

'We shall hang you, anyway,' said Mundt reassuringly. 'You murdered a guard. You tried to murder me.'

Leamas smiled drily.

'All cats are alike in the dark, Mundt . . . Smiley always said it could go wrong. He said it might start a reaction we couldn't stop. His nerve's gone – you know that. He's never been the same since the Fennan case – since the Mundt affair in London. They say something happened to him then – that's why he left the Circus. That's what I can't make out, why they paid off the bills, the girl and all that. It must have been Smiley wrecking the operation on purpose, it must have been. He must have had a crisis of conscience, thought it was wrong to kill or something. It was mad after all that preparation, all that work, to mess up an operation that way.

'But Smiley hated you, Mundt. We all did, I think, although we didn't say it. We planned the thing as if it was all a bit of a game . . . it's hard to explain now. We knew we had our backs to the wall: we'd failed against Mundt and now we were going to try and kill him. But it was still a game.' Turning to the Tribunal he said: 'You're wrong about Fiedler; he's not ours. Why would London take this kind of risk with a man in Fiedler's position? They counted on him, I admit. They knew he hated Mundt – why shouldn't he? Fiedler's a Jew, isn't he? You know, you must know, all of you, what Mundt's reputation is, what he thinks about Jews.

'I'll tell you something, no one else will, so I'll tell you: Mundt had Fiedler beaten up, and all the time, while it was going on, Mundt baited him and jeered at him for being a Jew. You all know what kind of man Mundt is, and you put up with him because he's good at his job. But . . .' he faltered for a second, then continued: 'But for God's sake . . . enough people have got mixed up in all this without Fiedler's head going into the basket. Fiedler's all right, I tell you . . . ideologically sound, that's the expression, isn't it?'

He looked at the Tribunal. They watched him impassively, curiously almost, their eyes steady and cold. Fiedler, who had returned to his chair and was listening with rather studied detachment, looked at Leamas blankly for a moment:

'And you messed it all up, Leamas, is that it?' he asked. 'An old dog like Leamas, engaged in the crowning operation of his career, falls for a . . . what did you call her? . . . a frustrated little girl in a crackpot library? London must have known; Smiley couldn't have done it alone.' Fiedler turned to Mundt: 'Here's an odd thing, Mundt; they must have known you'd check up on every part of his story. That was why Leamas lived the life. Yet afterwards they sent money to the grocer, paid up the rent; and they bought the lease for the girl. Of all the extraordinary things for them to do . . . people of their experience . . . to pay a thousand pounds, to a girl – *to a member of the Party* – who was supposed to believe he was broke. Don't tell me Smiley's conscience goes that far. London must have done it. What a risk!'

Leamas shrugged.

'Smiley was right. We couldn't stop the reaction. We never expected you to bring me here – Holland, yes – but not here.' He fell silent for a moment, then continued. 'And I never thought you'd bring the girl. I've been a bloody fool.'

'But Mundt hasn't,' Fiedler put in quickly. 'Mundt knew what to look for – he even knew the girl would provide the proof – very clever of Mundt I must say. He even knew about that lease – amazing really. I mean, how *could* he have found out; she didn't tell anyone. I know that girl; I understand her . . . she wouldn't tell anyone at all.' He glanced towards Mundt. 'Perhaps Mundt can tell us how he knew?'

Mundt hesitated, a second too long, Leamas thought.

'It was her subscription,' he said; 'a month ago she increased her Party contribution by ten shillings a month. I heard about it. And so I tried to establish how she could afford it. I succeeded.'

'A masterly explanation,' Fiedler replied coolly.

There was silence.

'I think,' said the President, glancing at her two colleagues, 'that the Tribunal is now in a position to make its report to the Praesidium. That is,' she added, turning her small, cruel eyes on Fiedler, 'unless you have anything more to say.'

Fiedler shook his head. Something still seemed to amuse him.

'In that case,' the President continued, 'my colleagues are agreed that Comrade Fiedler should be relieved of his duties until the disciplinary committee of the Praesidium has considered his position.

'Leamas is already under arrest. I would remind you all that the Tribunal has no executive powers. The people's prosecutor, in collaboration with Comrade Mundt, will no doubt consider what action is to be taken against a British *agent provocateur* and murderer.'

She glanced past Leamas at Mundt. But Mundt was looking at Fiedler with the dispassionate regard of a hangman measuring his subject for the rope.

And suddenly, with the terrible clarity of a man too long deceived, Leamas understood the whole ghastly trick.

Chapter 24

THE COMMISSAR

L iz stood at the window, her back to the wardress, and stared
blankly into the tiny yard outside. She supposed the prisoners
took their exercise there. She was in somebody's office; there was
food on the desk beside the telephone but she couldn't touch it.
She felt sick and terribly tired; physically tired. Her legs ached,
her face felt stiff and raw from weeping. She felt dirty and longed
for a bath.

'Why don't you eat?' the woman asked again. 'It's all over now.'
She said this without compassion, as if the girl were a fool not to
eat when the food was there.

'I'm not hungry.'

The wardress shrugged: 'You may have a long journey,' she
observed, 'and not much the other end.'

'What do you mean?'

'The workers are starving in England,' she declared complacently. 'The capitalists let them starve.'

Liz thought of saying something but there seemed no point.
Besides, she wanted to know; she had to know, and this woman
could tell her.

'What is this place?'

'Don't you know?' the wardress laughed. 'You should ask them
over there,' she nodded towards the window. 'They can tell you
what it is.'

'Who are they?'

'Prisoners.'

'What kind of prisoners?'

'Enemies of the state,' she replied promptly. 'Spies, agitators.'

'How do you know they are spies?'

'The Party knows. The Party knows more about people than
they know themselves. Haven't you been told that?' The wardress
looked at her, shook her head and observed, 'The English! The

rich have eaten your future and your poor have given them the food – that's what's happened to the English.'

'Who told you that?'

The woman smiled and said nothing. She seemed pleased with herself.

'And this is a prison for spies?' Liz persisted.

'It is a prison for those who fail to recognise Socialist reality; for those who think they have the right to err; for those who slow down the march. Traitors,' she concluded briefly.

'But what have they done?'

'We cannot build Communism without doing away with individualism. You cannot plan a great building if some swine builds his sty on your site.'

Liz looked at her in astonishment.

'Who told you all this?'

'I am Commissar here,' she said proudly, 'I work in the prison.'

'You are very clever,' Liz observed, approaching her.

'I am a worker,' the woman replied acidly. 'The concept of brain workers as a higher category must be destroyed. There are no categories, only workers; no antithesis between physical and mental labour. Haven't you read Lenin?'

'Then the people in this prison are intellectuals?'

The woman smiled. 'Yes,' she said, 'they are reactionaries who call themselves progressive: they defend the individual against the state. Do you know what Khrushchev said about the counter-revolution in Hungary?'

Liz shook her head. She must show interest, she must make the woman talk.

'He said it would never have happened if a couple of writers had been shot in time.'

'Who will they shoot now?' Liz asked quickly. 'After the trial?'

'Leamas,' she replied indifferently, 'and the Jew, Fiedler.' Liz thought for a moment she was going to fall but her hand found the back of a chair and she managed to sit down.

'What has Leamas done?' she whispered. The woman looked at her with her small, cunning eyes. She was very large; her hair was scant, stretched over her head to a bun at the nape of her thick neck. Her face was heavy, her complexion flaccid and watery.

'He killed a guard,' she said.

'Why?'

The woman shrugged.

'As for the Jew,' she continued, 'he made an accusation against a loyal comrade.'

'Will they shoot Fiedler for that?' asked Liz incredulously.

'Jews are all the same,' the woman commented. 'Comrade Mundt knows what to do with Jews. We don't need their kind here. If they join the Party they think it belongs to them. If they stay out, they think it is conspiring against them. It is said that Leamas and Fiedler plotted against Mundt. Are you going to eat that?' she enquired, indicating the food on the desk. Liz shook her head. 'Then I must,' she declared, with a grotesque attempt at reluctance. 'They have given you potato. You must have a lover in the kitchen.' The humour of this observation sustained her until she had finished the last of Liz's meal.

Liz went back to the window.

In the confusion of Liz's mind, in the turmoil of shame and grief and fear there predominated the appalling memory of Leamas, as she had last seen him in the courtroom, sitting stiffly in his chair, his eyes averted from her own. She had failed him and he dared not look at her before he died; would not let her see the contempt, the fear perhaps, that was written on his face.

But how could she have done otherwise? If Leamas had only told her what he had to do – even now it wasn't clear to her – she would have lied and cheated for him, anything, if he had only told her! Surely he understood that; surely he knew her well enough to realise that in the end she would do whatever he said, that she would take on his form and being, his will, life, his image, his pain, if she could; that she prayed for nothing more than the chance to do so? But how could she have known, if she was not told, how to answer those veiled, insidious questions? There seemed no end to the destruction she had caused. She remembered, in the fevered condition of her mind, how, as a child, she had been horrified to learn that with every step she made, thousands of minute creatures were destroyed beneath her foot; and now, whether she had lied or told the truth – or even, she was sure, had kept silent – she had been forced to destroy a human being; perhaps two, for was there not also the Jew, Fiedler, who had been gentle with her, taken her arm and told her to go back to England? They would shoot Fiedler; that's what the woman said. Why did it have to be Fiedler – why not the old man who asked the questions, or the fair one in the front row between the soldiers, the one who smiled all the time; whenever she turned round she had caught sight of his smooth, blond head and his smooth, cruel face smiling as if it were all a great joke. It comforted her that Leamas and Fiedler were on the same side. She turned to the woman again and asked:

'Why are we waiting here?'

The wardress pushed the plate aside and stood up.

'For instructions,' she replied. 'They are deciding whether you must stay.'

'Stay?' repeated Liz blankly.

'It is a question of evidence. Fiedler may be tried, I told you: they suspect conspiracy between Fiedler and Leamas.'

'But who against? How could he conspire in England? How did he come here? He's not in the Party.'

The woman shook her head.

'It is secret,' she replied. 'It concerns only the Praesidium. Perhaps the Jew brought him here.'

'But *you* know,' Liz insisted, a note of blandishment in her voice, 'you are Commissar at the prison. Surely they told *you*?'

'Perhaps,' the woman replied, complacently. 'It is very secret,' she repeated.

The telephone rang. The woman lifted the receiver and listened. After a moment she glanced at Liz.

'Yes, Comrade. At once,' she said, and put down the receiver.

'You are to stay,' she said shortly. 'The Praesidium will consider the case of Fiedler. In the meantime you will stay here. That is the wish of Comrade Mundt.'

'Who is Mundt?'

The woman looked cunning.

'It is the wish of the Praesidium,' she said.

'I don't want to stay,' Liz cried. 'I want . . .'

'The Party knows more about us than we know ourselves,' the woman replied. 'You must stay here. It is the Party's wish.'

'Who is Mundt?' Liz asked again, but still she did not reply.

Slowly Liz followed her along endless corridors, through grilles manned by sentries, past iron doors from which no sound came, down endless stairs, across whole courtyards far beneath the ground, until she thought she had descended to the bowels of hell itself, and no one would even tell her when Leamas was dead.

She had no idea what time it was when she heard the footsteps in the corridor outside her cell. It could have been five in the evening – it could have been midnight. She had been awake, staring blankly into the pitch darkness, longing for a sound. She had never imagined that silence could be so terrible. Once she had cried out, and there had been no echo, nothing. Just the memory of her own voice. She had visualised the sound breaking against the solid darkness like a fist against a rock. She had moved her hands about her as she sat on the bed, and it seemed to her that the darkness made them heavy, as if she were groping in the water. She knew the cell was small; that it contained the bed on which she sat, a handbasin without taps and a crude table: she had seen them when she first entered. Then the light had gone out, and she had run wildly to where she knew the bed had stood, and struck it with her shins, and had remained there, shivering with fright. Until she heard the footsteps, and the door of her cell was opened abruptly.

She recognised him at once, although she could only discern his silhouette against the pale blue light in the corridor. The trim, agile figure, the clear line of the cheek and the short fair hair just touched by the light behind him.

'It's Mundt,' he said. 'Come with me, at once.' His voice was contemptuous yet subdued, as if he were not anxious to be overheard.

Liz was suddenly terrified. She remembered the wardress: 'Mundt knows what to do with Jews.' She stood by the bed, staring at him, not knowing what to do.

'Hurry, you fool.' Mundt had stepped forward and seized her wrist. 'Hurry.' She let herself be drawn into the corridor. Bewildered, she watched Mundt quietly relock the door of her cell. Roughly he took her arm and forced her quickly along the first corridor, half running, half walking. She could hear the distant whirr of air conditioners; and now and then the sound of other footsteps from passages branching from their own. She noticed that Mundt hesitated, drew back even, when they came upon other corridors, would go ahead and confirm that no one was coming, then signal her forward. He seemed to assume that she would follow, that she knew the reason. It was almost as if he was treating her as an accomplice.

And suddenly he had stopped, was thrusting a key into the keyhole of a dingy metal door. She waited, panic-stricken. He pushed the door savagely outwards and the sweet, cold air of a winter's evening blew against her face. He beckoned to her again, still with the same urgency, and she followed him down two steps on to a gravel path which led through a rough kitchen garden.

They followed the path to an elaborate Gothic gateway which gave on to the road beyond. Parked in the gateway was a car. Standing beside it was Alec Leamas.

'Keep your distance,' Mundt warned her as she started to move forward:
'Wait here.'
Mundt went forward alone and for what seemed an age she watched the two men standing together, talking quietly between themselves. Her heart was beating madly, her whole body shivering with cold and fear. Finally Mundt returned.
'Come with me,' he said, and led her to where Leamas stood. The two men looked at one another for a moment.
'Good-bye,' said Mundt indifferently. 'You're a fool, Leamas,' he added. 'She's trash, like Fiedler.' And he turned without another word and walked quickly away into the twilight.
She put her hand out and touched him, and he half turned from her, brushing her hand away as he opened the car door. He nodded to her to get in, but she hesitated.
'Alec,' she whispered, 'Alec, what are you doing? Why is he letting you go?'
'Shut up!' Leamas hissed. 'Don't even think about it, d'you hear? Get in.'
'What is it he said about Fiedler? Alec, why is he letting us go?'
'He's letting us go because we've done our job. Get into the car, quick!' Under the compulsion of his extraordinary will she got into the car and closed the door. Leamas got in beside her.
'What bargain have you struck with him?' she persisted, suspicion and fear rising in her voice. 'They said you had tried to conspire against him, you and Fiedler. Then why is he letting you go?'
Leamas had started the car and was soon driving fast along the narrow road. On either side, bare fields; in the distance, dark monotonous hills were mingling with the gathering darkness. Leamas looked at his watch.
'We're five hours from Berlin,' he said. 'We've got to make Köpenick by quarter to one. We should do it easily.'
For a time Liz said nothing; she stared through the windscreen down the empty road, confused and lost in a labyrinth of half formed thoughts. A full moon had risen and the frost hovered in long shrouds across the fields. They turned on to an autobahn.

'Was I on your conscience, Alec?' she said at last. 'Is that why you made Mundt let me go?'

Leamas said nothing.

'You and Mundt are enemies, aren't you?'

Still he said nothing. He was driving fast now, the needle showed a hundred and twenty kilometres; the autobahn was pitted and bumpy. He had his headlights on full, she noticed, and didn't bother to dip for oncoming traffic on the other lane. He drove roughly, leaning forward, his elbows almost on the wheel.

'What will happen to Fiedler?' Liz asked suddenly and this time Leamas answered.

'He'll be shot.'

'Then why didn't they shoot you?' Liz continued quickly. 'You conspired with Fiedler against Mundt, that's what they said. You killed a guard. Why has Mundt let you go?'

'All right!' Leamas shouted suddenly. 'I'll tell you. I'll tell you what you were never, never to know, neither you nor I. Listen: Mundt is London's man, their agent; they bought him when he was in England. We are witnessing the lousy end to a filthy, lousy operation to save Mundt's skin. To save him from a clever little Jew in his own department who had begun to suspect the truth. They made us kill him, d'you see, kill the Jew. Now you know, and God help us both.'

Chapter 25

THE WALL

'I f that is so, Alec,' she said at last, 'what was my part in all this?'
Her voice was quite calm, almost matter-of-fact.

'I can only guess, Liz, from what I know and what Mundt told
me before we left. Fiedler suspected Mundt; had suspected him
ever since Mundt came back from England; he thought Mundt
was playing a double game. He hated him, of course – why
shouldn't he – but he was right too: Mundt was London's man.
Fiedler was too powerful for Mundt to eliminate alone, so London
decided to do it for him. I can see them working it out, they're so
damned academic; I can see them sitting round a fire in one of their
smart bloody clubs. They knew it was no good just eliminating
Fiedler – he might have told friends, published accusations: they
had to eliminate *suspicion*. Public rehabilitation, that's what they
organised for Mundt.'

He swung into the left-hand lane to overtake a lorry and trailer.
As he did so the lorry unexpectedly pulled out in front of him, so
that he had to brake violently on the pitted road to avoid being
forced into the crash-fence on his left.

'They told me to frame Mundt,' he said simply; 'they said he
had to be killed, and I was game. It was going to be my last
job. So I went to seed, and punched the grocer . . . you know all
that.'

'And made love?' she asked quietly. Leamas shook his head.
'But this is the point, you see,' he continued, 'Mundt knew it all;
he knew the plan; he had me picked up, he and Fiedler. Then he
let Fiedler take over, because he knew in the end Fiedler would
hang himself. My job was to let them think what in fact was the
truth: that Mundt was a British spy.' He hesitated. 'Your job was
to discredit me. Fiedler was shot and Mundt was saved, mercifully
delivered from a fascist plot. It's the old principle of love on the
rebound.'

'But how could they know about me; how could they know we

would come together?' Liz cried. 'Heavens above, Alec, can they even tell when people will fall in love?'

'It didn't matter – it didn't depend on that. They chose you because you were young and pretty and in the Party, because they knew you would come to Germany if they rigged an invitation. That man in the Labour Exchange, Pitt, he sent me up there; they knew I'd work at the library. Pitt was in the Service during the war and they squared him, I suppose. They only had to put you and me in contact, even for a day, it didn't matter; then afterwards they could call on you, send you the money, make it look like an affair even if it wasn't, don't you see? Make it look like an infatuation, perhaps. The only material point was that after bringing us together they should send you money as if it came at my request. As it was, we made it very easy for them . . .'

'Yes, we did.' And then she added, 'I feel dirty, Alec, as if I'd been put out to stud.'

Leamas said nothing.

'Did it ease your Department's conscience at all? Exploiting . . . somebody in the Party, rather than just anybody?' Liz continued.

Leamas said, 'Perhaps. They don't really think in those terms. It was an operational convenience.'

'I might have stayed in that prison, mightn't I? That's what Mundt wanted, wasn't it? He saw no point in taking the risk – I might have heard too much, guessed too much. After all, Fiedler was innocent, wasn't he? But then he's a Jew,' she added excitedly.'So that doesn't matter so much, does it?'

'Oh, for God's sake,' Leamas exclaimed.

'It seems odd that Mundt let me go, all the same – even as part of the bargain with you,' she mused. 'I'm a risk now, aren't I? When we get back to England, I mean: a Party member knowing all this . . . It doesn't seem logical that he should let me go.'

'I expect,' Leamas replied, 'he is going to use our escape to demonstrate to the Praesidium that there are other Fiedlers in his department who must be hunted down.'

'And other Jews?'

'It gives him a chance to secure his position,' Leamas replied curtly.

'By killing more innocent people? It doesn't seem to worry you much.'

'Of course it worries me. It makes me sick with shame and anger and . . . But I've been brought up differently, Liz; I can't see it in black and white. People who play this game take risks. Fiedler lost and Mundt won. London won – that's the point. It was a foul, foul operation. But it's paid off, and that's the only rule.' As he spoke his voice rose, until finally he was nearly shouting.

'You're trying to convince yourself,' Liz cried. 'They've done a wicked thing. How can you kill Fiedler – he was good, Alec? I know he was. And Mundt . . . '

'What the hell are you complaining about?' Leamas demanded roughly. 'Your Party's always at war, isn't it? Sacrificing the individual to the mass. That's what it says. Socialist reality: fighting night and day – the relentless battle – that's what they say, isn't it? At least you've survived. I never heard that Communists preached the sanctity of human life – perhaps I've got it wrong,' he added sarcastically. 'I agree, yes, I agree, you might have been destroyed. That was on the cards. Mundt's a vicious swine; he saw no point in letting you survive. His promise – I suppose he gave a promise to do his best by you – isn't worth a great deal. So you might have died – today, next year or twenty years on – in a prison in the worker's paradise. And so might I. But I seem to remember the Party is aiming at the destruction of a whole class. Or have I got it wrong?' Extracting a packet of cigarettes from his jacket he handed her two, together with a box of matches. Her fingers trembled as she lit them and passed one back to Leamas.

'You've thought it all out, haven't you?' she asked.

'We happened to fit the mould,' Leamas persisted, 'and I'm sorry. I'm sorry for the others too – the others who fit the mould. But don't complain about the terms, Liz; they're Party terms. A small price for a big return. One sacrificed for many. It's not pretty, I know, choosing who it'll be – turning the plan into people.'

She listened in the darkness, for a moment scarcely conscious of anything except the vanishing road before them, and the numb horror in her mind.

'But they let me love you,' she said at last. 'And you let me believe in you and love you.'

'They used us,' Leamas replied pitilessly. 'They cheated us both because it was necessary. It was the only way. Fiedler was bloody nearly home already, don't you see? Mundt would have been caught; can't you understand that?'

'How can you turn the world upside down?' Liz shouted suddenly. 'Fiedler was kind and decent; he was only doing his job, and now you've killed him. Mundt is a spy and a traitor and you

protect him. Mundt is a Nazi, do you know that? He hates Jews
. . . what side are you on? How can you . . . ?'

'There's only one law in this game,' Leamas retorted. 'Mundt
is their man; he gives them what they need. That's easy enough
to understand, isn't it? Leninism – the expediency of temporary
alliances. What do you think spies are: priests, saints and martyrs?
They're a squalid procession of vain fools, traitors too, yes; pansies,
sadists and drunkards, people who play cowboys and Indians to
brighten their rotten lives. Do you think they sit like monks in
London balancing the rights and wrongs? I'd have killed Mundt if
I could, I hate his guts; but not now. It so happens that they need
him. They need him so that the great moronic mass that you
admire can sleep soundly in their beds at night. They need him for
the safety of ordinary, crummy people like you and me.'

'But what about Fiedler – don't you feel anything for him?'

'This is a war,' Leamas replied. 'It's graphic and unpleasant
because it's fought on a tiny scale, at close range; fought with a
wastage of innocent life sometimes, I admit. But it's nothing,
nothing at all beside other wars – the last or the next.'

'Oh God,' said Liz softly. 'You don't understand. You don't
want to. You're trying to persuade yourself. It's far more terrible,
what they are doing; to find the humanity in people, in me and
whoever else they use, to turn it like a weapon in their hands, and
use it to hurt and kill . . .'

'Christ Almighty!' Leamas cried. 'What else have men done
since the world began? I don't believe in anything, don't you see
– not even destruction or anarchy. I'm sick, sick of killing but I
don't see what else they can do. They don't proselytise; they don't
stand in pulpits or on party platforms and tell us to fight for Peace
or for God or whatever it is. They're the poor sods who try to
keep the preachers from blowing each other sky high.'

'You're wrong,' Liz declared hopelessly; 'they're more wicked
than all of us.'

'Because I made love to you when you thought I was a tramp?'
Leamas asked savagely.

'Because of their contempt,' Liz replied; 'contempt for what is
real and good; contempt for love, contempt for . . .'

'Yes,' Leamas agreed, suddenly weary. 'That is the price they
pay; to despise God and Karl Marx in the same sentence. If that
is what you mean.'

'It makes you the same,' Liz continued; 'the same as Mundt and
all the rest . . . I should know, I was the one who was kicked

about, wasn't I? By them, by you because you don't care. Only Fiedler didn't . . . But the rest of you . . . you all treated me as if I was . . . nothing . . . just currency to pay with . . . You're all the same, Alec.'

'Oh, Liz,' he said desperately, 'for God's sake believe me. I hate it, I hate it all; I'm tired. But it's the world, it's mankind that's gone mad. We're a tiny price to pay . . . but everywhere's the same, people cheated and misled, whole lives thrown away, people shot and in prison, whole groups and classes of men written off for nothing. And you, your Party – God knows it was built on the bodies of ordinary people. You've never seen men die as I have, Liz . . .'

As he spoke Liz remembered the drab prison courtyard, and the wardress saying: 'It is a prison for those who slow down the march . . . for those who think they have the right to err.'

Leamas was suddenly tense, peering forward through the windscreen. In the headlights of the car Liz discerned a figure standing in the road. In his hand was a tiny light which he turned on and off as the car approached. 'That's him,' Leamas muttered; switched off the headlights and engine, and coasted silently forward. As they drew up, Leamas leant back and opened the rear door.

Liz did not turn round to look at him as he got in. She was staring stiffly forward, down the street at the falling rain.

'Drive at thirty kilometres,' the man said. His voice was taut, frightened. 'I'll tell you the way. When we reach the place you must get out and run to the wall. The searchlight will be shining at the point where you must climb. Stand in the beam of the searchlight. When the beam moves away begin to climb. You will have ninety seconds to get over. You go first,' he said to Leamas; 'and the girl follows. There are iron rungs in the lower part – after that you must pull yourself up as best you can. You'll have to sit on top and pull the girl up. Do you understand?'

'We understand,' said Leamas. 'How long have we got?'

'If you drive at thirty kilometres we shall be there in about nine minutes. The searchlight will be on the wall at five past one exactly. They can give you ninety seconds. Not more.'

'What happens after ninety seconds?' Leamas asked.

'They can only give you ninety seconds,' the man repeated; 'otherwise it is too dangerous. Only one detachment has been briefed. They think you are being infiltrated into West Berlin.

They've been told not to make it too easy. Ninety seconds are enough.'

'I bloody well hope so,' said Leamas drily. 'What time do you make it?'

'I checked my watch with the sergeant in charge of the detachment,' the man replied. A light went on and off briefly in the back of the car. 'It is twelve forty-eight. We must leave at five to one. Seven minutes to wait.'

They sat in total silence save for the rain pattering on the roof. The cobble road reached out straight before them, staged by dingy street lights every hundred metres. There was no one about. Above them the sky was lit with the unnatural glow of arclights. Occasionally the beam of a searchlight flickered overhead, and disappeared. Far to the left Leamas caught sight of a fluctuating light just above the sky-line, constantly altering in strength, like the reflection of a fire.

'What's that?' he asked, pointing towards it.

'Information Service,' the man replied. 'A scaffolding of lights. It flashes news headlines into East Berlin.'

'Of course,' Leamas muttered. They were very near the end of the road.

'There is no turning back,' the man continued; 'he told you that? There is no second chance.'

'I know,' Leamas replied.

'If something goes wrong – if you fall or get hurt – don't turn back. They shoot on sight within the area of the wall. You *must* get over.'

'We know,' Leamas repeated; 'he told me.'

'From the moment you get out of the car you are in the area.'

'We know. Now shut up,' Leamas retorted. And then he added: 'Are you taking the car back?'

'As soon as you get out of the car I shall drive it away. It is a danger for me, too,' the man replied.

'Too bad,' said Leamas drily.

Again there was silence; then Leamas asked: 'Have you got a gun?'

'Yes,' said the man; 'but I can't give it to you; he said I shouldn't give it to you . . . that you were sure to ask for it.'

Leamas laughed quietly. 'He would,' he said.

Leamas pulled the starter. With a noise that seemed to fill the street the car moved slowly forward.

They had gone about three hundred yards when the man

whispered excitedly, 'Go right here, then left.' They swung into a narrow side street. There were empty market stalls on either side so that the car barely passed between them.

'Left here, now!'

They turned again, fast, this time between two tall buildings into what looked like a cul-de-sac. There was washing across the street, and Liz wondered whether they would pass under it. As they approached what seemed to be the dead end the man said: 'Left again – follow the path.' Leamas mounted the curb, crossed the pavement, and they followed a broad footpath bordered by a broken fence to their left, and a tall, windowless building to their right. They heard a shout from somewhere above them, a woman's voice, and Leamas muttered: 'Oh, shut up,' as he steered clumsily round a right-angle bend in the path and came almost immediately upon a major road.

'Which way?' he demanded.

'Straight across – past the chemist – between the chemist and the post office – there!' The man was leaning so far forward that his face was almost level with theirs. He pointed now, reaching past Leamas, the tips of his fingers pressed against the windscreen.

'Get back,' Leamas hissed. 'Get your hand away. How the hell can I see if you wave your hand around like that?' Slamming the car into first gear he drove fast across the wide road. Glancing to his left he was astonished to glimpse the plump silhouette of the Brandenburg Gate three hundred yards away, and the sinister grouping of military vehicles at the foot of it.

'Where are we going?' asked Leamas suddenly.

'We're nearly there. Go slowly now . . . left, left, go left!' he cried, and Leamas jerked the wheel in the nick of time; they passed under a narrow archway into a courtyard. Half the windows were missing or boarded up; the empty doorways gaped sightlessly at them. At the other end of the yard was an open gateway. 'Through there,' came the whispered command, urgent in the darkness; 'then hard right. You'll see a street lamp on your right. The one beyond it is broken. When you reach the second lamp switch off the engine and coast until you see a fire hydrant. That's the place.'

'Why the hell didn't you drive yourself?'

'He said you should drive; he said it was safer.'

They passed through the gate and turned sharply to the right. They were in a narrow street, pitch dark.

'Lights out!'

Leamas switched off the car lights, drove slowly forwards

towards the first street lamp. Ahead, they could just see the second. It was unlit. Switching off the engine they coasted silently past it, until twenty yards ahead of them they discerned the dim outline of the fire hydrant. Leamas braked; the car rolled to a standstill.

'Where are we?' Leamas whispered. 'We crossed the Leninallee, didn't we?'

'Greifswalder Strasse. Then we turned north. We're north of Bernauerstrasse.'

'Pankow?'

'Just about. Look.' The man pointed down a side street to the left. At the far end they saw a brief stretch of wall, grey-brown in the weary arclight. Along the top ran a triple strand of barbed wire.

'How will the girl get over the wire?'

'It is already cut where you climb. There is a small gap. You have one minute to reach the Wall. Good-bye.'

They got out of the car, all three of them. Leamas took Liz by the arm, and she started from him as if he had hurt her.

'Good-bye,' said the German.

Leamas just whispered: 'Don't start that car till we're over.'

Liz looked at the German for a moment in the pale light. She had a brief impression of a young, anxious face; the face of a boy trying to be brave.

'Good-bye,' said Liz. She disengaged her arm and followed Leamas across the road and into the narrow street that led towards the Wall.

As they entered the street they heard the car start up behind them, turn and move quickly away in the direction they had come.

'Pull up the ladder, you bastard,' Leamas muttered, glancing back at the retreating car.

Liz hardly heard him.

Chapter 26

IN FROM
THE COLD

They walked quickly, Leamas glancing over his shoulder from time to time to make sure she was following. As he reached the end of the alley, he stopped, drew into the shadow of a doorway and looked at his watch.

'Two minutes,' he whispered.

She said nothing. She was staring straight ahead towards the wall, and the black ruins rising behind it.

'Two minutes,' Leamas repeated.

Before them was a strip of thirty yards. It followed the wall in both directions. Perhaps seventy yards to their right was a watch tower; the beam of its searchlight played along the strip. The thin rain hung in the air, so that the light from the arclamps was sallow and chalky, screening the world beyond. There was no one to be seen; not a sound. An empty stage.

The watch tower's searchlight began feeling its way along the wall towards them, hesitant; each time it rested they could see the separate bricks and the careless lines of mortar hastily put on. As they watched the beam stopped immediately in front of them. Leamas looked at his watch.

'Ready?' he asked.

She nodded.

Taking her arm he began walking deliberately across the strip. Liz wanted to run, but he held her so tightly that she could not. They were half-way towards the wall now, the brilliant semi-circle of light drawing them forward, the beam directly above them. Leamas was determined to keep Liz very close to him, as if he were afraid that Mundt would not keep his word and somehow snatch her away at the last moment.

They were almost at the wall when the beam darted to the north leaving them momentarily in total darkness. Still holding Liz's arm, Leamas guided her forward blindly, his left hand reaching ahead of him until suddenly he felt the coarse, sharp contact of the cinder brick. Now he could discern the wall and, looking upwards, the triple strand of wire and the cruel hooks which held it. Metal wedges, like climbers' pitons, had been driven into the brick. Seizing the highest one, Leamas pulled himself quickly upwards until he had reached the top of the wall. He tugged sharply at the lower strand of wire and it came towards him, already cut.

'Come on,' he whispered urgently, 'start climbing.'

Laying himself flat he reached down, grasped her upstretched hand and began drawing her slowly upwards as her foot found the first metal rung.

Suddenly the whole world seemed to break into flame; from everywhere, from above and beside them, massive lights converged, bursting upon them with savage accuracy.

Leamas was blinded, he turned his head away, wrenching wildly at Liz's arm. Now she was swinging free; he thought she had slipped and he called frantically, still drawing her upwards. He could see nothing – only a mad confusion of colour dancing in his eyes.

Then came the hysterical wail of sirens, orders frantically shouted. Half kneeling astride the wall he grasped both her arms in his, and began dragging her to him inch by inch, himself on the verge of falling.

Then they fired – single rounds, three or four, and he felt her shudder. Her thin arms slipped from his hands. He heard a voice in English from the Western side of the wall:

'Jump, Alec! Jump, man!'

Now everyone was shouting, English, French and German mixed; he heard Smiley's voice from quite close:

'The girl, where's the girl?'

Shielding his eyes he looked down at the foot of the wall and at last he managed to see her, lying still. For a moment he hesitated, then quite slowly he climbed back down the same rungs, until he was standing beside her. She was dead; her face was turned away, her black hair drawn across her cheek as if to protect her from the rain.

They seemed to hesitate before firing again; someone shouted an order, and still no one fired. Finally they shot him, two or three shots. He stood glaring round him like a blinded bull in the arena. As he fell, Leamas saw a small car smashed between great lorries, and the children waving cheerfully through the window.

THE LOOKING
GLASS WAR

To James Kennaway

'I wouldn't mind being a Pawn, if
only I might join' – Alice

AUTHOR'S NOTE

None of the characters, clubs, institutions nor intelligence organizations I have described here or elsewhere exists, or has existed to my knowledge in real life. I wish to make that very clear.

My thanks are due to the Radio Society of Great Britain and to Mr R. E. Molland, to the editors and staff of *Aviation Week and Space Technology* and to Mr Ronald Coles, all of whom provided me with valuable technical advice; and to Miss Elizabeth Tollinton for her secretarial help.

I must thank above all my wife for her untiring co-operation.

JOHN LE CARRÉ,
Agios Nikolaos,
Crete

May, 1964

Part One
TAYLOR'S RUN

Part Two
AVERY'S RUN
Prelude
Take-off
Homecoming

Part Three
LEISER'S RUN
Prelude
Take-off
Homecoming

'The carrying of a very heavy weight such as a large suitcase or trunk, immediately before sending practice, renders the muscles of the forearm, wrist and fingers too insensitive to produce good Morse.'

F. Tait's *Complete Morse Instructor*, Pitman.

Part One
TAYLOR'S RUN

'A fool lies here who tried to hustle the East'
KIPLING

Chapter 1

S now covered the airfield.

It had come from the north, in the mist, driven by the night wind, smelling of the sea. There it would stay all Winter, threadbare on the grey earth, an icy, sharp dust; not thawing and freezing, but static like a year without seasons. The changing mist, like the smoke of war, would hang over it, swallow up now a hangar, now the radar hut, now the machines; release them piece by piece, drained of colour, black carrion on a white desert.

It was a scene of no depth, no recession and no shadows. The land was one with the sky; figures and buildings locked in the cold like bodies in an icefloe.

Beyond the airfield there was nothing; no house, no hill, no road; not even a fence, a tree; only the sky pressing on the dunes, the running fog that lifted on the muddy Baltic shore. Somewhere inland were the mountains.

A group of children in school caps had gathered at the long observation window, chatting in German. Some wore ski clothes. Taylor gazed dully past them, holding a glass in his gloved hand. A boy turned round and stared at him, blushed and whispered to the other children. They fell silent.

He looked at his watch, making a wide arc with his arm, partly to free the sleeve of his overcoat and partly because it was his style; a military man, he wished you to say, decent regiment, decent club, knocked around in the war.

Ten to four. The plane was an hour late. They would have to announce the reason soon over the loudspeaker. He wondered what they would say: delayed by fog, perhaps; delayed take-off. They probably didn't even know – and they certainly would not admit – that she was two hundred miles off course, and south of Rostock. He finished his drink, turned to get rid of the empty glass. He had to admit that some of these foreign hooches, drunk in their own country, weren't at all bad. On the spot, with a couple of hours to kill and ten degrees of frost the other side of the window, you could do a lot worse than Steinhäger. He'd make them order it at the Alias Club when he got back. Cause quite a stir.

The loudspeaker was humming; it blared suddenly, faded out and began again, properly tuned. The children stared expectantly at it. First, the announcement in Finnish, then in Swedish, now in English. Northern Air Services regretted the delay to their charter flight two-nine-zero from Düsseldorf. No hint of how long, no hint of why. They probably didn't know themselves.

But Taylor knew. He wondered what would happen if he sauntered over to that pert little hostess in the glass box and told her: two-nine-zero will be a bit of time yet, my dear, she's been blown off course by heavy northerly gales over the Baltic, bearings all to Hades. The girl wouldn't believe him, of course, she'd think he was a crank. Later she'd know better. She'd realize he was something rather unusual, something rather special.

Outside it was already growing dark. Now the ground was lighter than the sky; the swept runways stood out against the snow like dykes, stained with the amber glow of marking lights. In the nearest hangars neon tubes shed a weary pallor over men and aeroplanes; the foreground beneath him sprang briefly to life as a beam from the control tower flicked across it. A fire engine had pulled away from the workshops on the left and joined the three ambulances already parked short of the centre runway. Simultaneously they switched on their blue rotating lights, and stood in line patiently flashing out their warning. The children pointed at them, chattering excitedly.

The girl's voice began again on the loudspeaker, it could only have been a few minutes since the last announcement. Once more the children stopped talking and listened. The arrival of flight two-nine-zero would be delayed at least another hour. Further information would be given as soon as it became available. There was something in the girl's voice, midway between surprise and anxiety, which seemed to communicate itself to the half-dozen people sitting at the other end of the waiting-room. An old woman said something to her husband, stood up, took her handbag and joined the group of children. For a time she peered stupidly into the twilight. Finding no comfort there, she turned to Taylor and said in English, 'What is become of the Düsseldorf plane?' Her voice had the throaty, indignant lilt of a Dutchwoman. Taylor shook his head. 'Probably the snow,' he replied. He was a brisk man; it went with his military way.

Pushing open the swing door, Taylor made his way downstairs to the reception hall. Near to the main entrance he recognized the yellow pennant of the Northern Air Services. The girl at the desk was very pretty.

'What's happened to the Düsseldorf flight?' His style was confiding; they said he had a knack with little girls. She smiled and shrugged her shoulders.

'I expect it is the snow. We are often having delays in Autumn.'

'Why don't you ask the boss?' he suggested, indicating with a nod the telephone in front of her.

'They will tell it on the loudspeaker,' she said, 'as soon as they know.'

'Who's the skipper, dear?'

'Please?'

'Who's the skipper, the captain?'

'Captain Lansen.'

'Is he any good?'

The girl was shocked. 'Captain Lansen is a very experienced pilot.'

Taylor looked her over, grinned and said, 'He's a very *lucky* pilot anyway, my dear.' They said he knew a thing or two, old Taylor did. They said it at the Alias on Friday nights.

Lansen. It was odd to hear a name spoken out like that. In the outfit they simply never did it. They favoured circumlocution, cover names, anything but the original: Archie boy, our flying friend, our friend up north, the chappie who takes the snapshots; they would even use the tortuous collection of figures and letters by which he was known on paper; but never in any circumstances the name.

Lansen. Leclerc had shown him a photograph in London: a boyish thirty-five, fair and goodlooking. He'd bet those hostesses went mad about him; that's all they were, anyway, cannon-fodder for the pilots. No one else got a look in. Taylor ran his right hand quickly over the outside of his overcoat pocket just to make sure the envelope was still there. He'd never carried this sort of money before. Five thousand dollars for one flight; seventeen hundred pounds, tax free, to lose your way over the Baltic. Mind you, Lansen didn't do that every day. This was special, Leclerc had said so. He wondered what she would do if he leant across the counter and told her who he was; showed her the money in that envelope. He'd never had a girl like that, a real girl, tall and young.

He went upstairs again to the bar. The barman was getting to know him. Taylor pointed to the bottle of Steinhäger on the centre shelf and said, 'Give me another of those, d'you mind? That's it, the fellow just behind you; some of your local poison.'

'It's German,' the barman said.

He opened his wallet and took out a banknote. In the Cellophane compartment there was a photograph of a girl, perhaps nine years old, wearing glasses and holding a doll. 'My daughter,' he explained to the barman, and the barman gave a watery smile.

His voice varied a lot, like the voice of a commercial traveller. His phoney drawl was more extravagant when he addressed his own class, when it was a matter of emphasizing a distinction which did not exist; or as now, when he was nervous.

He had to admit: he was windy. It was an eerie situation for a man of his experience and age, going over from routine courier work to operational stuff. This was a job for those swine in the Circus, not for his outfit at all. A different kettle of fish altogether, this was, from the ordinary run-of-the-mill stuff he was used to; stuck out on a limb, miles from nowhere. It beat him how they ever came to put an airport in a place like this. He quite liked the foreign trips as a rule: a visit to old Jimmy Gorton in Hamburg, for instance, or a night on the tiles in Madrid. It did him good to get away from Joanie. He'd done the Turkish run a couple of times, though he didn't care for wogs. But even that was a piece of cake compared to this: first-class travel and the bags on the seat beside him, a Nato pass in his pocket; a man had status, doing a job like that; good as the diplomatic boys, or nearly. But this was different, and he didn't like it.

Leclerc had said it was big, and Taylor believed him. They had got him a passport with another name. Malherbe. Pronounced Mallaby, they said. Christ alone knew who'd chosen it. Taylor couldn't even spell it; made a botch of the hotel register when he signed in that morning. The subsistence was fantastic, of course: fifteen quid a day operational expenses, no vouchers asked for. He'd heard the Circus gave seventeen. He could make a good bit on that, buy something for Joanie. She'd probably rather have the money.

He'd told her, of course: he wasn't supposed to, but Leclerc didn't know Joanie. He lit a cigarette, drew from it and held it in the palm of his hand like a sentry smoking on duty. How the hell was he supposed to push off to Scandinavia without telling his wife?

He wondered what those kids were doing, glued to the window

all this time. Amazing the way they managed the foreign language. He looked at his watch again, scarcely noticing the time, touched the envelope in his pocket. Better not have another drink; he must keep a clear head. He tried to guess what Joanie was doing now. Probably having a sit-down with a gin and something. A pity she had to work all day.

He suddenly realized that everything had gone silent. The barman was standing still, listening. The old people at the table were listening too, their silly faces turned towards the observation window. Then he heard it quite distinctly, the sound of an aircraft, still far away, but approaching the airfield. He made quickly for the window, was half-way there when the loudspeaker began; after the first few words of German the children, like a flock of pigeons, fluttered away to the reception lounge. The party at the table had stood up; the women were reaching for their gloves, the men for their coats and briefcases. At last the announcer gave the English. Lansen was coming in to land.

Taylor stared into the night. There was no sign of the plane. He waited, his anxiety mounting. It's like the end of the world, he thought, the end of the bloody world out there. Supposing Lansen crashed; supposing they found the cameras. He wished someone else were handling it. Woodford, why hadn't Woodford taken it over, or sent that clever college boy Avery? The wind was stronger; he could swear it was far stronger; he could tell from the way it stirred the snow, flinging it over the runway; the way it tore at the flares; the way it made white columns on the horizon, dashing them vehemently away like a hated creation. A gust struck suddenly at the windows in front of him, making him recoil, and there followed the rattle of ice grains and the short grunt of the wooden frame. Again he looked at his watch; it had become a habit with Taylor. It seemed to help, knowing the time.

Lansen will never make it in this, never.

His heart stood still. Softly at first, then rising swiftly to a wail, he heard the klaxons, all four together, moaning out over that godforsaken airfield like the howl of starving animals. Fire . . . the plane must be on fire. He's on fire and he's going to try and land . . . he turned frantically, looking for someone who could tell him.

The barman was standing beside him, polishing a glass, looking through the window.

'What's going on?' Taylor shouted. 'Why are the sirens going?'

'They always make the sirens in bad weather,' he replied. 'It is the law.'

'Why are they letting him land?' Taylor insisted. 'Why don't they route him farther south? It's too small, this place; why don't they send him somewhere bigger?'

The barman shook his head indifferently. 'It's not so bad,' he said indicating the airfield. 'Besides, he is very late. Maybe he has no petrol.'

They saw the plane low over the airfield, her lights alternating above the flares; her spotlights scanned the runway. She was down, safely down, and they heard the roar of her throttle as she began the long taxi to the reception point.

The bar had emptied. He was alone. Taylor ordered a drink. He knew his drill: stay put in the bar, Leclerc had said, Lansen will meet you in the bar. He'll take a bit of time; got to cope with his flight documents, clear his cameras. Taylor heard the children singing downstairs, and a woman leading them. Why the hell did he have to be surrounded by kids and women? He was doing a man's job, wasn't he, with five thousand dollars in his pocket and a phoney passport?

'There are no more flights today,' the barman said. 'They have forbidden all flying now.'

Taylor nodded. 'I know. It's bloody shocking out there, shocking.'

The barman was putting away bottles. 'There was no danger,' he added soothingly. 'Captain Lansen is a very good pilot.' He hesitated, not knowing whether to put away the Steinhäger.

'Of course there wasn't any danger,' Taylor snapped. 'Who said anything about danger?'

'Another drink?' the barman said.

'No, but you have one. Go on, have one yourself.'

The barman reluctantly gave himself a drink, locked the bottle away.

'All the same, how do they do it?' Taylor asked. His voice was conciliatory, putting it right with the barman. 'They can't see a thing in weather like this, not a damn thing.' He smiled knowingly. 'You sit there in the nose and you might just as well have your eyes shut for all the good they do. I've seen it,' Taylor added, his hands loosely cupped in front of him as though he were at the controls. 'I know what I'm talking about . . . and they're the first to catch it, those boys, if something *does* go wrong.' He shook his head. 'They can keep it,' he declared. 'They're entitled to every penny they earn. Specially in a kite that size. They're held together with string, those things; string.'

The barman nodded distantly, finished his drink, washed up the empty glass, dried it and put it on the shelf under the counter. He unbuttoned his white jacket.

Taylor made no move.

'Well,' said the barman with a mirthless smile, 'we have to go home now.'

'What do you mean *we*?' Taylor asked, opening his eyes wide and tilting back his head. 'What do you mean?' He'd take on anyone now; Lansen had landed.

'I have to close the bar.'

'Go home indeed. Give us another drink, come on. You can go home if you like. I happen to live in London.' His tone was challenging, half playful, half resentful, gathering volume. 'And since your aircraft companies are unable to *get* me to London, or any other damn place until tomorrow morning, it's a bit silly of you to tell me to go there, isn't it, old boy?' He was still smiling, but it was the short, angry smile of a nervous man losing his temper. 'And next time you accept a drink from me, chum, I'll trouble you to have the courtesy . . .'

The door opened and Lansen came in.

This wasn't the way it was supposed to happen; this wasn't the way they'd described it at all. Stay in the bar, Leclerc had said, sit at the corner table, have a drink, put your hat and coat on the other chair as if you're waiting for someone. Lansen always has a beer when he clocks in. He likes the public lounge, it's Lansen's style. There'll be people milling about, Leclerc said. It's a small place but there's always something going on at these airports. He'll look around for somewhere to sit – quite open and above board – then he'll come over and ask you if anyone's using the chair. You'll say you kept it free for a friend but the friend hadn't turned up: Lansen will ask if he can sit there. He'll order a beer, then say, 'Boy friend or girl friend?' You'll tell him not to be indelicate, and you'll both laugh a bit and get talking. Ask the two questions: height and airspeed. Research Section must know the height and airspeed. Leave the money in your overcoat pocket. He'll pick up your coat, hang his own beside it and help himself quietly, without any fuss, taking the envelope and dropping the film into your coat pocket. You finish your drinks, shake hands, and Bob's your uncle. In the morning you fly home. Leclerc had made it sound so simple.

Lansen strode across the empty room towards them, a tall, strong figure in a blue mackintosh and cap. He looked briefly at

Taylor and spoke past him to the barman: 'Jens, give me a beer.' Turning to Taylor he said, 'What's yours?'

Taylor smiled thinly. 'Some of your local stuff.'

'Give him whatever he wants. A double.'

The barman briskly buttoned up his jacket, unlocked the cupboard and poured out a large Steinhäger. He gave Lansen a beer from the cooler.

'Are you from Leclerc?' Lansen inquired shortly. Anyone could have heard.

'Yes.' He added tamely, far too late, 'Leclerc and Company, London.'

Lansen picked up his beer and took it to the nearest table. His hand was shaking. They sat down.

'Then you tell me,' he said fiercely, 'which damn fool gave me those instructions?'

'I don't know.' Taylor was taken aback. 'I don't even know what your instructions were. It's not my fault. I was sent to collect the film, that's all. It's not even my job, this kind of thing. I'm on the overt side – courier.'

Lansen leant forward, his hand on Taylor's arm. Taylor could feel him trembling. 'I was on the overt side too. Until today. There were kids on that plane. Twenty-five German school-children on Winter holidays. A whole load of kids.'

'Yes.' Taylor forced a smile. 'Yes, we had the reception committee in the waiting-room.'

Lansen burst out, 'What were we *looking* for, that's what I don't understand. What's so exciting about Rostock?'

'I tell you I'm nothing to do with it.' He added inconsistently: 'Leclerc said it wasn't Rostock but the area south.'

'The triangle south: Kalkstadt, Langdorn, Wolken. You don't have to tell me the area.'

Taylor looked anxiously towards the barman.

'I don't think we should talk so loud,' he said. 'That fellow's a bit anti.' He drank some Steinhäger.

Lansen made a gesture with his hand as if he were brushing something from in front of his face. 'It's finished,' he said. 'I don't want any more. It's finished. It was OK when we just stayed on course photographing whatever there was; but this is too damn much, see? Just too damn, damn much altogether.' His accent was thick and clumsy, like an impediment.

'Did you get any pictures?' Taylor asked. He must get the film and go.

Lansen shrugged, put his hand in his raincoat pocket and, to

Taylor's horror, extracted a zinc container for thirty-five-millimetre film, handing it to him across the table.

'What was it?' Lansen asked again. 'What were they after in such a place? I went under the cloud, circled the whole area. I didn't see any atom bombs.'

'Something important, that's all they told me. Something big. It's got to be done, don't you see? You can't make illegal flights over an area like that.' Taylor was repeating what someone had said. 'It has to be an airline, a registered airline, or nothing. There's no other way.'

'Listen. They picked us up as soon as we got into the place. Two MIGs. Where did they come from, that's what I want to know? As soon as I saw them I turned into cloud; they followed me. I put out a signal, asking for bearings. When we came out of the cloud, there they were again. I thought they'd force me down, order me to land. I tried to jettison the camera but it was stuck. The kids were all crowding the windows, waving at the MIGs. They flew alongside for a time, then peeled off. They came close, very close. It was bloody dangerous for the kids.' He hadn't touched his beer. 'What the hell did they want?' he asked. 'Why didn't they order me down?'

'I told you: it's not my fault. This isn't my kind of work. But whatever London are looking for, they know what they're doing.' He seemed to be convincing himself; he needed to believe in London. 'They don't waste their time. Or yours, old boy. They know what they're up to.' He frowned, to indicate conviction, but Lansen might not have heard.

'They don't believe in unnecessary risks either,' Taylor said. 'You've done a good job, Lansen. We all have to do our bit . . . take risks. We all do. I did in the war, you know. You're too young to remember the war. This is the same job; we're fighting for the same thing.' He suddenly remembered the two questions. 'What height were you doing when you took the pictures?'

'It varied. We were down to six thousand feet over Kalkstadt.'

'It was Kalkstadt they wanted most,' Taylor said with appreciation. 'That's first-class, Lansen, first-class. What was your airspeed?'

'Two hundred . . . two forty. Something like this. There was nothing there, I'm telling you, nothing.' He lit a cigarette.

'It's the end now,' Lansen repeated. 'However big the target is.' He stood up. Taylor got up too; he put his right hand in his overcoat pocket. Suddenly his throat went dry: the money, where was the money?

'Try the other pocket,' Lansen suggested.

Taylor handed him the envelope. 'Will there be trouble about this? About the MIGs, I mean?'

Lansen shrugged. 'I doubt it, it hasn't happened to me before. They'll believe me once; they'll believe it was the weather. I went off course about half-way. There could have been a fault in the ground control. In the hand-over.'

'What about the navigator? What about the rest of the crew? What do they think?'

'That's my business,' said Lansen sourly. 'You can tell London it's the end.'

Taylor looked at him anxiously. 'You're just upset,' he said, 'after the tension.'

'Go to hell,' said Lansen softly. 'Go to bloody hell.' He turned away, put a coin on the counter and strode out of the bar, stuffing carelessly into his raincoat pocket the long buff envelope which contained the money.

After a moment Taylor followed him. The barman watched him push his way through the door and disappear down the stairs. A very distasteful man, he reflected; but then he never had liked the English.

Taylor thought at first that he would not take a taxi to the hotel. He could walk it in ten minutes and save a bit on subsistence. The airline girl nodded to him as he passed her on his way to the main entrance. The reception hall was done in teak; blasts of warm air rose from the floor. Taylor stepped outside. Like the thrust of a sword the cold cut through his clothes; like the numbness of an encroaching poison it spread swiftly over his naked face, feeling its way into his neck and shoulders. Changing his mind, he looked round hastily for a taxi. He was drunk. He suddenly realized: the fresh air had made him drunk. The rank was empty. An old Citroën was parked fifty yards up the road, its engine running. He's got the heater on, lucky devil, thought Taylor and hurried back through the swing doors.

'I want a cab,' he said to the girl. 'Where can I get one, d'you know?' He hoped to God he looked all right. He was mad to have drunk so much. He shouldn't have accepted that drink from Lansen.

She shook her head. 'They have taken the children,' she said. 'Six in each car. That was the last flight today. We don't have many taxis in Winter.' She smiled. 'It's a very *little* airport.'

'What's that up the road, that old car? Not a cab, is it?' His voice was indistinct.

She went to the doorway and looked out. She had a careful balancing walk, artless and provocative.

'I don't see any car,' she said.

Taylor looked past her. 'There was an old Citroën. Lights on. Must have gone. I just wondered.' Christ, it went past and he'd never heard it.

'The taxis are all Volvos,' the girl remarked. 'Perhaps one will come back after he has dropped the children. Why don't you go and have a drink?'

'Bar's closed,' Taylor snapped. 'Barman's gone home.'

'Are you staying at the airport hotel?'

'The Regina, yes. I'm in a hurry, as a matter of fact.' It was easier now. 'I'm expecting a phone call from London.'

She looked doubtfully at his coat; it was of rainproof material in a pebble weave. 'You could walk,' she suggested. 'It is ten minutes, straight down the road. They can send your luggage later.'

Taylor looked at his watch, the same wide gesture. 'Luggage is already at the hotel. I arrived this morning.'

He had that kind of crumpled, worried face which is only a hair's breadth from the music halls and yet is infinitely sad; a face in which the eyes are paler than their environment, and the contours converge upon the nostrils. Aware of this, perhaps, Taylor had grown a trivial moustache, like a scrawl on a photograph, which made a muddle of his face without concealing its shortcoming. The effect was to inspire disbelief, not because he was a rogue but because he had no talent for deception. Similarly he had tricks of movement crudely copied from some lost original, such as an irritating habit which soldiers have of arching his back suddenly, as if he had discovered himself in an unseemly posture, or he would affect an agitation about the knees and elbows which feebly caricatured an association with horses. Yet the whole was dignified by pain, as if he were holding his little body stiff against a cruel wind.

'If you walk quickly,' she said, 'it takes less than ten minutes.'

Taylor hated waiting. He had a notion that people who waited were people of no substance: it was an affront to be seen waiting. He pursed his lips, shook his head, and with an ill-tempered 'Goodnight, lady,' stepped abruptly into the freezing air.

Taylor had never seen such a sky. Limitless, it curved downward to the snowbound fields, its destiny broken here and there by films of mist which frosted the clustered stars and drew a line round the yellow half moon. Taylor was frightened, like a landsman frightened by the sea. He hastened his uncertain step, swaying as he went.

He had been walking about five minutes when the car caught him up. There was no footpath. He became aware of its headlights first, because the sound of its engine was deadened by the snow, and he only noticed a light ahead of him, not realizing where it came from. It traced its way languidly over the snowfields and for a time he thought it was the beacon from the airport. Then he saw his own shadow shortening on the road, the light became suddenly brighter, and he knew it must be a car. He was walking on the right, stepping briskly along the edge of the icy rubble that lined the road. He observed that the light was unusually yellow and he guessed the headlamps were masked according to the French rule. He was rather pleased with this little piece of deduction; the old brain was pretty clear after all.

He didn't look over his shoulder because he was a shy man in his way and did not want to give the impression of asking for a lift. But it did occur to him, a little late perhaps, that on the continent they actually drove on the right, and that therefore strictly speaking he was walking on the wrong side of the road, and ought to do something about it.

The car hit him from behind, breaking his spine. For one dreadful moment Taylor described a classic posture of anguish, his head and shoulders flung violently backwards, fingers extended. He made no cry. It was as if his entire body and soul were concentrated in this final attitude of pain, more articulate in death than any sound the living man had made. It is quite possible that the driver was unaware of what he had done; that the impact of the body on the car was not to be distinguished from a thud of loose snow against the axle.

The car carried him for a yard or two then threw him aside, dead on the empty road, a stiff, wrecked figure at the fringe of the wilderness. His trilby hat lay beside him. A sudden blast seized it, carrying it across the snow. The shreds of his pebble-weave coat fluttered in the wind, reaching vainly for the zinc capsule as it rolled gently with the camber to lodge for a moment against the frozen bank, then to continue wearily down the slope.

Part Two
AVERY'S RUN

'There are some things that no one
has a right to ask of any white man'
JOHN BUCHAN, *MR STANDFAST*

Chapter 2
Prelude

I t was three in the morning.

Avery put down the telephone, woke Sarah and said, 'Taylor's dead.' He shouldn't have told her, of course.

'Who's Taylor?'

A bore, he thought; he only remembered him vaguely. A dreary English bore, straight off Brighton pier.

'A man in courier section,' he said. 'He was with them in the war. He was rather good.'

'That's what you always say. They're all good. How did he die, then? How did he die?' She had sat up in bed.

'Leclerc's waiting to hear.' He wished she wouldn't watch him while he dressed.

'And he wants you to help him wait?'

'He wants me to go to the office. He wants me. You don't expect me to turn over and go back to sleep, do you?'

'I was only asking,' Sarah said. 'You're always so considerate to Leclerc.'

'Taylor was an old hand. Leclerc's very worried.' He could still hear the triumph in Leclerc's voice: 'Come at once, get a taxi; we'll go through the files again.'

'Does this often happen? Do people often die?' There was indignation in her voice, as if no one ever told her anything; as if she alone thought it dreadful that Taylor had died.

'You're not to tell anyone,' said Avery. It was a way of keeping her from him. 'You're not even to say I've gone out in the middle of the night. Taylor was travelling under another name.' He added, 'Someone will have to tell his wife.' He was looking for his glasses.

She got out of bed and put on a dressing-gown. 'For God's sake stop talking like a cowboy. The secretaries know; why can't the wives? Or are they only told when their husbands die?' She went to the door.

She was of medium height and wore her hair long, a style at odds with the discipline of her face. There was a tension in her expression, an anxiety, an incipient discontent, as if tomorrow would only be worse. They had met at Oxford; she had taken a better degree than Avery. But somehow marriage had made her childish; dependence had become an attitude, as if she had given him something irredeemable, and were always asking for it back. Her son was less her projection than her excuse; a wall against the world and not a channel to it.

'Where are you going?' Avery asked. She sometimes did things to spite him, like tearing up a ticket for a concert. She said, 'We've got a child, remember?' He noticed Anthony crying. They must have woken him.

'I'll ring from the Office.'

He went to the front door. As she reached the nursery she looked back and Avery knew she was thinking they hadn't kissed.

'You should have stuck to publishing,' she said.

'You didn't like that any better.'

'Why don't they send a car?' she asked. 'You said they had masses of cars.'

'It's waiting at the corner.'

'Why, for God's sake?'

'More secure,' he replied.

'Secure against what?'

'Have you got any money? I seem to have run out.'

'What for?'

'Just money, that's all! I can't run around without a penny in my pocket.' She gave him ten shillings from her bag. Closing the door quickly behind him he went down the stairs into Prince of Wales Drive.

He passed the ground-floor window and knew without looking that Mrs Yates was watching him from behind her curtain, as she watched everybody night and day, holding her cat for comfort.

It was terribly cold. The wind seemed to come from the river, across the park. He looked up and down the road. It was empty. He should have telephoned the rank at Clapham but he wanted to get out of the flat. Besides, he had told Sarah the car was coming. He walked a hundred yards or so towards the Power Station, changed his mind and turned back. He was sleepy. It was a curious illusion that even in the street he still heard the telephone ringing. There was a cab that hung round Albert Bridge at all hours; that was the best bet. So he passed the entrance to his part of the Mansions, glanced up at the nursery window, and there was Sarah looking out. She must have been wondering where the car was. She had Anthony in her arms and he knew she was crying because he hadn't kissed her. He took half an hour to find a taxi to Blackfriars Road.

Avery watched the lamps come up the street. He was quite young, belonging to that intermediate class of contemporary Englishman which must reconcile an Arts degree with an uncertain provenance. He was tall and bookish in appearance, slow-eyed behind his spectacles, with a gently self-effacing manner which endeared him to his elders. The motion of the taxi comforted him, as rocking consoles a child.

He reached St George's Circus, passed the Eye Hospital and entered Blackfriars Road. Suddenly he was upon the house, but told the driver to drop him at the next corner because Leclerc had said be careful.

'Just here,' he called. 'This will do fine.'

The Department was housed in a crabbed, sooty villa of a place with a fire extinguisher on the balcony. It was like a house eternally for sale. No one knew why the Ministry put a wall round it; perhaps to protect it from the gaze of the people, like the wall round a cemetery; or the people from the gaze of the dead. Certainly not for the garden's sake, because nothing grew in it but grass which had worn away in patches like the coat of an old mongrel. The front door was painted dark green; it was never opened. By day anonymous vans of the same colour occasionally passed down the shabby drive, but they transacted their business in the back yard. The neighbours, if they referred to the place at all, spoke of the Ministry House, which was not accurate, for the Department was a separate entity, and the Ministry its master. The building had that unmistakable air of controlled dilapidation which characterizes government hirings all over the world. For those who worked in it, its mystery was like the mystery of motherhood, its survival like the mystery of England. It shrouded and contained them, cradled them and, with sweet anachronism, gave them the illusion of nourishment.

Avery could remember it when the fog lingered contentedly against its stucco walls, or in the Summer, when the sunlight would briefly peer through the mesh curtains of his room, leaving no warmth, revealing no secrets. And he would remember it on that Winter dawn, its façade stained black, the street lights catching the raindrops on the grimy windows. But however he remembered it, it was not as a place where he worked, but where he lived.

Following the path to the back, he rang the bell and waited for Pine to open the door. A light shone in Leclerc's window.

He showed Pine his pass. Perhaps both were reminded of the war: for Avery a vicarious pleasure, while Pine could look back on experience.

'A lovely moon, sir,' said Pine.

'Yes.' Avery stepped inside. Pine followed him in, locking up behind him.

'Time was, the boys would curse a moon like this.'

'Yes, indeed,' Avery laughed.

'Heard about the Melbourne test, sir? Bradley's out for three.'

'Oh dear,' said Avery pleasantly. He disliked cricket.

A blue lamp glowed from the hall ceiling like the night light in a Victorian hospital. Avery climbed the staircase; he felt cold and uneasy. Somewhere a bell rang. It was odd how Sarah had not heard the telephone.

Leclerc was waiting for him: 'We need a man,' he said. He spoke involuntarily, like someone waking. A light shone on the file before him.

He was sleek, small and very bland; a precise cat of a man, clean shaven and groomed. His stiff collars were cut away; he favoured ties of one colour, knowing perhaps that a weak claim was worse than none. His eyes were dark and quick; he smiled as he spoke, yet conveyed no pleasure. His jackets had twin vents, he kept his handkerchief in his sleeve. On Fridays he wore suède shoes, and they said he was going to the country. No one seemed to know where he lived. The room was in half darkness.

'We can't do another overflight. This was the last; they warned me at the Ministry. We'll have to put a man in. I've been going through the old cards, John. There's one called Leiser, a Pole. He would do.'

'What happened to Taylor? Who killed him?'

Avery went to the door and switched on the main light. They looked at one another awkwardly. 'Sorry. I'm still half asleep,' Avery said. They began again, finding the thread.

Leclerc spoke up. 'You took a time, John. Something go wrong at home?' He was not born to authority.

'I couldn't get a cab. I phoned the rank at Clapham but they didn't reply. Nor Albert Bridge; nothing there either.' He hated to disappoint Leclerc.

'You can charge for it,' Leclerc said distantly, 'and the phone calls, you realize. Your wife all right?'

'I told you: there was no reply. She's fine.'

'She didn't mind?'

'Of course not.'

They never talked about Sarah. It was as if they shared a single relationship to Avery's wife, like children who are able to share a toy they no longer care for. Leclerc said, 'Well, she's got that son of yours to keep her company.'

'Yes, rather.'

Leclerc was proud of knowing it was a son and not a daughter.

He took a cigarette from the silver box on his desk. He had told Avery once: the box was a gift, a gift from the war. The man who gave it to him was dead, the occasion for giving it was past; there was no inscription on the lid. Even now, he would say, he was not entirely certain whose side the man had been on, and Avery would laugh to make him happy.

Taking the file from his desk, Leclerc now held it directly under the light as if there was something in it which he must study very closely.

'John.'

Avery went to him, trying not to touch his shoulder.

'What do you make of a face like that?'

'I don't know. It's hard to tell from photographs.'

It was the head of a boy, round and blank, with long, fair hair swept back.

'Leiser. He *looks* all right, doesn't he? That was twenty years ago, of course,' Leclerc said. 'We gave him a very high rating.' Reluctantly he put it down, struck his lighter and held it to the cigarette. 'Well,' he said briskly, 'we seem to be up against something. I've no idea what happened to Taylor. We have a routine consular report, that's all. A car accident apparently. A few details, nothing informative. The sort of thing that goes out to next of kin. The Foreign Office sent us the teleprint as it came over the wire. They knew it was one of our passports.' He pushed a sheet of flimsy paper across the desk. He loved to make you read things while he waited. Avery glanced at it:

'Malherbe? Was that Taylor's cover name?'

'Yes. I'll have to get a couple of cars from the Ministry pool,' Leclerc said. 'Quite absurd not having our own cars. The Circus has a whole fleet.' And then, 'Perhaps the Ministry will believe me now. Perhaps they'll finally accept we're still an operational department.'

'Did Taylor collect the film?' Avery asked. 'Do we know whether he got it?'

'*I've* no inventory of his possessions,' Leclerc replied indignantly. 'At the moment, all his effects are impounded by the Finnish police. Perhaps the film is among them. It's a small place and I imagine they like to stick to the letter of the law.' And casually, so that Avery knew it mattered, 'The Foreign Office is afraid there may be a muddle.'

'Oh dear,' said Avery automatically. It was their practice in the Department: antique and understated.

Leclerc looked directly at him now, taking interest. 'The Resident Clerk at the Foreign Office spoke to the Assistant half an hour ago. They refuse to involve themselves. They say we're a clandestine service and must do it our own way. Somebody's got to go out there as next of kin; that is the course they favour. To claim the body and effects and get them back here. I want you to go.'

Avery was suddenly aware of the pictures round the room, of the boys who had fought in the war. They hung in two rows of six, either side of the model of a Wellington bomber, rather a dusty one, painted black with no insignia. Most of the photographs had been taken out of doors. Avery could see the hangars behind, and between the young, smiling faces the half-hidden fuselages of parked aircraft.

Beneath each photograph were signatures, already brown and faded, some fluent and racy, others – they must have been the other-ranks – self-conscious and elaborate, as if the writers had come unnaturally to fame. There were no surnames, but sobriquets from children's magazines: Jacko, Shorty, Pip and Lucky Joe. Only the Mae West was uniform, the long hair and the sunny, boyish smile. They seemed to like having their photographs taken, as if being together were an occasion for laughter which might not be repeated. The men in front were crouching comfortably, like men used to crouching in gun turrets, and those behind had put their arms carelessly over one another's shoulders. There was no affectation but a spontaneous goodwill which does not seem to survive war or photographs.

One face was common to every picture, right to the end; the face of a slim, bright-eyed man in a duffle coat and corduroy trousers. He wore no life jacket and stood a little apart from the men as if he were somehow extra. He was smaller than the rest, older. His features were formed; he had a purpose about him which the others lacked. He might have been their schoolmaster.

Avery had once looked for his signature to see if it had altered in the nineteen years, but Leclerc had not signed his name. He was still very like his photographs: a shade more set around the jaw perhaps, a shade less hair.

'But that would be an operational job,' said Avery uncertainly.

'Of course. We're an operational department, you know.' A little buck of the head. 'You are entitled to operational subsistence. All you have to do is collect Taylor's stuff. You're to bring back everything except the film, which you deliver to an address in Helsinki. You'll be instructed about that separately. You come back and you can help me with Leiser—'

'Couldn't the Circus take it on? I mean, couldn't they do it more simply?'

This smile came slowly. 'I'm afraid that wouldn't answer at all. It's our show, John: the commitment is within our competence. A military target. I would be shirking our responsibility if I gave it to the Circus. Their charter is political, exclusively political.'

His small hand ran over his hair, a short, concise movement, tense and controlled. 'So it's our problem. Thus far, the Ministry approves my reading' – a favourite expression – 'I can send someone else if you prefer – Woodford or one of the older men. I thought you'd enjoy it. It's an important job, you know; something new for you to tackle.'

'Of course. I'd like to go . . . if you trust me.'

Leclerc enjoyed that. Now he pushed a piece of blue draft paper into Avery's hand. It was covered with Leclerc's own writing, boyish and rounded. He had written 'Ephemeral' at the top and underlined it. In the left-hand margin were his initials, all four, and beneath them the word *Unclassified*. Once more Avery began reading.

'If you follow it carefully,' he said, 'you'll see that we don't specifically state that you *are* next of kin; we just quote from Taylor's application form. That's as far as the Foreign Office people are prepared to go. They've agreed to send this to the local consulate via Helsinki.'

Avery read: 'Following from Consular Department. Your Teleprint re Malherbe. John Somerton Avery, holder of British passport no—, half-brother of deceased, is named in Malherbe's passport application as next of kin. Avery informed and proposes to fly out today take over body and effects. NAS flight 201 via Hamburg, ETA 1820 local time. Please provide usual facilities and assistance.'

'I didn't know your passport number,' Leclerc said. 'The plane leaves at three this afternoon. It's only a small place; I imagine the Consul will meet you at the airport. There's a flight from Hamburg every other day. If you don't have to go to Helsinki you can take the same plane back.'

'Couldn't I be his brother?' Avery asked lamely. 'Half brother looks fishy.'

'There's no time to rig the passport. The Foreign Office are being very sticky about passports. We had a lot of trouble about Taylor's.' He had returned to the file. 'A *lot* of trouble. It would mean calling *you* Malherbe as well, you see. I don't think they'd like that.' He spoke without attention, paying out rope.

The room was very cold.

Avery said, 'What about our Scandinavian friend . . . ?' Leclerc looked uncomprehending. 'Lansen. Shouldn't someone contact him?'

'I'm attending to that.' Leclerc, hating questions, replied cautiously as if he might be quoted.

'And Taylor's wife?' It seemed pedantic to say widow. 'Are you attending to her?'

'I thought we'd go round first thing in the morning. She's not on the telephone. Telegrams are so cryptic.'

'We?' said Avery. 'Do we both need to go?'

'You're my aide, aren't you?'

It was too quiet. Avery longed for the sound of traffic and the buzz of telephones. By day they had people about them, the tramp of messengers, the drone of Registry trolleys. He had the feeling, when alone with Leclerc, that the third person was missing. No one else made him so conscious of behaviour, no one else had such a disintegrating effect on conversation. He wished Leclerc would give him something else to read.

'Have you heard anything about Taylor's wife?' Leclerc asked. 'Is she a secure sort of person?'

Seeing that Avery did not understand, he continued:

'She could make it awkward for us, you know. If she decided to. We shall have to tread carefully.'

'What will you say to her?'

'We shall play it by ear. The way we did in the war. She won't know, you see. She won't even know he was abroad.'

'He might have told her.'

'Not Taylor. Taylor's an old hand. He had his instructions and knew the rules. She must have a pension, that's most important. Active service.' He made another brisk, finite gesture with his hand.

'And the staff; what will you tell them?'

'I shall hold a meeting this morning for Heads of Sections. As for the rest of the Department, we shall say it was an accident.'

'Perhaps it was,' Avery suggested.

Leclerc was smiling again; an iron bar of a smile, like an affliction.

'In which case we shall have told the truth; and have more chance of getting that film.'

There was still no traffic in the street outside. Avery felt hungry. Leclerc glanced at his watch.

'You were looking at Gorton's report,' Avery said.

He shook his head, wistfully touched a file, revisiting a favourite album. 'There's nothing there. I've read it over and over again. I've had the other photographs blown up to every conceivable size. Haldane's people have been on them night and day. We just can't get any farther.'

Sarah was right: to help him wait.

Leclerc said – it seemed suddenly the point of their meeting – 'I've arranged for you to have a short talk with George Smiley at the Circus after this morning's conference. You've heard of him?'

'No,' Avery lied. This was delicate ground.

'He used to be one of their best men. Typical of the Circus in some ways, of the better kind. He resigns, you know, and he comes back. His conscience. One never knows whether he's there or not. He's a bit past it now. They say he drinks a good deal. Smiley has the North European desk. He can brief you about dropping the film. Our own courier service is disbanded, so there's no other way: the FO don't want to know us; after Taylor's death I can't allow you to run around with the thing in your pocket. How much do you know about the Circus?' He might have been asking about women, wary, an older man without experience.

'A bit,' said Avery. 'The usual gossip.'

Leclerc stood up and went to the window. 'They're a curious crowd. Some good, of course. Smiley was good. But they're cheats,' he broke out suddenly. 'That's an odd word, I know, to use about a sister service, John. Lying's second nature to them. Half of them don't know any longer when they're telling the truth.' He was inclining his head studiously this way and that to catch sight of whatever moved in the waking street below. 'What wretched weather. There was a lot of rivalry during the war, you know.'

'I heard.'

'That's all over now. I don't grudge them their work. They've more money and more staff than we have. They do a bigger job. However, I doubt whether they do a better one. Nothing can touch our Research Section, for example. Nothing.' Avery suddenly had the feeling that Leclerc had revealed something intimate, a failed marriage or a discreditable act, and that now it was all right.

'When you see Smiley, he may ask you about the operation. I don't want you to tell him *anything*, do you see, except that you are going to Finland and you may be handling a film for urgent dispatch to London. If he presses you, suggest it is a training matter. That's all you're authorized to say. The background, Gorton's report, future operations; none of that concerns them in the least. A training matter.'

'I realize that. But he'll know about Taylor, won't he, if the FO knows?'

'Leave that to me. And don't be misled into believing the Circus has a monopoly of agent running. We have the same right. We just don't use it unnecessarily.' He had restated his text.

Avery watched Leclerc's slim back against the lightening sky outside; a man excluded, a man without a card, he thought.

'Could we light a fire?' he asked, and went into the corridor where Pine had a cupboard for mops and brushes. There was kindling wood and some old newspaper. He came back and knelt in front of the fireplace, keeping the best pieces of cinder and coaxing the ash through the grate, just as he would in the flat at Christmas. 'I wonder if it was really wise to let them meet at the airport,' he asked.

'It was urgent. After Jimmy Gorton's report, it was very urgent. It still is. We haven't a moment to lose.'

Avery held a match to the newspaper and watched it burn. As the wood caught, the smoke began to roll gently into his face, causing his eyes to water behind his glasses. 'How could they know Lansen's destination?'

'It was a scheduled flight. He had to get clearance in advance.'

Tossing more coal on to the fire, Avery got up and rinsed his hands at the basin in the corner, drying them on his handkerchief.

'I keep asking Pine to put me out a towel,' said Leclerc. 'They haven't enough to do, that's half the trouble.'

'Never mind.' Avery put the wet handkerchief in his pocket. It felt cold against his thigh. 'Perhaps they will have now,' he added without irony.

'I thought I'd get Pine to make me up a bed here. A sort of ops room.' Leclerc spoke cautiously, as if Avery might deprive him of the pleasure. 'You can ring me here tonight from Finland. If you've got the film, just say the deal's come off.'

'And if not?'

'Say the deal's off.'

'It sounds rather alike,' Avery objected. 'If the line's bad, I mean. "Off" and "Come off".'

'Then say they're not interested. Say something negative. You know what I mean.'

Avery picked up the empty scuttle. 'I'll give this to Pine.'

He passed the duty-room. An Air Force clerk was half asleep beside the telephones. He made his way down the wooden staircase to the front door.

'The Boss wants some coal, Pine.' The porter stood up, as he always did when anyone spoke to him, at attention by his bed in a barrack-room.

'I'm sorry, sir. Can't leave the door.'

'For God's sake, I'll look after the door. We're freezing up there.'

Pine took the scuttle, buttoned his tunic and disappeared down the passage. He didn't whistle these days.

'And a bed made up in his room,' he continued when Pine returned. 'Perhaps you'd tell the duty clerk when he wakes up. Oh, and a towel. He must have a towel by his basin.'

'Yes, sir. Wonderful to see the old Department on the march again.'

'Where can we get breakfast round here? Is there anywhere near by?'

'There's the Cadena,' Pine replied doubtfully, 'but I don't know whether it would do for the Boss, sir.' A grin. 'We had the canteen in the old days. Slinger and wadge.'

It was quarter to seven. 'When does the Cadena open?'

'Couldn't say, sir.'

'Tell me, do you know Mr Taylor at all?' He nearly said 'did'.

'Oh yes, sir.'

'Have you met his wife?'

'No, sir.'

'What's she like? Have you any idea? Heard anything?'

'Couldn't say, I'm sure, sir. Very sad business indeed, sir.'

Avery looked at him in astonishment. Leclerc must have told him, he thought, and went upstairs. Sooner or later he would have to telephone Sarah.

Chapter 3

They breakfasted somewhere. Leclerc refused to go into the Cadena and they walked interminably until they found another café, worse than the Cadena and more expensive.

'I can't remember him,' Leclerc said. 'That's the absurd thing. He's a trained radio operator apparently. Or was in those days.'

Avery thought he was talking about Taylor. 'How old did you say he was?'

'Forty, something over. That's a good age. A Danzig Pole. They speak German, you know. Not as mad as the pure Slav. After the war he drifted for a couple of years, pulled himself together and bought a garage. He must have made a nice bit.'

'Then I don't suppose he'll . . .'

'Nonsense. He'll be grateful, or should be.'

Leclerc paid the bill and kept it. As they left the restaurant he said something about subsistence, and putting in a bill to Accounts. 'You can claim for night duty as well, you know. Or time in lieu.' They walked down the road. 'Your air ticket is booked. Carol did it from her flat. We'd better make you an advance for expenses. There'll be the business of having his body sent and that kind of thing. I understand it can be very costly. You'd better have him flown. We'll do a post-mortem privately over here.'

'I've never seen a dead man before,' Avery said.

They were standing on a street corner in Kennington, looking for a taxi; a gas works on one side of the road, nothing on the other: the sort of place they could wait all day.

'John, you've got to keep very quiet about that side of it; about putting a man in. No one's to know, not even in the Department, no one at all. I thought we'd call him Mayfly. Leiser, I mean. We'll call him Mayfly.'

'All right.'

'It's very delicate; a question of timing. I've no doubt there'll be opposition, within the Department as well as outside.'

'What about my cover and that kind of thing?' Avery asked. 'I'm not quite—' A taxi with its flag up passed them without stopping.

'Bloody man,' Leclerc snapped. 'Why didn't he pick us up?'

'He lives out here, I expect. He's making for the West End. About cover,' he prompted.

'You're travelling under your own name. I don't see that there's any problem. You can use your own address. Call yourself a publisher. After all you *were* one. The Consul will show you the ropes. What are you worried about?'

'Well – just the details.'

Leclerc, coming out of his reverie, smiled. 'I'll tell you something about cover; something you'll learn for yourself. Never volunteer information. People don't *expect* you to explain yourself. After all, what is there to explain? The ground's prepared; the Consul will have our teleprint. Show your passport and play the rest by ear.'

'I'll try,' said Avery.

'You'll succeed,' Leclerc rejoined with feeling, and they both grinned shyly.

'How far is it to the town?' Avery asked. 'From the airport?'

'About three miles. It feeds the main ski resorts. Heaven knows what the Consul does all day.'

'And to Helsinki?'

'I told you. A hundred miles. Perhaps more.'

Avery proposed they took a bus but Leclerc wouldn't queue, so they remained standing at the corner. He began talking about official cars again. 'It's utterly absurd,' he said. 'In the old days we had a pool of our own, now we have two vans and the Treasury won't let us pay the driver overtime. How can I run a Department under those conditions?'

In the end they walked. Leclerc had the address in his head; he made a point of remembering such things. It was awkward for Avery to walk beside him for long, because Leclerc adjusted his pace to that of the taller man. Avery tried to keep himself in check, but sometimes he forgot and Leclerc would stretch uncomfortably beside him thrusting upward with each stride. A fine rain was falling. It was still very cold.

There were times when Avery felt for Leclerc a deep, protective love. Leclerc had that indefinable quality of arousing guilt, as if his companion but poorly replaced a departed friend. Somebody had been there, and gone; perhaps a whole world, a generation; somebody had made him and disowned him, so that while at one moment Avery could hate him for his transparent manipulation, detest his prinking gestures as a child detests the affectations of a parent, at the next he ran to protect him, responsible and deeply caring. Beyond all the vicissitudes of their relationship, he was somehow grateful that Leclerc had engendered him; and thus they created that strong love which exists between the weak; each became the stage to which the other related his actions.

'It would be a good thing,' Leclerc said suddenly, 'if you shared the handling of Mayfly.'

'I'd like to.'

'When you get back.'

They had found the address on the map. Thirty-four Roxburgh Gardens; it was off Kennington High Street. The road soon became dingier, the houses more crowded. Gas lights burned yellow and flat like paper moons.

'In the war they gave us a hostel for the staff.'

'Perhaps they will again,' Avery suggested.

'It's twenty years since I did an errand like this.'

'Did you go alone then?' Avery asked, and wished at once that he had not. It was so easy to inflict pain on Leclerc.

'It was simpler in those days. We could say they'd died for their country. We didn't have to tell them the details; they didn't expect that.' So it *was* we, thought Avery. Some other boy, one of those laughing faces on the wall.

'They died every day then, the pilots. We did reconnaissance, you know, as well as special operations . . . I'm ashamed sometimes: I can't even remember their names. They were so young, some of them.'

There passed across Avery's mind a tragic procession of horror-struck faces; mothers and fathers, girl friends and wives, and he tried to visualize Leclerc standing among them, naïve yet footsure, like a politician at the scene of a disaster.

They stood at the top of a rise. It was a wretched place. The road led downward into a line of dingy, eyeless houses; above them rose a single block of flats: Roxburgh Gardens. A string of lights shone on to the glazed tiles, dividing and re-dividing the whole structure into cells. It was a large building, very ugly in its way, the beginning of a new world, and at its feet lay the black rubble of the old: crumbling, oily houses, haunted by sad faces which moved through the rain like driftwood in a forgotten harbour.

Leclerc's frail fists were clenched; he stood very still.

'There?' he said. 'Taylor lived there?'

'What's wrong? It's part of a scheme, redevelopment . . .' Then Avery understood. Leclerc was ashamed. Taylor had disgracefully deceived him. This was not the society they protected, these slums with their Babel's Tower: they had no place in Leclerc's scheme of things. To think that a member of Leclerc's staff should daily trudge from the breath and stink of such a place to the sanctuary of the Department: had he no money, no pension? Had he not a little bit beside, as we all have, just a hundred or two, to buy himself out of this squalor?

'It's no worse than Blackfriars Road,' Avery said involuntarily; it was meant to comfort him.

'Everyone knows we used to be in Baker Street,' Leclerc retorted.

They made their way quickly to the base of the block, past shop windows filled with old clothes and rusted electric fires, all the sad muddle of useless things which only the poor will buy. There was a chandler; his candles were yellow and dusty like fragments of a tomb.

'What number?' Leclerc asked.

'You said thirty-four.'

They passed between heavy pillars crudely ornamented with mosaics, followed plastic arrows marked with pink numbers; they squeezed between lines of aged, empty cars, until finally they came to a concrete entrance with cartons of milk on the step. There was no door, but a flight of rubberized steps which squeaked as they trod. The air smelt of food and that liquid soap they give in railway lavatories. On the heavy stucco wall a hand-painted notice discouraged noise. Somewhere a wireless played. They continued up two flights, and stopped before a green door, half-glazed. Mounted on it in letters of white bakelite was the number thirty-four. Leclerc took off his hat and wiped the sweat from his temples. He might have been entering church. It had been raining more than they realized; their coats were quite wet. He pressed the bell. Avery was suddenly very frightened; he glanced at Leclerc and thought: this is your show; you tell her.

The music seemed louder. They strained their ears to catch some other sound, but there was none.

'Why did you call him Malherbe?' Avery asked suddenly.

Leclerc pressed the bell again; and then they heard it, both of them, a whimper midway between the sob of a child and the whine of a cat, a throttled, metallic sigh. While Leclerc stepped back, Avery seized the bronze knocker on the letter box and banged it violently. The echo died away and they heard from inside the flat a light, reluctant tread; a bolt was slid from its housing, a spring lock disengaged. Then they heard again, much louder and more distinctly, the same plaintive monotone. The door opened a few inches and Avery saw a child, a frail, pallid rag of a girl not above ten years old. She wore steel-rimmed spectacles, the kind Anthony wore. In her arms, its pink limbs splayed stupidly about it, its painted eyes staring from between fringes of ragged cotton, was a doll. Its daubed mouth was lolling open, its head hung sideways as if it were broken or dead. It is called a talking doll, but no living thing uttered such a sound.

'Where is your mother?' asked Leclerc. His voice was aggressive, frightened.

The child shook her head. 'Gone to work.'

'Who looks after you, then?'

She spoke slowly as if she were thinking of something else. 'Mum comes back tea-times. I'm not to open the door.'

'Where is she? Where does she go?'

'Work.'

'Who gives you lunch?' Leclerc insisted.

'What?'

'Who gives you dinner?' Avery said quickly.

'Mrs Bradley. After school.'

Then Avery asked, 'Where's your father?' and she smiled and put a finger to her lips.

'He's gone on an aeroplane,' she said. 'To get money. But I'm not to say. It's a secret.'

Neither of them spoke. 'He's bringing me a present,' she added.

'Where from?' said Avery.

'From the North Pole, but it's a secret.' She still had her hand on the doorknob. 'Where Father Christmas comes from.'

'Tell your mother some men were here,' Avery said. 'From your Dad's office. We'll come again tea-time.'

'It's important,' said Leclerc.

She seemed to relax when she heard they knew her father.

'He's on an aeroplane,' she repeated. Avery felt in his pocket and gave her two half-crowns, the change from Sarah's ten shillings. She closed the door, leaving them on that damned staircase with the wireless playing dreamy music.

Chapter 4

They stood in the street not looking at one another. Leclerc said, 'Why did you ask that question, the question about her father?'

When Avery did not reply he added incongruously, 'It isn't a matter of liking people.'

Sometimes Leclerc seemed neither to hear nor to feel; he drifted away, listening for a sound, like a man who having learnt the steps had been deprived of the music; this mood read like a deep sadness, like the bewilderment of a man betrayed.

'I'm afraid I shan't be able to come back here with you this afternoon,' Avery said gently. 'Perhaps Bruce Woodford would be prepared—'

'Bruce is no good.' He added: 'You'll be at the meeting; at ten forty-five?'

'I may have to leave before the end to get to the Circus and collect my things. Sarah hasn't been well. I'll stay at the office as long as I can. I'm sorry I asked that question, I really am.'

'I don't want anyone to know. I must speak to her mother first. There may be some explanation. Taylor's an old hand. He knew the rules.'

'I shan't mention it, I promise I shan't. Nor Mayfly.'

'I must tell Haldane about Mayfly. He'll object, of course. Yes, that's what we'll call it . . . the whole operation. We'll call it Mayfly.' The thought consoled him.

They hurried to the office, not to work but for refuge; for anonymity, a quality they had come to need.

His room was one along from Leclerc's. It had a label on the door saying, 'Director's Aide'. Two years ago Leclerc had been invited to America, and the expression dated from his return. Within the Department, staff were referred to by the function they fulfilled. Hence Avery was known simply as Private Office;

though Leclerc might alter the title every week, he could not alter the vernacular.

At a quarter to eleven Woodford came into his room. Avery guessed he would: a little chat before the meeting began, a quiet word about some matter not strictly on the agenda.

'What's it all about, John?' He lit his pipe, tilted back his large head and extinguished the match with long, swinging movements of his hand. He had once been a schoolmaster; an athletic man.

'You tell me.'

'Poor Taylor.'

'Precisely.'

'I don't want to jump the gun,' he said, and settled himself on the edge of the desk, still absorbed in his pipe.

'I don't want to jump the gun, John,' he repeated. 'But there's another matter we ought to look at, tragic as Taylor's death is.' He stowed the tobacco tin in the pocket of his green suit and said, 'Registry.'

'That's Haldane's parish. Research.'

'I've got nothing against old Adrian. He's a good scout. We've been working together for over twenty years.' And therefore you're a good scout too, thought Avery.

Woodford had a way of coming close when he spoke; riding his heavy shoulder against you like a horse rubbing itself against a gate. He leaned forward and looked at Avery earnestly: a plain man perplexed, he was saying, a decent man choosing between friendship and duty. His suit was hairy, too thick to crease, forming rolls like a blanket; rough-cut buttons of brown bone.

'John, Registry's all to the devil; we both know that. Papers aren't being entered, files aren't brought up on the right dates.' He shook his head in despair. 'We've been missing a policy file on marine freight since mid-October. Just vanished into thin air.'

'Adrian Haldane put out a search notice,' Avery said. 'We were all involved, not just Adrian. Files do get lost – this is the first since April, Bruce. I don't think that's bad, considering the amount we handle. I thought Registry was one of our best things. The files are immaculate. I understand our Research index is unique. That's all Adrian's doing, isn't it? Still, if you're worried why not speak to Adrian about it?'

'No, no. It's not *that* important.'

Carol came in with the tea. Woodford had his in a pottery jumbo-cup, with his initials drawn large, embossed like icing. As Carol put it down, she remarked, 'Wilf Taylor's dead.'

'I've been here since one,' Avery lied, 'coping with it. We've been working all night.'

'The Director's very upset,' she said.

'What was his wife like, Carol?' She was a well-dressed girl, a little taller than Sarah.

'Nobody's met her.'

She left the room, Woodford watching her. He took his pipe from his mouth and grinned. Avery knew he was going to say something about sleeping with Carol and suddenly he'd had enough.

'Did your wife make that cup, Bruce?' he asked quickly. 'I hear she's quite a potter.'

'Made the saucer as well,' he said. He began talking about the classes she went to, the amusing way it had caught on in Wimbledon, how his wife was tickled to death.

It was nearly eleven; they could hear the others gathering in the corridor.

'I'd better go next door,' Avery said, 'and see if he's ready. He's taken quite a beating in the last eight hours.'

Woodford picked up his mug and took a sip of tea. 'If you get a chance, mention that Registry business to the Boss, John. I don't want to drag it up in front of everyone else. Adrian's getting a bit past it.'

'The Director's very tied up at the moment, Bruce.'

'Oh, quite.'

'He hates to interfere with Haldane, you know that.' As they reached the door of his room he turned to Woodford and asked, 'Do you remember a man called Malherbe in the Department?'

Woodford stopped dead. 'God, yes. A young chap, like you. In the war. Good Lord.' And earnestly, but quite unlike his usual manner: 'Don't mention that name to the Boss. He was very cut up about young Malherbe. One of the special fliers. The two of them were quite close in a way.'

Leclerc's room by daylight was not so much drab as of an impermanent appearance. You would think its occupant had requisitioned it hastily, under conditions of emergency, and had not known how long he would be staying. Maps lay sprawled over the trestle table, not in threes or fours but dozens, some of a scale large enough to show streets and buildings. Teletape, pasted in strips on pink paper, hung in batches on the notice board, fastened with a heavy bulldog clip like galley proofs awaiting correction. A bed had been put in one corner with a counterpane over it. A clean towel hung beside the basin. The desk was new, of grey steel, government issue. The walls were filthy. Here and there the cream paint had peeled, showing dark green beneath. It was a small, square room with Ministry of Works curtains. There had been a row about the curtains, a question of equating Leclerc's rank to the Civil Service scale. It was the one occasion, so far as Avery knew, when Leclerc had made any effort to improve the disorder of the room. The fire was nearly out. Sometimes when it was very windy the fire would not burn at all, and all through the day Avery could hear from next door the soot falling in the chimney.

Avery watched them come in; Woodford first, then Sandford, Dennison and McCulloch. They had all heard about Taylor. It was easy to imagine the news going round the Department, not as headlines, but as a small and gratifying sensation, passed from room to room, lending a briskness to the day's activity, as it had to these men; giving them a moment's optimism, like a rise in pay. They would watch Leclerc, watch him as prisoners watch a warder. They knew his routine by instinct, and they waited for him to break it. There would not be a man or woman in the Department but knew they had been called in the middle of the night, and that Leclerc was sleeping in the office.

They settled themselves at the table, putting their cups in front of them noisily like children at a meal, Leclerc at the head, the others on either side, an empty chair at the farther end. Haldane came in, and Avery knew as soon as he saw him that it would be Leclerc versus Haldane.

Looking at the empty chair, he said, 'I see I'm to take the draughtiest place.'

Avery rose, but Haldane had sat down. 'Don't bother, Avery. I'm a sick man already.' He coughed, just as he coughed all year. Not even the Summer could help him, apparently; he coughed in all seasons.

The others fidgeted uncomfortably; Woodford helped himself to a biscuit. Haldane glanced at the fire. 'Is that the best the Ministry of Works can manage?' he asked.

'It's the rain,' Avery said. 'The rain disagrees with it. Pine's had a go but he made no difference.'

'Ah.'

Haldane was a lean man with long, restless fingers; a man locked in himself, slow in his movements, agile in his features, balding, spare, querulous and dry; a man seemingly contemptuous of everything, keeping his own hours and his own counsel; addicted to crossword puzzles and nineteenth-century water colours.

Carol came in with files and maps, putting them on Leclerc's desk, which in contrast to the remainder of his room was very tidy. They waited awkwardly until she had gone. The door securely closed, Leclerc passed his hand cautiously over his dark hair as if he were not quite familiar with it.

'Taylor's been killed. You've all heard it by now. He was killed last night in Finland, travelling under another name.' Avery noticed he never mentioned Malherbe. 'We don't know the details. He appears to have been run over. I've told Carol to put it about that it was an accident. Is that clear?'

Yes, they said, it was quite clear.

'He went to collect a film from . . . a contact, a Scandinavian contact. You know whom I mean. We don't normally use the routine couriers for operational work, but this was different; something very special indeed. I think Adrian will back me up there.' He made a little upward gesture with his open hands, freeing the wrists from his white cuffs, laying the palms and fingers vertically together; praying for Haldane's support.

'Special?' Haldane repeated slowly. His voice was thin and sharp like the man himself, cultivated, without emphasis and without affectation; an enviable voice. 'It was different, yes. Not least because Taylor died. We should never have used him, never,' he observed flatly. 'We broke a first principle of intelligence. We used a man on the overt side for a clandestine job. Not that we have a clandestine side any more.'

'Shall we let our masters be the judges of that?' Leclerc suggested demurely. 'At least you'll agree the Ministry is pressing us daily for results.' He turned to those on either side of him, now to the left, now to the right, bringing them in like shareholders. 'It is time you all knew the details. We are dealing with something of exceptional security classification, you understand. I propose to limit to Heads of Sections. So far, only Adrian Haldane and one or two of his staff in Research have been initiated. And John Avery as my aide. I wish to emphasize that our sister service knows nothing whatever about it. Now about our own arrangements. The operation has the codeword Mayfly.' He was speaking in his clipped, effective voice. 'There is one action file, which will be returned to me personally, or to Carol if I am out, at the end of each day; and there is a library copy. That is the system we used in the war for operational files and I think you are all familiar with it. It's the system we shall use henceforth. I shall add Carol's name to the subscription list.'

Woodford pointed at Avery with his pipe, shaking his head.

Not young John there; John was not familiar with the system. Sandford, sitting beside Avery, explained. The library copy was kept in the cypher-room. It was against regulations to take it away. All new serials were to be entered on it as soon as they were made; the subscription list was the list of persons authorized to read it. No pins were allowed; all the papers had to be fast. The others looked on complacently.

Sandford was Administration; he was a fatherly man in gold-rimmed spectacles and came to the office on a motorbike. Leclerc had objected once, on no particular grounds, and now he parked it down the road opposite the hospital.

'Now, about the operation,' Leclerc said. The thin line of his joined hands bisected his bright face. Only Haldane was not watching him; his eyes were turned away towards the window. Outside, the rain was falling gently against the buildings like Spring rain in a dark valley.

Abruptly Leclerc rose and went to a map of Europe on the wall. There were small flags pinned to it. Stretching upwards with his arm, riding on his toes to reach the northern hemisphere, he said, 'We're having a spot of trouble with the Germans.' A little laugh went up. 'In the area south of Rostock; a place called Kalkstadt, just here.' His finger traced the Baltic coastline of Schleswig-Holstein, moved east and stopped an inch or two south of Rostock.

'To put it in a nutshell, we have three indicators which suggest – I cannot say prove – that something big is going on there in the way of military installations.'

He swung round to face them. He would remain at the map and say it all from there, to show he had the facts in his memory and didn't need the papers on the table.

'The first indicator came exactly a month ago when we received a report from our representative in Hamburg, Jimmy Gorton.'

Woodford smiled: Good God, was old Jimmy still going?

'An East German refugee crossed the border near Lübeck, swam the river; a railwayman from Kalkstadt. He went to our Consulate and offered to sell them information about a new rocket site near Rostock. I need hardly tell you the Consulate threw him out. Since the Foreign Office will not even give us the facilities of its bag service it is unlikely' – a thin smile – 'that they will assist us by buying military information.' A nice murmur greeted this joke. 'However, by a stroke of luck Gorton got to hear of the man and went to Flensburg to see him.'

Woodford would not let this pass. Flensburg? Was not that the place where they had located German submarines in 'forty-one? Flensburg had been a hell of a show.'

Leclerc nodded at Woodford indulgently, as if he too had been amused by the recollection. 'The wretched man had been to every Allied office in North Germany, but no one would look at him. Jimmy Gorton had a chat with him.' Implicit in Leclerc's way of describing things was an assumption that Gorton was the only intelligent man among a lot of fools. He crossed to his desk, took a cigarette from the silver box, lit it, picked up a file with a heavy red cross on the cover and laid it noiselessly on the table in front of them. 'This is Jimmy's report,' he said. 'It's a first-class bit of work by any standard.' The cigarette looked very long between his fingers. 'The defector's name,' he added inconsequentially, 'was Fritsche.'

'Defector?' Haldane put in quickly. 'The man's a low-grade refugee, a railwayman. We don't usually talk about men like that *defecting*.'

Leclerc replied defensively, 'The man's not only a railwayman. He's a bit of a mechanic and a bit of a photographer.'

McCulloch opened the file and began methodically turning over the serials. Sandford watched him through his gold-rimmed spectacles.

'On the first or second of September – we don't know which because he can't remember – he happened to be doing a double shift in the dumping sheds at Kalkstadt. One of his comrades was sick. He was to work from six till twelve in the morning, and four till ten at night. When he arrived to report for work there were a dozen Vopos, East German people's police, at the station entrance. All passenger traffic was forbidden. They checked his identity papers against a list and told him to keep away from the sheds on the eastern side of the station. They said,' Leclerc added deliberately, 'that if he approached the eastern sheds he was liable to be shot.'

This impressed them. Woodford said it was typical of the Germans.

'It's the Russians we're fighting,' Haldane put in.

'He's an odd fish, our man. He seems to have argued with them. He told them he was as reliable as they were, a good German and a Party member. He showed them his union card, photographs of his wife and Heaven knows what. It didn't do any good, of course, because they just told him to obey orders and keep away from the sheds. But he must have caught their fancy because when they brewed up some soup at ten o'clock they called him over and offered him a cup. Over the soup he asked them what was going on. They were cagey, but he could see they were excited. Then something happened. Something very important,' he continued. 'One of the younger ones blurted out that whatever they had in the sheds could blow the Americans out of West Germany in a couple of hours. At this point an officer came along and told them to get back to work.'

Haldane coughed a deep, hopeless cough, like an echo in an old vault.

What sort of officer, someone asked, was he German or Russian?

'German. That is most relevant. There were no Russians in evidence at all.'

Haldane interrupted sharply. 'The refugee saw none. That's all we know. Let us be accurate.' He coughed again. It was very irritating.

'As you wish. He went home and had lunch. He was disgruntled at being ordered around in his own station by a lot of young fellows playing soldiers. He had a couple of glasses of schnapps and sat there brooding about the dumping shed. Adrian, if your cough is troubling you . . . ?' Haldane shook his head. 'He remembered that on the northern side it abutted with an old storage hut, and that there was a shutter-type ventilator let into the party wall. He formed the notion of looking through the ventilator to see what was in the shed. As a way of getting his own back on the soldiers.'

Woodford laughed.

'Then he decided to go one further and photograph whatever was there.'

'He must have been mad,' Haldane commented. 'I find this part impossible to accept.'

'Mad or not, that's what he decided to do. He was cross because they wouldn't trust him. He felt he had a right to know what was in the shed.' Leclerc missed a beat then took refuge in technique. 'He had an Exa-two camera, single lens reflex. East German manufacture. It's cheap housing but takes all the Exakta range lenses; far fewer speeds than the Exakta, of course.' He looked inquiringly at the technicians, Dennison and McCulloch. 'Am I right, gentlemen?' he asked. 'You must correct me.' They smiled sheepishly because there was nothing to correct. 'He had a good wide-angle lens. The difficulty was the light. His next shift didn't begin till four, by which time dusk would be falling and there would be even less light inside the shed. He had one fast Agfa film which he'd been keeping for a special occasion; it had a DIN speed of twenty-seven. He decided to use that.' He paused, more for effect than for questions.

'Why didn't he wait till next morning?' Haldane asked.

'In the report,' Leclerc continued blandly, 'you'll find a very full account by Gorton of how the man got into the hut, stood on an oil drum and took his photographs through the ventilator. I'm not going to repeat all that now. He used the maximum aperture of two point eight, speeds ranging from a quarter of a second to two seconds. A fortunate piece of German thoroughness.' No one laughed. 'The speeds were guesswork, of course. He was bracketing an estimated exposure time of one second. Only the last three frames show anything. Here they are.'

Leclerc unlocked the steel drawer of his desk and extracted a set of high-gloss photographs twelve inches by nine. He was smiling a little, like a man looking at his own reflection. They gathered round, all but Haldane and Avery, who had seen them before.

Something was there.

You could see it if you looked quickly; something hid in the disintegrating shadows; but keep looking and the dark closed in and the shape was gone. Yet something was there; the muffled form of a gun barrel, but pointed and too long for its carriage, the suspicion of a transporter, a vague glint of what might have been a platform.

'They would put protective covers over them, of course,' Leclerc commented, studying their faces hopefully, waiting for their optimism.

Avery looked at his watch. It was twenty past eleven. 'I shall have to go soon, Director,' he said. He still hadn't rung Sarah. 'I have to see the accountant about my air ticket.'

'Stay another ten minutes,' Leclerc pleaded, and Haldane asked, 'Where's he going?'

Leclerc replied, 'To take care of Taylor. He has a date at the Circus first.'

'What do you mean, take care of him? Taylor's dead.'

There was an uncomfortable silence.

'You know very well that Taylor was travelling under an alias. Somebody has to collect his effects; recover the film. Avery is going out as next of kin. The Ministry has already given its approval; I wasn't aware that I needed yours.'

'To claim the body?'

'To get the film,' Leclerc repeated hotly.

'That's an operational job; Avery's not trained.'

'They were younger than he in the war. He can look after himself.'

'Taylor couldn't. What will he do when he's got it; bring it back in his sponge bag?'

'Shall we discuss that afterwards?' Leclerc suggested, and addressed himself once more to the others, smiling patiently as if to say old Adrian must be humoured.

'That was all we had to go on till ten days ago. Then came the second indicator. The area round Kalkstadt had been declared a prohibited area.' There was an excited murmur of interest. 'For a radius of – as far as we can establish – thirty kilometres. Sealed off; closed to all traffic. They brought in frontier guards.' He glanced round the table. 'I then informed the Minister. I cannot tell even you all the implications. But let me name one.' He said the last sentence quickly, at the same time flicking upwards the little horns of greying hair that grew above his ears.

Haldane was forgotten.

'What puzzled us in the beginning' – he nodded at Haldane, a conciliatory gesture at a moment of victory, but Haldane ignored it – 'was the absence of Soviet troops. They have units in Rostock, Witmar, Schwerin.' His finger darted among the flags. 'But none – this is confirmed by other agencies – none in the immediate area of Kalkstadt. If there *are* weapons there, weapons of high destructive capacity, why are there no Soviet troops?'

McCulloch made a suggestion: might there not be technicians, Soviet technicians in civilian dress?

'I regard that as unlikely.' A demure smile. 'In comparable cases where tactical weapons were being transported we have always identified at least one Soviet unit. On the other hand, five weeks ago a few Russian troops *were* seen at Gustweiler, farther south.' He was back to the map. 'They billeted for one night at a pub. Some wore artillery flashes; others had no shoulder-boards at all. One might conclude they had brought something, left it and gone away again.'

Woodford was becoming restless. What did it all add up to, he wanted to know, what did they make of it over at the Ministry? Woodford had no patience with riddles.

Leclerc adopted his academic tone. It had a bullying quality as if facts were facts and could not be disputed. 'Research Section have done a magnificent job. The overall length of the object in these photographs – they can compute it pretty exactly – is equal to the length of a Soviet middle-range rocket. On present information' – he lightly tapped the map with his knuckles so that it swung sideways on its hook – 'the Ministry believes it is *conceivable* we are dealing with Soviet missiles under East German control. Research,' he added quickly, 'are not prepared to go so far. Now if the Ministry view prevails, if they are right, that is, we would have on our hands' – this was his moment – 'a sort of Cuba situation all over again, only' – he tried to sound apologetic, to make it a throw-away line – 'more dangerous.'

He had them.

'It was at this point,' Leclerc explained, 'that the Ministry felt entitled to authorize an overflight. As you know, for the last four years the Department has been limited to aerial photographs along orthodox civilian or military air routes. Even these required Foreign Office approval.' He drifted away. 'It really was too bad.' His eyes seemed to be searching for something not in the room. The others watched him anxiously, waiting for him to continue.

'For once the Ministry agreed to waive the ruling, and I am pleased to say the task of mounting the operation was given to this Department. We selected the best pilot we could find on our books: Lansen.' Someone looked up in surprise; agents' names were never used that way. 'Lansen undertook, for a price, to go off course on a charter flight from Düsseldorf to Finland. Taylor was dispatched to collect the film; he died at the landing field. A road accident, apparently.'

Outside they could hear the sound of cars moving through the rain like the rustling of paper in the wind. The fire had gone out; only the smoke remained, hanging like a shroud over the table.

Sandford had raised his hand. What kind of missile was this supposed to be?

'A Sandal, Medium Range. I am told by Research that it was first shown in Red Square in November 'sixty-two. It has achieved a certain notoriety since then. It was the Sandal which the Russians installed in Cuba. The Sandal is also' – a glance at Woodford – 'the linear descendant of the wartime German V2.'

He fetched other photographs from the desk and laid them on the table.

'Here is a Research Section photograph of the Sandal missile. They tell me it is distinguished by what is called a flared skirt' – he pointed to the formation at the base – 'and by small fins. It is about forty foot long from base to cone. If you look carefully you will see tucks near the clamp – just here – which hold the protective cloth cover in position. There is, ironically, no extant picture of the Sandal in protective covers. Possibly the Americans have one, but I don't feel able to approach them at this stage.'

Woodford reacted quickly. 'Of course not,' he said.

'The Minister was anxious that we shouldn't alarm them prematurely. One only has to *suggest* rockets to the Americans to get the most drastic reaction. Before we know where we are they'll be flying U2's over Rostock.' Encouraged by their laughter, Leclerc continued: 'The Minister made another point which I think I might pass on to you. The country which comes under maximum threat from these rockets – they have a range of around eight hundred miles – might well be our own. It is certainly not the United States. Politically, this would be a bad moment to go hiding our faces in the Americans' skirts. After all, as the Minister put it, we still *have* one or two teeth of our own.'

Haldane said sarcastically, 'That is a charming notion,' and Avery turned on him with all the anger he had fought away.

'I think you might do better than that,' he said. He nearly added: have a little mercy.

Haldane's cold gaze held Avery for a moment, then released him, his case not forgiven but suspended.

Someone asked what they would do next: suppose Avery did not find Taylor's film? Suppose it just wasn't there? Could they mount another overflight?

'No,' Leclerc replied. 'Another overflight is out of the question. Far too dangerous. We shall have to try something else.' He seemed disinclined to go further, but Haldane said, 'What, for instance?'

'We may have to put a man in. It seems to be the only way.'

'This Department?' Haldane asked incredulously. 'Put a man in? The Ministry would never tolerate such a thing. You mean, surely, you'll ask the Circus to do it?'

'I have already told you the position. Heaven knows, Adrian, you're not going to tell me we can't do it?' He looked appealingly round the table. 'Every one of us here except young Avery has been in the business twenty years or more. You yourself have forgotten more about agents than half those people in the Circus ever knew.'

'Hear, hear!' Woodford cried.

'Look at your own section, Adrian; look at Research. There must have been half a dozen occasions in the last five years when the Circus actually came to you, asked you for advice, used your facilities and skills. The time may come when they do the same with agents! The Ministry granted us an overflight. Why not an agent too?'

'You mentioned a third indicator. I don't follow you. What was that?'

'Taylor's death,' said Leclerc.

Avery got up, nodded goodbye and tiptoed to the door. Haldane watched him go.

Chapter 5

There was a note on his desk from Carol: 'Your wife rang.' He walked into her office and found her sitting at her type-writer but not typing. 'You wouldn't talk about poor Wilf Taylor like that,' she said, 'if you'd known him better.'

'Like what? I haven't talked about him at all.'

He thought he should comfort her, because sometimes they touched one another; he thought she might expect that now.

He bent forward, advancing until the sharp ends of her hair touched his cheek. Inclining his head inwards so that their temples met, he felt her skin travel slightly across the flat bone of her skull. For a moment they remained thus, Carol sitting upright, looking straight ahead of her, her hands either side of the typewriter, Avery awkwardly stooping. He thought of putting his hand beneath her arm and touching her breast, but did not; both gently recoiling, they separated and were alone again. Avery stood up.

'Your wife telephoned,' she said. 'I told her you were at the meeting. She wants to talk to you urgently.'

'Thanks. I'm on my way.'

'John, what *is* going on? What's all this about the Circus? What's Leclerc up to?'

'I thought you knew. He said he'd put you on the list.'

'I don't mean that. Why's he lying to them again? He's dictated a memorandum to Control about some training scheme and you going abroad. Pine took it round by hand. He's gone mad about her pension; Mrs Taylor's; looking up precedents and Heaven knows what. Even the application is Top Secret. He's building one of his card houses, John, I know he is. Who's Leiser, for instance?'

'You're not supposed to know. He's an agent; a Pole.'

'Does he work for the Circus?' She changed her tack. 'Well, why are *you* going? That's another thing I don't under-stand. For that matter, why did Taylor have to go? If the Circus has couriers in Finland, why couldn't we have used them in the first place? Why send poor Taylor? Even now the FO could iron it out. I'm sure they could. He just won't give them a chance: he *wants* to send you.'

'You don't understand,' Avery said shortly.

'Another thing,' she demanded as he was going, 'why does Adrian Haldane hate you so?'

He visited the accountant then took a taxi to the Circus. Leclerc had said he could claim for it. He was cross that Sarah had tried to reach him at such a moment. He had told her never to ring him at the Department. Leclerc said it was insecure.

'What did you read at Oxford? It was Oxford, wasn't it?' Smiley asked, and gave him a cigarette, rather a muddled one from a packet of ten.

'Languages.' Avery patted his pockets for a match. 'German and Italian.' When Smiley said nothing he added, 'German principally.'

Smiley was a small, distracted man with plump fingers and a shadowy, blinking way with him which suggested discomfort. Whatever Avery had expected, it was not this.

'Well, well.' Smiley nodded to himself, a very private comment. 'It's a question of a courier, I believe, in Helsinki. You want to give him a film. A training scheme.'

'Yes.'

'It's a most unusual request. You're sure . . . do you know the *size* of the film?'

'No.'

A long pause.

'You should try to find out that kind of thing,' Smiley said kindly. 'I mean, the courier may want to conceal it, you see.'

'I'm sorry.'

'Oh, it doesn't matter.'

Avery was reminded of Oxford, and reading essays to his tutor.

'Perhaps,' said Smiley thoughtfully, 'I might say one thing. I'm sure Leclerc has already had it from Control. We want to give you all the help we can – *all* the help. There used to be a time,' he mused, with that curious air of indirection which seemed to characterize all his utterances, 'when our departments *competed*. I always found that very painful. But I wondered whether you could tell me a *little*, just a little . . . Control was so anxious to help. We should hate to do the wrong thing out of ignorance.'

'It's a training exercise. Full dress. I don't know much about it myself.'

'We want to help,' Smiley repeated simply. 'What is your target country, your *putative* target?'

'I don't know. I'm only playing a small part. It's training.'

'But if it's training, why so much secrecy?'

'Well, Germany,' Avery said.

'Thank you.'

Smiley seemed embarrassed. He looked at his hands folded lightly on the desk before him. He asked Avery whether it was still raining. Avery said he was afraid so.

'I'm sorry to hear about Taylor,' he said. Avery said yes he was a good man.

'Do you know what time you'll have your film? Tonight? Tomorrow? Leclerc rather thought tonight, I gather.'

'I don't know. It depends how it goes. I just can't tell at the moment.'

'No.' There followed a long, unexplained silence. He's like an old man, thought Avery, he forgets he's not alone. 'No, there are so many imponderables. Have you done this kind of thing before?'

'Once or twice.' Again Smiley said nothing and did not seem to notice the gap.

'How *is* everyone in Blackfriars Road? Do you know Haldane at all?' Smiley asked. He didn't care about the reply.

'He's Research now.'

'Of course. A good brain. Your Research people enjoy quite a reputation, you know. We have consulted them ourselves more than once. Haldane and I were contemporaries at Oxford. Then in the war we worked together for a while. A Greats man. We'd have taken him here after the war; I think the medical people were worried about his chest.'

'I hadn't heard.'

'Hadn't you?' The eyebrows rose comically. 'There's a hotel in Helsinki called the Prince of Denmark. Opposite the main station. Do you know it by any chance?'

'No. I've never been to Helsinki.'

'Haven't you, now?' Smiley peered at him anxiously. 'It's a very *strange* story. This Taylor: was he training too?'

'I don't know. But I'll find the hotel,' Avery said with a touch of impatience.

'They sell magazines and postcards just inside the door. There's only the one entrance.' He might have been talking about the house next door. 'And flowers. I think the best arrangement would be for you to go there once you have the film. Ask the people at the flower stall to send a dozen red roses to Mrs Avery at the Imperial Hotel at Torquay. Or half a dozen would be enough, we don't want to waste money, do we? Flowers are so expensive up there. Are you travelling under your own name?'

'Yes.'

'Any particular reason? I don't mean to be curious,' he added hastily, 'but one has such a short life anyway . . . I mean before one's blown.'

'I gather it takes a bit of time to get a fake passport. The Foreign Office . . .' He shouldn't have answered. He should have told him to mind his own business.

'I'm sorry,' said Smiley, and frowned as if he had made an error of tact. 'You can always come to us, you know. For passports, I mean.' It was meant as a kindness. 'Just send the flowers. As you leave the hotel, check your watch by the hall clock. Half an hour later return to the main entrance. A taxi driver will recognize you and open the door of his car. Get in, drive around, give him the film. Oh, and pay him please. Just the ordinary fare. It's so easy to forget the *little* things. What *kind* of training precisely?'

'What if I don't get the film?'

'In that case do nothing. Don't go near the hotel. Don't go to Helsinki. Forget about it.' It occurred to Avery that his instructions had been remarkably clear.

'When you were reading German, did you touch on the seventeenth century by any chance?' Smiley inquired hopefully as Avery rose to go. 'Gryphius, Lohenstein; those people?'

'It was a special subject. I'm afraid I didn't.'

'*Special*,' muttered Smiley. 'What a *silly* word. I suppose they mean extrinsic; it's a very impertinent notion.'

As they reached the door he said, 'Have you a briefcase or anything?'

'Yes.'

'When you have that film, put it in your pocket,' he suggested, 'and carry the briefcase in your hand. If you *are* followed, they tend to watch the briefcase. It's natural, really. If you just drop the briefcase somewhere, they may go looking for that instead. I don't think the Finns are very *sophisticated* people. It's only a training hint, of course. But don't *worry*. It's such a mistake, I always feel, to put one's trust in *technique*.' He saw Avery to the door, then made his way ponderously along the corridor to Control's room.

Avery walked upstairs to the flat, guessing how Sarah would react. He wished he had telephoned after all because he hated to find her in the kitchen, and Anthony's toys all over the drawing-room carpet. It never worked, turning up without warning. She took fright as if she expected him to have done something dreadful.

He did not carry a key; Sarah was always in. She had no friends of her own as far as he knew; she never went to coffee parties or took herself shopping. She seemed to have no talent for independent pleasure.

He pressed the bell, heard Anthony calling Mummy, Mummy, and waited to hear her step. The kitchen was at the end of the passage, but this time she came from the bedroom, softly as though she were barefooted.

She opened the door without looking at him. She was wearing a cotton nightdress and a cardigan.

'God, you took your time,' she said, turned and walked uncertainly back to the bedroom. 'Something wrong?' she asked over her shoulder. 'Someone else been murdered?'

'What's the matter, Sarah? Aren't you well?'

Anthony was running about shouting because his father had come home. Sarah climbed back into bed. 'I rang the doctor. *I* don't know what it is,' she said, as if illness were not her subject.

'Have you a temperature?'

She had put a bowl of cold water and the bathroom flannel beside her. He wrung out the flannel and laid it on her head. 'You'll have to cope,' she said. 'I'm afraid it's not as exciting as spies. Aren't you going to ask me what's wrong?'

'When's the doctor arriving?'

'He has surgery till twelve. He'll turn up after that, I suppose.'

He went to the kitchen, Anthony following. The breakfast things were still on the table. He telephoned her mother in Reigate and asked her to come straight away.

It was just before one when the doctor arrived. A fever, he said; some germ that was going the rounds.

He thought she would weep when he told her he was going abroad; she took it in, reflected for a while and then suggested he went and packed.

'Is it important?' she said suddenly.

'Of course. Terribly.'

'Who for?'

'You, me. All of us, I suppose.'

'And for Leclerc?'

'I told you. For all of us.'

He promised Anthony he would bring him something.

'Where are you going?' Anthony asked.

'In an aeroplane.'

'Where?'

He was going to tell him it was a great secret when he remembered Taylor's little girl.

He kissed her goodbye, took his suitcase to the hall and put it on the mat. There were two locks on the door for Sarah's sake and they had to be turned simultaneously. He heard her say:

'Is it dangerous too?'

'I don't know. I only know it's very big.'

'You're really sure of that, are you?'

He called almost in despair, 'Look, how far am I supposed to think? It isn't a question of politics, don't you see? It's a question of fact. Can't you believe? Can't you tell me for once in my life that I'm doing something good?' He went into the bedroom, reasoning. She held a paperback in front of her and was pretending to read. 'We all have to, you know, we all have to draw a line round our lives. It's no good asking me the whole time, "Are you sure?" It's like asking whether we should have children, whether we should have married. There's just no point.'

'Poor John,' she observed, putting down the book and analysing him. 'Loyalty without faith. It's very hard for you.' She said this with total dispassion as if she had identified a social evil. The kiss was like a betrayal of her standards.

Haldane watched the last of them leave the room: he had arrived late, he would leave late, never with the crowd.

Leclerc said, 'Why do you do that to me?' He spoke like an actor tired from the play. The maps and photographs were strewn on the table with the empty cups and ashtrays.

Haldane didn't answer.

'What are you trying to prove, Adrian?'

'What was that you said about putting a man in?'

Leclerc went to the basin and poured himself a glass of water from the tap. 'You don't care for Avery, do you?' he asked.

'He's young. I'm tired of that cult.'

'I get a sore throat, talking all the time. Have some yourself. Do your cough good.'

'How old is Gorton?' Haldane accepted the glass, drank, and handed it back.

'Fifty.'

'He's more. He's our age. He was our age in the war.'

'One forgets. Yes, he must be fifty-five or six.'

'Established?' Haldane persisted.

Leclerc shook his head. 'He's not qualified. Broken service. He went to the Control Commission after the war. When that packed up he wanted to stay in Germany. German wife, I think. He came to us and we gave him a contract. We could never afford to keep him there if he were established.' He took a sip of water, delicately, like a girl. 'Ten years ago we'd thirty men in the field. Now we've nine. We haven't even got our own couriers, not clandestine ones. They all knew it this morning; why didn't they say so?'

'How often does he put in a refugee report?'

Leclerc shrugged. 'I don't see all his stuff,' he said. 'Your people should know. The market's dwindling, I suppose, now they've closed the Berlin border.'

'They only put the better reports up to me. This must be the first I've seen from Hamburg for a year. I always imagined he had some other function.'

Leclerc shook his head. Haldane asked, 'When does his contract come up for renewal?'

'I don't know. I just don't know.'

'I suppose he must be fairly worried. Does he get a gratuity on retirement?'

'It's just a three-year contract. There's no gratuity. No frills. He has the chance of going on after sixty, of course, if we want him. That's the advantage of being a temporary.'

'When was his contract last renewed?'

'You'd better ask Carol. It must be two years ago. Maybe longer.'

Haldane said again, 'You talked about putting a man in.'

'I'm seeing the Minister again this afternoon.'

'You've sent Avery already. You shouldn't have done that, you know.'

'Somebody had to go. Did you want me to ask the Circus?'

'Avery was very impertinent,' Haldane observed.

The rain was running in the gutters, tracing grey tracks on the dingy panes. Leclerc seemed to want Haldane to speak, but Haldane had nothing to say. 'I don't know yet what the Minister thinks about Taylor's death. He'll ask me this afternoon and I shall give him my opinion. We're all in the dark, of course.' His voice recovered its strength. 'But he may instruct me – it's on the cards, Adrian – he may *instruct* me to get a man in.'

'Well?'

'Suppose I asked you to form an operations section, make the research, prepare papers and equipment; suppose I asked you to find, train and field the agent. Would you do it?'

'Without telling the Circus?'

'Not in detail. We may need their facilities from time to time. That doesn't mean we need tell them the whole story. There's the question of security: *need to know*.'

'Then without the Circus?'

'Why not?'

Haldane shook his head. 'Because it isn't our work. We're just not equipped. Give it to the Circus and help them out with the military stuff. Give it to an old hand, someone like Smiley or Leamas . . .'

'Leamas is dead.'

'All right then, Smiley.'

'Smiley is blown.'

Haldane coloured. 'Then Guillam or one of the others. One of the pros. They've got a big enough stable these days. Go and see Control, let him have the case.'

'No,' Leclerc said firmly, putting the glass on the table. 'No, Adrian. You've been in the Department as long as I have, you know our brief. *Take all necessary steps* – that's what it says – *all necessary steps for the procurement, analysis and verification of military intelligence in those areas where the requirement cannot be met from conventional military resources.*' He beat out the words with his little fist as he spoke. 'How else do you think I got authority for the overflight?'

'All right,' Haldane conceded. 'We have our brief. But things have changed. It's a different game now. In those days we were top of the tree – rubber boats on a moonless night; a captured enemy plane; wireless and all that. You and I know; we did it together. But it's changed. It's a different war; a different kind of fighting. They know that at the Ministry perfectly well.' He added, 'And don't place too much trust in the Circus; you'll get no charity from those people.'

They looked at one another in surprise, a moment of recognition. Leclerc said, his voice scarcely above a whisper: 'It began with the networks, didn't it? Do you remember how the Circus swallowed them up one by one? The Ministry would say: "We're in danger of duplication on the Polish desks, Leclerc. I've decided Control should look after Poland." When was that? July 'forty-eight. Year after year it's gone on. Why do you think they patronize your Research Section? Not just for your beautiful files; they've got us where they want us, don't you see? Satellites! Non-operational! It's a way of putting us to sleep! You know what they call us in Whitehall these days? The Grace and Favour boys.'

There was a long silence.

Haldane said, 'I'm a collator, not an operational man.'

'You *used* to be operational, Adrian.'

'So did we all.'

'You know the target. You know the whole background. There's no one else. Take whom you want – Avery, Woodford, whoever you want.'

'We're not used to people any more. Handling them, I mean.' Haldane had become unusually diffident. 'I'm a Research man. I work with files.'

'We've had nothing else to give you until now. How long is it? Twenty years.'

'Do you know what it means, a rocket site?' Haldane demanded. 'Do you know how much mess it makes? They need launch pads, blast shields, cable troughs, control buildings; they need bunkers for storing the warheads, trailers for fuel and oxidizers. All those things come first. Rockets don't creep about in the night; they move like a travelling fair; we'd have other indicators before now; or the Circus would. As for Taylor's death—'

'For Heaven's sake, Adrian, do you think Intelligence consists of unassailable philosophical truths? Does every priest have to *prove* that Christ was born on Christmas Day?'

His little face was thrust forward as he tried to draw from Haldane something he seemed to know was there. 'You can't do it all by sums, Adrian. We're not academics, we're Civil Servants. We have to deal with things as they are. We have to deal with people, with events!'

'Very well, events then: if he swam the river, how did he preserve the film? How did he *really* take the pictures? Why isn't there any trace of camera shake? He'd been drinking, he was balancing on tiptoe; they're long enough exposures, you know, time exposures, he said.' Haldane seemed afraid, not of Leclerc, not of the operation, but of himself. 'Why did he give Gorton for nothing what he'd offered elsewhere for money? Why did he risk his life at all, taking those photographs? I sent Gorton a list of supplementaries. He's still trying to find the man, he says.'

His eyes drifted to the model aeroplane and the files on Leclerc's desk. 'You're thinking of Peenemünde, aren't you?' he continued. 'You want it to be like Peenemünde.'

'You haven't told me what you'll do if I get those instructions.'

'You never will. You never, never will.' He spoke with great finality, almost triumph. 'We're dead, don't you see? You said it yourself. They want us to go to sleep, not go to war.' He stood up. 'So it doesn't matter. It's all academic, after all. Can you *really* imagine Control would help us?'

'They've agreed to help us with a courier.'

'Yes. I find that most odd.'

Haldane stopped before a photograph by the door. 'That's Malherbe, isn't it? The boy who died. Why did you choose that name?'

'I don't know. It just came into my head. One's memory plays odd tricks.'

'You shouldn't have sent Avery. We've no business to use him for a job like that.'

'I went through the cards last night. We've got a man who'd do. A man we could send, I mean.' Daring, he added, 'An agent. Trained wireless operator, German speaker, unmarried.' Haldane stood quite still.

'Age?' he asked at last.

'Forty. A bit over.'

'He must have been very young.'

'He put up a good show. They caught him in Holland and he got away.'

'How did he get caught?'

The slightest pause. 'It isn't recorded.'

'Intelligent?'

'He seems quite well qualified.'

The same long silence.

'So am I. Let's see what Avery brings back.'

'Let's see what the Ministry says.'

Leclerc waited till the sound of coughing had faded down the corridor before he put on his coat. He would go for a walk, take some fresh air and have lunch at his club; the best they had. He wondered what it would be; the place had gone off badly in the last few years. After lunch he would go round to Taylor's widow. Then to the Ministry.

Woodford, lunching with his wife at Gorringe's, said, 'Young Avery's on his first run. Clarkie sent him. He should make a good job of it.'

'Perhaps he'll get himself killed, too,' she said nastily. She was off the drink, doctor's orders. 'Then you can have a real ball.

Christ, that would be a party and a half! Come to the Black Friars'
Ball!' Her lower lip was quivering. 'Why are the young ones
always so bloody marvellous? We were young, weren't we? . . .
Christ, we still are! What's wrong with us? We can't wait to grow
old, can we? We can't—'

'All right, Babs,' he said. He was afraid she might cry.

Chapter 6
Take-off

Avery sat in the aeroplane remembering the day when Haldane
failed to appear. It was, by coincidence, the first of the
month, July it must have been, and Haldane did not come to
the office. Avery knew nothing of it until Woodford rang him
on the internal telephone to tell him. Haldane was probably ill,
Avery had said; some personal matter had cropped up. But
Woodford was adamant. He had been to Leclerc's room, he
said, and had looked at the leave roster: Haldane was not due
for leave till August.

'Telephone his flat, John, telephone his flat,' he had urged.
'Speak to his wife. Find out what's become of him.' Avery was
so astonished that he did not know what to say: those two had
worked together for twenty years, and even he knew Haldane was
a bachelor.

'Find out where he is,' Woodford had persisted. 'Go on, I order
you: ring his flat.'

So he did. He might have told Woodford to do it himself, but
he hadn't the heart. Haldane's sister answered. Haldane was in
bed, his chest was playing him up; he had refused to tell her
the Department's telephone number. As Avery's eye caught the
calendar, he realized why Woodford had been so agitated: it
was the beginning of a quarter. Haldane might have got a new
job and left the Department without telling Woodford. A day or
two later, when Haldane returned, Woodford was uncommonly
warm towards him, bravely ignoring his sarcasm; he was grateful to him for coming back. For some time after that, Avery
had been frightened. His faith shaken, he examined more closely
its object.

He noticed that they ascribed – it was a plot in which all but
Haldane compounded – legendary qualities to one another.
Leclerc, for instance, would seldom introduce Avery to a member
of his parent Ministry without some catchword. 'Avery is the

brightest of our new stars' – or, to more senior men, 'John is my memory. You must ask John.' For the same reason they lightly forgave one another their trespasses, because they dared not think, for their own sakes, that the Department had room for fools. He recognized that it provided shelter from the complexities of modern life, a place where frontiers still existed. For its servants, the Department had a religious quality. Like monks, they endowed it with a mystical identity far away from the hesitant, sinful band which made up its ranks. While they might be cynical of the qualities of one another, contemptuous of their own hierarchical preoccupations, their faith in the Department burned in some separate chapel and they called it patriotism.

For all that, as he glanced at the darkening sea beneath him, at the cold sunlight slanting on the waves, he felt his heart thrilling with love. Woodford with his pipe and his plain way became part of that secret élite to which Avery now belonged; Haldane, Haldane above all, with his crosswords and his eccentricities, fitted into place as the uncompromising intellectual, irritable and aloof. He was sorry he had been rude to Haldane. He saw Dennison and McCulloch as the matchless technicians, quiet men, not articulate at meetings, but tireless and, in the end, right. He thanked Leclerc, thanked him warmly, for the privilege of knowing these men, for the excitement of this mission; for the opportunity to advance from the uncertainty of the past towards experience and maturity, to become a man, shoulder to shoulder with the others, tempered in the fire of war; he thanked him for the precision of command, which made order out of the anarchy of his heart. He imagined that when Anthony grew up, he too might be led into those dowdy corridors, and be presented to old Pine, who with tears in his eyes would stand up in his box and warmly grasp the child's tender hand.

It was a scene in which Sarah played no part.

Avery lightly touched a corner of the long envelope in his inside pocket. It contained his money: two hundred pounds in a blue envelope with the Government crest. He had heard of people in the war sewing such things into the lining of their clothes, and he rather wished they had done that for him. It was a childish conceit, he knew; he even smiled to discover himself given to such fancies.

He remembered Smiley that morning; in retrospect he was just a little frightened of Smiley. And he remembered the child at the door. A man must steel himself against sentiment.

★   ★   ★

'Your husband did a very good job,' Leclerc was saying, 'I cannot tell you the details. I am sure that he died very gallantly..'

Her mouth was stained and ugly. Leclerc had never seen anyone cry so much; it was like a wound that would not close.

'What do you mean, gallantly?' she blinked. 'We're not fighting a war. That's finished, all that fancy talk. He's dead,' she said stupidly, and buried her face in her crooked arm, slouching across the dining-room table like a puppet abandoned. The child was staring from a corner.

'I trust,' Leclerc said, 'that I have your permission to apply for a pension. You must leave all that to us. The sooner we take care of it the better. A pension,' he declared, as if it were the maxim of his house, 'can make a lot of difference.'

The Consul was waiting beside the Immigration Officer; he came forward without a smile, doing his duty. 'Are you Avery?' he asked. Avery had the impression of a tall man in a trilby and a dark overcoat; red-faced and severe. They shook hands.

'You're the British Consul, Mr Sutherland.'

'H.M. Consul, actually,' he replied, a little tartly. 'There's a difference you know.' He spoke with a Scottish accent. 'How did you know my name?'

They walked together towards the main entrance. It was all very simple. Avery noticed the girl at the desk; fair and rather pretty.

'It's kind of you to come all this way,' Avery said.

'It's only three miles from the town.' They got into the car.

'He was killed just up the road,' said Sutherland. 'Do you want to see the spot?'

'I might as well. To tell my mother.' He was wearing a black tie.

'Your name *is* Avery, isn't it?'

'Of course it is; you saw my passport at the desk.' Sutherland didn't like that, and Avery rather wished he hadn't said it. He started the engine. They were about to pull into the centre of the road when a Citroën swung out and overtook them.

'Damn fool,' Sutherland snapped. 'Roads are like ice. One of these pilots, I suppose. No idea of speed.' They could see a peak cap silhouetted against the windscreen as the car hurried down the long road across the dunes, throwing up a small cloud of snow behind it.

'Where do you come from?' he asked.

'London.'

Sutherland pointed straight ahead: 'That's where your brother died. Up there on the brow. The police reckon the driver must have been tight. They're very hot on drunken driving here, you know.' It sounded like a warning. Avery stared at the flat reaches of snowbound country on either side and thought of lonely, English Taylor struggling along the road, his weak eyes streaming from the cold.

'We'll go to the police afterwards,' said Sutherland. 'They're expecting us. They'll tell you all the details. Have you booked yourself a room here?'

'No.'

As they reached the top of the rise Sutherland said with grudging deference, 'It was just here, if you want to get out.'

'It's all right.'

Sutherland accelerated a little as if he wanted to get away from the place.

'Your brother was walking to the hotel. The Regina, just here. There was no taxi.' They descended the slope on the other side; Avery caught sight of the long lights of a hotel across the valley.

'No distance at all, really,' Sutherland commented. 'He'd have done it in fifteen minutes. Less. Where does your mother live?'

The question took Avery by surprise.

'Woodbridge, in Suffolk.' There was a by-election going on there; it was the first town that came into his head, though he had no interest in politics.

'Why didn't he put her down?'

'I'm sorry, I don't understand.'

'As next of kin. Why didn't Malherbe put his mother down instead of you?'

Perhaps it was not meant as a serious question; perhaps he just wanted to keep Avery talking because he was upset; nevertheless, it was unnerving. He was still strung up from the journey, he wanted to be taken for granted, not subjected to this interrogation. He realized, too, that he had not sufficiently worked out the supposed relationship between Taylor and himself. What had Leclerc written in the teleprint; half-brother or step-brother? Hastily he tried to visualize a train of family events, death, remarriage or estrangement, which would lead him to the answer to Sutherland's question.

'There's the hotel,' the Consul said suddenly, and then, 'it's nothing to do with me, of course. He can put down whoever he wants.' Resentment had become a habit of speech with Sutherland, a philosophy. He spoke as if everything he said were the contradiction of a popular view.

'She's old,' Avery replied at last. 'It's a question of protecting her from shock. I expect that's what he had in mind when he filled in his passport application. She's been ill; a bad heart. She's had an operation.' It sounded very childish.

'Ah.'

They had reached the outskirts of the town.

'There has to be a post-mortem,' Sutherland said. 'It's the law here, I'm afraid, in the case of violent death.'

Leclerc was going to be angry about that. Sutherland continued, 'For us, it makes the formalities more complicated. The Criminal Police take over the body until the post-mortem is complete. I asked them to be quick, but one can't insist.'

'Thanks. I thought I'd have the body flown back.' As they turned off the main road into the market square, Avery asked casually, as if he had no personal interest in the outcome, 'What about his effects? I'd better take them with me, hadn't I?'

'I doubt whether the police will hand them over until they've had the go-ahead from the public prosecutor. The post-mortem report goes to him; he gives clearance. Did your brother leave a will?'

'I've no idea.'

'You'd not happen to know whether you're an executor?'

'No.'

Sutherland gave a dry, patient laugh. 'I can't help feeling you're a little premature. Next of kin is not quite the same as executor,' he said. 'It gives you no legal rights, I'm afraid, apart from the disposal of the body.' He paused, looking back over his seat while he reversed the car into a parking space. 'Even if the police hand your brother's effects over to me, I'm not allowed to release them until I've had instructions from the Office, and *they*,' he continued quickly, for Avery was about to interrupt him, 'won't issue such instructions to *me* until a grant of probate has been made or a Letter of Administration issued. But I can give you a death certificate,' he added consolingly, opening his door, 'if the insurance companies require it.' He looked at Avery sideways, as if wondering whether he stood to inherit anything. 'It'll cost you five shillings for the Consular registration and five shillings per certified copy. What was that you said?'

'Nothing.' Together they climbed the steps to the police station.

'We'll be seeing Inspector Peersen,' Sutherland explained. 'He's quite well disposed. You'll kindly let me handle him.'

'Of course.'

'He's been a lot of help with my DBS problems.'

'Your what?'

'Distressed British Subjects. We get one a day in Summer. They're a disgrace. Did your brother drink a lot, incidentally? There's some suggestion he was—'

'It's possible,' Avery said. 'I hardly knew him in the last few years.' They entered the building.

Leclerc himself was walking carefully up the broad steps of the Ministry. It lay between Whitehall Gardens and the river; the doorway was large and new, surrounded with that kind of Fascist statuary which is admired by local authorities. Partly modernized, the building was guarded by sergeants in red sashes and contained two escalators; the one which descended was full, for it was half past five.

'Under Secretary,' Leclerc began diffidently. 'I shall have to ask the Minister for another overflight.'

'You'll be wasting your time,' he replied with satisfaction. 'He was most apprehensive about the last one. He's made a policy decision; there'll be no more.'

'Even with a target like this?'

'Particularly with a target like this.'

The Under Secretary lightly touched the corners of his in-tray as a bank manager might touch a statement. 'You'll have to think of something else,' he said. 'Some other way. Is there no *painless* method?'

'None. I suppose we could try to stimulate a defection from the area. That's a lengthy business. Leaflets, propaganda broadcasts, financial inducements. It worked well in the war. We would have to approach a lot of people.'

'It sounds a most improbable notion.'

'Yes. Things are different now.'

'What other ways are there, then?' he insisted.

Leclerc smiled again, as if he would like to help a friend, but could not work miracles. 'An agent. A short-term operation. In and out: a week altogether perhaps.'

The Under Secretary said, 'But who could you find for a job like that? These days?'

'Who indeed? It's a very long shot.'

The Under Secretary's room was large but dark, with rows of bound books. Modernization had encroached as far as his Private Office, which was done in the contemporary style, but there the process had stopped. They could wait till he retired to do his room. A gas fire burned in the marble fireplace. On the wall hung an oil painting of a battle at sea. They could hear the sound of barges in the fog. It was an oddly maritime atmosphere.

'Kalkstadt's pretty close to the border,' Leclerc suggested. 'We wouldn't have to use a scheduled airline. We could do a training flight, lose our way. It's been done before.'

'Precisely,' said the Under Secretary, then: 'This man of yours who died.'

'Taylor?'

'I'm not concerned with names. He was murdered, was he?'

'There's no proof,' Leclerc said.

'But you assume it?'

Leclerc smiled patiently. 'I think we both know, Under Secretary, that it is very dangerous to make broad assumptions when decisions of policy are involved. I'm still asking for another overflight.'

The Under Secretary coloured.

'I told you it's out of the question. No! Does that make it clear? We were talking of alternatives.'

'There's one alternative, I suppose, which would scarcely touch on my Department. It's more a matter for yourselves and the Foreign Office.'

'Oh?'

'Drop a hint to the London newspapers. Stimulate publicity. Print the photographs.'

'And?'

'Watch them. Watch the East German and Soviet diplomacy, watch their communications. Throw a stone into the nest and see what comes out.'

'I can tell you exactly what would come out. A protest from the Americans that would ring through these corridors for another twenty years.'

'Of course. I was forgetting that.'

'Then you're very lucky. You suggested putting an agent in.'

'Only tentatively. We've no one in mind.'

'Look,' said the Under Secretary, with the finality of a man much tried. 'The Minister's position is very simple. You have produced a report. If it is true, it alters our entire defence position. In fact it alters everything. I detest sensation, so does the Minister. Having put up the hare, the least you can do is have a shot at it.'

Leclerc said, 'If I found a man there's the problem of resources.

Money, training and equipment. Extra staff perhaps. Transport. Whereas an overflight . . .'

'Why do you raise so many difficulties? I understood you people existed for this kind of thing.'

'We have the expertise, Under Secretary. But I cut down, you know. I have cut down a lot. Some of our functions have lapsed: one must be honest. I have never tried to put the clock back. This is, after all' – a delicate smile – 'a slightly *anachronistic* situation.'

The Under Secretary glanced out of the window at the lights along the river.

'It seems pretty contemporary to me. Rockets and that kind of thing. I don't think the Minister considers it anachronistic.'

'I'm not referring to the target but the method of attack: it would have to be a crash operation at the border. That has scarcely been done since the war. Although it is a form of clandestine warfare with which my Department is traditionally at home. Or used to be.'

'What are you getting at?'

'I'm only thinking aloud, Under Secretary. I wonder whether the Circus might not be better equipped to deal with this. Perhaps you should approach Control. I can promise him the support of my armaments people.'

'You mean you don't think you can handle it?'

'Not with my existing organization. Control can. As long, that is, as the Minister doesn't mind bringing in another Department. Two, really. I didn't realize you were so worried about publicity.'

'Two?'

'Control will feel bound to inform the Foreign Office. It's his duty. Just as I inform you. And from then on, we must accept that it will be their headache.'

'If *those* people know,' the Under Secretary said with contempt, 'it'll be round every damned club by tomorrow.'

'There is that danger,' Leclerc conceded. 'More particularly, I wonder whether the Circus has the *military* skills. A rocket site is a complicated affair: launch pads, blast shields, cable troughs; all these things require proper processing and evaluation. Control and I could combine forces, I suppose—'

'That's out of the question. You people make poor bed-fellows. Even if you succeeded in co-operating, it would be against policy: no monolith.'

'Ah yes. Of course.'

'Assume you do it yourself, then; assume you find a man, what would that involve?'

'A supplementary estimate. Immediate resources. Extra staff. A training establishment. Ministerial protection; special passes and authority.' The knife again: 'And *some* help from Control . . . we could obtain that under a pretext.'

A foghorn echoed mournfully across the water.

'If it's the only way . . .'

'Perhaps you'd put it to the Minister,' Leclerc suggested.

Silence. Leclerc continued, 'In practical terms we need the best part of thirty thousand pounds.'

'Accountable?'

'Partially. I understood you wanted to be spared details.'

'Except where the Treasury's concerned. I suggest that you make a minute about costs.'

'Very well. Just an outline.'

The silence returned.

'That is hardly a large sum when set against the risk,' the Under Secretary said, consoling himself.

'The potential risk. We want to clarify. I don't pretend to be convinced. Merely suspicious, heavily suspicious.' He couldn't resist adding, 'The Circus would ask twice as much. They're very free with money.'

'Thirty thousand pounds, then, and our protection?'

'And a man. But I must find him for myself.' A small laugh. The Under Secretary said abruptly: 'There are certain details the Minister will not want to know. You realize that?'

'Of course. I imagine you will do most of the talking.'

'I imagine the Minister will. You've succeeded in worrying him a good deal.'

Leclerc remarked with impish piety, 'We should never do that to our master; our common master.'

The Under Secretary did not seem to feel they had one. They stood up.

'Incidentally,' Leclerc said, 'Mrs Taylor's pension. I'm making an application to the Treasury. They feel the Minister should sign it.'

'Why, for God's sake?'

'It's a question of whether he was killed in action.'

The Under Secretary froze. 'That is most presumptuous. You're asking for Ministerial confirmation that Taylor was murdered.'

'I'm asking for a widow's pension,' Leclerc protested gravely. 'He was one of my best men.'

'Of course. They always are.'

The Minister did not look up as they came in.

But the Police Inspector rose from his chair, a short, plump man with a shaven neck. He wore plain clothes. Avery supposed him to be a detective. He shook their hands with an air of professional bereavement, sat them in modern chairs with teak arms and offered cigars out of a tin. They declined, so he lit one himself, and used it thereafter both as a prolongation of his short fingers when making gestures of emphasis, and as a drawing instrument to describe in the smoke-filled air objects of which he was speaking. He deferred frequently to Avery's grief by thrusting his chin downwards into his collar and casting from the shadow of his lowered eyebrows confiding looks of sympathy. First he related the circumstances of the accident, praised in tiresome detail the efforts of the police to track down the car, referred frequently to the personal concern of the President of Police, whose anglophilia was a byword, and stated his own conviction that the guilty man would be found out, and punished with the full severity of Finnish law. He dwelt for some time on his own admiration of the British, his affection for the Queen and Sir Winston Churchill, the charms of Finnish neutrality and finally he came to the body.

The post-mortem, he was proud to say, was complete, and Mr Public Prosecutor (his own words) had declared that the circumstances of Mr Malherbe's death gave no grounds for suspicion despite the presence of a considerable amount of alcohol in the blood. The barman at the airport accounted for five glasses of Steinhäger. He returned to Sutherland.

'Does he want to see his brother?' he inquired, thinking it apparently a delicacy to refer the question to a third party.

Sutherland was embarrassed. 'That's up to Mr Avery,' he said, as if the matter were outside his competence. They both looked at Avery.

'I don't think so,' Avery said.

'There is one difficulty. About the identification,' Peersen said.

'Identification?' Avery repeated. 'Of my brother?'

'You saw his passport,' Sutherland put in, 'before you sent it up to me. What's the difficulty?'

The policeman nodded. 'Yes, yes.' Opening a drawer he took out a handful of letters, a wallet and some photographs.

'His name was Malherbe,' he said. He spoke fluent English with a heavy American accent which somehow suited the cigar. 'His passport was Malherbe. It was a *good* passport, wasn't it?' Peersen glanced at Sutherland. For a second Avery thought he detected in Sutherland's clouded face a certain honest hesitation.

– 66 –

'Of course.'

Peersen began to sort through the letters, putting some in a file before him and returning others to the drawer. Every now and then, as he added to the pile, he muttered: 'Ah, so,' or 'Yes, yes.' Avery could feel the sweat running down his body; it drenched his clasped hands.

'And your brother's name was Malherbe?' he asked again, when he had finished his sorting.

Avery nodded. 'Of course.'

Peersen smiled. 'Not of course,' he said, pointing his cigar and nodding in a friendly way as if he were making a debating point. 'All his possessions, his letters, his clothes, driving licence, all belong to Mr Taylor. You know anything of Taylor?'

A dreadful block was forming in Avery's mind. The envelope, what should he do with the envelope? Go to the lavatory, destroy it now before it was too late? He doubted whether it would work: the envelope was stiff and shiny. Even if he tore it, the pieces would float. He was aware of Peersen and Sutherland looking at him, waiting for him to speak and all he could think of was the envelope weighing so heavily in his inside pocket.

He managed to say, 'No, I don't. My brother and I . . .' Step-brother or half-brother? '. . . my brother and I did not have much to do with one another. He was older. We didn't really grow up together. He had a lot of different jobs, he could never quite settle down to anything. Perhaps this Taylor was a friend of his . . . who . . .' Avery shrugged, bravely trying to imply that Malherbe had been something of a mystery to him also.

'How old are you?' Peersen asked. His respect for the bereaved seemed to be dwindling.

'Thirty-two.'

'And Malherbe?' he threw out conversationally. 'He was how many years older, please?'

Sutherland and Peersen had seen his passport and knew his age. One remembers the age of people who die. Only Avery, his brother, had no idea how old the dead man was.

'Twelve,' he hazarded. 'My brother was forty-four.' Why did he have to say so much?

Peersen raised his eyebrows. 'Only forty-four? Then the pass-port is wrong as well.'

Peersen turned to Sutherland, poked his cigar towards the door at the far end of the room and said happily, as if he had ended an old argument between friends, 'Now you are seeing why I have a problem about identification.'

Sutherland was looking very angry.

'It would be nice if Mr Avery looked at the body,' Peersen suggested, 'then we can be sure.'

Sutherland said, 'Inspector Peersen. The identity of Mr Malherbe has been established from his passport. The Foreign Office in London has ascertained that Mr Avery's name was quoted by Mr Malherbe as his next of kin. You tell me there is nothing suspicious about the circumstances of his death. The customary procedure is now for you to release his effects to me for custody pending the completion of formalities in the United Kingdom. Mr Avery may presumably take charge of his brother's body.'

Peersen seemed to deliberate. He extracted the remainder of Taylor's papers from the steel drawer of his desk, added them to the pile already in front of him. He telephoned somebody and spoke in Finnish. After some minutes an orderly brought in an old leather suitcase with an inventory which Sutherland signed. Throughout all this, neither Avery nor Sutherland exchanged a word with the Inspector.

Peersen accompanied them all the way to the front door. Sutherland insisted on carrying the suitcase and papers himself. They went to the car. Avery waited for Sutherland to speak, but he said nothing. They drove for about ten minutes. The town was poorly lit. Avery noticed there was chemical on the road, in two lanes. The crown and gutters were still covered with snow. He was reminded of riding in the Mall, a thing he had never done. The street lamps were neon, shedding a sickly light which seemed to shrink before the gathering darkness. Now and then Avery was aware of steep timbered roofs, the clanging of a tram or the tall white hat of a policeman.

Occasionally he stole a glance through the rear window.

Chapter 7

Woodford stood in the corridor smoking his pipe, grinning at the staff as they left. It was his hour of magic. The mornings were different. Tradition demanded that the junior staff arrived at half past nine; officer grades at ten or quarter past. Theoretically, senior members of the Department stayed late in the evening, clearing their papers. A gentleman, Leclerc would say, never watched the clock. The custom dated from the war, when officers spent the early hours of the morning debriefing reconnaissance pilots back from a run, or the late hours of the night despatching an agent. The junior staff had worked shift in those days, but not the officers, who came and went as their work allowed. Now tradition fulfilled a different purpose. Now there were days, often weeks, when Woodford and his colleagues scarcely knew how to fill the time until five thirty; all but Haldane, who supported on his stooping shoulders the Department's reputation for research. The rest would draft projects which were never submitted, bicker gently among themselves about leave, duty rosters and the quality of their official furniture, give excessive attention to the problems of their section staff.

Berry, the cypher clerk, came into the corridor, stooped and put on his bicycle clips.

'How's the missus, Berry?' Woodford asked. A man must keep his finger on the pulse.

'Doing very nicely, thank you, sir.' He stood up, ran a comb through his hair. 'Shocking about Wilf Taylor, sir.'

'Shocking. He was a good scout.'

'Mr Haldane's locking up Registry, sir. He's working late.'

'Is he? Well, we all have our hands full now.'

Berry lowered his voice. 'And the Boss is sleeping in, sir. Quite a crisis, really. I hear he's gone to see the Minister. They sent a car for him.'

'Goodnight, Berry.' They hear too much, Woodford reflected with satisfaction, and began sauntering along the passage.

The illumination in Haldane's room came from an adjustable reading-lamp. It threw a brief, intense beam on to the file in front of him, touching the contours of his face and hands.

'Working late?' Woodford inquired.

Haldane pushed one file into his out-tray and picked up another.

'Wonder how young Avery's faring; he'll do well, that boy. I hear the Boss isn't back yet. Must be a long session.' As he spoke Woodford settled himself in the leather armchair. It was Haldane's own, he had brought it from his flat and sat in it to do his cross-word after luncheon.

'Why should he do well? There is no particular precedent,' Haldane said, without looking up.

'How did Clarkie get on with Taylor's wife?' Woodford now asked. 'How'd she take it?'

Haldane sighed and put his file aside.

'He broke it to her. That's all I know.'

'You didn't hear how she took it? He didn't tell you?'

Woodford always spoke a little louder than necessary, for he was used to competing with his wife.

'I've really no idea. He went alone, I understand. Leclerc prefers to keep these things to himself.'

'I thought perhaps with you . . .'

Haldane shook his head. 'Only Avery.'

'It's a big thing, this, isn't it, Adrian . . . could be?'

'It could be. We shall see,' Haldane said gently. He was not always unkind towards Woodford.

'Anything new on the Taylor front?'

'The Air Attaché at Helsinki has located Lansen. He confirms that he handed Taylor the film. Apparently the Russians intercepted him over Kalkstadt; two MIGs. They buzzed him, then let him go.'

'God,' said Woodford stupidly. 'That clinches it.'

'It does nothing of the kind; it's consistent with what we know. If they declare the area closed why shouldn't they patrol it? They probably closed it for manoeuvres, ground-air exercises. Why didn't they force Lansen down? The whole thing is entirely inconclusive.'

Leclerc was standing in the doorway. He had put on a clean collar for the Minister and a black tie for Taylor.

'I came by car,' he said. 'They've given us one from the Ministry pool on indefinite loan. The Minister was quite distressed to hear we hadn't one. It's a Humber, chauffeur-driven like Control's. They tell me the chauffeur is a secure sort of person.' He looked at Haldane. 'I've decided to form Special Section, Adrian. I want you to take it over. I'm giving Research to Sandford for the time being. The change will do him good.' His face broke into a smile as if he could contain himself no longer. He was very excited. 'We're putting a man in. The Minister's given his consent. We go to work at once. I want to see Heads of Sections first thing tomorrow. Adrian, I'll give you Woodford and Avery. Bruce, you keep in touch with the boys; get on to the old training people. The Minister will support three-month contracts for temporary staff. No peripheral liabilities, of course. The usual programme: wireless, weapon training, cyphers, observation, unarmed combat and cover. Adrian, we'll need a house. Perhaps Avery could go into that when he comes back. I'll approach Control about documentation; the forgers all went over to him. We'll want frontier records for the Lübeck area, refugee reports, details of minefields and obstructions.' He glanced at his watch. 'Adrian, shall we have a word?'

'Tell me one thing,' Haldane said. 'How much does the Circus know about this?'

'Whatever we choose to tell them. Why?'

'They know Taylor is dead. It's all over Whitehall.'

'Possibly.'

'They know Avery's picking up a film in Finland. They may very well have noticed the Air Safety Centre report on Lansen's plane. They have a way of noticing things . . .'

'Well?'

'So it isn't only a question of what we tell them is it?'

'You'll come to tomorrow's meeting?' Leclerc asked a little pathetically.

'I think I have the meat of my instructions. If you have no objection I would like to make one or two inquiries. This evening and tomorrow perhaps.'

Leclerc, bewildered, said, 'Excellent. Can we help you?'

'Perhaps I might have the use of your car for an hour?'

'Of course. I want us all to use it – to our common benefit. Adrian – this is for you.'

He handed him a green card in a Cellophane folder.

'The Minister signed it, personally.' He implied that, like a Papal blessing, there were degrees of authenticity in a Ministerial signature. 'Then you'll do it, Adrian? You'll take the job?'

Haldane might not have heard. He had reopened the file and

was looking curiously at the photograph of a Polish boy who had fought the Germans twenty years ago. It was a young, strict face; humourless. It seemed to be concerned not with living but with survival.

'Why, Adrian,' Leclerc cried with sudden relief, 'you've taken the second vow!'

Reluctantly Haldane smiled, as if the phrase had called to mind something he thought he had forgotten. 'He seems to have a talent for survival,' he observed, finally indicating the file. 'Not an easy man to kill.'

'As next of kin,' Sutherland began, 'you have the right to state your wishes concerning the disposal of your brother's body.'

'Yes.'

Sutherland's house was a small building with a picture window full of potted plants. Only these distinguished it, either externally or internally, from its model in the dormitory areas of Aberdeen. As they walked down the drive, Avery caught sight of a middle-aged woman in the window. She wore an apron and was dusting something. She reminded him of Mrs Yates and her cat.

'I have an office at the back,' said Sutherland, as if to emphasize that the place was not wholly given over to luxury. 'I suggest we tie up the rest of the details now. I shan't keep you long.' He was telling Avery he needn't expect to stay to supper. 'How do you propose to get him back to England?'

They sat down either side of the desk. Behind Sutherland's head hung a water colour of mauve hills reflected in a Scottish loch.

'I should like it flown home.'

'You know that is an expensive business?'

'I should like him flown all the same.'

'For burial?'

'Of course.'

'It isn't "of course" at all,' Sutherland countered with distaste. 'If your brother' – he said it in inverted commas now, but he would play the game to the end – 'were to be cremated, the flight regulations would be totally different.'

'I see. I'm sorry.'

'There is a firm of undertakers in the town, Barford and Company. One of the partners is English, married to a Swedish girl. There is a substantial Swedish minority here. We do our best to support the British community. In the circumstances I would prefer you to return to London as soon as you can. I suggest you empower me to use Barford.'

'All right.'

'As soon as he has taken over the body, I will provide him with your brother's passport. He will have to obtain a medical certificate regarding the cause of death. I'll put him in touch with Peersen.'

'Yes.'

'He will also require a death certificate issued by a local registrar. It is cheaper if one attends to that side of things oneself. If money matters to your people.'

Avery said nothing.

'When he has found out a suitable flight he will look after the freight warrant and bill of lading. I understand these things are usually moved at night. The freight rate is cheaper and . . .'

'That's all right.'

'I'm glad. Barford will make sure the coffin is airtight. It may be of metal or wood. He will also append his own certificate that the coffin contains nothing but the body – and the same body as that to which the passport and the death certificate refer. I mention this for when you take delivery in London. Barford will do all this very quickly. I shall see to that. He has some pull with the charter companies here. The sooner he—'

'I understand.'

'I'm not sure you do.' Sutherland raised his eyebrows, as if Avery had been impertinent. 'Peersen has been very reasonable. I don't wish to test his patience. Barford will have a correspondent firm in London – it *is* London, isn't it?'

'London, yes.'

'I imagine he will expect some payment in advance. I suggest you leave the money with me against a receipt. As regards your brother's effects, I take it that whoever sent you wished you to recover these letters?' He pushed them across the table.

Avery muttered, 'There was a film, an undeveloped film.' He put the letters in his pocket.

Deliberately Sutherland extracted a copy of the inventory which he had signed at the police station, spread it out before him and ran his finger down the left-hand column, suspiciously, as if he were checking someone else's figures.

'There is no film entered here. Was there a camera too?'

'No.'

'Ah.'

He saw Avery to the door. 'You'd better tell whoever sent you that Malherbe's passport was not valid. The Foreign Office sent out a circular about a group of numbers, twenty-odd. Your brother's was one of them. There must have been a slip-up. I was about to report it when a Foreign Office teleprint arrived empowering you to take over Malherbe's effects.' He gave a short laugh. He was very angry. 'That was nonsense, of course. The Office would never have sent that on their own. They've no authority, not unless you'd Letters of Administration, and you couldn't have got *those* in the middle of the night. Have you somewhere to stay? The Regina's quite good, near the airport. Out of town, too. I assume you can find your own way. I gather you people get excellent subsistence.'

Avery made his way quickly down the drive, carrying in his memory the indelible image of Sutherland's thin, bitter face set angrily against the Scottish hills. The wooden houses beside the road shone half white in the darkness like shadows round an operating table.

Somewhere not far from Charing Cross, in the basement of one of those surprising eighteenth-century houses between Villiers Street and the river, is a club with no name on the door. You reach it by descending a curving stone staircase. The railing, like the woodwork of the house in Blackfriars Road, is painted dark green and needs replacing.

Its members are an odd selection. Some of a military kind, some in the teaching profession, others clerical; others again from that no-man's-land of London society which lies between the bookmaker and the gentleman, presenting to those around them, and perhaps even to themselves, an image of vacuous courage; conversing in codes and phrases which a man with a sense of language can only listen to at a distance. It is a place of old faces and young bodies; of young faces and old bodies; where the tensions of war have become the tensions of peace, and voices are raised to drown the silence, and glasses to drown the loneliness; it is the place where the searchers meet, finding no one but each other and the comfort of a shared pain; where the tired watchful eyes have no horizon to observe. It is their battlefield still; if there is love, they find it here in one another, shyly like adolescents, thinking all the time of other people.

From the war, none but the dons were missing.

It is a small place, run by a thin, dry man called Major Dell; he has a moustache and a tie with blue angels on a black background. He stands the first drink, and they buy him the others. It is called the Alias Club, and Woodford was a member.

It is open in the evenings. They come at about six, detaching themselves with pleasure from the moving crowd, furtive but determined, like men from out of town visiting a disreputable theatre. You notice first the things that are not there: no silver cups behind the bar, no visitors' book nor list of membership; no insignia, crest or title. Only on the white-washed brick walls a few photographs hang, framed in passe-partout, like the photographs in Leclerc's room. The faces are indistinct, some enlarged, apparently from a passport, taken from the front with both ears showing according to the regulation; some are of women, a few of them attractive, with high square shoulders and long hair after the fashion of the war years. The men are wearing a variety of uniforms; Free French and Poles mingle with their British comrades. Some are fliers. Of the English faces one or two, grown old, still haunt the club.

When Woodford came in everyone looked round and Major Dell, much pleased, ordered his pint of beer. A florid, middle-aged man was talking about a sortie he once made over Belgium but he stopped when he lost the attention of his audience.

'Hello, Woodie,' somebody said in surprise. 'How's the lady?'

'Fit,' Woodford smiled genially. 'Fit.' He drank some beer. Cigarettes were passed round. Major Dell said, 'Woodie's jolly shifty tonight.'

'I'm looking for someone. It's all a bit top secret.'

'We know the form,' the florid man replied. Woodford glanced round the bar and asked quietly, a note of mystery in his voice, 'What did Dad do in the war?'

A bewildered silence. They had been drinking for some time.

'Kept Mum, of course,' said Major Dell uncertainly and they all laughed.

Woodford laughed with them, savouring the conspiracy, reliving the half-forgotten ritual of secret mess nights somewhere in England.

'And where did he keep her?' he demanded, still in the same confiding tone: this time two or three voices called in unison, 'Under his blooming hat!'

They were louder, happier.

'There was a man called Johnson,' Woodford continued quickly, 'Jack Johnson. I'm trying to find out what became of him. He was a trainer in wireless transmission; one of the best. He was at Bovingdon first with Haldane until they moved him up to Oxford.'

'Jack Johnson!' the florid man cried excitedly. 'The WT man? I bought a car radio from Jack two weeks ago! Johnson's Fair Deal in the Clapham Broadway, that's the fellow. Drops in here from time to time. Amateur wireless enthusiast. Little bloke, speaks out of the side of his face?'

'That's him,' someone else said. 'He knocks off twenty per cent for the old gang.'

'He didn't for me,' the florid man said.

'That's Jack; he lives at Clapham.'

The others took it up; that was the fellow and he ran this shop, at Clapham; king of ham radio, been a ham before the war even when he was a kid; yes, on the Broadway, hung out there for years; must be worth a ransom. Liked to come into the club round Christmas time. Woodford, flushed with pleasure, ordered drinks.

In the bustle that followed, Major Dell took Woodford gently by the arm and guided him to the other end of the bar.

'Woodie, is it true about Wilf Taylor? Has he really bought it?'

Woodford nodded, his face grave. 'He was on a job. We think someone's been a little bit naughty.'

Major Dell was all solicitude. 'I haven't told the boys. It would only worry them. Who's caring for the Missus?'

'The Boss is taking that up now. It looks pretty hopeful.'

'Good,' said the Major. 'Good.' He nodded, patting Woodford's arm in a gesture of consolation. 'We'll keep it from the boys, shall we?'

'Of course.'

'He had one or two bills. Nothing very big. He liked to drop in Friday nights.' The Major's accent slipped from time to time like a made-up tie.

'Send them along. We'll take care of those.'

'There was a kid, wasn't there? A little girl?' They were moving back to the bar. 'How old was she?'

'Eightish. Maybe more.'

'He talked about her a lot,' said the Major.

Somebody called, 'Hey, Bruce, when are you chaps going to take another crack at the Jerries? They're all over the bloody place. Took the wife to Italy in the Summer – full of arrogant Germans.'

Woodford smiled. 'Sooner than you think. Now let's try this one.' The conversation died. Woodford was real. He still did the job.

'There was an unarmed combat man, a staff sergeant; a Welshman. He was short too.'

'Sounds like Sandy Lowe,' the florid man suggested.

'Sandy, that's him!' They all turned to the florid man in admiration. 'He was a Taffy. Randy Sandy we called him.'

'Of course,' said Woodford contentedly. 'Now didn't he go off to some public school as a boxing instructor?' He was looking at them narrowly, holding a good deal back, playing it long because it was so secret.

'That's him, that's Sandy!'

Woodford wrote it down, taking care because he had learnt from experience that he tended to forget things which he entrusted to memory.

As he was going, the Major asked, 'How's Clarkie?'

'Busy,' Woodford said. 'Working himself to death, as always.'

'The boys talk about him a lot, you know. I wish he'd come here now and then; give them a hell of a boost, you know. Perk them up.'

'Tell me,' said Woodford. They were by the door. 'Do you remember a fellow called Leiser? Fred Leiser, a Pole? Used to be with our lot. He was in the Holland show.'

'Still alive?'

'Yes.'

'Sorry,' said the Major vaguely. 'The foreigners have stopped coming; I don't know why. I don't discuss it with the boys.'

Closing the door behind him, Woodford stepped into the London night. He looked about him, loving all he saw – the mother city in his rugged care. He walked slowly, an old athlete on an old track.

Chapter 8

Avery, on the other hand, walked fast. He was afraid. There is no terror so consistent, so elusive to describe, as that which haunts a spy in a strange country. The glance of a taxi driver, the density of people in the street, the variety of official uniform – was he a policeman or a postman? – the obscurity of custom and language, and the very noises which comprised the world into which Avery had moved contributed to a state of constant anxiety, which, like a nervous pain, became virulent now that he was alone. In the shortest time his spirit ranged between panic and cringing love, responding with unnatural gratitude to a kind glance or word. It was part of an effeminate dependence upon those whom he deceived. Avery needed desperately to win from the uncaring faces around him the absolution of a trusting smile. It was no help that he told himself: you do them no harm, you are their protector. He moved among them like a hunted man in search of rest and food.

He took a cab to the hotel and asked for a room with a bath. They gave him the register to sign. He had actually put his pen to the page when he saw, not ten lines above, done in a laborious hand, the name Malherbe, broken in the middle as if the writer could not spell it. His eye followed the entry along the line: Address, London; Profession, Major (retired); Destination, London. His last vanity, Avery thought, a false profession, a false rank, but little English Taylor had stolen a moment's glory. Why not Colonel? Or Admiral? Why not give himself a peerage and an address in Park Lane? Even when he dreamed, Taylor had known his limits.

The concierge said, 'The valet will take your luggage.'

'I'm sorry,' said Avery, a meaningless apology, and signed his name, while the man watched him curiously.

He gave the valet a coin and it occurred to him as he did so that he had given him eight and six. He closed the bedroom door. For a while he sat on his bed. It was a carefully planned room but bleak and without sympathy. On the door was a notice in several languages warning against the perils of theft, and by the bed another which explained the financial disadvantages of failing to breakfast in the hotel. There was a magazine about travel on the writing-desk, and a Bible bound in black. There was a small bathroom, very clean, and a built-in wardrobe with one coat-hanger. He had forgotten to bring a book. He had not anticipated having to endure leisure.

He was cold and hungry. He thought he would have a bath. He ran it and undressed. He was about to get into the water when he remembered Taylor's letters in his pocket. He put on a dressing-gown, sat on the bed and looked through them. One from his bank about an overdraft, one from his mother, one from a friend which began Dear Old Wilf, the rest from a woman. He was suddenly frightened of the letters: they were evidence. They could compromise him. He determined to burn them all. There was a second basin in the bedroom. He put all the papers into it and held a match to them. He had read somewhere that was the thing to do. There was a membership card for the Alias Club made out in Taylor's name so he burnt that too, then broke up the ash with his fingers and turned on the water; it rose swiftly. The plug was a built-in metal affair operated by a lever between the taps. The sodden ash was packed beneath it. The basin was blocked.

He looked for some instrument to probe under the lip of the plug. He tried his fountain pen but it was too fat, so he fetched the nail file. After repeated attempts he persuaded the ash into the outlet. The water ran away, revealing a heavy brown stain on the enamel. He rubbed it, first with his hand then with the scrubbing brush, but it wouldn't go. Enamel didn't stain like that, there must have been some quality in the paper, tar or something. He went into the bathroom, looking vainly for a detergent.

As he re-entered his bedroom he became aware that it was filled with the smell of charred paper. He went quickly to the window and opened it. A blast of freezing wind swept over his naked limbs. He was gathering the dressing-gown more closely about him when there was a knock on the door. Paralyzed with fear, he stared at the door handle, heard another knock, called, watched the handle turn. It was the man from Reception.

'Mr Avery?'

'Yes?'

'I'm sorry. We need your passport. For the police.'

'Police.'

'It's the customary procedure.'

Avery had backed against the basin. The curtains were flapping wildly beside the open window.

'May I close the window?' the man asked.

'I wasn't well. I wanted some fresh air.'

He found his passport and handed it over. As he did so, he saw the man's gaze fixed upon the basin, on the brown mark and the small flakes which still clung to the sides.

He wished as never before that he was back in England.

The row of villas which lines Western Avenue is like a row of pink graves in a field of grey; an architectural image of middle age. Their uniformity is the discipline of growing old, of dying without violence and living without success. They are houses which have got the better of their occupants, whom they change at will, and do not change themselves. Furniture vans glide respectfully among them like hearses, discreetly removing the dead and introducing the living. Now and then some tenant will raise his hand, expending pots of paint on the woodwork or labour on the garden, but his efforts no more alter the house than flowers a hospital ward, and the grass will grow its own way, like grass on a grave.

Haldane dismissed the car and turned off the road towards South Park Gardens, a crescent five minutes from the Avenue. A school, a post office, four shops and a bank. He stooped a little as he walked; a black briefcase hung from his thin hand. He made his way quietly along the pavement; the tower of a modern church rose above the houses; a clock struck seven. A grocer's on the corner, new façade, self-service. He looked at the name: Smethwick. Inside, a youngish man in a brown overall was completing a pyramid of cereal foods. Haldane rapped on the glass. The man shook his head and added a packet to the pyramid. He knocked again, sharply. The grocer came to the door.

'I'm not allowed to sell you anything,' he shouted, 'so it's no good knocking, is it?' He noticed the briefcase and asked, 'Are you a rep, then?'

Haldane put his hand in his inside pocket and held something to the window – a card in a Cellophane wrapper like a season ticket. The grocer stared at it. Slowly he turned the key.

'I want a word with you in private,' Haldane said, stepping inside.

'I've never seen one of those,' the grocer observed uneasily. 'I suppose it's all right.'

'It's quite all right. A security inquiry. Someone called Leiser, a Pole. I understand he worked here long ago.'

'I'll have to call my Dad,' the grocer said. 'I was only a kid then.'

'I see,' said Haldane, as if he disliked youth.

It was nearly midnight when Avery rang Leclerc. He answered straight away. Avery could imagine him sitting up in the steel bed, the Air Force blankets thrown back, his small, alert face anxious for the news.

'It's John,' he said cautiously.

'Yes, yes, I know who you are.' He sounded cross that Avery had mentioned his name.

'The deal's off I'm afraid. They're not interested . . . negative. You'd better tell the man I saw; the little, fat man . . . tell him we shan't need the services of his friend here.'

'I see. Never mind.' He sounded utterly uninterested.

Avery didn't know what to say; he just didn't know. He needed desperately to go on talking to Leclerc. He wanted to tell him about Sutherland's contempt and the passport that wasn't right. 'The people here, the people I'm negotiating with, are rather worried about the whole deal.'

He waited.

He wanted to call him by his name but he had no name for him. They did not use 'Mister' in the Department; the elder men addressed one another by their surnames and called the juniors by their Christian names. There was no established style of addressing one's superior. So he said, 'Are you still there?' and Leclerc replied, 'Of course. Who's worried? What's gone wrong?' Avery thought: I could have called him 'Director', but that would have been insecure.

'The representative here, the man who looks after our interests . . . he's found out about the deal,' he said. 'He seems to have guessed.'

'You stressed it was highly confidential?'

'Yes, of course.' How could he ever explain about Sutherland?

'Good. We don't want any trouble with the Foreign Office just now.' In an altered tone Leclerc continued, 'Things are going very well over here, John, very well. When do you get back?'

'I've got to cope with the . . . with bringing our friend home. There are a lot of formalities. It's not as easy as you'd think.'

'When will you be finished?'

'Tomorrow.'

'I'll send a car to meet you at Heathrow. A lot's happened in the last few hours; a lot of improvements. We need you badly.' Leclerc added, throwing him a coin, 'And well done, John, well done indeed.'

'All right.'

He expected to sleep heavily that night, but after what might have been an hour he woke, alert and watchful. He looked at his watch; it was ten past one. Getting out of bed he went to the window and looked on to the snow-covered landscape, marked by the darker lines of the road which led to the airport; he thought he could discern the little rise where Taylor had died.

He was desolate and afraid. His mind was obsessed by confused visions: Taylor's dreadful face, the face he so nearly saw, drained of blood, wide-eyed as if communicating a crucial discovery; Leclerc's voice, filled with vulnerable optimism; the fat policeman, staring at him in envy, as if he were something he could not afford to buy. He realized he was a person who did not take easily to solitude. Solitude saddened him, made him sentimental. He found himself thinking, for the first time since he had left the flat that morning, of Sarah and Anthony. Tears came suddenly to his tired eyes when he recalled his boy, the steel-rimmed spectacles like tiny irons; he wanted to hear his voice, he wanted Sarah, and the familiarity of his home. Perhaps he could telephone the flat, speak to her mother, ask after her. But what if she were ill? He had suffered enough pain that day, he had given enough of his energy, fear and invention. He had lived a nightmare: he could not be expected to ring her now. He went back to bed.

Try as he might, he could not sleep. His eyelids were hot and heavy, his body deeply tired, but still he could not sleep. A wind rose, rattling the double windows; now he was too hot, now too cold. Once he dozed, only to be woken violently from his uneasy rest by the sound of crying, it might have been in the next room, it might have been Anthony, or it might have been – since he did not hear it properly, but only half knew in waking what kind of a sound it had been – the metallic sobbing of a child's doll.

And once, it was shortly before dawn, he heard a footfall outside his room, a single tread in the corridor, not imagined but real, and he lay in chill terror waiting for the handle of his door to turn or the peremptory knocking of Inspector Peersen's men. As he strained his ears he swore he detected the faintest rustle of clothing, the subdued intake of human breath, like a tiny sigh; then silence.

Though he listened for minutes on end, he heard nothing more.

Putting on the light, he went to the chair, felt in his jacket for his fountain pen. It was by the basin. From his briefcase he took a leather holdall which Sarah had given him.

Settling himself at the flimsy table in front of the window, he began writing a love letter to a girl, it might have been to Carol. When at last morning came, he destroyed it, tearing it into small pieces and flushing them down the lavatory. As he did so he caught sight of something white on the floor. It was a photograph of Taylor's child carrying a doll; she was wearing glasses, the kind Anthony wore. It must have been among his papers. He thought of destroying it but somehow he couldn't. He slipped it into his pocket.

Chapter 9
Homecoming

Leclerc was waiting at Heathrow as Avery knew he would be, standing on tiptoe, peering anxiously between the heads of the waiting crowd. He had squared the customs somehow, he must have got the Ministry to do it, and when he saw Avery he came forward into the hall and guided him in a managing way as if he were used to being spared formalities. This is the life we lead, Avery thought; the same airport with different names; the same hurried, guilty meetings; we live outside the walls of the town, black friars from a dark house in Lambeth. He was desperately tired. He wanted Sarah. He wanted to say sorry, make it up with her, get a new job, try again; play with Anthony more. He felt ashamed.

'I'll just make a telephone call. Sarah wasn't too well when I left.'

'Do it from the Office,' Leclerc said. 'Do you mind? I have a meeting with Haldane in an hour.' Thinking he detected a false note in Leclerc's voice, Avery looked at him suspiciously, but the other's eyes were turned away towards the black Humber standing in the privilege car park. Leclerc let the driver open the door for him; a silly muddle took place until Avery sat on his left as protocol apparently demanded. The driver seemed tired of waiting. There was no partition between him and themselves.

'This is a change,' Avery said, indicating the car.

Leclerc nodded in a familiar way as if the acquisition were no longer new. 'How are things?' he asked, his mind elsewhere.

'All right. There's nothing the matter, is there? With Sarah, I mean.'

'Why should there be?'

'Blackfriars Road?' the driver inquired, without turning his head, as a sense of respect might have indicated.

'Headquarters, yes, please.'

'There was a hell of a mess in Finland,' Avery observed brutally. 'Our friend's papers . . . Malherbe's . . . weren't in order. The Foreign Office had cancelled his passport.'

'Malherbe? Ah yes. You mean Taylor. We know all about that. It's all right now. Just the usual jealousy. Control is rather upset about it, as a matter of fact. He sent round to apologize. We've a lot of people on our side now, John, you've no idea. You're going to be very useful, John; you're the only one who's seen it on the ground.' Seen what? Avery wondered. They were together again. The same intensity, the same physical unease, the same absences. As Leclerc turned to him Avery thought for one sickening moment he was going to put a hand on his knee. 'You're tired, John, I can tell. I know how it feels. Never mind – you're back with us now. Listen, I've good news for you. The Ministry's woken up to us in a big way. We're to form a special operational unit to mount the next phase.'

'Next phase?'

'Of course. The man I mentioned to you. We can't leave things as they are. We're clarifiers, John, not simply collators. I've revived Special Section; do you know what that is?'

'Haldane ran it during the war; training . . .'

Leclerc interrupted quickly for the driver's sake: '. . . training the travelling salesmen. And he's going to run it again now. I've decided you're to work with him. You're the two best brains I've got.' A sideways glance.

Leclerc had altered. There was a new quality to his bearing, something more than optimism or hope. When Avery had seen him last he had seemed to be living against adversity; now he had a freshness about him, a purpose, which was either new or very old.

'And Haldane accepted?'

'I told you. He's working night and day. You forget, Adrian's a professional. A real technician. Old heads are the best for a job like this. With one or two young heads among them.'

Avery said, 'I want to talk to you about the whole operation . . . about Finland. I'll come to your office after I've rung Sarah.'

'Come straight away, then I can put you in the picture.'

'I'll phone Sarah first.'

Again Avery had the unreasonable feeling that Leclerc was trying to keep him from communicating with Sarah.

'She *is* all right, isn't she?'

'So far as I know. Why do you ask?' Leclerc went on, charming him: 'Glad to be back, John?'

'Yes, of course.'

He sank back into the cushions of the car. Leclerc, noticing his hostility, abandoned him for a time; Avery turned his attention to the road and the pink, healthy villas drifting past in the light rain.

Leclerc was talking again, his committee voice. 'I want you to start straight away. Tomorrow if you can. We've got your room ready. There's a lot to be done. This man: Haldane has him in play. We should hear something when we get home. From now on you're Adrian's creature. I trust that pleases you. Our masters have agreed to provide you with a special Ministry pass. The same kind of thing that they have in the Circus.'

Avery was familiar with Leclerc's habit of speech; there were times when he resorted entirely to oblique allusion, offering a raw material which the consumer, not the purveyor, must refine.

'I want to talk to you about the whole thing. When I've rung Sarah.'

'That's right,' Leclerc replied nicely. 'Come and talk to me about it. Why not come now?' He looked at Avery, offering his whole face; a thing without depth, a moon with one side. 'You've done well,' he said generously, 'I hope you'll keep it up.' They entered London. 'We're getting some help from the Circus,' he added. 'They seem to be quite willing. They don't know the whole picture of course. The Minister was very firm on that point.'

They passed down Lambeth Road, where the God of Battles presides; the Imperial War Museum one end, schools the other, hospitals in between; a cemetery wired off like a tennis court. You cannot tell who lives there. The houses are too many for the people, the schools too large for the children. The hospitals may be full, but the blinds are drawn. Dust hangs everywhere, like the dust of war. It hangs over the hollow façades, chokes the grass in the graveyard: it has driven away the people, save those who loiter in the dark places like the ghosts of soldiers, or wait sleepless behind their yellow-lighted windows. It is a road which people seem to have left often. The few who returned brought something of the living world, according to their voyages. One a piece of field, another a broken Regency terrace, a warehouse or dumping yard; or a pub called the Flowers of the Forest.

It is a road filled with faithful institutions. Over one presides our Lady of Consolation, over another, Archbishop Amigo. Whatever is not hospital, school, pub or seminary is dead, and the dust has got its body. There is a toyshop with a padlocked door. Avery looked into it every day on the way to the office; the toys were rusting on the shelves. The window looked dirtier than ever; the lower part was striped with children's fingermarks. There is a place that mends your teeth while you wait. He glimpsed them now from the car, counting them off as they drove past, wondering whether he would ever see them again as a member of the Department. There are warehouses with barbed wire across their gates, and factories which produce nothing. In one of them a bell rang but no one heard. There is a broken wall with posters on it. You are somebody today in the Regular Army. They rounded St George's Circus and entered Blackfriars Road for the home run.

As they approached the building, Avery sensed that things had changed. For a moment he imagined that the very grass on the wretched bit of lawn had thickened and revived during his brief absence; that the concrete steps leading to the front door, which even in Midsummer managed to appear moist and dirty, were now clean and inviting. Somehow he knew, before he entered the building at all, that a new spirit had infected the Department.

It had reached the most humble members of the staff. Pine, impressed no doubt by the black staff car and the sudden passage of busy people, looked spruce and alert. For once he said nothing about cricket scores. The staircase was daubed with wax polish.

In the corridor they met Woodford. He was in a hurry. He was carrying a couple of files with red caution notices on the cover.

'Hullo, John! You've landed safely, then? Good party?' He really did seem pleased to see him. 'Sarah all right now?'

'He's done well,' said Leclerc quickly. 'He had a very difficult run.'

'Ah yes; poor Taylor. We shall need you in the new section. Your wife will have to spare you for a week or two.'

'What was that about Sarah?' Avery asked. Suddenly he was frightened. He hastened down the corridor. Leclerc was calling but he took no notice. He entered his room and stopped dead. There was a second telephone on his desk, and a steel bed like Leclerc's along the side wall. Beside the new telephone was a piece of military board with a list of emergency telephone numbers pinned to it. The numbers for use during the night were printed in red. On the back of the door hung a two-colour poster depicting in profile the head of a man. Across his skull was written, 'Keep it here', and across his mouth, 'Don't let it out here'. It took him a moment or two to realize that the poster was an exhortation to security, and not some dreadful joke about Taylor. He lifted the receiver and waited. Carol came in with a tray of papers for signature.

'How did it go?' she asked. 'The Boss seems pleased.' She was standing quite close to him.

'Go? There's no film. It wasn't among his things. I'm going to resign; I've decided. What the hell's wrong with this phone?'

'They probably don't know you're back. There's a thing from Accounts about your claim for a taxi. They've queried it.'

'Taxi?'

'From your flat to the office. The night Taylor died. They say it's too much.'

'Look, go and stir up the exchange, will you, they must be fast asleep.'

Sarah answered the telephone herself.

'Oh, thank God it's you.'

Avery said yes, he had got in an hour ago. 'Sarah, look, I've had enough, I'm going to tell Leclerc—' But before he could finish she burst out, 'John, for *God's* sake, what *have* you been doing? We had the police here, detectives; they want to talk to you about a body that's arrived at London Airport; somebody called Malherbe. They say it was sent from Finland on a false passport.'

He closed his eyes. He wanted to put down the receiver, he held it away from his ear but he still heard her voice, saying John, John. 'They say he's your brother; it's addressed to *you*, John; some London undertaker was supposed to be doing it all for you . . . John, John, are you still there?'

'Listen,' he said, 'it's all right. I'll take care of it now.'

'I told them about Taylor: I had to.'

'Sarah!'

'What else could I do? They thought I was a criminal or something; they didn't believe me, John! They asked how they could get hold of you; I had to say I didn't know; I didn't even know which country or which plane; I was ill, John, I felt awful, I've got this damn 'flu and I'd forgotten to take my pills. They came in the middle of the night, two of them. John, why did they come in the night?'

'What did you tell them? For Christ's sake, Sarah, what else did you say to them?'

'Don't swear at me! I should be swearing at you and your beastly Department! I said you were doing something secret; you'd had to go abroad for the Department – John, I don't even know its *name*! – that you'd been rung in the night and you'd gone away. I said it was about a courier called Taylor.'

'You're mad,' Avery shouted, 'you're absolutely mad. I told you never to say!'

'But, John, they were *policemen*! There can't be any harm in telling them.' She was crying, he could hear the tears in her voice. 'John, *please* come back. I'm so frightened. You've got to get out of this, go back to publishing; I don't care what you do but . . .'

'I can't. It's terribly big. More important than you can possibly understand. I'm sorry, Sarah. I just can't leave the office.' He added savagely, a useful lie, 'You may have wrecked the whole thing.'

There was a very long silence.

'Sarah, I'll have to sort this out. I'll ring you later.'

When at last she answered he detected in her voice the same flat resignation with which she had sent him to pack his things. 'You took the cheque book. I've no money.'

He told her he would send it round. 'We've got a car,' he added, ''specially for this thing, chauffeur driven.' As he rang off he heard her say, 'I thought you'd got lots of cars.'

He ran into Leclerc's room. Haldane was standing behind the desk; his coat still wet from the rain. They were bent over a file. The pages were faded and torn.

'Taylor's body!' he blurted out. 'It's at London Airport. You've messed the whole thing up. They've been on to Sarah! In the middle of the night!'

'Wait!' It was Haldane who spoke. 'You have no business to come running in here,' he declared furiously. 'Just wait.' He did not care for Avery.

He returned to the file, ignoring him. 'None at all,' he muttered, adding to Leclerc: 'Woodford has already had some success, I gather. Unarmed combat's all right; he's heard of a wireless operator, one of the best. I remember him. The garage is called the King of Hearts; it is clearly prosperous. We inquired at the bank; they were quite helpful if not specific. He's unmarried. He has a reputation for women; the usual Polish style. No political interests, no known hobbies, no debts, no complaints. He seems to be something of a nonentity. They say he's a good mechanic. As for character—' he shrugged. 'What do we know about anybody?'

'But what did they *say*? Good Heavens, you can't be fifteen years in a community without leaving *some* impression. There was a grocer wasn't there – Smethwick? – he lived with them after the war.'

Haldane allowed himself a smile. 'They said he was a good worker and very polite. Everyone says he's polite. They remember one thing only: he had a passion for hitting a tennis ball round their backyard.'

'Did you take a look at the garage?'

'Certainly not. I didn't go near it. I propose to call there this evening. I don't see that we have any other choice. After all, the man's been on our cards for twenty years.'

'Is there nothing more you can find out?'

'We would have to do the rest through the Circus.'

'Then let John Avery clear up the details.' Leclerc seemed to have forgotten Avery was in the room. 'As for the Circus, I'll deal with them myself.' His interest had been arrested by a new map on the wall, a town plan of Kalkstadt showing the church and railway station. Beside it hung an older map of Eastern Europe. Rocket bases whose existence had already been confirmed were here related to the putative site south of Rostock. Supply routes and chains of command, the order of battle of supporting arms, were indicated with lines of thin wool stretched between pins. A number of these led to Kalkstadt.

'It's good, isn't it? Sandford put it together last night,' Leclerc said. 'He does that kind of thing rather well.'

On his desk lay a new whitewood pointer like a giant bodkin threaded with a loop of barrister's ribbon. He had a new telephone, green, smarter than Avery's, with a notice on it saying 'Speech on this telephone is NOT secure.' For a time Haldane and Leclerc studied the map, referring now and then to a file of telegrams which Leclerc held open in both hands as a choirboy holds a psalter.

Finally Leclerc turned to Avery and said, 'Now, John.' They were waiting for him to speak.

He could feel his anger dying. He wanted to hold on to it but it was slipping away. He wanted to cry out in indignation: how dare you involve my wife? He wanted to lose control, but he could not. His eyes were on the map.

'Well?'

'The police have been round to Sarah. They woke her in the middle of the night. Two men. Her mother was there. They came about the body at the airport: Taylor's body. They knew the passport was phoney and thought she was involved. They woke her up,' he repeated lamely.

'We know all about that. It's straightened out. I wanted to tell you but you wouldn't let me. The body's been released.'

'It was wrong to drag Sarah in.'

Haldane lifted his head quickly: 'What do you mean by that?'

'We're not competent to handle this kind of thing.' It sounded very impertinent. 'We shouldn't be doing it. We ought to give it to the Circus. Smiley or someone – they're the people, not us.' He struggled on: 'I don't even believe that report. I don't believe it's true! I wouldn't be surprised if that refugee never existed; if Gorton made the whole thing up! I don't believe Taylor was murdered.'

'Is that all?' Haldane demanded. He was very angry.

'It's not something I want to go on with. The operation, I mean. It isn't right.'

He looked at the map and at Haldane, then laughed a little stupidly. 'All the time I've been chasing a dead man you've been after a live one! It's easy here, in the dream factory . . . but they're people out there, real people!'

Leclerc touched Haldane lightly on the arm as if to say he would handle this himself. He seemed undisturbed. He might almost have been gratified to recognize symptoms which he had previously diagnosed. 'Go to your room, John, you're suffering from strain.'

'But what do I tell Sarah?' He spoke with despair.

'Tell her she won't be troubled any more. Tell her it was a mistake . . . tell her whatever you like. Get some hot food and come back in an hour. These airline meals are useless. Then we'll hear the rest of your news.' Leclerc was smiling, the same neat, bland smile with which he had stood among the dead fliers. As Avery reached the door he heard his name called softly, with affection: he stopped and looked back.

Leclerc raised one hand from the desk and with a semi-circular movement indicated the room in which they were standing.

'I'll tell you something, John. During the war we were in Baker Street. We had a cellar and the Ministry fixed it up as an emergency operations room. Adrian and I spent a lot of time down there. A *lot* of time.' A glance at Haldane. 'Remember how the oil lamp used to swing when the bombs fell? We had to face situations where we had one rumour, John, no more. One indicator and we'd take the risk. Send a man in, two if necessary, and maybe they wouldn't come back. Maybe there wouldn't be anything there. Rumours, a guess, a hunch one follows up; it's easy to forget what intelligence consists of: luck, and speculation. Here and there a windfall, here and there a scoop. Sometimes you stumbled on a thing like this: it could be very big, it could be a shadow. It may have been from a peasant in Flensburg, or it may come from the Provost of King's, but you're left with a possibility you dare not discount. You get instructions: find a man, put him in. So we did. And many *didn't* come back. They were sent to resolve doubt, don't you see? We sent them because we didn't know. All of us have moments like this, John. Don't think it's always easy.' A reminiscent smile. 'Often we had scruples like you. We had to overcome them. We used to call that the second vow.' He leant against the desk, informally. 'The second vow,' he repeated.

'Now, John, if you want to wait until the bombs are falling, till people are dying in the street . . .' He was suddenly serious, as if revealing his faith. 'It's a great deal harder, I know, in peacetime. It requires courage. Courage of a different kind.'

Avery nodded. 'I'm sorry,' he said.

Haldane was watching him with distaste.

'What the Director means,' he said acidly, 'is that if you wish to stay in the Department and do the job, do it. If you wish to cultivate your emotions, go elsewhere and do so in peace. We are too old for your kind here.'

Avery could still hear Sarah's voice, see the rows of little houses hanging in the rain; he tried to imagine his life without the Department. He realized that it was too late, as it always had been, because he had gone to them for the little they could give him, and they had taken the little he had. Like a doubting cleric, he had felt that whatever his small heart contained was safely locked in the place of his retreat: now it was gone. He looked at Leclerc, then at Haldane. They were his colleagues. Prisoners of silence, the three of them would work side by side, breaking the arid land all four seasons of the year, strangers to each other, needing each other, in a wilderness of abandoned faith.

'Did you hear what I said?' Haldane demanded.

Avery muttered: 'Sorry.'

'You didn't fight in the war, John,' Leclerc said kindly. 'You don't understand how these things take people. You don't understand what real duty is.'

'I know,' said Avery. 'I'm sorry. I'd like to borrow the car for an hour . . . send something round to Sarah, if that's all right.'

'Of course.'

He realized he had forgotten Anthony's present. 'I'm sorry,' he said again.

'Incidentally—' Leclerc opened a drawer of the desk and took out an envelope. Indulgently he handed it to Avery. 'That's your pass, a special one from the Ministry. To identify yourself. It's in your own name. You may need it in the weeks to come.'

'Thanks.'

'Open it.'

It was a piece of thick pasteboard bound in cellophane, green, the colour washed downwards, darker at the bottom. His name was printed across it in capitals with an electric typewriter: Mr John Avery. The legend entitled the bearer to make inquiries on behalf of the Ministry. There was a signature in red ink.

'Thanks.'

'You're safe with that,' Leclerc said. 'The Minister signed it. He uses red ink, you know. It's tradition.'

He went back to his room. There were times when he confronted his own image as a man confronts an empty valley, and the vision propelled him forward again to experience, as despair compels us to extinction. Sometimes he was like a man in flight, but running towards the enemy, desperate to feel upon his vanishing body the blows that would prove his being; desperate to imprint upon his sad conformity the mark of real purpose, desperate perhaps, as Leclerc had hinted, to abdicate his conscience in order to discover God.

Part Three
LEISER'S RUN

'To turn as swimmers into cleanness leaping
Glad from a world grown old and cold and weary'
RUPERT BROOKE, *1914*

Chapter 10
Prelude

The Humber dropped Haldane at the garage.

'You needn't wait. You have to take Mr Leclerc to the Ministry.'

He picked his way reluctantly over the tarmac, past the yellow petrol pumps and the advertisement shields rattling in the wind. It was evening; there was rain about. The garage was small but very smart; showrooms one end, workshops the other, in the middle a tower where somebody lived. Swedish timber and open plan; lights on the tower in the shape of a heart, changing colour continuously. From somewhere came the whine of a metal lathe. Haldane went into the office. It was empty. There was a smell of rubber. He rang the bell and began coughing wretchedly. Sometimes when he coughed he held his chest, and his face betrayed the submissiveness of a man familiar with pain. Calendars with showgirls hung on the wall beside a small handwritten notice, like an amateur advertisement, which read, 'St Christopher and all his angels, please protect us from road accidents. F.L.' At the window a budgerigar fluttered nervously in its cage. The first drops of rain thumped lazily against the panes. A boy came in, about eighteen, his fingers black with engine oil. He wore an overall with a red heart sewn to the breast pocket with a crown above it.

'Good evening,' said Haldane. 'Forgive me. I'm looking for an old acquaintance; a friend. We knew one another long ago. A Mr Leiser. Fred Leiser. I wondered if you had any idea . . .'

'I'll get him,' the boy said, and disappeared.

Haldane waited patiently, looking at the calendars and wondering whether it was the boy or Leiser who had hung them there. The door opened a second time. It was Leiser. Haldane recognized him from his photograph. There was really very little change. The twenty years were not drawn in forceful lines but in tiny webs beside each eye, in marks of discipline around the mouth. The light above him was diffuse and cast no shadow. It was a face which at first sight recorded nothing but loneliness. Its complexion was pale.

'What can I do for you?' Leiser asked. He stood almost at attention.

'Hullo, I wonder if you remember me?'

Leiser looked at him as if he were being asked to name a price, blank but wary.

'Sure it was me?'

'Yes.'

'It must have been a long time ago,' he said at last. 'I don't often forget a face.'

'Twenty years.' Haldane coughed apologetically.

'In the war then, was it?'

He was a short man, very straight; in build he was not unlike Leclerc. He might have been a waiter. His sleeves were rolled up a little way, there was a lot of hair on the forearms. His shirt was white and expensive; a monogram on the pocket. He looked like a man who spent a good deal on his clothes. He wore a gold ring; a golden wristband to his watch. He took great care of his appearance; Haldane could smell the lotion on his skin. His long brown hair was full, the line along the forehead straight. Bulging a little at the sides, the hair was combed backwards. He wore no parting; the effect was definitely Slav. Though very upright, he had about him a certain swagger, a looseness of the hips and shoulders, which suggested a familiarity with the sea. It was here that any comparison with Leclerc abruptly ceased. He looked, despite himself, a practical man, handy in the house or starting the car on a cold day; and he looked an innocent man, but travelled. He wore a tartan tie.

'Surely you remember me?' Haldane pleaded.

Leiser stared at the thin cheeks, touched with points of high colour, at the hanging, restless body and the gently stirring hands, and there passed across his face a look of painful recognition, as if he were identifying the remains of a friend.

'You're not Captain Hawkins, are you?'

'That's right.'

'God Christ,' said Leiser, without moving. 'You're the people who've been asking about me.'

'We're looking for someone with your experience, a man like you.'

'What do you want him for, sir?'

He still hadn't moved. It was very hard to tell what he was thinking. His eyes were fixed on Haldane.

'To do a job, one job.'

Leiser smiled, as if it all came back to him. He nodded his head towards the window. 'Over there?' He meant somewhere beyond the rain.

'Yes.'

'What about getting back?'

'The usual rules. It's up to the man in the field. The war rules.'

He pushed his hands into his pockets, discovered cigarettes and a lighter. The budgerigar was singing.

'The war rules. You smoke?' He gave himself a cigarette and lit it, his hands cupped round the flame as if there were a high wind. He dropped the match on to the floor for someone else to pick up.

'God Christ,' he repeated. 'Twenty years. I was a kid in those days, just a kid.'

Haldane said, 'You don't regret it, I trust. Shall we go and have a drink?' He handed Leiser a card. It was newly printed: Captain A. Hawkins. Written underneath was a telephone number.

Leiser read it and shrugged. 'I don't mind,' he said and fetched his coat. Another smile, incredulous this time. 'But you're wasting your time, Captain.'

'Perhaps you know someone. Someone else from the war who might take it on.'

'I don't know a lot of people,' Leiser replied. He took a jacket from the peg and a nylon raincoat of dark blue. Going ahead of Haldane to the door, he opened it elaborately as if he valued formality. His hair was laid carefully upon itself like the wings of a bird.

There was a pub on the other side of the Avenue. They reached it by crossing a footbridge. The rush hour traffic thundered beneath them; the cold, plump raindrops seemed to go with it. The bridge trembled to the drumming of the cars. The pub was Tudor with new horse brasses and a ship's bell very highly polished. Leiser asked for a White Lady. He never drank anything else, he said. 'Stick to one drink, Captain, that's my advice. Then you'll be all right. Down the hatch.'

'It's got to be someone who knows the tricks,' Haldane observed. They sat in a corner near the fire. They might have been talking about trade. 'It's a very important job. They pay far more than in the war.' He gave a gaunt smile. 'They pay a lot of money these days.'

'Still, money's not everything, is it?' A stiff phrase, borrowed from the English.

'They remembered you. People whose names you've forgotten, if you even knew them.' An unconvincing smile of reminiscence crossed his thin lips: it might have been years since he had lied. 'You left quite an impression behind you, Fred; there weren't many as good as you. Even after twenty years.'

'They remember me then, the old crowd?' He seemed grateful for that, but shy, as if it were not his place to be held in memory. 'I was only a kid then,' he repeated. 'Who's there still, who's left?'

Haldane, watching him, said, 'I warned you: we play the same rules, Fred. *Need to know*, it's all the same.' It was very strict.

'God Christ,' Leiser declared. 'All the same. Big as ever, then, the outfit?'

'Bigger.' Haldane fetched another White Lady. 'Take much interest in politics?'

Leiser lifted a clean hand and let it fall.

'You know the way we are,' he said. 'In Britain, you know.' His voice carried the slightly impertinent assumption that he was as good as Haldane.

'I mean,' Haldane prompted, 'in a *broad* sense.' He coughed his dusty cough. 'After all, they took over your country, didn't they?' Leiser said nothing. 'What did you think of Cuba, for instance?'

Haldane did not smoke, but he had bought some cigarettes at the bar, the brand Leiser preferred. He removed the Cellophane with his slim, ageing fingers, and offered them across the table. Without waiting for an answer, he continued, 'The point was, you see, in the Cuba thing the Americans *knew*. It was a matter of information. Then they could act. Of course *they* made overflights. One can't always do that.' He gave another little laugh. 'One wonders what they would have done without them.'

'Yes, that's right.' He nodded his head like a dummy. Haldane paid no attention.

'They might have been stuck,' Haldane suggested and sipped his whisky. 'Are you married, by the way?'

Leiser grinned, held his hand out flat, tipped it briskly to left and right, like a man talking about aeroplanes. 'So, so,' he said. His tartan tie was fastened to his shirt with a heavy gold pin in

the shape of a riding crop against a horse's head. It was very
incongruous.

'How about you, Captain?'

Haldane shook his head.

'No,' Leiser observed thoughtfully. 'No.'

'Then there have been other occasions,' Haldane went on,
'where very serious mistakes were made because they hadn't the
right information, or not enough. I mean not even we can have
people permanently everywhere.'

'No, of course,' Leiser said politely.

The bar was filling up.

'I wonder whether you know of a different place where we
might talk?' Haldane inquired. 'We could eat, chat about some of
the old gang. Or have you another engagement?' The lower classes
eat early.

Leiser glanced at his watch. 'I'm all right till eight,' he said. 'You
want to do something about that cough, sir. It can be dangerous, a
cough like that.' The watch was of gold; it had a black face and a
compartment for indicating phases of the moon.

The Under Secretary, similarly conscious of the time, was bored
to be kept so late.

'I think I mentioned to you,' Leclerc was saying, 'that the
Foreign Office has been awfully sticky about providing operational passports. They've taken to consulting the Circus in every
case. We have no status, you understand; it's hard for me to make
myself unpleasant about these things – they have only the vaguest
notion of how we work. I wondered whether the best system
might not be for my Department to route passport requisitions
through your Private Office. That would save the bother of going
to the Circus every time.'

'What do you mean, sticky?'

'You will remember we sent poor Taylor out under another
name. The Office revoked his operational passport a matter of
hours before he left London. I fear the Circus made an administrative blunder. The passport which accompanied the body was therefore challenged on arrival in the United Kingdom. It gave us a lot
of trouble. I had to send one of my best men to sort it out,' he
lied. 'I'm sure that if the Minister insisted, Control would be quite
agreeable to a new arrangement.'

The Under Secretary jabbed a pencil at the door which led to
his Private Office. 'Talk to them in there. Work something out.

It sounds very stupid. Who do you deal with at the Office?'

'De Lisle,' said Leclerc with satisfaction, 'in General Department. He's the Assistant. And Smiley at the Circus.'

The Under Secretary wrote it down. 'One never knows *who* to talk to in that place; they're so top-heavy.'

'Then I may have to approach the Circus for technical resources. Wireless and that kind of thing. I propose to use a cover story for security reasons: a notional training scheme is the most appropriate.'

'Cover story? Ah yes: a lie. You mentioned it.'

'It's a precaution, no more.'

'You must do as you think fit.'

'I imagined you would prefer the Circus not to know. You said yourself: no monolith. I have proceeded on that assumption.'

The Under Secretary glanced again at the clock above the door. 'He's been in rather a difficult mood: a dreary day with the Yemen. I think it's partly the Woodbridge by-election: he gets so upset about the marginals. How's this thing going, by the way? It's been very worrying for him, you know. I mean, what's he to believe?' He paused. 'It's these Germans who terrify me . . . You mentioned you'd found a fellow who fitted the bill.' They moved to the corridor.

'We're on to him now. We've got him in play. We shall know tonight.'

The Under Secretary wrinkled his nose very slightly, his hand on the Minister's door. He was a churchman and disliked irregular things.

'What makes a man take on a job like that? Not you; him, I mean.'

Leclerc shook his head in silence, as if the two of them were in close sympathy. 'Heaven knows. It's something we don't even understand ourselves.'

'What kind of person is he? What sort of class? Only generally, you appreciate.'

'Intelligent. Self-educated. Polish extraction.'

'Oh, I see.' He seemed relieved. 'We'll keep it gentle, shall we? Don't paint it too black. He loathes drama. I mean any fool can see what the *dangers* are.'

They went in.

Haldane and Leiser took their places at a corner table, like lovers in a coffee bar. It was one of those restaurants which rely on empty Chianti bottles for their charm and on very little else for their custom. It would be gone tomorrow, or the next day, and scarcely anyone would notice, but while it was there and new and full of hope, it was not at all bad. Leiser had steak, it seemed to be habit, and sat primly while he ate it, his elbows firmly at his side.

At first Haldane pretended to ignore the purpose of his visit. He talked badly about the war and the Department; about operations he had half forgotten until that afternoon, when he had refreshed his memory from the files. He spoke – no doubt it seemed desirable – mainly of those who had survived.

He referred to the courses Leiser had attended; had he kept up his interest in radio at all? Well, no, as a matter of fact. How about unarmed combat? There hadn't been the opportunity, really.

'You had one or two rough moments in the war, I remember,' Haldane prompted. 'Didn't you have some trouble in Holland?' They were back to vanity and old times' sake.

A stiff nod. 'I had a spot of trouble,' he conceded. 'I was younger then.'

'What happened exactly?'

Leiser looked at Haldane, blinking, as if the other had woken him, then began to talk. It was one of those wartime stories which have been told with variations since war began, as remote from the neat little restaurant as hunger or poverty, less credible for being articulate. He seemed to tell it at second hand. It might have been a big fight he had heard on the wireless. He had been caught, he had escaped, he had lived for days without food, he had killed, been taken into refuge and smuggled back to England. He told it well; perhaps it was what the war meant to him now, perhaps it was true, but as with a Latin widow relating the manner of her husband's death, the passion had gone out of his heart and into the telling. He seemed to speak because he had been told to; his affectations, unlike Leclerc's, were designed less to impress others than to protect himself. He seemed a very private man whose speech was exploratory; a man who had been a long time alone and had not reckoned with society; poised, not settled. His accent was good but exclusively foreign, lacking the slur and the elision which escapes even gifted imitators; a voice familiar with its environment, but not at home there.

Haldane listened courteously. When it was over he asked, 'How did they pick you up in the first place, do you know?' The space between them was very great.

'They never told me,' he said blankly, as if it were not proper to inquire.

'Of course you *are* the man we need. You've got the German background, if you understand me. You know them, don't you; you have the German experience.'

'Only from the war,' Leiser said.

They talked about the training school. 'How's that fat one? George somebody. Little sad bloke.'

'Oh . . . he's well, thank you.'

'He married a pretty girl.' He laughed obscenely, raising his right forearm in an Arab gesture of sexual prowess. 'God Christ,' he said, laughing again. 'Us little blokes! Go for anything.' It was an extraordinary lapse. It seemed to be what Haldane had been waiting for.

He watched Leiser for a long time. The silence became remarkable. Deliberately he stood up; he seemed suddenly very angry; angry at Leiser's silly grin and this whole cheap, incompetent flirtation; at these meaningless repetitive blasphemies and this squalid derision of a person of quality.

'Do you mind not saying that? George Smiley happens to be a friend of mine.'

He called the waiter and paid the bill, stalked quickly from the restaurant, leaving Leiser bewildered and alone, his White Lady held delicately in his hand, his brown eyes turned anxiously towards the doorway through which Haldane had so abruptly vanished.

Eventually he left, making his way back by the footbridge, slowly through the dark and the rain, staring down on the double alley of streetlamps and the traffic passing between them. Across the road was his garage, the line of illuminated pumps, the tower crowned with its neon heart of sixty-watt bulbs alternating green and red. He entered the brightly lit office, said something to the boy, walked slowly upstairs towards the blare of music.

Haldane waited till he had disappeared from sight, then hurried back to the restaurant to order a taxi.

She had put the gramophone on. She was listening to dance music, sitting in his chair, drinking.

'Christ, you're late,' she said. 'I'm starving.'

He kissed her.

'You've eaten,' she said. 'I can smell the food.'

'Just a snack, Bett. I had to. A man called; we had a drink.'

'Liar.'

He smiled. 'Come off it, Betty. We've got a dinner date, remember?'

'What man?'

The flat was very clean. Curtains and carpets were flowered, the polished surfaces protected with lace. Everything was protected; vases, lamps, ashtray, all were carefully guarded, as if Leiser expected nothing from nature but stark collision. He favoured a suggestion of the antique: it was reflected in the scrolled wood-work of the furniture and the wrought iron of the lamp brackets. He had a mirror framed in gold and a picture made of fretwork and plaster; a new clock with weights which turned in a glass case.

When he opened the cocktail cabinet it played a brief tune on a music box.

He mixed himself a White Lady, carefully, like a man making up medicine. She watched him, moving her hips to the record, holding her glass away to one side as if it were her partner's hand, and the partner were not Leiser.

'What man?' she repeated.

He stood at the window, straight-backed like a soldier. The flashing heart on the roof played over the houses, caught the staves of the bridge and quivered in the wet surface of the Avenue. Beyond the houses was the church, like a cinema with a spire, fluted brick with vents where the bells rang. Beyond the church was the sky. Sometimes he thought the church was all that remained, and the London sky was lit with the glow of a burning city.

'Christ, you're really gay tonight.'

The church bells were recorded, much amplified to drown the noise of traffic. He sold a lot of petrol on Sundays. The rain was running harder against the road; he could see it shading the beams of the car lights, dancing green and red on the tarmac.

'Come on, Fred, dance.'

'Just a minute, Bett.'

'Oh, for Christ's sake, what's the matter with you? Have another drink and forget it.'

He could hear her feet shuffling across the carpet to the music; the tireless jingle of her charm bracelet.

'Dance, for Christ's sake.'

She had a slurred way of talking, slackly dragging the last syllable of a sentence beyond its natural length; it was the same calculated disenchantment with which she gave herself, sullenly, as if she were giving money, as if men had all the pleasure and women the pain.

She stopped the record, careless as she pulled the arm. The needle scratched in the loudspeaker.

'Look, what the hell goes on?'

'Nothing, I tell you. I've just had a hard day, that's all. Then this man called, somebody I used to know.'

'I keep asking you: who? Some woman, wasn't it? Some tart.'

'No, Betty, it was a man.'

She came to the window, nudging him indifferently. 'What's so bloody marvellous about the view, anyway? Just a lot of rotten little houses. You always said you hated them. Well, who was it?'

'He's from one of the big companies.'

'And they want you?'

'Yes . . . they want to make me an offer.'

'Christ, who'd want a bloody Pole?'

He hardly stirred. 'They do.'

'Someone came to the bank, you know, asking about you. They all sat together in Mr Dawnay's office. You're in trouble, aren't you?'

He took her coat and helped her into it, very correct, elbows wide.

She said: 'Not that new place with waiters, for Christ's sake.'

'It's nice there, isn't it? I thought you fancied it there. You can dance too; you like that. Where do you want to go then?'

'With you? For Christ's sake! Somewhere where there's a bit of life, that's all.'

He stared at her. He was holding the door open. Suddenly he smiled.

'OK, Bett. It's your night. Slip down and start the car, I'll book a table.' He gave her the key. 'I know a place, a real place.'

'What the hell's come over you now?'

'You can drive. We'll have a night out.' He went to the telephone.

It was shortly before eleven when Haldane returned to the Department. Leclerc and Avery were waiting for him. Carol was typing in the Private Office.

'I thought you'd be here earlier,' Leclerc said.

'It's no good. He said he wouldn't play. I think you'd better try the next one yourself. It's not my style any more.' He seemed undisturbed. He sat down. They stared at him incredulously.

'Did you offer money?' Leclerc asked finally. 'We have clearance for five thousand pounds.'

'Of course I offered money. I tell you he's just not interested. He was a singularly unpleasant person.'

'I'm sorry.' He didn't say why.

They could hear the tapping of Carol's typewriter. Leclerc said, 'Where do we go from here?'

'I have no idea.' He glanced restlessly at his watch.

'There must be others, there must be.'

'Not on our cards. Not with his qualifications. There are Belgians, Swedes, Frenchmen. But Leiser was the only German speaker with technical experience. On paper, he's the only one.'

'Still young enough. Is that what you mean?'

'I suppose so. It would have to be an old hand. We haven't the time to train a new man, nor the facilities. We'd better ask the Circus. They'll have someone.'

'We can't do that,' Avery said.

'What kind of man was he?' Leclerc persisted, reluctant to abandon hope.

'Common, in a Slav way. Small. He plays the Rittmeister. It's most unattractive.' He was looking in his pockets for the bill. 'He dresses like a bookie, but I suppose they all do that. Do I give this to you or Accounts?'

'Secure?'

'I don't see why not.'

'And you spoke about the urgency? New loyalties and that kind of thing?'

'He found the old loyalties more attractive.' He put the bill on the table.

'And politics . . . some of these exiles are very . . .'

'We spoke about politics. He's not that sort of exile. He considers himself integrated, naturalized British. What do you expect him to do? Swear allegiance to the Polish royal house?' Again he looked at his watch.

'You never wanted to recruit him!' Leclerc cried, angered by Haldane's indifference. 'You're pleased, Adrian, I can see it in your face! Good God, what about the Department! Didn't that mean anything to him? You don't believe in it any more, you don't care! You're sneering at me!'

'Who of us does believe?' asked Haldane with contempt. 'You said yourself: we do the job.'

'I believe,' Avery declared.

Haldane was about to speak when the green telephone rang.

'That will be the Ministry,' Leclerc said. 'Now what do I tell them?' Haldane was watching him.

He picked up the receiver, put it to his ear then handed it across the table. 'It's the exchange. Why on earth did they come through on green? Somebody asking for Captain Hawkins. That's you, isn't it?'

Haldane listened, his thin face expressionless. Finally he said, 'I imagine so. We'll find someone. There should be no difficulty. Tomorrow at eleven. Kindly be punctual,' and rang off. The light in Leclerc's room seemed to ebb towards the thinly curtained window. The rain fell ceaselessly outside.

'That was Leiser. He's decided he'll do the job. He wants to know whether we can find someone to take care of his garage while he's away.'

Leclerc looked at him in astonishment. Pleasure spread comically over his face. 'You expected it!' he cried. He stretched out his small hand. 'I'm sorry, Adrian. I misjudged you. I congratulate you warmly.'

'Why did he accept?' Avery asked excitedly. 'What made him change his mind?'

'Why do agents ever do anything? Why do any of us?' Haldane sat down. He looked old but inviolate, like a man whose friends had already died. 'Why do they consent or refuse, why do they lie or tell the truth? Why do any of us?' He began coughing again. 'Perhaps he's under-employed. It's the Germans: he hates them. That's what he says. I place no value on that. Then he said he couldn't let us down. I assume he means himself.'

To Leclerc he added, 'The war rules: that was right, wasn't it?'

But Leclerc was dialling the Ministry.

Avery went into the Private Office. Carol was standing up.

'What's going on?' she said quickly. 'What's the excitement?'

'It's Leiser.' Avery closed the door behind him. 'He's agreed to go.' He stretched out his arms to embrace her. It would be the first time.

'Why?'

'Hatred of the Germans, he says. My guess is money.'

'Is that a good thing?'

Avery grinned knowingly. 'As long as we pay him more than the other side.'

'Shouldn't you go back to your wife?' she said sharply. 'I can't believe you need to sleep here.'

'It's operational.' Avery went to his room. She did not say goodnight.

★   ★   ★

Leiser put down the telephone. It was suddenly very quiet. The lights on the roof went out, leaving the room in darkness. He went quickly downstairs. He was frowning, as if his entire mental force were concentrated on the prospect of eating a second dinner.

Chapter 11

They chose Oxford as they had done in the war. The variety of nationalities and occupations, the constant coming and going of visiting academics and the resultant anonymity, the proximity of open country, all perfectly suited their needs. Besides, it was a place they could understand. The morning after Leiser had rung, Avery went ahead to find a house. The following day he telephoned Haldane to say he had taken one for a month in the north of the town, a large Victorian affair with four bedrooms and a garden. It was very expensive. It was known in the Department as the Mayfly house and carded under Live Amenities.

As soon as Haldane heard, he told Leiser. At Leiser's suggestion it was agreed that he should put it about that he was attending a course in the Midlands.

'Don't give any details,' Haldane had said. 'Have your mail sent *post restante* to Coventry. We'll get it picked up from there.' Leiser was pleased when he heard it was Oxford.

Leclerc and Woodford had searched desperately for someone to run the garage in Leiser's absence; suddenly they thought of McCulloch. Leiser gave him power of attorney and spent a hasty morning showing him the ropes. 'We'll offer you some kind of guarantee in return,' Haldane said.

'I don't need it,' Leiser replied, explaining quite seriously, 'I'm working for English gentlemen.'

On the Friday night Leiser had telephoned his consent; by the Wednesday preparations were sufficiently advanced for Leclerc to convene a meeting of Special Section and outline his plans. Avery and Haldane were to be with Leiser in Oxford; the two of them would leave the following evening, by which time he understood that Haldane would be ready with his syllabus. Leiser would arrive in Oxford a day or two later, as soon as his own arrangements were complete. Haldane was to supervise his training, Avery to act as Haldane's assistant. Woodford would remain in London.

Among his tasks was that of consulting with the Ministry (and Sandford of Research) in order to assemble instructional material on the external specifications of short- and medium-range rockets, and thus provided come himself to Oxford.

Leclerc had been tireless, now at the Ministry to report on progress, now at the Treasury to argue the case for Taylor's widow, now, with Woodford's aid, engaging former instructors in wireless transmission, photography and unarmed combat.

Such time as remained to Leclerc he devoted to Mayfly Zero: the moment at which Leiser was to be infiltrated into Eastern Germany. At first he seemed to have no firm idea of how this was to be done. He talked vaguely of a sea operation from Denmark; small fishing craft and a rubber dinghy to evade radar detection; he discussed illegal frontier crossing with Sandford and telegraphed Gorton for information on the border area round Lübeck. In veiled terms he even consulted the Circus. Control was remarkably helpful.

All this took place in that atmosphere of heightened activity and optimism which Avery had observed on his return. Even those who were kept, supposedly, in ignorance of the operation were infected by the air of crisis. The little lunch group that gathered daily at a corner table of the Cadena café was alive with rumours and speculation. It was said, for instance, that a man named Johnson, known in the war as Jack Johnson, a wireless instructor, had been taken on to the strength of the Department. Accounts had paid him subsistence and – most intriguing of all – they had been asked to draft a three-month contract for submission to the Treasury. Who ever heard, they asked, of a three-month contract? Johnson had been concerned with the French drops during the war; a senior girl remembered him. Berry, the cypher clerk, had asked Mr Woodford what Johnson was up to (Berry was always the cheeky one) and Mr Woodford had grinned and told him to mind his own business, but it was for an operation, he'd said, a very secret one they were running in Europe . . . northern Europe, as a matter of fact, and it might interest Berry to know that poor Taylor had not died in vain.

There was now a ceaseless traffic of cars and Ministry messengers in the front drive; Pine requested and received from another Government establishment a junior whom he treated with sovereign brutality. In some oblique way he had learnt that Germany was the target, and the knowledge made him diligent.

It was even rumoured among the local tradesmen that the Ministry House was changing hands; private buyers were named and great hopes placed upon their custom. Meals were sent for at all hours, lights burned day and night; the front door, hitherto permanently sealed for reasons of security, was opened, and the sight of Leclerc with bowler hat and briefcase entering his black Humber became a familiar one in Blackfriars Road.

And Avery, like an injured man who would not look at his own wound, slept within the walls of his little office, so that they became the boundary of his life. Once he sent out Carol to buy Anthony a present. She came back with a toy milk lorry with plastic bottles. You could lift the caps off and fill the bottles with water. They tried it out one evening, then sent it round to Battersea in the Humber.

When all was ready Haldane and Avery travelled to Oxford first class on a Ministry Warrant. At dinner on the train they had a table to themselves. Haldane ordered half a bottle of wine and drank it while he completed *The Times* crossword. They sat in silence, Haldane occupied, Avery too diffident to interrupt him.

Suddenly Avery noticed Haldane's tie; before he had time to think, he said, 'Good Lord, I never knew you were a cricketer.'

'Did you expect me to tell you?' Haldane snapped. 'I could hardly wear it in the Office.'

'I'm sorry.'

Haldane looked at him closely. 'You shouldn't apologize so much,' he observed. 'You both do it.' He helped himself to some coffee and ordered a brandy. Waiters noticed Haldane.

'Both?'

'You and Leiser. He does it by implication.'

'It's going to be different with Leiser, isn't it?' Avery said quickly. 'Leiser's a professional.'

'Leiser is not one of us. Never make that mistake. We touched him long ago, that's all.'

'What's he like? What sort of man is he?'

'He's an agent. He's a man to be handled, not known.'

He returned to his crossword.

'He must be loyal,' Avery said. 'Why else would he accept?'

'You heard what the Director said: the two vows. The first is often quite frivolously taken.'

'And the second?'

'Ah, that is different. We shall be there to help him take it.'

'But why did he accept the first time?'

'I mistrust reasons. I mistrust words like loyalty. And above all,' Haldane declared, 'I mistrust *motive*. We're running an agent; the arithmetic is over. You read German, didn't you? In the beginning was the deed.'

Shortly before they arrived Avery ventured one more question. 'Why *was* that passport out of date?'

Haldane had a way of inclining his head when addressed.

'The Foreign Office used to allocate a series of passport numbers to the Department for operational purposes. The arrangement ran from year to year. Six months ago the Office said they wouldn't issue any more without reference to the Circus. It seems Leclerc had been making insufficient claims on the facility and Control cut him out of the market. Taylor's passport was one of the old series. They revoked the whole lot three days before he left. There was no time to do anything about it. It might never have been noticed. The Circus has been very devious.' A pause. 'Indeed I find it hard to understand what Control *is* up to.'

They took a taxi to North Oxford and got out at the corner of their road. As they walked along the pavement Avery looked at the houses in the half darkness, glimpsed grey-haired figures moving across the lighted windows, velvet-covered chairs trimmed with lace, Chinese screens, music stands and a bridge-four sitting like bewitched courtiers in a castle. It was a world he had known about once; for a time he had almost fancied he was part of it; but that was long ago.

They spent the evening preparing the house. Haldane said Leiser should have the rear bedroom overlooking the garden, they themselves would take the rooms on the street side. He had sent some academic books in advance, a typewriter and some imposing files. These he unpacked and arranged on the dining-room table for the benefit of the landlord's housekeeper who would come each day. 'We shall call this room the study,' he said. In the drawing-room he installed a tape-recorder.

He had some tapes which he locked in a cupboard, meticulously adding the key to his key ring. Other luggage was still waiting in the hall: a projector, Air Force issue, a screen, and a suitcase of green canvas, securely fastened, with leather corners.

The house was spacious and well kept; the furniture was of mahogany, with brass inlay. The walls were filled with pictures of some unknown family: sketches in sepia, miniatures, photographs faded with age. There was a bowl of pot-pourri on the sideboard and a palm cross pinned to the mirror; chandeliers hung from the ceiling, clumsy, but inoffensive; in one corner, a bible table; in another a small cupid, very ugly, its face turned to the dark. The whole house gently asserted an air of old age; it had a quality, like incense, of courteous but inconsolable sadness.

By midnight they had finished unpacking. They sat down in the drawing-room. The marble fireplace was supported by blacka-moors of ebony; the light of the gas fire played over the gilded rose-chains which linked their thick ankles. The fireplace came from an age, it might have been the seventeenth century, it might have been the nineteenth, when blackamoors had briefly replaced borzois as the decorative beasts of society; they were quite naked, as a dog might be, and chained with golden roses. Avery gave himself a whisky, then went to bed, leaving Haldane sunk in his own thoughts.

His room was large and dark; above the bed hung a light shade of blue china; there were embroidered covers on the tables and a small enamelled notice saying, 'God's blessing on this house'; beside the window a picture of a child saying its prayers while his sister ate breakfast in bed.

He lay awake, wondering about Leiser; it was like waiting for a girl. From across the passage he could hear Haldane's solitary cough, on and on. It had not ended when he fell asleep.

Leclerc thought Smiley's club a very strange place; not at all the kind of thing he had expected. Two half-basement rooms and a dozen people dining at separate tables before a large fire. Some of them were vaguely familiar. He suspected they were connected with the Circus.

'This is rather a good spot. How do you join?'

'Oh, you don't,' said Smiley apologetically, then blushed and continued, 'I mean, they don't have new members. Just one gener-ation . . . several went in the war, you know, some have died or gone abroad. What was it you had in mind, I wonder?'

'You were good enough to help young Avery out.'

'Yes . . . yes of course. How did that go, by the way? I never heard.'

'It was just a training run. There was no film in the end.'

'I'm sorry,' Smiley spoke hastily, covering up, as if someone were dead and he had not known.

'We didn't really expect there would be. It was just a precaution. How much did Avery tell you, I wonder? We're training up one or two of the old hands . . . and some of the new boys too. It's something to do,' Leclerc explained, 'during the slack season . . . Christmas, you know. People on leave.'

'I know.'

Leclerc noticed that the claret was very good. He wished he had joined a smaller club; his own had gone off terribly. They had such difficulty with staff.

'You have probably heard,' Leclerc added, officially, as it were, 'that Control has offered me full assistance for training purposes.'

'Yes, yes, of course.'

'My Minister was the moving spirit. He likes the idea of a pool of trained agents. When the plan was first mooted I went and spoke to Control myself. Later, Control called on me. You knew that, perhaps?'

'Yes. Control wondered . . .'

'He has been most helpful. Don't think I am unappreciative. It has been agreed – I think I should give you the background, your own office will confirm it – that if the training is to be effective, we must create as nearly as possible an operational atmosphere. What we used to call battle conditions.' An indulgent smile. 'We've chosen an area in Western Germany. It's bleak and unfamiliar ground, ideal for frontier crossing exercises and that kind of thing. We can ask for the Army's co-operation if we need it.'

'Yes, indeed. What a good idea.'

'For elementary reasons of security, we all accept that your office should only be briefed in the aspects of this exercise in which you are good enough to help.'

'Control told me,' said Smiley. 'He wants to do whatever he can. He didn't know you touched this kind of thing any more. He was pleased.'

'Good,' Leclerc said shortly. He moved his elbows forward a little across the polished table. 'I thought I might pick your brains . . . quite informally. Rather as you people from time to time have made use of Adrian Haldane.'

'Of course.'

'The first thing is false documents. I looked up our old forgers in the index. I see Hyde and Fellowby went over to the Circus some years ago.'

'Yes. It was the change in emphasis.'

'I've written down a personal description of a man in our employment; he is supposedly resident at Magdeburg for the purposes of the scheme. One of the men under training. Do you think they could prepare documents, Identity Card, Party Membership and that kind of thing? Whatever is necessary.'

'The man would have to sign them,' Smiley said. 'We would then stamp on top of his signature. We'd need photographs too.

He'd have to be briefed on how the documents worked; perhaps Hyde could do that on the spot with your agent?'

A slight hesitation. 'No doubt. I have selected a cover name. It closely approximates his own; we find that a useful technique.'

'I might just make the point,' Smiley said, with a rather comic frown, 'since this is such an *elaborate* exercise, that forged papers are of very *limited* value. I mean, one telephone call to the Magdeburg Town Administration and the best forgery in the world is blown sky high . . .'

'I think we know about that. We want to teach them cover, submit them to interrogation . . . you know the kind of thing.'

Smiley sipped his claret. 'I just thought I'd make the point. It's so easy to get hypnotized by *technique*. I didn't mean to imply . . . How is Haldane, by the way? He read Greats, you know. We were up together.'

'Adrian is well.'

'I liked your Avery,' Smiley said politely. His heavy small face contracted in pain. 'Do you realize,' he asked impressively, 'they *still* don't include the Baroque period in the German syllabus? They call it a special subject.'

'Then there is the question of clandestine wireless. We haven't used that kind of thing much since the war. I understand it has all become a great deal more sophisticated. Highspeed transmission and so on. We want to keep up with the times.'

'Yes. Yes, I believe the message is taped on a miniature recorder and sent over the air in a matter of seconds.' He sighed. 'But no one really tells us much. The technical people hold their cards very close to their chests.'

'Is that a method in which our people could profitably be trained . . . in a month, say?'

'And use under operational conditions?' Smiley asked in astonishment. 'Straight away, after a month's training?'

'Some are technically minded, you understand. People with wireless experience.'

Smiley was watching Leclerc incredulously. 'Forgive me. Would he, would they,' he inquired, 'have *other* things to learn in that month as well?'

'For some it's more a refresher course.'

'Ah.'

'What do you mean?'

'Nothing, nothing,' Smiley said vaguely and added, 'I don't *think* our technical people would be very keen to part with this kind of equipment unless . . .'

'Unless it were their own training operation?'

'Yes,' Smiley blushed. 'Yes, that's what I mean. They're very particular, you know; jealous.'

Leclerc lapsed into silence, lightly tapping the base of his wine glass on the polished surface of the table. Suddenly he smiled and said, as if he had shaken off depression, 'Oh well. We shall just have to use a conventional set. Have direction-finding methods also improved since the war? Interception, location of an illegal transmitter?'

'Oh yes. Yes, indeed.'

'We would have to incorporate that. How long can a man remain on the air before they spot him?'

'Two or three minutes, perhaps. It depends. Often it's a matter of luck how soon they hear him. They can only pin him down while he's transmitting. Much depends on the frequency. Or so they tell me.'

'In the war,' said Leclerc reflectively, 'we gave an agent several crystals. Each vibrated at a fixed frequency. Every so often he changed the crystal; that was usually a safe enough method. We could do that again.'

'Yes. Yes, I remember that. But there was the headache of retuning the transmitter . . . possibly changing the coil . . . matching the aerial.'

'Suppose a man is used to a conventional set. You tell me the chances of interception are greater now than they were in the war? You say allow two or three minutes?'

'Or less,' said Smiley, watching him. 'It depends on a lot of things . . . luck, reception, amount of signal traffic, density of population . . .'

'Supposing he changed his frequency after every two and a half minutes on the air. Surely that would meet the case?'

'It could be a slow business.' His sad, unhealthy face was wrinkled in concern. 'You're quite sure this *is* only training?'

'As far as I remember,' Leclerc persisted, courting his own idea, 'these crystals are the size of a small matchbox. We could give them several. We're only aiming at a few transmissions; perhaps only three or four. Would you consider my suggestion impractical?'

'It's hardly my province.'

'What is the alternative? I asked Control; he said speak to you. He said you'd help, find me the equipment. What else can I do? Can I *talk* to your technical people?'

'I'm sorry. Control rather agreed with the technical side, that we should give all the help we can, but not compromise new equipment. *Risk* compromising it, I mean. After all, it *is* only training. I think he felt that if you hadn't full technical resources you should . . .'

'Hand over the commitment?'

'No, no,' Smiley protested, but Leclerc interrupted him. 'These people would eventually be used against military targets,' he said angrily. 'Purely military. Control accepts that.'

'Oh quite.' He seemed to have given up. 'And if you want a conventional set, no doubt we can dig one up.'

The waiter brought a decanter of port. Leclerc watched Smiley pour a little into his glass, then slide the decanter carefully across the polished table.

'It's quite good, but I'm afraid it's nearly finished. When this is gone we shall have to break into the younger ones. I'm seeing Control first thing tomorrow. I'm sure he'll have no objection. About the documents, I mean. And crystals. We could advise you on frequencies, I'm sure. Control made a point of that.'

'Control's been very good,' Leclerc confessed. He was slightly drunk. 'It puzzles me sometimes.'

Chapter 12

Two days later, Leiser arrived at Oxford. They waited anxiously for him on the platform, Haldane peering among the hurrying faces in the crowd. It was Avery, curiously, who saw him first: a motionless figure in a camel-hair coat at the window of an empty compartment.

'Is that him?' Avery asked.

'He's travelling first class. He must have paid the difference.' Haldane spoke as if it were an affront.

Leiser lowered the window and handed out two pigskin cases shaped for the boot of a car, a little too orange for nature. They greeted one another briskly, shaking hands for everyone to see. Avery wanted to carry the luggage to the taxi, but Leiser preferred to take it himself, a piece in each hand, as if it were his duty. He walked a little away from them, shoulders back, staring at the people as they went by, startled by the crowd. His long hair bounced with each step.

Avery, watching him, felt suddenly disturbed.

He was a man; not a shadow. A man with force to his body and purpose to his movement, but somehow theirs to direct. There seemed to be nowhere he would not walk. He was recruited; and had assumed already the anxious, brisk manner of an enlisted man. Yet, Avery accepted, no single factor wholly accounted for Leiser's recruitment. Avery was already familiar, during his short association with the Department, with the phenomenon of organic motivation; with operations which had no discernible genesis and no conclusion, which formed part of an unending pattern of activity until they ceased to have any further identity; with that progress of fruitless courtships which, in the aggregate, passed for an active love life. But as he observed this man bobbing beside him, animate and quick, he recognized that hitherto they had courted ideas, incestuously among themselves; now they had a human being upon their hands, and this was he.

They climbed into the taxi, Leiser last because he insisted. It was mid-afternoon, a slate sky behind the plane trees. The smoke rose from the North Oxford chimneys in ponderous columns like proof of a virtuous sacrifice. The houses were of a modest stateliness; romantic hulls redecked, each according to a different legend. Here the turrets of Avalon, there the carved trellis of a pagoda; between them the monkey-puzzle trees, and the half-hidden washing like butterflies in the wrong season. The houses sat decently in their own gardens, the curtains drawn, first lace and then brocade, petticoats and skirts. It was like a bad water colour, the dark things drawn too heavy, the sky grey and soiled in the dusk, the paint too worked.

They dismissed the taxi at the corner of the street. A smell of leaf mould lingered in the air. If there were children they made no noise. The three men walked to the gate. Leiser, his eyes on the house, put down his suitcases.

'Nice place,' he said with appreciation. He turned to Avery: 'Who chose it?'

'I did.'

'That's nice.' He patted his shoulder. 'You did a good job.' Avery, pleased, smiled and opened the gate; Leiser was determined that the others should pass through first. They took him upstairs and showed him his room. He still carried his own luggage.

'I'll unpack later,' he said. 'I like to make a proper job of it.'

He walked through the house in a critical way, picking things up and looking at them; he might have come to bid for the place.

'It's a nice spot,' he repeated finally; 'I like it.'

'Good,' said Haldane, as if he didn't give a damn.

Avery went with him to his room to see if he could help.

'What's your name?' Leiser asked. He was more at ease with Avery; more vulgar.

'John.'

They shook hands again.

'Well, hullo, John; glad to meet you. How old are you?'

'Thirty-four,' he lied.

A wink. 'Christ, I wish I was thirty-four. Done this kind of thing before, have you?'

'I finished my own run last week.'

'How did it go?'

'Fine.'

'That's the boy. Where's your room?'

Avery showed him.

'Tell me, what's the set-up here?'

'What do you mean?'

'Who's in charge?'

'Captain Hawkins.'

'Anyone else?'

'Not really. I shall be around.'

'All the time?'

'Yes.'

He began unpacking. Avery watched. He had brushes backed with leather, hair lotion, a whole range of little bottles of things for men, an electric shaver of the newest kind and ties, some in tartan, others in silk, to match his costly shirts. Avery went downstairs. Haldane was waiting. He smiled as Avery came in. 'Well?'

Avery shrugged, too big a gesture. He felt elated, ill at ease. 'What do *you* make of him?' he asked.

'I hardly know him,' Haldane said drily. He had a way of terminating conversations. 'I want you to be always in his company. Walk with him, shoot with him, drink with him if you must. He's not to be alone.'

'What about his leave in between?'

'We'll see about that. Meanwhile, do as I say. You will find he enjoys your company. He's a very *lonely* man. And remember he's British: British to the core. One more thing – this is most important – do not let him think we have changed since the war. The Department has remained exactly as it was: that is an illusion you must foster even' – he did not smile – 'even though you are too young to make the comparison.'

They began next morning. Breakfast over, they assembled in the drawing-room and Haldane addressed them.

The training would be divided into two periods of a fortnight each, with a short rest in between. The first was to be a refresher course; in the second, old skills, now revived, would be related to the task which lay ahead. Not until the second period would Leiser be told his operational name, his cover and the nature of his mission; even then, the information would reveal neither the target area nor the means by which he was to be infiltrated.

In communications as in all other aspects of his training he would graduate from the general to the particular. In the first period he would familiarize himself once more with the technique of cyphers, signal plans and schedules. In the second he would spend much time actually transmitting under semi-operational conditions. The instructor would arrive during that week.

Haldane explained all this with pedagogic acrimony while Leiser listened carefully, now and then briskly nodding his assent. Avery found it strange that Haldane took so little care to conceal his distaste.

'In the first period we shall see what you remember. We shall give you a lot of running about, I'm afraid. We want to get you fit. There'll be small arms training, unarmed combat, mental exercises, tradecraft. We shall try to take you walking in the afternoons.'

'Who with? Will John come?'

'Yes. John will take you. You should regard John as your adviser on all minor matters. If there is anything you wish to discuss, any complaint or anxiety, I trust you will not hesitate to mention it to either one of us.'

'All right.'

'On the whole, I must ask you not to venture out alone. I should prefer John to accompany you if you wish to go to the cinema, do some shopping or whatever else the time allows. But I fear you may not have much chance of recreation.'

'I don't expect it,' Leiser said; 'I don't need it.' He seemed to mean he didn't want it.

'The wireless instructor, when he comes, will not know your name. That is a customary precaution: please observe it. The daily woman believes we are participating in an academic conference. I cannot imagine you will have occasion to talk to her, but if you do, remember that. If you wish to make inquiries about your business, kindly consult me first. You should not telephone without my consent. Then there will be other visitors: photographers, medical people, technicians. They are what we call ancillaries and are not in the picture. Most of them believe you're here as part of a wider training scheme. Please remember this.'

'OK,' said Leiser. Haldane looked at his watch.

'Our first appointment is at ten o'clock. A car will collect us from the corner of the road. The driver is not one of us: no conversation on the journey, please. Have you no other clothes?' he asked. 'Those are scarcely suitable for the range.'

'I've got a sports coat and a pair of flannels.'

'I could wish you less conspicuous.'

As they went upstairs to change, Leiser smiled wryly at Avery. 'He's a real boy, isn't he? The old school.'

'But good,' Avery said.

Leiser stopped. 'Of course. Here, tell me something. Was this place always here? Have you used it for many people?'

'You're not the first,' Avery said.

'Look, I know you can't tell me much. Is the outfit still like it was . . . people everywhere . . . the same set-up?'

'I don't think you'd find much difference. I suppose we've expanded a bit.'

'Are there many young ones like you?'

'Sorry, Fred.'

Leiser put his open hand on Avery's back. He used his hands a lot.

'You're good, too,' he said. 'Don't bother about me. Not to worry, eh, John?'

They went to Abingdon: the Ministry had made arrangements with the parachute base. The instructor was expecting them.

'Used to any particular gun, are you?'

'Browning three-eight automatic, please,' Leiser said, like a child ordering groceries.

'We call it the nine-millimetre now. You'll have had the Mark One.'

Haldane stood in the gallery at the back while Avery helped wind in the man-sized target to a distance of ten yards and paste squares of gum-strip over the old holes.

'You call me "Staff",' the instructor said and turned to Avery. 'Like to have a go as well, sir?'

Haldane put in quickly, 'Yes, they are both shooting, please, Staff.'

Leiser took first turn. Avery stood beside Haldane while Leiser, his long back towards them, waited in the empty range, facing the plywood figure of a German soldier. The target was black, framed against the crumbling whitewash of the walls; over its belly and groin a heart had been crudely described in chalk, its interior extensively repaired with fragments of paper. As they watched, he began testing the weight of the gun, raising it quickly to the level of his eye, then lowering it slowly; pushing home the empty magazine, taking it out and thrusting it in again. He glanced over his shoulder at Avery, with his left hand brushing from his forehead a strand of brown hair which threatened to impede his view. Avery smiled encouragement, then said quickly to Haldane, talking business, 'I still can't make him out.'

'Why not? He's a perfectly ordinary Pole.'

'Where does he come from? What part of Poland?'

'You've read the file. Danzig.'

'Of course.'

The instructor began. 'We'll just try it with the empty gun first, both eyes open, and look along the line of sight, feet nicely apart now, thank you, that's lovely. Relax now, be nice and comfy, it's not a drill movement, it's a firing position, oh yes, we've done *this* before! Now traverse the gun, point it but never aim. Right!' The instructor drew breath, opened a wooden box and took out four magazines. 'One in the gun and one in the left hand,' he said and handed the other two up to Avery, who watched with fascination as Leiser deftly slipped a full magazine into the butt of the automatic and advanced the safety catch with his thumb.

'Now cock the gun, pointing it at the ground three yards ahead of you. Now take up a firing position, keeping the arm straight. Pointing the gun but not aiming it, fire off one magazine, two shots at a time, remembering that we don't regard the automatic as a weapon of science but more in the order of a stopping weapon for close combat. Now slowly, very slowly . . .'

Before he could finish the range was vibrating with the sound of Leiser's shooting – he shot fast, standing very stiff, his left hand holding the spare magazine precisely at his side like a grenade. He shot angrily, a mute man finding expression. Avery could feel with rising excitement the fury and purpose of his shooting; now two shots, and another two, then three, then a long volley, while the haze gathered round him and the plywood soldier shook and Avery's nostrils filled with the sweet smell of cordite.

'Eleven out of thirteen on the target,' the instructor declared. 'Very nice, very nice indeed. Next time, stick to two shots at a time, please, and wait till I give the fire order.' To Avery, the subaltern, he said, 'Care to have a go, sir?'

Leiser had walked up to the target and was lightly tracing the bullet holes with his slim hands. The silence was suddenly oppressive. He seemed lost in meditation, feeling the plywood here and there, running a finger thoughtfully along the outline of the German helmet, until the instructor called:

'Come on. We haven't got all day.'

Avery stood on the gym mat, measuring the weight of the gun. With the instructor's help he inserted one magazine, clutching the other nervously in his left hand. Haldane and Leiser looked on.

Avery fired, the heavy gun thudding in his ears, and he felt his young heart stir as the silhouette flicked passively to his shooting.

'Good shot, John, good shot!'

'Very good,' said the instructor automatically. 'A very good first effort, sir.' He turned to Leiser: 'Do you mind not shouting like that?' He knew a foreigner when he saw one.

'How many?' Avery asked eagerly, as he and the sergeant gathered round the target, touching the blackened perforations scattered thinly over the chest and belly. 'How many, Staff?'

'You'd better come with me, John,' Leiser whispered, throwing his arm over Avery's shoulder. 'I could do with you over there.' For a moment Avery recoiled. Then, with a laugh, he put his own arm round Leiser, feeling the warm, crisp cloth of his sports jacket in the palm of his hand.

The instructor led them across the parade ground to a brick barrack like a theatre with no windows, tall at one end. There were walls half crossing one another like the entrance to a public lavatory.

'Moving targets,' Haldane said, 'and shooting in the dark.'

At lunch they played the tapes.

The tapes were to run like a theme through the first two weeks of his training. They were made from old gramophone records; there was a crack in one which recurred like a metronome. Together, they comprised a massive parlour game in which things to be remembered were not listed but mentioned, casually, obliquely, often against a distracting background of other noises, now contradicted in conversation, now corrected or contested. There were three principal voices, one female and two male. Others would interfere. It was the woman who got on their nerves.

She had that antiseptic voice which air hostesses seem to acquire. In the first tape she read from lists, quickly; first it was a shopping-list, two pounds of this, one kilo of that; without warning she was talking about coloured skittles – so many green so many ochre; then it was weapons, guns, torpedoes, ammunition of this and that calibre; then a factory with capacity, waste and production figures, annual targets and monthly achievements. In the second tape she had not abandoned these topics, but unfamiliar voices distracted her and led the dialogue into unexpected paths.

While shopping she entered into an argument with the grocer's wife about certain merchandise which did not meet with her approval; eggs that were not sound, the outrageous cost of butter. When the grocer himself attempted to mediate he was accused of favouritism; there was talk of points and ration cards, the extra allowance of sugar for jam-making; a hint of undisclosed treasures under the counter. The grocer's voice was raised in anger but he stopped when the child intervened, talking about skittles. 'Mummy, Mummy, I've knocked over the three green ones, but when I tried to put them up, seven black ones fell down; Mummy, why are there only eight black ones left?'

The scene shifted to a public house. It was the woman again. She was reciting armaments statistics; other voices joined in. Figures were disputed, new targets stated, old ones recalled; the performance of a weapon – a weapon unnamed, undescribed – was cynically questioned and heatedly defended.

Every few minutes a voice shouted 'break!' – it might have been a referee – and Haldane stopped the tape and made Leiser talk about football or the weather, or read aloud from a newspaper for five minutes by his watch (the clock on the mantelpiece was broken). The tape recorder was switched on again, and they heard a voice, vaguely familiar, trailing a little like a parson's; a young voice, deprecating and unsure, like Avery's: 'Now here are the four questions. Discounting those eggs which were not sound, how many has she bought in the last three weeks? How many skittles are there altogether? What was the annual overall output of proved and calibrated gun barrels for the years 1937 and 1938? Finally, put in telegraph form any information from which the length of the barrels might be computed.'

Leiser rushed into the study – he seemed to know the game – to write down his answers. As soon as he had left the room Avery said accusingly, 'That was you. That was your voice speaking at the end.'

'Was it?' Haldane replied. He might not have known.

There were other tapes too, and they had the smell of death; the running of feet on a wooden staircase, the slamming of a door, a click, and a girl's voice asking – she might have been offering lemon or cream – 'Catch of a door, cocking of a gun?'

Leiser hesitated. 'A door,' he said. 'It was just the door.'

'It was a gun,' Haldane retorted. 'A Browning nine-millimetre automatic. The magazine was being slid into the butt.'

In the afternoon they went for their first walk, the two of them, Leiser and Avery, through Port Meadow and into the country beyond. Haldane had sent them. They walked fast, striding over the whip grass, the wind catching at Leiser's hair and throwing it wildly about his head. It was cold but there was no rain; a clear, sunless day when the sky above the flat fields was darker than the earth.

'You know your way round here, don't you?' Leiser asked. 'Were you at school here?'

'I was an undergraduate here, yes.'

'What did you study?'

'I read languages. German principally.'

They climbed a stile and emerged in a narrow lane.

'You married?' he asked.

'Yes.'

'Kids?'

'One.'

'Tell me something, John. When the Captain turned up my card
. . . what happened?'

'What do you mean?'

'What does it look like, an index for so many? It must be a big
thing in an outfit like ours.'

'It's in alphabetical order,' Avery said helplessly. 'Just cards.
Why?'

'He said they remembered me: the old hands. I was the best, he
said. Well, *who* remembered?'

'They all did. There's a special index for the best people. Practically everyone in the Department knows Fred Leiser. Even the
new ones. You can't have a record like yours and get forgotten,
you know.' He smiled. 'You're part of the furniture, Fred.'

'Tell me something else, John. I don't want to rock the boat,
see, but tell me this . . . Would I be any good on the inside?'

'The inside?'

'In the Office, with you people. I suppose you've got to be born
to it really, like the Captain.'

'I'm afraid so, Fred.'

'What cars do you use up there, John?'

'Humbers.'

'Hawk or Snipe?'

'Hawk.'

'Only four-cylinder? The Snipe's a better job, you know.'

'I'm talking about non-operational transport,' Avery said.
'We've a whole range of stuff for the special work.'

'Like the van?'

'That's it.'

'How long before . . . how long does it take to train you? You,
for instance; you just did a run. How long before they let you
go?'

'Sorry, Fred. I'm not allowed . . . not even you.'

'Not to worry.'

They passed a church set back on a rise above the road, skirted
a field of plough and returned, tired and radiant, to the cheerful
embrace of the Mayfly house and the gas fire playing on the golden
roses.

In the evening, they had the projector for visual memory: they would be in a car, passing a marshalling yard; or in a train beside an airfield; they would be taken on a walk through a town, and suddenly they would become aware that a vehicle or a face had reappeared, and they had not remembered its features. Sometimes a series of disconnected objects were flashed in rapid succession on to the screen, and there would be voices in the background, like the voices on the tape, but the conversation was not related to the film, so that the student must consult both his senses and retain what was valuable from each.

Thus the first day ended, setting the pattern for those that followed: carefree, exciting days for them both, days of honest labour and cautious but deepening attachment as the skills of boyhood became once more the weapons of war.

For the unarmed combat they had rented a small gymnasium near Headington which they had used in the war. An instructor had come by train. They called him Sergeant.

'Will he be carrying a knife at all? Not wanting to be curious,' he asked respectfully. He had a Welsh accent.

Haldane shrugged. 'It depends what he likes. We don't want to clutter him up.'

'There's a lot to be said for a knife, sir.' Leiser was still in the changing-room. 'If he knows how to use it. And the Jerries don't like them, not one bit.' He had brought some knives in a handcase, and he unpacked them in a private way, like a traveller unpacking his samples. 'They never could take cold steel,' he explained. 'Nothing too long, that's the trick of it, sir. Something flat with the two cutting edges.' He selected one and held it up. 'You can't do much better than this, as a matter of fact.' It was wide and flat like a laurel leaf, the blade unpolished, the handle waisted like an hour-glass, cross-hatched to prevent slip. Leiser was walking towards them, smoothing a comb through his hair.

'Used one of these, have you?'

Leiser examined the knife and nodded. The sergeant looked at him carefully. 'I know you, don't I? My name's Sandy Lowe. I'm a bloody Welshman.'

'You taught me in the war.'

'Christ,' said Lowe softly, 'so I did. You haven't changed much, have you?' They grinned shyly at one another, not knowing whether to shake hands. 'Come on, then, see what you remember.' They walked to the coconut matting in the centre of the floor. Lowe threw the knife at Leiser's feet and he snatched it up, grunting as he bent.

Lowe wore a jacket of torn tweed, very old. He stepped quickly back, took it off and with a single movement wrapped it round his left forearm, like a man preparing to fight a dog. Drawing his own knife he moved slowly round Leiser, keeping his weight steady but riding a little from one foot to the other. He was stooping, his bound arm held loosely in front of his stomach, fingers outstretched, palm facing the ground. He had gathered his body behind the guard, letting the blade play restlessly in front of it while Leiser kept steady, his eyes fixed upon the sergeant. For a time they feinted back and forth; once Leiser lunged and Lowe sprang back, allowing the knife to cut the cloth of the jacket on his arm. Once Lowe dropped to his knees, as if to drive the knife upwards beneath Leiser's guard, and it was Leiser's turn to spring back, but too slowly, it seemed, for Lowe shook his head, shouted 'Halt!' and stood upright.

'Remember that?' He indicated his own belly and groin, pressing his arms and elbows in as if to reduce the width of his body. 'Keep the target small.' He made Leiser put his knife away and showed him holds, crooking his left arm round Leiser's neck and pretending to stab him in the kidneys or the stomach. Then he asked Avery to stand as a dummy, and the two of them moved round him with detachment, Lowe indicating the places with his knife and Leiser nodding, smiling occasionally when a particular trick came back to him.

'You didn't weave with the blade enough. Remember thumb on top, blade parallel to the ground, forearm stiff, wrist loose. Don't let his eye settle on it, not for a moment. And left hand in over your own target, whether you've got the knife or not. Never be generous about offering the body, that's what I say to my daughter.' They laughed dutifully, all but Haldane.

After that, Avery had a turn. Leiser seemed to want it. Removing his glasses, he held the knife as Lowe showed him, hesitant, alert, while Leiser trod crabwise, feinted and darted lightly back, the sweat running off his face, his small eyes alight with concentration. All the time Avery was conscious of the sharp grooves of the haft against the flesh of his palm, the aching in his calves and buttocks as he kept his weight forward on his toes, and Leiser's angry eyes searching his own. Then Leiser's foot had hooked round his ankle; as he lost balance he felt the knife being wrenched from his hand; he fell back, Leiser's full weight upon him, Leiser's hand clawing at the collar of his shirt.

They helped him up, all laughing, while Leiser brushed the dust from Avery's clothes. The knives were put away while they did physical training; Avery took part.

When it was over Lowe said: 'We'll just have a spot of unarmed combat and that will do nicely.'

Haldane glanced at Leiser. 'Have you had enough?'

'I'm all right.'

Lowe took Avery by an arm and stood him in the centre of the gym mat. 'You sit on the bench,' he called to Leiser, 'while I show you a couple of things.'

He put a hand on Avery's shoulder. 'We're only concerned with five marks, whether we got a knife or not. What are they?'

'Groin, kidneys, belly, heart and throat,' Leiser replied wearily.

'How do you break a man's neck?'

'You don't. You smash his windpipe at the front.'

'What about a blow on the back of the neck?'

'Not with the bare hand. Not without a weapon.' He had put his face in his hands.

'Correct.' Lowe moved his open palm in slow motion towards Avery's throat. 'Hand open, fingers straight, right?'

'Right,' Leiser said.

'What else do you remember?'

A pause. 'Tiger's Claw. An attack on the eyes.'

'Never use it,' the sergeant replied shortly. 'Not as an attacking blow. You leave yourself wide open. Now for the strangle holds. All from behind, remember? Bend the head back, so, hand on the throat, so, and *squeeze*.' Lowe looked over his shoulder: 'Look this way, please. I'm not doing this for my own benefit . . . come on, then, if you know it all, show us some throws!'

Leiser stood up, locking arms with Lowe, and for a while they struggled back and forth, each waiting for the other to offer an opening. Then Lowe gave way, Leiser toppled and Lowe's hand slapped the back of his head, thrusting it down so that Leiser fell face forward heavily on to the mat.

'You fall a treat,' said Lowe with a grin, and then Leiser was upon him, twisting Lowe's arm savagely back and throwing him very hard so that his little body hit the carpets like a bird hitting the windscreen of a car.

'You play fair!' Leiser demanded. 'Or I'll damn well hurt you.'

'Never lean on your opponent,' Lowe said shortly. 'And don't lose your temper in the gym.'

He called across to Avery. 'You have a turn now, sir; give him some exercise.'

Avery stood up, took off his jacket and waited for Leiser to approach him. He felt the strong grasp upon his arms and was suddenly conscious of the frailty of his body when matched against this adult force. He tried to seize the forearms of the older man, but his hands could not encompass them; he tried to break free, but Leiser held him; Leiser's head was against his own, filling his nostrils with the smell of hair oil. He felt the damp stubble of his cheek and the close, rank heat of his thin, straining body. Putting his hands on Leiser's chest he forced himself back, throwing all his energy into one frantic effort to escape the suffocating constriction of the man's embrace. As he drew away they caught sight of one another, it might have been for the first time, across the heaving cradle of their entangled arms; Leiser's face, contorted with exertion, softened into a smile; the grip relaxed.

Lowe walked over to Haldane. 'He's foreign, isn't he?'

'A Pole. What's he like?'

'I'd say he was quite a fighter in his day. Nasty. He's a good build. Fit too, considering.'

'I see.'

'How are you these days, sir, in yourself. All right, then?'

'Yes, thank you.'

'That's right. Twenty years. Amazing really. Kiddies all grown up.'

'I'm afraid I have none.'

'Mine, I mean.'

'Ah.'

'See any of the old crowd, then, sir? How about Mr Smiley?'

'I'm afraid I have not kept in touch. I am not a gregarious kind of person. Shall we settle up?'

Lowe stood lightly to attention while Haldane prepared to pay him; travelling money, salary and thirty-seven and six for the knife, plus twenty-two shillings for the sheath, a flat metal one with a spring to facilitate extraction. Lowe wrote him a receipt, signing it S.L. for reasons of security. 'I got the knife at cost,' he explained. 'It's a fiddle we work through the sports club.' He seemed proud of that.

Haldane gave Leiser a trenchcoat and Wellingtons and Avery took him for a walk. They went by bus as far as Headington, sitting on the top deck.

'What happened this morning?' Avery asked.

'I thought we were fooling about, that's all. Then he threw me.'

'He remembered you, didn't he?'

'Of course he did: then why did he hurt me?'

'He didn't mean to.'

'Look, it's all right, see.' He was still upset.

They got out at the terminus and began trudging through the rain. Avery said, 'It's because he wasn't one of us; that's why you didn't like him.'

Leiser laughed, slipped his arm through Avery's. The rain drifting in slow waves across the empty street, ran down their faces and trickled into the collars of their mackintoshes. Avery pressed his arm to his side, holding Leiser's hand captive, and they continued their walk in shared contentment, forgetting the rain or playing with it, treading in the deepest parts and not caring about their clothes.

'Is the Captain pleased, John?'

'Very. He says it's going fine. We begin the wireless soon, just the elementary stuff. Jack Johnson's expected tomorrow.'

'It's coming back to me, John, the shooting and that. I hadn't forgotten.' He smiled. 'The old three-eight.'

'Nine-millimetre. You're doing fine, Fred. Just fine. The Captain said so.'

'Is that what he said, John, the Captain?'

'Of course. And he's told London. London's pleased too. We're only afraid you're a bit too . . .'

'Too what?'

'Well – too English.'

Leiser laughed. 'Not to worry, John.'

The inside of Avery's arm, where he held Leiser's hand, felt dry and warm.

They spent a morning on cyphers. Haldane acted as instructor. He had brought pieces of silk cloth imprinted with a cypher of the type Leiser would use, and a chart backed with cardboard for converting letters into numerals. He put the chart on the chimney-piece, wedging it behind the marble clock, and lectured them, rather as Leclerc would have done, but without affectation. Avery and Leiser sat at the table, pencils in hand, and under Haldane's tuition converted one passage after another into numbers according to the chart, deducted the result from figures on the silk cloth, finally re-translating into letters. It was a process which demanded application rather than concentration, and perhaps because Leiser was trying too hard he became bothered and erratic.

'We'll have a timed run over twenty groups,' Haldane said, and dictated from the sheet of paper in his hand a message of eleven words with the signature Mayfly. 'From next week you will have to manage without the chart. I shall put it in your room and you must commit it to memory. Go!'

He pressed the stopwatch and walked to the window while the two men worked feverishly at the table, muttering almost in unison while they jotted elementary calculations on the scrap paper in front of them. Avery could detect the increasing flurry of Leiser's movements, the suppressed sighs and imprecations, the angry erasures; deliberately slowing down, he glanced over the other's arm to ascertain his progress and noticed that the stub of pencil buried in his little hand was smeared with sweat. Without a word, he silently changed his paper for Leiser's. Haldane, turning round, might not have seen.

Even in these first few days, it had become apparent that Leiser looked to Haldane as an ailing man looks to his doctor; a sinner to his priest. There was something terrible about a man who derived his strength from such a sickly body.

Haldane affected to ignore him. He adhered stubbornly to the habits of his private life. He never failed to complete his crossword. A case of burgundy was delivered from the town, half bottles, and he drank one alone at each meal while they listened to the tapes. So complete, indeed, was his withdrawal that one might have thought him revolted by the man's proximity. Yet the more elusive, the more aloof Haldane became, the more surely he drew Leiser after him. Leiser, by some obscure standards of his own, had cast him as the English gentleman, and whatever Haldane did or said only served, in the eyes of the other, to fortify him in the part.

Haldane grew in stature. In London he was a slow-walking man; he picked his way pedantically along the corridors as if he were looking for footholds; clerks and secretaries would hover impatiently behind him, lacking the courage to pass. In Oxford he betrayed an agility which would have astonished his London colleagues. His parched frame had revived, he held himself erect. Even his hostility acquired the mark of command. Only the cough remained, that racked, abandoned sob too heavy for such a narrow chest, bringing dabs of red to his thin cheeks and causing Leiser the mute concern of a pupil for his admired master.

'Is the Captain sick?' he once asked Avery, picking up an old copy of Haldane's *Times*.

'He never speaks of it.'

'I suppose that would be bad form.' His attention was suddenly arrested by the newspaper. It was unopened. Only the crossword had been done, the margins round it sparsely annotated with permutations of a nine-letter anagram. He showed it to Avery in bewilderment.

'He doesn't read it,' he said. 'He's only done the competition.'

That night, when they went to bed, Leiser took it with him, furtively as if it contained some secret which study could reveal.

So far as Avery could judge, Haldane was content with Leiser's progress. In the great variety of activities to which Leiser was now subjected, they had been able to observe him more closely; with the corrosive perception of the weak they discovered his failing and tested his power. He acquired, as they gained his trust, a disarming frankness; he loved to confide. He was their creature; he gave them everything, and they stored it away as the poor do. They saw that the Department had provided direction for his energy: like a man of uncommon sexual appetite, Leiser had found in his new employment a love which he could illustrate with his gifts. They saw that he took pleasure in their command, giving in return his strength as homage for fulfilment. They even knew perhaps that between them they constituted for Leiser the poles of absolute authority: the one by his bitter adherence to standards which Leiser could never achieve, the other by his youthful accessibility, the apparent sweetness and dependence of his nature.

He liked to talk to Avery. He talked about his women or the war. He assumed – it was irritating for Avery, but nothing more – that a man in his middle thirties, whether married or not, led an intense and varied love life. Later in the evening when the two of them had put on their coats and hurried to the pub at the end of the road, he would lean his elbows on the small table, thrust his bright face forward and relate the smallest detail of his exploits, his hand beside his chin, his slim fingertips rapidly parting and closing in unconscious imitation of his mouth. It was not vanity which made him thus but friendship. These betrayals and confessions, whether truth or fantasy, were the simple coinage of their intimacy. He never mentioned Betty.

Avery came to know Leiser's face with an accuracy no longer related to memory. He noticed how its features seemed structurally to alter shape according to his mood, how when he was tired or depressed at the end of a long day the skin on his cheekbones was drawn upwards rather than down, and the corners of his eyes and mouth rose tautly so that his expression was at once more Slav and less familiar.

He had acquired from his neighbourhood or his clients certain turns of phrase which, though wholly without meaning, impressed his foreign ear. He would speak, for instance, of 'some measure of satisfaction', using an impersonal construction for the sake of dignity. He had assimilated also a variety of clichés. Expressions like 'not to worry', 'don't rock the boat', 'let the dog see the rabbit', came to him continually, as if he were aspiring after a way of life which he only imperfectly understood, and these were the offerings that would buy him in. Some expressions, Avery remarked, were out of date.

Once or twice Avery suspected that Haldane resented his intimacy with Leiser. At other times it seemed that Haldane was deploying emotions in Avery over which he himself no longer disposed. One evening at the beginning of the second week, while Leiser was engaged in that lengthy toilet which preceded almost any recreational engagement, Avery asked Haldane whether he did not wish to go out himself.

'What do you expect me to do? Make a pilgrimage to the shrine of my youth?'

'I thought you might have friends there; people you still know.'

'If I do, it would be insecure to visit them. I am here under another name.'

'I'm sorry. Of course.'

'Besides' – a dour smile – 'we are not all so prolific in our friendships.'

'You told me to stay with him!' Avery said hotly.

'Precisely; and you have. It would be churlish of me to complain. You do it admirably.'

'Do what?'

'Obey instructions.'

At that moment the door bell rang and Avery went downstairs to answer it. By the light of the streetlamp he could see the familiar shape of a Department van in the road. A small, homely figure stood on the doorstep. He was wearing a brown suit and overcoat. There was a high shine on the toes of his brown shoes. He might have come to read the meter.

'Jack Johnson's my name,' he said uncertainly. 'Johnson's Fair Deal, that's me.'

'Come in,' Avery said.

'This is the right place, isn't it? Captain Hawkins . . . and all that?'

He carried a soft leather bag which he laid carefully on the floor as if it contained all he possessed. Half closing his umbrella he shook it expertly to rid it of the rain, then placed it on the stand beneath his overcoat.

'I'm John.'

Johnson took his hand and squeezed it warmly.

'Very pleased to meet you. The Boss has talked a lot about you. You're quite the blue-eyed boy, I hear.'

They laughed.

He took Avery by the arm in a quick confiding gesture. 'Using your own name, are you?'

'Yes. Christian name.'

'And the Captain?'

'Hawkins.'

'What's he like, Mayfly? How's he bearing up?'

'Fine. Just fine.'

'I hear he's quite a one for the girls.'

While Johnson and Haldane talked in the drawing-room Avery slipped upstairs to Leiser.

'It's no go, Fred. Jack's come.'

'Who's Jack?'

'Jack Johnson, the wireless chap.'

'I thought we didn't start that till next week.'

'Just the elementary this week, to get your hand in. Come down and say hello.'

He was wearing a dark suit and held a nail file in one hand.

'What about going out, then?'

'I told you; we can't tonight, Fred; Jack's here.'

Leiser went downstairs and shook Johnson briefly by the hand, without formality, as if he did not care for latecomers. They talked awkwardly for quarter of an hour until Leiser, protesting tiredness, went sullenly to bed.

Johnson made his first report. 'He's slow,' he said. 'He hasn't worked a key for a long time, mind. But I daren't try him on a set till he's quicker on the key. I know it's all of twenty years, sir; you can't blame him. But he *is* slow, sir, very.' He had an attentive, nursery-rhyme way of talking as if he spent much time in the company of children. 'The Boss says I'm to play him all the time – when he starts the job, too. I understand we're all going over to Germany, sir.'

'Yes.'

'Then we shall have to get to know each other,' he insisted, 'Mayfly and me. We ought to be together a lot, sir, the moment I begin working him on the set. It's like handwriting, this game, we've got to get used to one another's handwriting. Then there's schedules, times for coming up and that; signal plans for his frequencies. Safety devices. That's a lot to learn in a fortnight.'

'Safety devices?' Avery asked.

'Deliberate mistakes, sir; like a misspelling in a particular group, an E for an A or something of that kind. If he wants to tell us he's been caught and is transmitting under control, he'll miss the safety device.' He turned to Haldane. 'You know the kind of thing, Captain.'

'There was talk in London of teaching him high-speed transmission on tape. Do you know what became of that idea?'

'The Boss did mention it to me, sir. I understand the equipment wasn't available. I can't say I know much about it, really; since my time, the transistorized stuff. The Boss said we were to stick to the old methods but change the frequency every two and a half minutes, sir; I understand the Jerries are very hot on the direction-finding these days.'

'What set did they send down? It seemed very heavy for him to carry about.'

'It's the kind Mayfly used in the war, sir, that's the beauty of it. The old B 2 in the waterproof casing. If we've only got a couple of weeks there doesn't hardly seem time to go over anything else. Not that he's ready to work it yet—'

'What does it weigh?'

'About fifty pound, sir, all in. The ordinary suitcase set. It's the waterproofing that adds the weight, but he's got to have it if he's going over rough country. Specially at this time of year.' He hesitated. 'But he's slow on his Morse, sir.'

'Quite. Do you think you can bring him up to scratch in the time?'

'Can't tell yet, sir. Not till we really get cracking on the set. Not till the second period, when he's had his little bit of leave. I'm just letting him handle the buzzer at present.'

'Thank you,' said Haldane.

Chapter 13

At the end of the first two weeks they gave him forty-eight hours leave of absence. He had not asked for it and when they offered it to him he seemed puzzled. In no circumstances was he to visit his own neighbourhood. He could depart for London on the Friday but he said he preferred to go on Saturday. He could return on Monday morning but he said it depended and he might come back late on Sunday. They stressed that he was to keep clear of anyone who might know him, and in some curious fashion this seemed to console him.

Avery, worried, went to Haldane.

'I don't think we should send him off into the blue. You've told him he can't go back to South Park; or visit his friends, even if he's got any; I don't see quite where he can go.'

'You think he'll be lonely?'

Avery blushed. 'I think he'll just want to come back all the time.'

'We can hardly object to that.'

They gave him subsistence money in old notes, fives and ones. He wanted to refuse it, but Haldane pressed it on him as if a principle were involved. They offered to book him a room but he declined. Haldane assumed he was going to London, so in the end he went, as if he owed it to them.

'He's got some woman,' said Johnson with satisfaction.

He left on the midday train, carrying one pigskin suitcase and wearing his camel-hair coat; it had a slightly military cut, and leather buttons, but no person of breeding could ever have mistaken it for a British warm.

He handed in his suitcase to the depository at Paddington Station and wandered out into Praed Street because he had nowhere to go. He walked about for half an hour, looking at the shop windows and reading the tarts' advertisements on the glazed notice boards. It was Saturday afternoon: a handful of old men in trilby hats and raincoats hovered between the pornography shops and the pimps on the corner. There was very little traffic: an atmosphere of hopeless recreation filled the street.

The cinema club charged a pound and gave him a predated membership card because of the law. He sat among ghost figures on a kitchen chair. The film was very old; it might have come over from Vienna when the persecutions began. Two girls, quite naked, took tea. There was no sound track and they just went on drinking tea, changing position a little as they passed their cups. They would be sixty now, if they had survived the war. He got up to go because it was after half past five and the pubs were open. As he passed the kiosk at the doorway, the manager said: 'I know a girl who likes a gay time. Very young.'

'No, thanks.'

'Two and a half quid; she likes foreigners. She gives it foreign if you like. French.'

'Run away.'

'Don't you tell me to run away.'

'Run away.' Leiser returned to the kiosk, his small eyes suddenly alight. 'Next time you offer me a girl, make it something English, see.'

The air was warmer, the wind had dropped, the street emptied; pleasures were indoors now. The woman behind the bar said, 'Can't mix it for you now, dear, not till the rush dies down. You can see for yourself.'

'It's the only thing I drink.'

'Sorry, dear.'

He ordered gin and Italian instead and got it warm with no cherry. Walking had made him tired. He sat on the bench which ran along the wall, watching the darts four. They did not speak, but pursued their game with quiet devotion, as if they were deeply conscious of tradition. It was like the film club. One of them had a date, and they called to Leiser, 'Make a four, then?'

'I don't mind,' he said, pleased to be addressed, and stood up; but a friend came in, a man called Henry, and Henry was preferred. Leiser was going to argue but there seemed no point.

Avery too had gone out alone. To Haldane he had said he was taking a walk, to Johnson that he was going to the cinema. Avery had a way of lying which defied rational explanation. He found himself drawn to the old places he had known; his college in the Turl; the bookshops, pubs and libraries. The term was just ending. Oxford had a smell of Christmas about it, and acknowledged it with prudish ill will, dressing the shop windows with last year's tinsel.

He took the Banbury Road until he reached the street where he and Sarah had lived for the first year of marriage. The flat was in darkness. Standing before it, he tried to detect in the house, in himself, some trace of the sentiment, or affection, or love, or whatever it was that explained their marriage, but it was not to be found and he supposed it had never been. He sought desperately, wanting to find the motive of youth; but there was none. He was staring into an empty house. He hastened home to the place where Leiser lived.

'Good film?' Johnson asked.

'Fine.'

'I thought you were going for a walk,' Haldane complained, looking up from his crossword.

'I changed my mind.'

'Incidentally,' Haldane said, 'Leiser's gun. I understand he prefers the three-eight.'

'Yes. They call it the nine-millimetre now.'

'When he returns he should start to carry it with him; take it everywhere, unloaded of course.' A glance at Johnson. 'Particularly when he begins transmission exercises on any scale. He must have it on him all the time; we want him to feel lost without it. I have arranged for one to be issued; you'll find it in your room, Avery, with various holsters. Perhaps you'd explain it to him, would you?'

'Won't you tell him yourself?'

'You do it. You get on with him so nicely.'

He went upstairs to telephone Sarah. She had gone to stay with her mother. Conversation was very formal.

Leiser dialled Betty's number, but there was no reply.

Relieved, he went to a cheap jewellers, near the station, which was open on Saturday afternoon and bought a gold coach and horses for a charm bracelet. It cost eleven pounds, which was what they had given him for subsistence. He asked them to send it by registered mail to her address in South Park. He put a note in saying 'Back in two weeks. Be good', signing it, in a moment of aberration, F. Leiser, so he crossed it out and wrote 'Fred'.

He walked for a bit, thought of picking up a girl, and finally booked in at the hotel near the station. He slept badly because of the noise of traffic. In the morning he rang her number again; there was no reply. He replaced the receiver quickly; he might have waited a little longer. He had breakfast, went out and bought the Sunday papers, took them to his room and read the football reports till lunch time. In the afternoon he went for a walk, it had become a habit, right through London, he hardly knew where. He followed the river as far as Charing Cross and found himself in an empty garden filled with drifting rain. The tarmac paths were strewn with yellow leaves. An old man sat on the bandstand, quite alone. He wore a black overcoat and a rucksack of green webbing like the case of a gas mask. He was asleep, or listening to music.

He waited till evening in order not to disappoint Avery, then caught the last train home to Oxford.

Avery knew a pub behind Balliol where they let you play bar billiards on Sundays. Johnson liked a game of bar billiards. Johnson was on Guinness, Avery was on whisky. They were laughing a good deal; it had been a tough week. Johnson was winning; he went for the lower numbers, methodically, while Avery tried cushion shots at the hundred pocket.

'I wouldn't mind a bit of what Fred's having,' Johnson said with a snigger. He played a shot; a white ball dropped dutifully into its hole. 'Poles are dead randy. Go up anything, a Pole will. Specially Fred, he's a real terror. He's got the walk.'

'Are you that way, Jack?'

'When I'm in the mood. I wouldn't mind a little bit now, as a matter of fact.'

They played a couple of shots, each lost in an alcoholic euphoria of erotic fancy.

'Still,' said Johnson gratefully, 'I'd rather be in our shoes, wouldn't you?'

'Any day.'

'You know,' Johnson said, chalking his cue, 'I shouldn't be speaking to you like this, should I? You've had college and that. You're different class, John.'

They drank to each other, both thinking of Leiser.

'For Christ's sake,' Avery said. 'We're fighting the same war, aren't we?'

'Quite right.'

Johnson poured the rest of the Guinness out of the bottle. He took great care, but a little ran over the side on to the table.

'Here's to Fred,' Avery said.

'To Fred. On the nest. And bloody good luck to him.'

'Good luck, Fred.'

'I don't know how he'll manage the B 2,' Johnson murmured. 'He's got a long way to go.'

'Here's to Fred.'

'Fred. He's a lovely boy. Here: do you know this bloke Woodford, the one who picked me up?'

'Of course. He'll be coming down next week.'

'Met his wife at all; Babs? She was a girl, she was; give it to anyone . . . Christ! Past it now, I suppose. Still, many a good tune, eh?'

'That's right.'

'To him that hath shalt be given,' Johnson declared.

They drank; that joke went astray.

'She used to go with the admin bloke, Jimmy Gorton. What happened to him then?'

'He's in Hamburg. Doing very well.'

They got home before Leiser. Haldane was in bed.

It was after midnight when Leiser hung his wet camel-hair coat in the hall, on a hanger because he was a precise man: tiptoed to the drawing-room and put on the light. His eye ran fondly over the heavy furniture, the tallboy elaborately decorated with fretwork and heavy brass handles; the escritoire and the bible table. Lovingly he revisited the handsome women at croquet, handsome men at war, disdainful boys in boaters, girls at Cheltenham; a whole long history of discomfort and not a breath of passion. The clock on the chimney-piece was like a pavilion in blue marble. The hands were of gold, so ornate, so fashioned, so flowered and spreading that you had to look twice to see where the points of them lay. They had not moved since he went away, perhaps not since he was born, and somehow that was a great achievement for an old clock.

He picked up his suitcase and went upstairs. Haldane was coughing but no light came from his room. He tapped on Avery's door.

'You there, John?'

After a moment he heard him sit up. 'Nice time, Fred?'

'You bet.'

'Woman all right?'

'Just the job. See you tomorrow, John.'

'See you in the morning. Night, Fred. Fred . . .'

'Yes, John?'

'Jack and I had a bit of a session. You should have been there.'

'That's right, John.'

Slowly he made his way along the corridor, content in his weariness, entered his room, took off his jacket, lit a cigarette and threw himself gratefully into the armchair. It was tall and very comfortable, with wings on the side. As he did so he caught sight of something. A chart hung on the wall for turning letters into figures, and beneath it, on the bed, lying in the middle of the eiderdown, was an old suitcase of continental pattern, dark green canvas with leather on the corners. It was open; inside were two boxes of grey steel. He got up, staring at them in mute recognition; reached out and touched them, wary as if they might be hot; turned the dials, stooped and read the legend by the switches. It could have been the set he had in Holland: transmitter and receiver in one box; power unit, key and earphones in the other. Crystals, a dozen of them, in a bag of parachute silk with a green drawstring threaded through the top. He tested the key with his finger; it seemed much smaller than he remembered.

He returned to the armchair, his eyes still fixed upon the suitcase; sat there, stiff and sleepless, like a man conducting a wake.

He was late for breakfast. Haldane said, 'You spend all day with Johnson. Morning and afternoon.'

'No walk?' Avery was busy with his egg.

'Tomorrow perhaps. From now on we're concerned with technique. I'm afraid walks take second place.'

Control quite often stayed in London on Monday nights, which he said was the only time he could get a chair at his club; Smiley suspected he wanted to get away from his wife.

'I hear the flowers are coming out in Blackfriars Road,' he said. 'Leclerc's driving around in a Rolls-Royce.'

'It's a perfectly ordinary Humber,' Smiley retorted. 'From the Ministry pool.'

'Is that where it comes from?' Control asked, his eyebrows very high. 'Isn't it fun? So the black friars have won the pool.'

Chapter 14

'You know the set, then?' Johnson asked.
  'The B 2.'
  'OK. Official title, Type three, Mark two; runs on AC or a six-volt car battery, but you'll be using the mains, right? They've queried the current where you're going and it's AC. Your mains consumption with this set is fifty-seven watts on transmit and twenty-five on receive. So if you *do* end up somewhere and they've only got DC, you're going to have to borrow a battery, right?'
  Leiser did not laugh.
  'Your mains lead is provided with adaptors for all continental sockets.'
  'I know.'
  Leiser watched Johnson prepare the set for operation. First he linked the transmitter and receiver to the power pack by means of six-pin plugs, adjusting the twin claws to the terminals; having plugged in the set and turned it on, he joined the miniature Morse key to the transmitter and the earphones to the receiver.
  'That's a smaller key than we had in the war,' Leiser objected. 'I tried it last night. My fingers kept slipping.'
  Johnson shook his head.
  'Sorry, Fred; same size.' He winked. 'Perhaps your finger's grown.'
  'All right, come on.'
  Now he extracted from the spares box a coil of multi-stranded wire, plastic covered, attaching one end to the aerial terminals. 'Most of your crystals will be around the three megacycle mark, so you may not have to change your coil – get a nice stretch on your aerial and you'll be a hundred per cent, Fred; specially at night. Now watch the tuning. You've connected up your aerial, earth, key, headphones and power pack. Look at your signal plan and see what frequency you're on; fish out the corresponding

crystal, right?' He held up a small capsule of black bakelite, guided the pins into the double socket – 'Shoving the male ends into the doodahs, like so. All right so far, Fred? Not hurrying you, am I?'

'I'm watching. Don't keep asking.'

'Now turn the crystal selector dial to "fundamental all crystals", and adjust your wave band to match your frequency. If you're on three and a half megs you want the wave-band knob on three to four, like so. Now insert your plug-in coil either way round, Fred; you've got a nice overlap there.'

Leiser's head was supported in his hand as he tried desperately to remember the sequence of movements which once had come so naturally to him. Johnson proceeded with the method of a man born to his trade. His voice was soft and easy, very patient, his hands moving instinctively from one dial to another with perfect familiarity. All the time the monologue continued:

'TRS switch on T for tune; put your anode tuning and aerial matching on ten; now you can switch on your power pack, right?' He pointed to the meter window. 'You should get the three hundred reading, near enough, Fred. Now I'm ready to have a go: I shove my meter selector on three and twiddle the PA tuning till I get maximum meter reading; now I put her on six—'

'What's PA?'

'Power Amplifier, Fred: didn't you know that?'

'Go on.'

'Now I move the anode tuning knob till I get my minimum value – here you are! She's a hundred with the knob on two, right? Now push your TRS over to S – S for send, Fred – and you're ready to tune the aerial. Here – press the key. That's right, see? You get a bigger reading because you're putting power into the aerial, follow it?'

Silently he performed the brief ritual of tuning the aerial until the meter obediently dipped to the final reading.

'And Bob's your uncle!' he declared triumphantly. 'Now it's Fred's turn. Here, your hand's sweating. You must have had a week-end, you must. Wait a minute, Fred!' He left the room, returning with an oversized white pepperpot, from which he carefully sprinkled french chalk over the black lozenge on the key lever.

'Take my advice,' Johnson said, 'just leave the girls in peace, see, Fred? Let it grow.'

Leiser was looking at his open hand. Particles of sweat had gathered in the grooves. 'I couldn't sleep.'

'I'll bet you couldn't.' He slapped the case affectionately. 'From

now on you sleep with *her*. She's Mrs Fred, see, and no one else!'
He dismantled the set and waited for Leiser to begin. With childish
slowness Leiser painfully reassembled the equipment. It was all so
long ago.

Day after day Leiser and Johnson sat at the small table in the
bedroom tapping out their messages. Sometimes Johnson would
drive away in the van leaving Leiser alone, and they would work
back and forth till early morning. Or Leiser and Avery would go
– Leiser was not allowed out alone – and from a borrowed house
in Fairford they would pass their signals, encoding, sending and
receiving *en clair* trivialities disguised as amateur transmissions.
Leiser discernibly changed. He became nervy and irritable; he
complained to Haldane about the complications of transmitting
on a series of frequencies, the difficulty of constant retuning, the
shortage of time. His relationship to Johnson was always uneasy.
Johnson had arrived late, and for some reason Leiser insisted on
treating him as an outsider, not admitting him properly to the
companionship which he fancied to exist between Avery, Haldane
and himself.

There was a particularly absurd scene one breakfast. Leiser
raised the lid of a jam-pot, peered inside and, turning to Avery,
asked, 'Is this bee-honey?'

Johnson leant across the table, knife in one hand, bread and
butter in the other.

'We don't say that, Fred. We just call it honey.'

'That's right, honey. Bee-honey.'

'Just honey,' Johnson repeated. 'In England we just call it
honey.'

Leiser carefully replaced the lid, pale with anger. 'Don't you tell
me what to say.'

Haldane looked up sharply from his paper. 'Be quiet, Johnson.
Bee-honey is perfectly accurate.'

Leiser's courtesy had something of the servant, his quarrels with
Johnson something of the backstairs.

Despite such incidents as this, like any two men engaged daily
upon a single project, they came gradually to share their hopes,
moods and depressions. If a lesson had gone well, the meal that
followed it would be a happy affair. The two of them would
exchange esoteric remarks about the state of the ionosphere, the
skip distance on a given frequency, or an unnatural meter reading
which had occurred during tuning. If badly, they would speak
little or not at all, and everyone but Haldane would hasten through
his food for want of anything to say. Occasionally Leiser would

ask whether he might not take a walk with Avery, but Haldane shook his head and said there was no time. Avery, a guilty lover, made no move to help.

As the two weeks neared their end, the Mayfly house was several times visited by specialists of one kind or another from London. A photographic instructor came, a tall, hollow-eyed man, who demonstrated a sub-miniature camera with interchangeable lenses; there was a doctor, benign and wholly incurious, who listened to Leiser's heart for minutes on end. The Treasury had insisted upon it; there was the question of compensation. Leiser declared he had no dependants, but he was examined all the same to satisfy the Treasury.

With the increase in these activities Leiser came to derive great comfort from his gun. Avery had given it to him after his weekend's leave. He favoured a shoulder holster (the drape of his jackets nicely concealed the bulge) and sometimes at the end of a long day he would draw the gun and finger it, looking down the barrel, raising it and lowering it as he had done on the range. 'There isn't a gun to beat it,' he would say. 'Not for the size. You can have your continental types any time. Women's guns, they are, like their cars. Take my advice, John, a three-eight's best.'

'Nine-millimetre they call it now.'

His resentment of strangers reached its unexpected climax in the visit of Hyde, a man from the Circus. The morning had gone badly. Leiser had been making a timed run, encoding and transmitting forty groups; his bedroom and Johnson's were now linked on an internal circuit; they played back and forth behind closed doors. Johnson had taught him a number of international code signs: QRJ, your signals are too weak to read: QRW, send faster: QSD, your keying is bad: QSM, repeat the last message: QSZ, send each word twice: QRU, I have nothing for you. As Leiser's transmission became increasingly uneven, Johnson's comments, thus cryptically expressed, added to his confusion, until with a shout of irritation he switched off his set and stalked downstairs to Avery. Johnson followed him.

'It's no good giving up, Fred.'

'Leave me alone.'

'Look, Fred, you did it all wrong. I *told* you to send the number of groups *before* you send the message. You can't remember a thing, can you—'

'Look, leave me alone, I said!' He was about to add something when the door bell rang. It was Hyde. He had brought an assistant, a plump man who was sucking something against the weather.

They did not play the tapes at lunch. Their guests sat side by side, eating glumly as if they had the same food every day because of the calories. Hyde was a meagre, dark-faced man without a trace of humour who reminded Avery of Sutherland. He had come to give Leiser a new identity. He had papers for him to sign, identity documents, a form of ration card, a driving licence, a permit to enter the border zone along a specified area, and an old shirt in a briefcase. After lunch he laid them all out on the drawing-room table while the photographer put up his camera.

They dressed Leiser in the shirt and took him full face with both ears showing according to the German regulations, then led him to sign the papers. He seemed nervous.

'We're going to call you Freiser,' Hyde said, as if that were an end to the matter.

'Freiser? That's like my own name.'

'That's the idea. That's what your people wanted. For signatures and things, so that there's no slip-up. You'd better practise it a bit before you sign.'

'I'd rather have it different. Quite different.'

'We'll stick to Freiser, I think,' said Hyde. 'It's been decided at high level.' Hyde was a man who leaned heavily upon the Passive Voice.

There was an uncomfortable silence.

'I want it different. I don't like Freiser and I want it different.' He didn't like Hyde either, and in half a minute he was going to say so.

Haldane intervened. 'You're under instructions. The Department has taken the decision. There is no question of altering it now.'

Leiser was very pale.

'Then they can bloody well change the instructions. I want a different name, that's all. Christ, it's only a little thing, isn't it? That's all I'm asking for: another name, a proper one, not a half-cock imitation of my own.'

'I don't understand,' Hyde said. 'It's only training, isn't it?'

'You don't have to understand! Just change it, that's all. Who the hell d'you think you are, coming in here and ordering me about?'

'I'll telephone London,' Haldane said, and went upstairs. They waited awkwardly until he came down.

'Will you accept Hartbeck?' Haldane inquired. There was a note of sarcasm in his voice.

Leiser smiled. 'Hartbeck. That's fine.' He spread out his hands in a gesture of apology. 'Hartbeck's fine.'

Leiser spent ten minutes practising a signature then signed the papers, with a little flourish each time as if there were dust on them. Hyde gave them a lecture on the documents. It took a very long time. There were no actual ration cards in East Germany, Hyde said, but there existed a system of registration with food shops, who provided a certificate. He explained the principle of travel permits and the circumstances under which they were granted, he talked at length about the obligation on Leiser to show his identity card, unasked, when he bought a railway ticket or put up at an hotel. Leiser argued with him and Haldane attempted to terminate the meeting. Hyde paid no attention. When he had finished he nodded and went away with his photographer, folding the old shirt into his briefcase as if it were part of his equipment.

This outburst of Leiser's appeared to cause Haldane some concern. He telephoned to London and ordered his assistant, Gladstone, to go over Leiser's file for any trace of the name Freiser; he had a search made in all the indices, but without success. When Avery suggested Haldane was making too much of the incident the other shook his head. 'We're waiting for the second vow,' he said.

Following upon Hyde's visit, Leiser now received daily briefings about his cover. Stage by stage he, Avery and Haldane constructed in tireless detail the background of the man Hartbeck, establishing him in his work, his tastes and recreations, in his love life and choice of friends. Together, they entered the most obscure corners of the man's conjectured existence, gave him skills and attributes which Leiser himself barely possessed.

Woodford came with news of the Department.

'The Director's putting up a marvellous show.' From the way he spoke, Leclerc might have been fighting an illness. 'We leave for Lübeck a week today. Jimmy Gorton's been on to the German frontier people – he says they're pretty reliable. We've got a crossing point lined up and we've taken a farmhouse on the outskirts of the town. He's let it be known that we're a team of academics wanting a quiet time and a bit of fresh air.' Woodford looked confidingly at Haldane. 'The Department is working wonderfully. As one man. And what a *spirit*, Adrian! No watching the clock these days. And no *rank*. Dennison, Sandford . . . we're just a single team. You should see the way Clarkie's going for the Ministry about poor Taylor's pension. How's Mayfly bearing up?' he added in a low voice.

'All right. He's doing wireless upstairs.'

'Any more signs of nerves? Outbreaks or anything?'

'None so far as I know,' Haldane replied, as if he were unlikely to know anyway.

'Is he getting frisky? Sometimes they want a girl about now.'

Woodford had brought drawings of Soviet rockets. They had been made by Ministry draughtsmen from photographs held in Research Section, enlarged to about two foot by three, neatly mounted on showcards. Some were stamped with a security classification. Prominent features were marked with arrows; the nomenclature was curiously childish: fin, cone, fuel compartment, payload. Beside each rocket stood a gay little figure like a penguin in a flying helmet, and printed beneath him: 'size of average man'. Woodford arranged them round the room as if they were his own work; Avery and Haldane watched in silence.

'He can look at them after lunch,' Haldane said. 'Put them together till then.'

'I've brought along a film to give him some background. Launchings, transportation, a bit about destructive capacity. The Director said he should have an idea what these things can do. Give him a shot in the arm.'

'He doesn't need a shot in the arm,' Avery said.

Woodford remembered something. 'Oh – and your little Gladstone wants to talk to you. He said it was urgent – didn't know how to get hold of you. I told him you'd give him a ring when you had time. Apparently you asked him to do a job on the Mayfly area. Industry, was it, or manoeuvres? He says he's got the answer ready for you in London. He's the best type of NCO, that fellow.' He glanced at the ceiling. 'When's Fred coming down?'

Haldane said abruptly, 'I don't want you to meet him, Bruce.' It was unusual in Haldane to use a Christian name. 'I'm afraid you must take luncheon in the town. Charge it to Accounts.'

'Why on earth not?'

'Security. I see no point in his knowing more of us than is strictly necessary. The charts speak for themselves; so, presumably, does the film.'

Woodford, profoundly insulted, left. Avery knew then that Haldane was determined to preserve Leiser in the delusion that the Department housed no fools.

For the last day of the course, Haldane had planned a full-scale exercise to last from ten in the morning until eight in the evening, a combined affair including visual observation in the town, clandestine photography and listening to tapes. The information which Leiser assembled during the day was to be made into a report, encoded and communicated by wireless to Johnson in the evening. A certain hilarity infected the briefing that morning. Johnson made a joke about not photographing the Oxford Constabulary by mistake; Leiser laughed richly and even Haldane allowed himself a wan smile. It was the end of term; the boys were going home.

The exercise was a success. Johnson was pleased; Avery enthusiastic; Leiser manifestly delighted. They had made two faultless transmissions, Johnson said, Fred was steady as a rock. At eight o'clock they assembled for dinner wearing their best suits. A special menu had been arranged. Haldane had presented the rest of his burgundy; toasts were made; there was talk of an annual reunion in years to come. Leiser looked very smart in a dark blue suit and a pale tie of watered silk.

Johnson got rather drunk and insisted on bringing down Leiser's wireless set, raising his glass to it repeatedly and calling it Mrs Hartbeck. Avery and Leiser sat together: the estrangement of the last week over.

The next day, a Saturday, Avery and Haldane returned to London. Leiser was to remain in Oxford with Johnson until the whole party left for Germany on Monday. On the Sunday, an Air Force van would call at the house to collect the suitcase. This would be independently conveyed to Gorton in Hamburg together with Johnson's own base equipment, and thence to the farmhouse near Lübeck from which Operation Mayfly would be launched. Before he left the house Avery took a last look round, partly for reasons of sentiment, and partly because he had signed the lease and was concerned about the inventory.

Haldane was ill at ease on the journey to London. He was still waiting, apparently, for some unknown crisis in Leiser.

Chapter 15

It was the same evening. Sarah was in bed. Her mother had brought her to London.

'If you ever want me,' he said, 'I'll come to you, wherever you are.'

'You mean when I'm dying.' Analysing, she added, 'I'll do the same for you, John. Now can I repeat my question?'

'Monday. There's a group of us going.' It was like children: parallel playing.

'Which part of Germany?'

'Just Germany, West Germany. For a conference.'

'More bodies?'

'Oh, for God's sake, Sarah, do you think I want to keep it from you?'

'Yes, John, I do,' she said simply. 'I think if you were allowed to tell me you wouldn't care about the job. You've got a kind of licence I can't share.'

'I can only tell you it's a big thing . . . a big operation. With agents. I've been training them.'

'Who's in charge?'

'Haldane.'

'Is that the one who confides in you about his wife? I think he's utterly disgusting.'

'No, that's Woodford. This man's quite different. Haldane's odd. Donnish. Very good.'

'But they're all good, aren't they? Woodford's good too.'

Her mother came in with tea.

'When are you getting up?' he asked.

'Monday, probably. It depends on the doctor.'

'She'll need quiet,' her mother said, and went out.

'If you believe in it, do it,' Sarah said. 'But don't . . .' she broke off, shook her head, little girl now.

– 152 –

'You're jealous. You're jealous of my job and the secrecy. You don't *want* me to believe in my work!'

'Go on. Believe in it if you can.'

For a while they did not look at one another. 'If it weren't for Anthony I really would leave you,' Sarah declared at last.

'What for?' Avery asked hopelessly, and then, seeing the opening, 'Don't let Anthony stop you.'

'You never talk to me: any more than you talk to Anthony. He hardly knows you.'

'What is there to talk about?'

'Oh, God.'

'I can't talk about my work, you know that. I tell you more than I should as it is. That's why you're always sneering at the Department, isn't it? You can't understand it, you don't want to; you don't *like* it being secret but you despise me when I break the rules.'

'Don't go over that again.'

'I'm not coming back,' Avery said. 'I've decided.'

'This time, perhaps you'll remember Anthony's present.'

'I bought him that milk lorry.'

They sat in silence again.

'You ought to meet Leclerc,' said Avery; 'I think you ought to talk to him. He keeps suggesting it. Dinner . . . he might convince you.'

'What of?'

She found a piece of cotton hanging from the seam of her bed-jacket. Sighing, she took a pair of nail scissors from the drawer in the bedside table and cut it off.

'You should have drawn it through at the back,' Avery said. 'You ruin your clothes that way.'

'What are they like?' she asked. 'The agents? Why do they do it?'

'For loyalty, partly. Partly money, I suppose.'

'You mean you bribe them?'

'Oh shut up!'

'Are they English?'

'One of them is. Don't ask me any more, Sarah; I can't tell you.' He advanced his head towards her. 'Don't ask me, Sweet.' He took her hand; she let him.

'And they're all men?'

'Yes.'

Suddenly she said, it was a complete break, no tears, no precision, but quickly, with compassion, as if the speeches were over and this were the choice: 'John, I want to know, I've got to know, now, before you go. It's an awful, unEnglish question, but all the time you've been telling me something, ever since you took this job. You've been telling me people don't matter, that *I* don't, Anthony doesn't; that the agents don't. You've been telling me you've found a vocation. Well, who calls you, that's what I mean: what *sort* of vocation? That's the question you never answer: that's why you hide from me. Are you a martyr, John? Should I admire you for what you're doing? Are you making sacrifices?'

Flatly, avoiding her, Avery replied, 'It's nothing like that. I'm doing a job. I'm a technician; part of the machine. You want me to say double-think, don't you? You want to demonstrate the paradox.'

'No. You've said what I want you to say. You've got to draw a circle and not go outside it. That's not double-think, it's unthink. It's very humble of you. Do you really believe you're that small?'

'You've made me small. Don't sneer. You're making me small now.'

'John, I swear it, I don't mean to. When you came back last night you looked as though you'd fallen in love. The kind of love that gives you comfort. You looked free and at peace. I thought for a moment you'd found a woman. That's why I asked, really it is, whether they were all men . . . I thought you were in love. Now you tell me you're nothing, and you seem proud of that too.'

He waited, then smiling, the smile he gave Leiser, he said, 'Sarah, I missed you terribly. When I was in Oxford I went to the house, the house in Chandos Road, remember? It was fun there, wasn't it?' He gave her hand a squeeze. 'Real fun. I thought about it, our marriage and you. And Anthony. I love you, Sarah; I love you. For everything . . . the way you bring up our baby.' A laugh. 'You're both so vulnerable, sometimes I can hardly tell you apart.'

She remained silent, so he continued, 'I thought perhaps if we lived in the country, bought a house . . . I'm established now: Leclerc would arrange a loan. Then Anthony could run about more. It's only a matter of increasing our range. Going to the theatre, like we used to at Oxford.'

She said absently, 'Did we? We can't go to the theatre in the country, can we?'

'The Department gives me something, don't you understand? It's a real job. It's important, Sarah.'

She pushed him gently away. 'My mother's asked us to Reigate for Christmas.'

'That'll be fine. Look . . . about the office. They owe me something now, after all I've done. They accept me on equal terms. As a colleague. I'm one of them.'

'Then you're not responsible, are you? Just one of the team. So there's no sacrifice.' They were back to the beginning. Avery, not realizing this, continued softly. 'I can tell him, can't I? I can tell him you'll come to dinner?'

'For pity's sake, John,' she snapped, 'don't try to run me like one of your wretched agents.'

Haldane, meanwhile, sat at his desk, going through Gladstone's report.

There had twice been manoeuvres in the Kalkstadt area; in 1952 and 1960. On the second occasion the Russians had staged an infantry attack on Rostock with heavy armoured support but no air cover. Little was known of the 1952 exercise, except that a large detachment of troops had occupied the town of Wolken. They were believed to be wearing magenta shoulder-boards. The report was unreliable. On both occasions the area had been declared closed; the restriction had been enforced as far as the northern coast. There followed a long recitation of the principal industries. There was some evidence – it came from the Circus, who refused to release the source – that a new refinery was being constructed on a plateau to the east of Wolken, and that the machinery for it had been transported from Leipzig. It was conceivable (but unlikely) that it had come by rail and been sent by way of Kalkstadt. There was no evidence of civil or industrial unrest, nor of any incident which could account for a temporary closure of the town.

A note from Registry lay in his in-tray. They had put up the files he had asked for, but some were Subscription Only; he would have to read them in the library.

He went downstairs, opened the combination lock on the steel door of General Registry, groped vainly for the light switch. Finally he made his way in the dark between the shelves to the small, windowless room at the back of the building where documents of special interest or secrecy were kept. It was pitch dark. He struck a match, put on the light. On the table were two sets of files: *Mayfly*, heavily restricted, now in its third volume, with a subscription list pasted on the cover, and Deception (*Soviet and*

East Germany), an immaculately kept collection of papers and photographs in hard folders.

After glancing briefly at the Mayfly files he turned his attention to the folders, thumbing his way through the depressing miscellany of rogues, double agents and lunatics who in every conceivable corner of the earth, under every conceivable pretext, had attempted, sometimes successfully, to delude the Western intelligence agencies. There was the boring similarity of technique; the grain of truth carefully reconstructed, culled from newspaper reports and bazaar gossip; the follow-up, less carefully done, betraying the deceiver's contempt for the deceived; and finally the flight of fancy, the stroke of artistic impertinence which wantonly terminated a relationship already under sentence.

On one report he found a flag with Gladstone's initials; written above them in his cautious, rounded hand were the words: 'Could be of interest to you.'

It was a refugee report of Soviet tank trials near Gustweiler. It was marked: 'Should not issue. Fabrication.' There followed a long justification citing passages in the report which had been abstracted almost verbatim from a 1949 Soviet military manual. The originator appeared to have enlarged every dimension by a third, and added some ingenious flavouring of his own. Attached were six photographs, very blurred, purporting to have been taken from a train with a telephoto lens. On the back of the photographs was written in McCulloch's careful hand: 'Claims to have used Exa-two camera, East German manufacture. Cheap housing. Exakta range lens. Low shutter speed. Negatives very blurred owing to camera shake from train. Fishy.' It was all very inconclusive. The same make of camera, that was all. He locked up the Registry and went home. Not his duty, Leclerc had said, to prove that Christ was born on Christmas Day; any more, Haldane reflected, that it was his business to prove that Taylor had been murdered.

Woodford's wife added a little soda to her Scotch, a splash: it was habit rather than taste.

'Sleep in the office, my foot,' she said. 'Do you get operational subsistence?'

'Yes, of course.'

'Well, it *isn't* a conference then, is it? A conference isn't operational. Not unless,' she added with a giggle, 'you're having it in the Kremlin.'

'All right, it's not a conference. It's an operation. That's why I'm getting subsistence.'

She looked at him cruelly. She was a thin, childless woman, her eyes half shut from the smoke of the cigarette in her mouth.

'There's nothing going on at all. You're making it up.' She began laughing, a hard false laugh. 'You poor sod,' she said and laughed again, derisively. 'How's little Clarkie? You're all scared of him, aren't you? Why don't you ever say anything against him? Jimmy Gorton used to: *he* saw through him.'

'Don't mention Jimmy Gorton to me!'

'Jimmy's *lovely*.'

'Babs, I warn you!'

'Poor Clarkie. Do you remember,' his wife asked reflectively, 'that nice little dinner he gave us in his club? The time he remembered it was our turn for welfare? Steak and kidney and frozen peas.' She sipped her whisky. 'And warm gin.' Something struck her. 'I wonder if he's ever had a woman,' she said. 'Christ, I wonder why I never thought of that before?'

Woodford returned to safer ground.

'All right, so nothing's going on.' He got up, a silly grin on his face, collected some matches from the desk.

'You're not smoking that damn pipe in here,' she said automatically.

'So nothing's going on,' he repeated smugly, and lit his pipe, sucking noisily.

'God, I hate you.'

Woodford shook his head, still grinning. 'Never mind,' he urged, 'just never mind. You said it, my dear, I didn't. I'm not sleeping in the office so everything's fine, isn't it? So I didn't go to Oxford either; I didn't even go to the Ministry; I haven't got a car to bring me home at night.'

She leant forward, her voice suddenly urgent, dangerous. 'What's happening?' she hissed. 'I've got a right to know, haven't I? I'm your wife, aren't I? You tell those little tarts in the office, don't you? Well, tell me!'

'We're putting a man over the border,' Woodford said. It was his moment of victory. 'I'm in charge of the London end. There's a crisis. There could even be a war. It's a damn ticklish thing.' The match had gone out, but he was still swinging it up and down with long movements of his arm, watching her with triumph in his eyes.

'You bloody liar,' she said. 'Don't give me that.'

Back in Oxford, the pub at the corner was three-quarters empty. They had the saloon bar to themselves. Leiser sipped a White Lady while the wireless operator drank best bitter at the Department's expense.

'Just take it gently, that's all you got to do, Fred,' he urged kindly. 'You came up lovely on the last run through. We'll hear you, don't worry about that – you're only eighty miles from the border. It's a piece of cake as long as you remember your procedure. Take it gently on the tuning or we're all done for.'

'I'll remember. Not to worry.'

'Don't get all bothered about the Jerries picking it up; you're not sending love letters, just a handful of groups. Then a new call sign and a different frequency. They'll never home on that, not for the time you're there.'

'Perhaps they can, these days,' Leiser said. 'Maybe they got better since the war.'

'There'll be all sorts of other traffic getting in their hair; shipping, military, air control, Christ knows what. They're not supermen, Fred; they're like us. A dozy lot. Don't worry.'

'I'm not worried. They didn't get me in the war; not for long.'

'Now listen, Fred, how about this? One more drink and we'll slip home and just have a nice run through with Mrs Hartbeck. No lights, mind. In the dark: she's shy, see? Get it a hundred per cent before we turn in. Then tomorrow we'll take it easy. After all, it's Sunday tomorrow, isn't it?' he added solicitously.

'I want to sleep. Can't I sleep a little, Jack?'

'Tomorrow, Fred. Then you can have a nice rest.' He nudged Leiser's elbow. 'You're married now, Fred. Can't always go to sleep, you know. You've taken the vow, that's what we used to say.'

'All right, forget about it, will you?' Leiser sounded on edge. 'Just leave it alone, see?'

'Sorry, Fred.'

'When do we go to London?'

'Monday, Fred.'

'Will John be there?'

'We meet him at the airport. And the Captain. They wanted us to have a bit more practice . . . on the routine and that.'

Leiser nodded, drumming his second and third fingers lightly on the table as if he were tapping the key.

'Here – why don't you tell us about one of those girls you had on your week-end in London?' Johnson suggested.

Leiser shook his head.

'Come on, then, let's have the other half and you give us a nice game of billiards.'

Leiser smiled shyly, his irritation forgotten. 'I got a lot more money than you, Jack. White Lady's an expensive drink. Not to worry.'

He chalked his cue and put in the sixpence. 'I'll play you double or quits; for last night.'

'Look, Fred,' Johnson pleaded gently. 'Don't always go for the big money, see, trying to put the red into the hundred slot. Just take the twenties and fifties – they mount up, you know. Then you'll be home and dry.'

Leiser was suddenly angry. He put his cue back in the cradle and took down his camel-hair coat from its peg.

'What's the matter, Fred, what the hell's the matter now?'

'For Christ's sake let me loose! Stop behaving like a bloody gaoler. I'm going on a job, like we all did in the war. I'm not sitting in the hanging cell.'

'Don't you be daft,' Johnson said gently, taking his coat and putting it back on the peg. 'Anyway we don't say hanging, we say condemned.'

Carol put the coffee on the desk in front of Leclerc. He looked up brightly and said thank you, tired but well drilled, like a child at the end of a party.

'Adrian Haldane's gone home,' Carol observed. Leclerc went back to the map.

'I looked in his room. He might have said goodnight.'

'He never does,' Leclerc said proudly.

'Is there anything I can do?'

'I never remember how you turn yards into metres.'

'Neither do I.'

'The Circus say this gully is two hundred metres long. That's about two hundred and fifty yards, isn't it?'

'I think so. I'll get the book.'

She went to her room and took a ready-reckoner from the bookcase.

'One metre is thirty-nine point three seven inches,' she read. 'A hundred metres is a hundred and nine yards and thirteen inches.'

Leclerc wrote it down.

'I think we should make a confirmatory telegram to Gorton. Have your coffee first, then come in with your pad.'

'I don't want any coffee.'

'Routine Priority will do, we don't want to haul old Jimmy out of bed.' He ran his small hand briskly over his hair. 'One. Advance party, Haldane, Avery, Johnson and Mayfly arrive BEA flight so and so, such and such a time December nine.' He glanced up. 'Get the details from Administration. Two. All will travel under their own names and proceed by train to Lübeck. For security reasons you will not repeat not meet party at airport but you may discreetly contact Avery by telephone at Lübeck base. We can't put him on to old Adrian,' he observed with a short laugh. 'The two of them don't hit it off at all . . .' He raised his voice: 'Three. Party number two consisting of Director only arriving morning flight December ten. You will meet him at airport for short conference before he proceeds to Lübeck. Four. Your role is discreetly to provide advice and assistance at all stages in order to bring operation Mayfly to successful conclusion.'

She stood up.

'Does John Avery have to go? His poor wife hasn't seen him for weeks.'

'Fortunes of war,' Leclerc replied without looking at her. 'How long does a man take to crawl two hundred and twenty yards?' he muttered. 'Oh, Carol – put another sentence on to that telegram: Five. Good Hunting. Old Jimmy likes a bit of encouragement, stuck out there all on his own.'

He picked a file from the in-tray and looked critically at the cover, aware perhaps of Carol's eyes upon him.

'Ah.' A controlled smile. 'This must be the Hungarian report. Did you ever meet Arthur Fielden in Vienna?'

'No.'

'A nice fellow. Rather your type. One of our best chaps . . . knows his way around. Bruce tells me he's done a very good report on unit changes in Budapest. I must get Adrian to look at it. Such a *lot* going on just now.' He opened the file and began reading.

Control said: 'Did you speak to Hyde?'

'Yes.'

'Well, what did he say? What have they got down there?'

Smiley handed him a whisky and soda. They were sitting in Smiley's house in Bywater Street. Control was in the chair he preferred, nearest the fire.

'He said they'd got first-night nerves.'

'Hyde said that? Hyde used an expression like that? How extraordinary.'

'They've taken over a house in North Oxford. There was just this one agent, a Pole of about forty, and they wanted him documented as a mechanic from Magdeburg, a name like Freiser. They wanted travel papers to Rostock.'

'Who else was there?'

'Haldane and that new man, Avery. The one who came to me about the Finnish courier. And a wireless operator, Jack Johnson. We had him in the war. No one else at all. So much for their big team of agents.'

'What *are* they up to? And whoever gave them all that money just for *training*? We lent them some equipment, didn't we?'

'Yes, a B 2.'

'What on earth's that?'

'A wartime set,' Smiley replied with irritation. 'You said it was all they could have. That and the crystals. Why on earth did you bother with the crystals?'

'Just charity. A B 2 was it? Oh well,' Control observed with apparent relief. 'They wouldn't get far with *that*, would they?'

'Are you going home tonight?' Smiley asked impatiently.

'I thought you might give me a bed here,' Control suggested. 'Such a *fag* always traipsing home. It's the people . . . They seem to get worse every time.'

Leiser sat at the table, the taste of the White Ladies still in his mouth. He stared at the luminous dial of his watch, the suitcase open in front of him. It was eleven eighteen; the second hand struggled jerkily towards twelve. He began tapping, JAJ, JAJ, – you can remember that, Fred, my name's Jack Johnson, see? – he switched over to receive, and there was Johnson's reply, steady as a rock.

Take your time, Johnson had said, don't rush your fences. We'll be listening all night, there are plenty more schedules. By the beam of a small torch he counted the encoded groups. There were thirty-eight. Putting out the torch he tapped a three and an eight; numerals were easy but long. His mind was very clear. He could hear Jack's gentle repetitions all the time: You're too quick on your shorts, Fred, a dot is one third of a dash, see? That's longer than you think. Don't rush the gaps, Fred; five dots between each word, three dots between each letter. Forearm horizontal, in a straight line with the key lever; elbow just clear of the body. It's like knife fighting, he thought with a little smile, and began keying. Fingers loose, Fred, relax, wrist clear of the table. He tapped out the first two groups, slurring a little on the gaps, but not as much as he usually did. Now came the third group: put in the safety signal. He tapped an S, cancelled it and tapped the next ten groups, glancing now and then at the dial of his watch. After two and a half minutes he went off the air, groped for the small capsule which contained the crystal, discovered with the tips of his fingers the twin sockets of the housing, inserted it, then stage by stage followed the tuning procedure, moving the dials, flashing his torch on the crescent window to watch the black tongue tremble across it.

He tapped out the second call sign, PRE, PRE, switched quickly to receive and there was Johnson again, QRK 4, your signal readable. For the second time he began transmitting, his hand moving slowly but methodically as his eye followed the meaningless letters, until with a nod of satisfaction he heard Johnson's reply: Signal received. QRU: I have nothing for you.

When they had finished Leiser insisted on a short walk. It was bitterly cold. They followed Walton Street as far as the main gates of Worcester, thence by way of Banbury Road once more to the respectable sanctuary of their dark North Oxford house.

Chapter 16
Take-off

It was the same wind. The wind that had tugged at Taylor's frozen body and drove the rain against the blackened walls of Blackfriars Road, the wind that flailed the grass of Port Meadow now ran headlong against the shutters of the farmhouse.

The farmhouse smelt of cats. There were no carpets. The floors were of stone: nothing would dry them. Johnson lit the tiled oven in the hall as soon as they arrived but the damp still lay on the flagstones, collecting in the dips like a tired army. They never saw a cat all the time they were there, but they smelt them in every room. Johnson left corned beef on the doorstep: it was gone in ten minutes.

It was built on one floor with a high granary roof, of brick, and lay against a small coppice beneath a vast Flemish sky, a long, rectangular building with cattle sheds on the sheltered side. It was two miles north of Lübeck. Leclerc had said they were not to enter the town.

A ladder led to the loft, and there Johnson installed his wireless, stretching the aerial between the beams, thence through a skylight to an elm tree beside the road. He wore plimsolls in the house, brown ones of military issue, and a blazer with a squadron crest. Gorton had had food delivered from the Naafi in Celle. It covered the kitchen floor in old cardboard boxes, with an invoice marked 'Mr Gorton's party'. There were two bottles of gin and three of whisky. They had two bedrooms; Gorton had sent army beds, two to each room, and reading lights with standard green shades. Haldane was very angry about the beds. 'He must have told every damned department in the area,' he complained. 'Cheap whisky, Naafi food, army beds. I suppose we shall find he requisitioned the house next. God, what a way to mount an operation.'

It was late afternoon when they arrived. Johnson, having put up his set, busied himself in the kitchen. He was a domesticated man; he cooked and washed up without complaint, treading lightly over the flagstones in his neat plimsolls. He assembled a hash of bully beef and egg, and gave them cocoa with a great deal of sugar. They ate in the hall in front of the stove. Johnson did most of the talking; Leiser, very quiet, scarcely touched his food.

'What's the matter, Fred? Not hungry, then?'

'Sorry, Jack.'

'Too many sweets on the plane, that's your trouble.' Johnson winked at Avery. 'I saw you giving that air hostess a look. You shouldn't do it, Fred, you know, you'll break her heart.' He frowned round the table in mock disapproval. 'He really looked her over, you know. A proper tip-to-toe job.'

Avery grinned dutifully. Haldane ignored him.

Leiser was concerned about the moon, so after supper they stood at the back door in a small shivering group, staring at the sky. It was strangely light; the clouds drifted like black smoke, so low that they seemed to mingle with the swaying branches of the coppice and half obscure the grey fields beyond.

'It will be darker at the border, Fred,' said Avery. 'It's higher ground; more hills.'

Haldane said they should have an early night; they drank another whisky and at quarter past ten they went to bed, Johnson and Leiser to one room, Avery and Haldane to the other. No one dictated the arrangement. Each knew, apparently, where he belonged.

It was after midnight when Johnson came into their room. Avery was woken by the squeak of his rubber shoes.

'John, are you awake?'

Haldane sat up.

'It's about Fred. He's sitting alone in the hall. I told him to try and sleep, sir; gave him a couple of tablets, the kind my mother takes; he wouldn't even get into bed at first, now he's gone along to the hall.'

Haldane said, 'Leave him alone. He's all right. None of us can sleep with this damned wind.'

Johnson went back to his room. An hour must have passed; there was still no sound from the hall. Haldane said, 'You'd better go and see what he's up to.'

Avery put on his overcoat and went along the corridor, past tapestries of Biblical quotations and an old print of Lübeck harbour. Leiser was sitting on a chair beside the tiled oven.

'Hello, Fred.'

He looked old and tired.

'It's near here, isn't it, where I cross?'

'About five kilometres. The Director will brief us in the morning. They say it's quite an easy run. He'll give you all your papers and that kind of thing. In the afternoon we'll show you the place. They've done a lot of work on it in London.'

'In London,' Leiser repeated, and suddenly: 'I did a job in Holland in the war. The Dutch were good people. We sent a lot of agents to Holland. Women. They were all picked up. You were too young.'

'I read about it.'

'The Germans caught a radio operator. Our people didn't know. They just went on sending more agents. They said there was nothing else to do.' He was talking faster. 'I was only a kid then; just a quick job they wanted, in and out. They were short of operators. They said it didn't matter me not speaking Dutch, the reception party would meet me at the drop. All I had to do was work the set. There'd be a safe house ready.' He was far away. 'We fly in and nothing moves, not a shot or a searchlight, and I'm jumping. And when I land, there they are: two men and a woman. We say the words and they take me to the road to get the bikes. There's no time to bury the parachute – we aren't bothering by then. We find the house and they give me food. After supper we go upstairs where the set is – no schedules, London listened all the time those days. They give the message: I'm sending a call sign – "Come in TYR, come in TYR" – then the message in front of me, twenty-one groups, four-letter.'

He stopped.

'Well?'

'They were following the message, you see; they wanted to know where the safety signal came. It was in the ninth letter; a back shift of one. They let me finish the message and then they were on me, one hitting me, men all over the house.'

'But *who*, Fred? Who's *they*?'

'You can't talk about it like that: you never know. It's never that easy.'

'But for God's sake, whose fault was it? Who did it? Fred!'

'Anyone's. You can never tell. You'll learn that.' He seemed to have given up.

'You're alone this time. Nobody has been told. Nobody's expecting you.'

'No. That's right.' His hands were clasped on his lap. He made a hunched figure, small and cold. 'In the war it was easier because, however bad it got, you thought one day we'd win. Even if you were picked up, you thought, "They'll come and get me, they'll drop some men or make a raid." You knew they never would, see, but you could think it. You just wanted to be left alone to think it. But nobody wins this one, do they?'

'It's not the same. But more important.'

'What do you do if I'm caught?'

'We'll get you back. Not to worry, eh, Fred?'

'Yes, but how?'

'We're a big outfit, Fred. A lot goes on you don't know about. Contacts here and there. You can't see the whole picture.'

'Can you?'

'Not all of it, Fred. Only the Director sees it all. Not even the Captain.'

'What's he like, the Director?'

'He's been in it a long time. You'll see him tomorrow. He's a very remarkable man.'

'Does the Captain fancy him?'

'Of course.'

'He never talks about him,' Leiser said.

'None of us talk about him.'

'There was this girl I had. She worked in the bank. I told her I was going away. If anything goes wrong I don't want anything said, see. She's just a kid.'

'What was her name?'

A moment of mistrust. 'Never mind. But if she turns up just keep it all right with her.'

'What do you mean, Fred?'

'Never mind.'

Leiser didn't talk after that. When the morning came Avery returned to his room.

'What's it all about?' Haldane asked.

'He was in some mess in the war, in Holland. He was betrayed.'

'But he's giving us a second chance. How nice. Just what they always said.' And then: 'Leclerc arrives this morning.'

His taxi came at eleven. Leclerc was getting out almost before it had pulled up. He was wearing a duffle coat, heavy brown shoes for rough country and a soft cap. He looked very well.

'Where's Mayfly?'

'With Johnson,' Haldane said.

'Got a bed for me?'

'You can have Mayfly's when he's gone.'

At eleven thirty Leclerc held a briefing; in the afternoon they were to make a tour of the border.

The briefing took place in the hall. Leiser came in last. He stood in the doorway, looking at Leclerc, who smiled at him winningly, as if he liked what he saw. They were about the same height.

Avery said, 'Director, this is Mayfly.'

His eyes still on Leiser, Leclerc replied, 'I think I'm allowed to call him Fred. Hullo.' He advanced and shook him by the hand, both formal, two weather men coming out of a box.

'Hullo,' said Leiser.

'I hope they haven't been working you too hard?'

'I'm all right, sir.'

'We're all very impressed,' Leclerc said. 'You've done a grand job.' He might have been talking to his constituents.'

'I haven't started yet.'

'I always feel the training is three-quarters of the battle. Don't you, Adrian?'

'Yes.'

They sat down. Leclerc stood a little away from them. He had hung a map on the wall. By some indefinable means – it may have been his maps, it may have been the precision of his language, or it may have been his strict deportment, which so elusively combined purpose with restraint – Leclerc evoked in that hour that same nostalgic, campaigning atmosphere which had informed the briefing in Blackfriars Road a month before. He had the illusionist's gift, whether he spoke of rockets or wireless transmission, of cover or the point at which the border was to be crossed, of implying great familiarity with his subject.

'Your target is Kalkstadt' – a little grin – 'hitherto famous only for a remarkably fine fourteenth-century church.' They laughed, Leiser too. It was so good, Leclerc knowing about old churches.

He had brought a diagram of the crossing point, done in different inks, with the border drawn in red. It was all very simple. On the western side, he said, there was a low, wooded hill overgrown with gorse and bracken. This ran parallel to the border until the southern end curved eastwards in a narrow arm stopping about two hundred and twenty yards short of the border, directly opposite an observation tower. The tower was set well back from the demarcation line: at its foot ran a fence of barbed wire. It had been observed that this wire was laid out in a single apron and only loosely fixed to its staves. East German guards had been seen to detach it in order to pass through and patrol the undefended strip of territory which lay between the demarcation line and the physi-

- 167 -

cal border. That afternoon Leclerc would indicate the precise staves. Mayfly, he said, should not be alarmed at having to pass so close to the tower; experience had shown that the attention of the guards was concentrated on the more distant parts of their area; the night was ideal; a high wind was forecast; there would be no moon. Leclerc had set the crossing time for 0235 hours; the guard changed at midnight, each watch lasted three hours. It was reasonable to suppose that the sentries would not be as alert after two and a half hours on duty as they would be at the start of their watches. The relief guard, which had to approach from a barrack some distance to the north, would not yet be under way.

Much attention had been given, Leclerc continued, to the possibility of mines. They would see from the map – the little forefinger traced the green dotted line from the end of the rise across the border – that there was an old footpath which did indeed follow the very route which Leiser would be taking. The frontier guards had been seen to avoid this path, striking a track of their own some ten yards to the south of it. The assumption was, Leclerc said, that the path was mined, while the area to the side of it had been left clear for the benefit of patrols. Leclerc proposed that Leiser should use the track made by the frontier guards.

Wherever possible over the two hundred odd yards between the foot of the hill and the tower, Leiser should crawl, keeping his head below the level of the bracken. This eliminated the small danger that he would be sighted from the tower. He would be comforted to hear, Leclerc added with a smile, that there was no record of any patrol operating on the western side of the wire during the hours of darkness. The East German guards seemed to fear that one of their own number might slip away unseen.

Once across the border Leiser should keep clear of any path. The country was rough, partly wooded. The going would be hard but all the safer for that; he was to head south. The reason for this was simple. To the south, the border turned westward for some ten kilometres. Thus Leiser, by moving southwards, would put himself not two but fifteen kilometres from the border, and more quickly escape the zonal patrols which guarded the eastern approaches. Leclerc would advise him thus – he withdrew one hand casually from the pocket of his duffle coat and lit a cigarette, conscious all the time of their eyes upon him – march east for half an hour, then turn due south, making for the Marienhorst lake. At the eastern end of the lake was a disused boathouse. There he could lie up for an hour and give himself some food. By that time

Leiser might care for a drink – relieved laughter – and he would find a little brandy in his rucksack.

Leclerc had a habit, when making a joke, of holding himself at attention and lifting his heels from the ground as if to launch his wit upon the higher air.

'I couldn't have something with gin, could I?' Leiser asked. 'White Lady's my drink.'

There was a moment's bewildered silence.

'That wouldn't do at all,' Leclerc said shortly, Leiser's master.

Having rested, he should walk to the village of Marienhorst and look around for transport to Schwerin. From then on, Leclerc added lightly, he was on his own.

'You have all the papers necessary for a journey from Magdeburg to Rostock. When you reach Schwerin, you are on the legitimate route. I don't want to say too much about cover because you have been through that with the Captain. Your name is Fred Hartbeck, you are an unmarried mechanic from Magdeburg with an offer of employment at the State Co-operative ship-building works at Rostock.' He smiled, undeterred. 'I am sure you have all been through every detail of this already. Your love life, your pay, medical history, war service and the rest. There is just one thing that I might add about cover. Never *volunteer* information. People don't *expect* you to explain yourself. If you are cornered, play it by ear. Stick as closely to the truth as you can. Cover,' he declared, stating a favourite maxim, 'should never be *fabricated* but only an extension of the truth.' Leiser laughed in a reserved way. It was as if he could have wished Leclerc a taller man.

Johnson brought coffee from the kitchen, and Leclerc said briskly, 'Thank you, Jack,' as if everything were quite as it should be.

Leclerc now addressed himself to the question of Leiser's target; he gave a résumé of the indicators, implying somehow that they only confirmed suspicions which he himself had long harboured. He employed a tone which Avery had not heard in him before. He sought to imply, as much by omission and inference as by direct allusion, that theirs was a Department of enormous skill and knowledge, enjoying in its access to money, its intercourse with other services and in the unchallenged authority of its judgements an unearthly, oracular immunity, so that Leiser might well have wondered why, if all this were so, he need bother to risk his life at all.

'The rockets are in the area now,' Leclerc said. 'The Captain has told you what signs to look for. We want to know what they look like, where they are and above all who mans them.'

'I know.'

'You must try the usual tricks. Pub gossip, tracing an old soldier friend, you know the kind of thing. When you find them, come back.'

Leiser nodded.

'At Kalkstadt there's a workers' hostel.' He unfolded a chart of the town. 'Here. Next to the church. Stay there if you can. You may run into people who have actually been engaged . . .'

'I know,' Leiser repeated. Haldane stirred, glanced at him anxiously.

'You might even hear something of a man who used to be employed at the station, Fritsche. He gave us some interesting details about the rockets, then disappeared. If you get the chance, that is. You could ask at the station, say you're a friend of his . . .'

There was a very slight pause.

'Just disappeared,' Leclerc repeated, for them, not for himself. His mind was elsewhere. Avery watched him anxiously, waiting for him to go on. At last he said, rapidly, 'I have deliberately avoided the question of communication,' indicating by his tone that they were nearly done. 'I imagine you have gone over that enough times already.'

'No worries there,' Johnson said. 'All the schedules are at night. That leaves the frequency range pretty simple. He'll have a clear hand during the day, sir. We've had some very nice dummy runs, haven't we, Fred?'

'Oh yes. Very nice.'

'As regards getting back,' Leclerc said, 'we play the war rules. There are no submarines any more, Fred; not for this kind of thing. When you return, you should report at once to the nearest British Consulate or Embassy, give your proper name and ask to be repatriated. You should represent yourself as a distressed British subject. My instinct would be to advise you to come out the way you went in. If you're in trouble, don't necessarily move west straight away. Lie up for a bit. You're taking plenty of money.'

Avery knew he would never forget that morning, how they had sat at the farmhouse table like sprawling boys at the Nissen hut desks, their strained faces fixed upon Leclerc as in the stillness of a church he read the liturgy of their devotion, moving his little hand across the map like a priest with the taper. All of them in that room — but Avery perhaps best of all — knew the fatal disproportion between the dream and reality, between motive and action. Avery had talked to Taylor's child, stammered out his half-formed lies to Peersen and the Consul: he had heard that dreadful footfall in the hotel, and returned from a nightmare journey to see his own experiences remade into the images of Leclerc's world. Yet Avery, like Haldane and Leiser, listened to Leclerc with the piety of an agnostic, feeling perhaps that this was how, in some clean and magic place, it really ought to be.

'Excuse me,' said Leiser. He was looking at the plan of Kalkstadt. He was very much the small man just then. He might have been pointing to a fault in an engine. The station, hostel and church were marked in green; an inset at the bottom left-hand corner depicted the railway warehouses and dumping sheds. At each side, the point of the compass was given adjectivally: Western Prospect, Northern Prospect.

'What's a prospect, sir?' Leiser inquired.

'A view, an outlook.'

'What's it for? What's it for on the map, please?'

Leclerc smiled patiently. 'For purposes of orientation, Fred.'

Leiser got up and examined the chart closely. 'And this is the church?'

'That's right, Fred.'

'Why does it face north? Churches go from east to west. You've got the entrance on the eastern side where the altar should be.'

Haldane leaned forward, the index finger of his right hand resting on his lip.

'It's only a sketch map,' Leclerc said. Leiser returned to his place and sat to attention, straighter than ever. 'I see. Sorry.'

When the meeting was over Leclerc took Avery on one side. 'Just one point, John, he's not to take a gun. It's quite out of the question. The Minister was adamant. Perhaps you'll mention it to him.'

'No gun?'

'I think we can allow the knife. That could be a general-purpose thing; I mean if anything went wrong we could say it was general purpose.'

After lunch they made a tour of the border – Gorton had provided a car. Leclerc brought with him a handful of notes he had made from the Circus frontier report, and these he kept on his knee, together with a folded map.

The extreme northern part of the frontier which divides the two halves of Germany is largely a thing of depressing inconsequence.

Those who look eagerly for dragon's teeth and substantial fortifications will be disappointed. It crosses land of considerable variety; gullies and small hills overgrown with bracken and patches of untended forest. Often the Eastern defences are set so far behind the demarcation line as to be hidden from Western eyes – only a forward pillbox, crumbling roads, a vacated farmhouse or an occasional observation tower excite the imagination.

By way of emphasis the Western side is adorned with the grotesque statuary of political impotence: a plywood model of the Brandenburg Gate, the screws rusting in their sockets, rises absurdly from an untended field; notice boards, broken by wind and rain, display fifteen-year-old slogans across an empty valley. Only at night, when the beam of a searchlight springs from the darkness and draws its wavering finger across the cold earth, does the heart chill for the captive crouching like a hare in the plough, waiting to break cover and run in terror till he fall.

They followed an unmade road along the top of a hill, and wherever it ran close to the frontier they stopped the car and got out. Leiser was shrouded in a mackintosh and hat. The day was very cold. Leclerc wore his duffle coat and carried a shooting stick – Heaven knows where he had found it. The first time they stopped, and the second, and again at the next, Leclerc said quietly, 'Not this one.' As they got into the car for the fourth time he declared, 'The next stop is ours.' It was the kind of brave joke favoured in battle.

Avery would not have recognized the place from Leclerc's sketch map. The hill was there, certainly, turning inwards towards the frontier, then descending sharply to the plain below. But the land beyond it was hilly and partly wooded, its horizon fringed with trees against which, with the aid of glasses, they could discern the brown shape of a wooden tower. 'It's the three staves to the left,' Leclerc said. As they scanned the ground, Avery could make out here and there the worn mark of the old path.

'It's mined. The path is mined the whole way. Their territory begins at the foot of the hill.' Leclerc turned to Leiser. 'You start from here.' He pointed with his shooting stick. 'You proceed to the brow of the hill and lie up till take-off time. We'll have you here early so that your eyes grow used to the light. I think we should go now. We mustn't attract attention, you know.'

As they drove back to the farmhouse the rain came bursting against the windscreen, thundering on the roof of the car. Avery, sitting next to Leiser, was sunk in his own thoughts. He realized with what he took to be utter detachment that, while his own mission had unfolded as comedy, Leiser was to play the same part as tragedy; that he was witnessing an insane relay race in which each contestant ran faster and longer than the last, arriving nowhere but at his own destruction.

'Incidentally,' he said suddenly, addressing himself to Leiser, 'hadn't you better do something about your hair? I don't imagine they have much in the way of lotions over there. A thing like that could be insecure.'

'He needn't cut it,' Haldane observed. 'The Germans go in for long hair. Just wash it, that's all that's needed. Get the oil out. A nice point, John, I congratulate you.'

Chapter 17

The rain had stopped. The night came slowly, struggling with the wind. They sat at the table in the farmhouse, waiting; Leiser was in his bedroom. Johnson made tea and attended to his equipment. No one talked. The pretending was over. Not even Leclerc, master of the public-school catchword, bothered any more. He seemed to resent being made to wait, that was all, at the tardy wedding of an unloved friend. They had relapsed into a state of somnolent fear, like men in a submarine, while the lamp over their heads rocked gently. Now and then Johnson would be sent to the door to look for the moon, and each time he announced that there was none.

'The met reports were pretty good,' Leclerc observed, and drifted away to the attic to watch Johnson check his equipment.

Avery, alone with Haldane, said quickly, 'He says the Ministry's ruled against the gun. He's not to take it.'

'And what bloody fool told him to consult the Ministry in the first place?' Haldane demanded, beside himself with anger. Then: 'You'll have to tell him. It depends on you.'

'Tell Leclerc?'

'No, you idiot; Leiser.'

They had some food and afterwards Avery and Haldane took Leiser to his bedroom.

'We must dress you up,' they said.

They made him strip, taking from him piece by piece his warm, expensive clothes: jacket and trousers of matching grey, cream silk shirt, black shoes without toecaps, socks of dark blue nylon. As he loosened the knot of his tartan tie his fingers discovered the gold pin with the horse's head. He unclipped it carefully and held it out to Haldane.

'What about this?'

Haldane had provided envelopes for valuables. Into one of these he slipped the tie-pin, sealed it, wrote on the back, tossed it on the bed.

'You washed your hair?'

'Yes.'

'We had difficulty in obtaining East German soap. I'm afraid you'll have to try and get some when you're over there. I understand it's in short supply.'

'All right.'

He sat on the bed naked except for his watch, crouched forward, his broad arms folded across his hairless thighs, his white skin mottled from the cold. Haldane opened a trunk and extracted a bundle of clothes and half a dozen pairs of shoes.

As Leiser put on each unfamiliar thing, the cheap, baggy trousers of coarse serge, broad at the foot and gathered at the waist, the grey, threadbare jacket with arched pleats, the shoes, brown with a bright unhealthy finish, he seemed to shrink before their eyes, returning to some former estate which they had only guessed at. His brown hair, free from oil, was streaked with grey and fell undisciplined upon his head. He glanced shyly at them, as if he had revealed a secret; a peasant in the company of his masters.

'How do I look?'

'Fine,' Avery said. 'You look marvellous, Fred.'

'What about a tie?'

'A tie would spoil it.'

He tried the shoes one after another, pulling them with difficulty over the coarse woollen socks.

'They're Polish,' Haldane said, giving him a second pair. 'The Poles export them to East Germany. You'd better take these as well – you don't know how much walking you'll have to do.'

Haldane fetched from his own bedroom a heavy cashbox and unlocked it.

First he took a wallet, a shabby brown one with a centre compartment of Cellophane which held Leiser's identity card, fingered and stamped it; it lay open behind its flat frame, so that the photograph of Leiser looked outwards, a little prison picture. Beside it was an authority to travel and a written offer of employment from the State Co-operative for ship-building in Rostock. Haldane emptied one pocket of the wallet and then replaced the contents paper for paper, describing each in turn.

'Food registration card – driving licence . . . Party card. How long have you been a Party member?'

'Since 'forty-nine.'

He put in a photograph of a woman and three or four grimy letters, some still in their envelopes.

'Love letters,' he explained shortly.

Next came a Union card and a cutting from a Magdeburg newspaper about production figures at a local engineering works; a photograph of the Brandenburg Gate before the war, a tattered testimonial from a former employer.

'That's the wallet, then,' Haldane said. 'Except for the money. The rest of your equipment is in the rucksack. Provisions and that kind of thing.'

He handed Leiser a bundle of banknotes from the box. Leiser stood in the compliant attitude of a man being searched, his arms raised a little from his sides and his feet slightly apart. He would accept whatever Haldane gave him, put it carefully away, then resume the same position. He signed a receipt for the money. Haldane glanced at the signature and put the paper in a black briefcase which he had put separately on a side table.

Next came the odds and ends which Hartbeck would plausibly have about him: a bunch of keys on a chain – the key to the suitcase was among them – a comb, a khaki handkerchief stained with oil and a couple of ounces of substitute coffee in a twist of newspaper; a screwdriver, a length of fine wire and fragments of metal ends newly turned – the meaningless rubble of a working man's pockets.

'I'm afraid you can't take that watch,' Haldane said.

Leiser unbuckled the gold armband and dropped the watch into Haldane's open palm. They gave him a steel one of Eastern manufacture and set it with great precision by Avery's bedside clock.

Haldane stood back. 'That will do. Now remain there and go through your pockets. Make sure things are where you would naturally keep them. Don't touch anything else in the room, do you understand?'

'I know the form,' said Leiser, glancing at his gold watch on the table. He accepted the knife and hooked the black scabbard into the waistband of his trousers.

'What about my gun?'

Haldane guided the steel clip of the briefcase into its housing and it snapped like the latch of a door.

'You don't take one,' Avery said.

'No gun?'

'It's not on, Fred. They reckon it's too dangerous.'

'Who for?'

'It could lead to a dangerous situation. Politically, I mean. Sending an armed man into East Germany. They're afraid of an incident.'

'Afraid.'

For a long time he stared at Avery, his eyes searching the young, unfurrowed face for something that was not there. He turned to Haldane.

'Is that true?'

Haldane nodded.

Suddenly he thrust out his empty hands in front of him, cupped in a terrible gesture of poverty, the fingers crooked and pressed together as if to catch the last water, his shoulders trembling in the cheap jacket, his face drawn, half in supplication, half in panic.

'The gun, John! You can't send a man without a gun! For mercy's sake, let me have the gun!'

'Sorry, Fred.'

His hands still extended, he swung round to Haldane. 'You don't know what you're doing!'

Leclerc had heard the noise and came to the doorway. Haldane's face was arid as rock; Leiser could have beaten his empty fists upon it for all the charity it held. His voice fell to a whisper. 'What are you doing? God Christ, what are you trying to do?' To both of them he cried in revelation, 'You hate me, don't you! What have I done to you? John, what have I done? We were pals, weren't we?'

Leclerc's voice, when at last he spoke, sounded very pure, as if he were deliberately emphasizing the gulf between them.

'What's the trouble?'

'He's worried about the gun,' Haldane explained.

'I'm afraid there's nothing we can do. It's out of our hands. You know how we feel about it, Fred. Surely you know that. It's an order, that's all. Have you forgotten how it used to be?' He added stiffly, a man of duty and decision, 'I can't question my orders: what do you want me to say?'

Leiser shook his head. His hands fell to his sides. The discipline had gone out of his body.

'Never mind.' He was looking at Avery.

'A knife's better in some ways, Fred,' Leclerc added consolingly, 'quieter.'

'Yes.'

Haldane picked up Leiser's spare clothes. 'I must put these into the rucksack,' he said, and with a sideways glance at Avery, walked quickly from the room, taking Leclerc with him. Leiser and Avery looked at one another in silence. Avery was embarrassed to see him so ugly. At last Leiser spoke.

'It was us three. The Captain, you and me. It was all right, then. Don't worry about the others, John. They don't matter.'

'That's right, Fred.'

Leiser smiled. 'It was the best ever, that week, John. It's funny, isn't it: we spend all our time chasing girls, and it's the men that matter; just the men.'

'You're one of us, Fred. You always were; all the time your card was there, you were one of us. We don't forget.'

'What does it look like?'

'It's two pinned together. One for then, one for now. It's in the index . . . live agents, we call it. Yours is the first name. You're the best man we've got.' He could imagine it now; the index was something they had built together. He could believe in it, like love.

'You said it was alphabetical order,' Leiser said sharply. 'You said it was a special index for the best.'

'Big cases go to the front.'

'And men all over the world?'

'Everywhere.'

Leiser frowned as if it were a private matter, a decision to be privately taken. He stared slowly round the bare room, then at the cuffs on his coarse jacket, then at Avery, interminably at Avery, until, taking him by the wrist, but lightly, more to touch than to lead, he said under his breath, 'Give us something. Give me something to take. From you. Anything.'

Avery felt in his pockets, pulling out a handkerchief, some loose change and a twist of thin cardboard, which he opened. It was the photograph of Taylor's little girl.

'Is that your kid?' Leiser looked over the other's shoulder at the small, bespectacled face; his hand closed on Avery's. 'I'd like that.' Avery nodded. Leiser put it in his wallet, then picked up his watch from the bed. It was gold with a black dial for the phases of the moon. 'You have it,' he said. 'Keep it. I've been trying to remember,' he continued, 'at home. There was this school. A big courtyard like a barracks with nothing but windows and drainpipes. We used to bang a ball round after lunch. Then a gate, and a path to the church, and the river on the other side . . .' He was laying out the town with his hands, placing bricks. 'We went Sunday, through the side door, the kids last, see?' A smile of success. 'That church was facing north,' he declared, 'not east at all.' Suddenly he asked: 'How long; how long have you been in, John?'

'In the outfit?'

'Yes.'

'Four years.'

'How old were you then?'

'Twenty-eight. It's the youngest they take you.'

'You told me you were thirty-four.'

'They're waiting for us,' Avery said.

In the hall they had the rucksack and the suitcase, green canvas with leather corners. He tried the rucksack on, adjusting the straps until it sat high on his back, like a German schoolboy's satchel. He lifted the suitcase and felt the weight of the two things together.

'Not too bad,' he muttered.

'It's the minimum,' Leclerc said. They had begun to whisper, though no one could hear. One by one they got into the car.

A hurried handshake and he walked away towards the hill. There were no fine words; not even from Leclerc. It was as if they had all taken leave of Leiser long ago. The last they saw of him was the rucksack gently bobbing as he disappeared into the darkness. There had always been a rhythm about the way he walked.

Chapter 18

L eiser lay in the bracken on the spur of the hill, stared at the luminous dial of his watch. Ten minutes to wait. The key chain was swinging from his belt. He put the keys back in his pocket, and as he drew his hand away he felt the links slip between his thumb and finger like the beads of a rosary. For a moment he let them linger there; there was comfort in their touch; they were where his childhood was. St Christopher and all his angels, please preserve us from road accidents.

Ahead of him the ground descended sharply, then evened out. He had seen it; he knew. But now, as he looked down, he could make out nothing in the darkness below him. Suppose it were marshland down there? There had been rain; the water had drained into the valley. He saw himself struggling through mud to his waist, carrying the suitcase above his head, the bullets splashing round him.

He tried to discern the tower on the opposite hill, but if it was there it was lost against the blackness of the trees.

Seven minutes. Don't worry about the noise, they said, the wind will carry it south. They'll hear nothing in a wind like this. Run beside the path, on the south side, that means to the right, keep on the new trail through the bracken, it's narrow but clear. If you meet anyone, use your knife, but for the love of Heaven don't go near the path.

His rucksack was heavy. Too heavy. So was the case. He'd quarrelled about it with Jack. He didn't care for Jack. 'Better be on the safe side, Fred,' Jack had explained. 'These little sets are sensitive as virgins: all right for fifty miles, dead as mutton on sixty. Better to have the margin, Fred, then we know where we are. They're experts, real experts where this one comes from.'

One minute to go. They'd set his watch by Avery's clock.

He was frightened. Suddenly he couldn't keep his mind from it any more. Perhaps he was too old, too tired, perhaps he'd done enough. Perhaps the training had worn him out. He felt his heart pounding his chest. His body wouldn't stand any more; he hadn't the strength. He lay there, talking to Haldane: Christ, Captain, can't you see I'm past it? The old body's cracking up. That's what he'd tell them; he would stay there when the minute hand came up, he would stay there too heavy to move. 'It's my heart, it's packed in,' he'd tell them. 'I've had a heart attack, skipper, didn't tell you about my dickie heart, did I? It just came over me as I lay here in the bracken.'

He stood up. Let the dog see the rabbit.

Run down the hill, they'd said; in this wind they won't hear a thing; run down the hill, because that's where they may spot you, they'll be looking at that hillside hoping for a silhouette. Run fast through the moving bracken, keep low and you'll be safe. When you reach level ground, lie up and get your breath back, then begin the crawl.

He was running like a madman. He tripped and the rucksack brought him down, he felt his knee against his chin and the pain as he bit his tongue, then he was up again and the suitcase swung him round. He half fell into the path and waited for the flash of a bursting mine. He was running down the slope, the ground gave way beneath his heels, the suitcase rattling like an old car. Why wouldn't they let him take the gun? The pain rose in his chest like fire, spreading under the bone, burning the lungs: he counted each step, he could feel the thump of each footfall and the slowing drag of the case and rucksack. Avery had lied. Lied all the way. Better watch that cough, Captain; better see a doctor, it's like barbed wire in your guts. The ground levelled out; he fell again and lay still, panting like an animal, feeling nothing but fear and the sweat that drenched his woollen shirt.

He pressed his face to the ground. Arching his body, he slid his hand beneath his belly and tightened the belt of his rucksack.

He began crawling up the hill, dragging himself forward with his elbows and his hands, pushing the suitcase in front of him, conscious all the time of the hump on his back rising above the undergrowth. The water was seeping through his clothes; soon it ran freely over his thighs and knees. The stink of leaf mould filled his nostrils; twigs tugged at his hair. It was as if all nature conspired to hold him back. He looked up the slope and caught sight of the observation tower against the line of black trees on the horizon. There was no light on the tower.

He lay still. It was too far: he could never crawl so far. It was quarter to three by his watch. The relief guard would be coming from the north. He unbuckled his rucksack, stood up, holding it under his arm like a child. Taking the suitcase in his other hand he began walking cautiously up the rise, keeping the trodden path to his left, his eyes fixed upon the skeleton outline of the tower. Suddenly it rose before him like the dark bones of a monster.

The wind clattered over the brow of the hill. From directly above him he could hear the slats of old timber banging, and the long creak of a casement. It was not a single apron but double; when he pulled, it came away from the staves. He stepped across, reattached the wire and stared into the forest ahead. He felt even in that moment of unspeakable terror while the sweat blinded him and the throbbing of his temples drowned the rustling of the wind, a full, confiding gratitude towards Avery and Haldane, as if he knew they had deceived him for his own good.

Then he saw the sentry, like the silhouette in the range, not ten yards from him, back turned, standing on the old path, his rifle slung over his shoulder, his bulky body swaying from left to right as he stamped his feet on the sodden ground to keep them from freezing. Leiser could smell tobacco – it was past him in a second – and coffee warm like a blanket. He put down the rucksack and suitcase and moved instinctively towards him; he might have been in the gymnasium at Headington. He felt the haft sharp in his hand, cross-hatched to prevent slip. The sentry was quite a young boy under his greatcoat; Leiser was surprised how young. He killed him hurriedly, one blow, as a fleeing man might shoot into a crowd; shortly; not to destroy but to preserve; impatiently, for he had to get along; indifferently because it was a fixture.

'Can you see anything?' Haldane repeated.

'No.' Avery handed him the glasses. 'He just went into the dark.'

'Can you see a light from the watch-tower? They'd shine a light if they heard him.'

'No, I was looking for Leiser,' Avery answered.

'You should have called him Mayfly,' Leclerc objected from behind. 'Johnson knows his name now.'

'I'll forget it, sir.'

'He's over, anyway,' Leclerc said and walked back to the car. They drove home in silence.

As they entered the house Avery felt a friendly touch upon his shoulder and turned, expecting to see Johnson; instead he found himself looking into the hollow face of Haldane, but so altered, so manifestly at peace, that it seemed to possess the youthful calm of a man who has survived a long illness; the last pain had gone out of him.

'I am not given to eulogies,' Haldane said.

'Do you think he's safely over?'

'You did well.' He was smiling.

'We'd have heard, wouldn't we? Heard the shots or seen the lights?'

'He's out of our care. Well done.' He yawned. 'I propose we go early to bed. There is nothing more for us to do. Until tomorrow night, of course.' At the door he stopped, and without turning his head he remarked, 'You know, it doesn't seem real. In the war, there was no question. They went or they refused. Why did he go, Avery? Jane Austen said money or love, those were the only two things in the world. Leiser didn't go for money.'

'You said one could never know. You said so the night he telephoned.'

'He told me it was hate. Hatred for the Germans; and I didn't believe him.'

'He went anyway. I thought that was all that mattered to you, you said you didn't trust motive.'

'He wouldn't do it for hatred, we know that. What is he, then? We never knew him, did we? He's near the mark, you know; he's on his deathbed. What does he think of? If he dies now, tonight, what will be in his mind?'

'You shouldn't speak like that.'

'Ah.' At last he turned and looked at Avery and the peace had not left his face. 'When we met him he was a man without love. Do you know what love is? I'll tell you: it is whatever you can still betray. We ourselves live without it in our profession. We don't force people to do things for us. We let them discover love. And, of course, Leiser did, didn't he? He married us for money, so to speak, and left us for love. He took his second vow. I wonder when.'

Avery said quickly, 'What do you mean, for money?'

'I mean whatever we gave to him. Love is what he gave to us. I see you have his watch, incidentally.'

'I'm keeping it for him.'

'Ah. Goodnight. Or good morning, I suppose.' A little laugh. 'How quickly one loses one's sense of time.' Then he commented, as if to himself: 'And the Circus helped us all the way. It's most strange. I wonder why.'

★ ★ ★

Very carefully Leiser rinsed the knife. The knife was dirty and must be washed. In the boathouse, he ate the food and drank the brandy in the flask. 'After that,' Haldane had said, 'you live off the land; you can't run around with tinned meat and French brandy.' He opened the door and stepped outside to wash his hands and face in the lake.

The water was quite still in the darkness. Its unruffled surface was like a perfect skin shrouded with floating veils of grey mist. He could see the reeds along the bank; the wind, subdued by the approach of dawn, touched them as it moved across the water. Beyond the lake hung the shadow of low hills. He felt rested and at peace. Until the memory of the boy passed over him like a shudder.

He threw the empty meat can and the brandy bottle far out, and as they hit the water a heron rose languidly from the reeds. Stooping, he picked up a stone and sent it skimming across the lake. He heard it bounce three times before it sank. He threw another but he couldn't beat three. Returning to the hut he fetched his rucksack and suitcase. His right arm was aching painfully, it must have been from the weight of the case. From somewhere came the bellow of cattle.

He began walking east, along the track which skirted the lake. He wanted to get as far as he could before morning came.

He must have walked through half a dozen villages. Each was empty of life, quieter than the open road because they gave a moment's shelter from the rising wind. There were no signposts and no new buildings, it suddenly occurred to him. That was where the peace came from, it was the peace of no innovation – it might have been fifty years ago, a hundred. There were no street lights, no gaudy signs on the pubs or shops. It was the darkness of indifference, and it comforted him. He walked into it like a tired man breasting the sea; it cooled and revived him like the wind; until he remembered the boy. He passed a farmhouse. A long drive led to it from the road. He stopped. Half-way up the drive stood a motorbike, an old mackintosh thrown over the saddle. There was no one in sight.

The oven smoked gently.

'When did you say his first schedule was?' Avery asked. He had asked already.

'Johnson said twenty-two twenty. We start scanning an hour before.'

'I thought he was on a fixed frequency,' Leclerc muttered, but without much interest.

'He may start with the wrong crystal. It's the kind of thing that happens under strain. It's safest for base to scan with so many crystals.'

'He must be on the road by now.'

'Where's Haldane?'

'Asleep.'

'How can anyone sleep at a time like this?'

'It'll be daylight soon.'

'Can't you do something about that fire?' Leclerc asked. 'It shouldn't smoke like that, I'm sure.' He shook his head, suddenly, as if shaking off water and said, 'John, there's a most interesting report from Fielden. Troop movements in Budapest. Perhaps when you get back to London . . .' He lost the thread of his sentence and frowned.

'You mentioned it,' Avery said softly.

'Yes, well you must take a look at it.'

'I'd like to. It sounds very interesting.'

'It does, doesn't it?'

'Very.'

'You know,' he said – he seemed to be reminiscing – 'they *still* won't give that wretched woman her pension.'

He sat very straight on the motorbike, elbows in as if he were at table. It made a terrible noise; it seemed to fill the dawn with sound, echoing across the frosted fields and stirring the roosting poultry. The mackintosh had leather pieces on the shoulders; as he bounced along the unmade road its skirts fluttered behind, rattling against the spokes of the rear wheel. Daylight came.

Soon he would have to eat. He couldn't understand why he was so hungry. Perhaps it was the exercise. Yes, it must be the exercise. He would eat, but not in a town, not yet. Not in a café where strangers came. Not in a café where the boy had been.

He drove on. His hunger taunted him. He could think of nothing else. His hand held down the throttle and drove his ravening body forward. He turned on to a farm track and stopped.

The house was old, falling with neglect; the drive overgrown with grass, pitted with cart tracks. The fences were broken. There was a terraced garden once partly under plough, now left as if it were beyond all use.

A light burned in the kitchen window. Leiser knocked at the door. His hand was trembling from the motorbike. No one came;

he knocked again, and the sound of his knocking frightened him. He thought he saw a face, it might have been the shadow of the boy sinking across the window as he fell, or the reflection of a swaying branch.

He returned quickly to his motorbike, realizing with terror that his hunger was not hunger at all but loneliness. He must lie up somewhere and rest. He thought: I've forgotten how it takes you. He drove on until he came to the wood, where he lay down. His face was hot against the bracken.

It was evening; the fields were still light but the wood in which he lay gave itself swiftly to the darkness, so that in a moment the red pines had turned to columns of black.

He picked the leaves from his jacket and laced up his shoes. They pinched badly at the instep. He never had a chance to wear them in. He caught himself thinking, it's all right for them, and he remembered that nothing ever bridged the gulf between the man who went and the man who stayed behind, between the living and the dying.

He struggled into the harness of his rucksack and once again felt gratefully the hot, raw pain in his shoulders as the straps found the old bruises. Picking up the suitcase he walked across the field to the road where the motorbike was waiting; five kilometres to Langdorn. He guessed it lay beyond the hill: the first of the three towns. Soon he would meet the road block; soon he would have to eat.

He drove slowly, the case across his knees, peering ahead all the time along the wet road, straining his eyes for a line of red lights or a cluster of men and vehicles. He rounded a bend and saw to his left a house with a beer sign propped in the window. He entered the forecourt; the noise of the engine brought an old man to the door. Leiser lifted the bike on to its stand.

'I want a beer,' he said, 'and some sausage. Have you got that here?'

The old man showed him inside, sat him at a table in the front room from which Leiser could see his motorbike parked in the yard. He brought him a bottle of beer, some sliced sausage and a piece of black bread; then stood at the table watching him eat.

'Where are you making for?' His thin face was shaded with beard.

'North.' Leiser knew this game.

'Where are you from?'

'What's the next town?'

'Langdorn.'

'Far?'

'Five kilometres.'

'Somewhere to stay?'

The old man shrugged. It was a gesture not of indifference nor of refusal, but of negation, as if he rejected everything and everything rejected him.

'What's the road like?' Leiser asked.

'It's all right.'

'I heard there was a diversion.'

'No diversion,' the old man said, as if a diversion were hope, or comfort, or companionship; anything that might warm the damp air or lighten the corners of the room.

'You're from the east,' the man declared. 'One hears it in the voice.'

'My parents,' he said. 'Any coffee?'

The old man brought him coffee, very black and sour, tasting of nothing.

'You're from Wilmsdorf,' the old man said. 'You've got a Wilmsdorf registration.'

'Much custom?' Leiser asked, glancing at the door.

The old man shook his head.

'Not a busy road, eh?' Still the old man said nothing. 'I've got a friend near Kalkstadt. Is that far?'

'Not far. Forty kilometres. They killed a boy near Wilmsdorf.'

'He runs a café. On the northern side. The Tom Cat. Know it at all?'

'No.'

Leiser lowered his voice. 'They had trouble there. A fight. Some soldiers from the town. Russians.'

'Go away,' the old man said.

He tried to pay him but he only had a fifty-mark note.

'Go away,' the old man repeated.

Leiser picked up the suitcase and rucksack. 'You old fool,' he said roughly. 'What do you think I am?'

'You are either good or bad, and both are dangerous. Go away.'

There was no road block. Without warning he was in the centre of Langdorn; it was already dark; the only lights in the main street stole from the shuttered windows, barely reaching the wet cobbles. There was no traffic. He was alarmed by the din of his motorbike; it sounded like a trumpet blast across the market square. In the war, Leiser thought, they went to bed early to keep warm; perhaps they still did.

It was time to get rid of the motorbike. He drove through the town, found a disused church and left it by the vestry door. Walking back into the town he made for the railway station. The official wore uniform.

'Kalkstadt. Single.'

The official held out his hand. Leiser took a banknote from his wallet and gave it to him. The official shook it impatiently. For a moment Leiser's mind went blank while he looked stupidly at the flicking fingers in front of him and the suspicious, angry face behind the grille.

Suddenly the official shouted: 'Identity card!'

Leiser smiled apologetically. 'One forgets,' he said, and opened his wallet to show the card in the Cellophane window.

'Take it out of the wallet,' the official said. Leiser watched him examine it under the light on his desk.

'Travel authority?'

'Yes, of course.' Leiser handed him the paper.

'Why do you want to go to Kalkstadt if you are travelling to Rostock?'

'Our co-operative in Magdeburg sent some machinery by rail to Kalkstadt. Heavy turbines and some tooling equipment. It has to be installed.'

'How did you come this far?'

'I got a lift.'

'The granting of lifts is forbidden.'

'One must do what one can these days.'

'These days?'

The man pressed his face against the glass, looking down at Leiser's hands.

'What's that you're fiddling with down there?' he demanded roughly.

'A chain; a key chain.'

'So the equipment has to be installed. Well? Go on!'

'I can do the job on the way. The people in Kalkstadt have been waiting six weeks already. The consignment was delayed.'

'So?'

'We made inquiries . . . of the railway people.'

'And?'

'They didn't reply.'

'You've got an hour's wait. It leaves at six thirty.' A pause. 'You heard the news? They've killed a boy at Wilmsdorf,' he said. 'Swine.' He handed him his change.

He had nowhere to go; he dared not deposit his luggage. There was nothing else to do. He walked for half an hour, then returned to the station. The train was late.

'You both deserve great credit,' Leclerc said, nodding gratefully at Haldane and Avery. 'You too, Johnson. From now on there's nothing any of us can do: it's up to Mayfly.' A special smile for Avery: 'How about you, John; you've been keeping very quiet? Do you think you've profited from the experience?' He added with a laugh, appealing to the other two, 'I do hope we shan't have a divorce on our hands; we must get you home to your wife.'

He was sitting at the edge of the table, his small hands folded tidily on his knee. When Avery said nothing he declared brightly, 'I had a ticking off from Carol, you know, Adrian; breaking up the young home.'

Haldane smiled as if it were an amusing notion. 'I'm sure there's no danger of that,' he said.

'He made a great hit with Smiley, too; we must see they don't poach him away!'

Chapter 19

When the train reached Kalkstadt, Leiser waited until the other passengers had left the platform. An elderly guard collected the tickets. He looked a kindly man.

'I'm looking for a friend,' Leiser said. 'A man called Fritsche. He used to work here.'

The guard frowned.

'Fritsche?'

'Yes.'

'What was his first name?'

'I don't know.'

'How old, then; how old about?'

He guessed: 'Forty.'

'Fritsche, here, at this station?'

'Yes. He had a small house down by the river; a single man.'

'A whole house? And worked at this station?'

'Yes.'

The guard shook his head. 'Never heard of him.' He peered at Leiser. 'Are you sure?' he said.

'That's what he told me.' Something seemed to come back to him. 'He wrote to me in November . . . he complained that Vopos had closed the station.'

'You're mad,' the guard said. 'Goodnight.'

'Goodnight,' Leiser replied; as he walked away he was conscious all the time of the man's gaze upon his back.

There was an inn in the main street called the Old Bell. He waited at the desk in the hall and nobody came. He opened a door and found himself in a big room, dark at the farther end. A girl sat at a table in front of an old gramophone. She was slumped forward, her head buried in her arms, listening to the music. A single light burned above her. When the record stopped she played it again, moving the arm of the record player without lifting her head.

'I'm looking for a room,' Leiser said. 'I've just arrived from Langdorn.'

There were stuffed birds round the room: herons, pheasants and a kingfisher. 'I'm looking for a room,' he repeated. It was dance music, very old.

'Ask at the desk.'

'There's no one there.'

'They have nothing, anyway. They're not allowed to take you. There's a hostel near the church. You have to stay there.'

'Where's the church?'

With an exaggerated sigh she stopped the record, and Leiser knew she was glad to have someone to talk to.

'It was bombed,' she declared. 'We just talk about it still. There's only the tower left.'

Finally he said, 'Surely they've got a bed here? It's a big place.' He put his rucksack in a corner and sat at the table next to her. He ran a hand through his thick dry hair.

'You look all in,' the girl said.

His blue trousers were still caked with mud from the border. 'I've been on the road all day. Takes a lot out of you.'

She stood up self-consciously and went to the end of the room where a wooden staircase led upwards towards a glimmer of light. She called out but no one came.

'Steinhäger?' she asked him from the dark.

'Yes.'

She returned with a bottle and a glass. She was wearing a mackintosh, an old brown one of military cut with epaulettes and square shoulders.

'Where are you from?' she asked.

'Magdeburg. I'm making north. Got a job in Rostock.' How many more times would he say it? 'This hostel; do I get a room to myself?'

'If you want one.'

The light was so poor that at first he could scarcely make her out. Gradually she came alive. She was about eighteen, and heavily built; quite a pretty face but bad skin. The same age as the boy; older perhaps.

'Who are you?' he asked. She said nothing. 'What do you do?'

She took his glass and drank from it, looking at him precociously over the brim as if she were a great beauty. She put it down slowly, still watching him, touched the side of her hair. She seemed to think her gestures mattered. Leiser began again:

'Been here long?'

'Two years.'

'What do you do?'

'Whatever you want.' Her voice was quite earnest.

'Much going on here?'

'It's dead. Nothing.'

'No boys?'

'Sometimes.'

'Troops?' A pause.

'Now and then. Don't you know it's forbidden to ask that?'

Leiser helped himself to more Steinhäger from the bottle.

She took his glass, fumbling with his fingers.

'What's wrong with this town?' he asked. 'I tried to come here six weeks ago. They wouldn't let me in. Kalkstadt, Langdorn, Wolken, all closed, they said. What was going on?'

Her fingertips played over his hand.

'What was up?' he repeated.

'Nothing was closed.'

'Come off it,' Leiser laughed. 'They wouldn't let me near the place, I tell you. Road blocks here and on the Wolken road.' He thought: 'It's eight twenty; only two hours till the first schedule.'

'Nothing was closed.' Suddenly she added, 'So you came from the west: you came by road. They're looking for someone like you.'

He stood up to go. 'I'd better find the hostel.' He put some money on the table. The girl whispered, 'I've got my own room. In a new flat behind the Friedensplatz. A workers' block. They don't mind. I'll do whatever you want.'

Leiser shook his head. He picked up his luggage and went to the door. She was still looking at him and he knew she suspected him.

'Goodbye,' he said.

'I won't say anything. Take me with you.'

'I had a Steinhäger,' Leiser muttered. 'We didn't even talk. You played your record all the time.' They were both frightened.

The girl said, 'Yes. Records all the time.'

'It was never closed, you are sure of that? Langdorn, Wolken, Kalkstadt, six weeks ago?'

'What would anyone close this place for?'

'Not even the station?'

She said quickly, 'I don't know about the station. The area was closed for three days in November. No one knows why. Russian troops stayed, about fifty. They were billeted in the town. Mid November.'

'Fifty? Any equipment?'

'Lorries. There were manoeuvres farther north, that's the rumour. Stay with me tonight. Stay with me! Let me come with you. I'll go anywhere.'

'What colour shoulder-boards?'

'I don't remember.'

'Where did they come from?'

'They were new. Some came from Leningrad, two brothers.'

'Which way did they go?'

'North. Listen, no one will ever know. I don't talk, I'm not the kind. I'll give it to you, anything you want.'

'Towards Rostock?'

'They said they were going to Rostock. They said not to tell. The Party came round all the houses.'

Leiser nodded. He was sweating. 'Goodbye,' he said.

'What about tomorrow, tomorrow night? I'll do whatever you want.'

'Perhaps. Don't tell anyone, do you understand?'.

She shook her head. 'I won't tell them,' she said, 'because I don't care. Ask for the Hochhaus behind the Friedensplatz. Apartment nineteen. Come any time. I'll open the door. You give two rings and they know it's for me. You needn't pay. Take care,' she said. 'There are people everywhere. They've killed a boy in Wilmsdorf.'

He walked to the market square, correct again because everything was closing in, looking for the church tower and the hostel. Huddled figures passed him in the darkness; some wore pieces of uniform; forage caps and the long coats they had in the war. Now and then he would glimpse their faces, catching them in the pale glow of a street light and he would seek in their locked, unseeing features the qualities he hated. He would say to himself, 'Hate him – he is old enough,' but it did not stir him. They were nothing. Perhaps in some other town, some other place, he would find them and hate them; but not here. These were old and nothing; poor, like him, and alone. The tower was black and empty. It reminded him suddenly of the turret on the border, and the garage after eleven, of the moment when he killed the sentry: just a kid, like himself in the war; even younger than Avery.

'He should be there by now,' Avery said.

'That's right, John. He should be there, shouldn't he? One hour to go. One more river to cross.' He began singing. No one took him up.

They looked at each other in silence.

– 193 –

'Know the Alias Club at all?' Johnson asked suddenly. 'Off Villiers Street? A lot of the old gang meet up there. You ought to come along one evening, when we get home.'

'Thanks,' Avery replied. 'I'd like to.'

'It gets nice Christmas time,' he said. 'That's when I go. A good crowd. There's even one or two come in uniform.'

'It sounds fine.'

'They have a mixed do at New Year. You could take your wife.'

'Grand.'

Johnson winked. 'Or your fancy-girl.'

'Sarah's the only girl for me,' Avery said.

The telephone was ringing. Leclerc rose to answer it.

Chapter 20
Homecoming

He put down the rucksack and the suitcase and looked round the walls. There was an electric point beside the window. The door had no lock so he pushed the armchair against it. He took off his shoes and lay on the bed. He thought of the girl's fingers on his hands and the nervous movement of her lips; he remembered her deceitful eyes watching him from the shadows and he wondered how long it would be before she betrayed him.

He remembered Avery: the warmth and English decency of their early companionship; he remembered his young face glistening in the rain, and his shy, dazzled glance as he dried his spectacles, and he thought: he must have said thirty-two all the time. I misheard.

He looked at the ceiling. In an hour he would put up the aerial.

The room was large and bare with a round marble basin in one corner. A single pipe ran from it to the floor and he hoped to God it would do for the earth. He ran some water and to his relief it was cold, because Jack had said a hot pipe was dicey. He drew his knife and carefully scraped the pipe clean on one side. The earth was important; Jack had said so. If you can't do anything else, he'd said, lay your earth wire zig-zag fashion under the carpet, the same length as the aerial. But there was no carpet; the pipe would have to do. No carpet, no curtains.

Opposite him stood a heavy wardrobe with bow doors. The place must once have been the main hotel. There was a smell of Turkish tobacco and rank, unscented disinfectant. The walls were of grey plaster; the damp had spread over them in dark shadows, arrested here and there by some mysterious inner property of the house which had dried a path across the ceiling. In some places the plaster had crumbled with the damp, leaving a ragged island of white mildew; in others it had contracted and the plasterer had returned to fill the cavities with paste which described white rivers along the corners of the room. Leiser's eye followed them carefully while he listened for the smallest sound outside.

There was a picture on the wall of workers in a field, leading a horse plough. On the horizon was a tractor. He heard Johnson's benign voice running on about the aerial: 'If it's indoors it's a headache, and indoors it'll be. Now listen: zig-zag fashion across the room, quarter the length of your wave and one foot below the ceiling. Space them wide as possible, Fred, and not parallel to metal girders, electric wires and that. And don't double her back on herself, Fred, or you'll muck her up properly, see?' Always the joke, the copulative innuendo to aid the memory of simple men.

Leiser thought: I'll take it to the picture frame, then back and forth to the far corner. I can put a nail into that soft plaster; he looked around for a nail or pin, and noticed a bronze hanger on one of the pelmets. He got up, unscrewed the handle of his razor. The thread began to the right, it was considered an ingenious detail, so that a suspicious man who gave the handle a casual twist to the left would be going against the thread. From the recess he extracted the knot of silk cloth which he smoothed carefully over his knee with his thick fingers. He found a pencil in his pocket and sharpened it, not moving from the edge of his bed because he did not want to disturb the silk cloth. Twice the point broke; the shavings collected on the floor at his feet. He began writing in the notebook, capital letters, like a prisoner writing to his wife, and every time he made a full stop he drew a ring round it the way he was taught long ago.

The message composed, he drew a line after every two letters, and beneath each compartment he entered the numerical equivalent according to the chart he had memorized: sometimes he had to resort to a mnemonic rhyme in order to recall the numbers; sometimes he remembered wrong and had to rub out and begin again. When he had finished he divided the line of numbers into groups of four and deducted each in turn from the groups on the silk cloth; finally he converted the figures into letters again and wrote out the result, redividing them into groups of four.

Fear like an old pain had again taken hold of his belly so that with every imagined sound he looked sharply towards the door, his hand arrested in the middle of writing. But he heard nothing; just the creaking of an ageing house, like the noise of wind in the rigging of a ship.

He looked at the finished message, conscious that it was too long, and that if he were better at that kind of thing, if his mind were quicker, he could reduce it, but just now he couldn't think of a way, and he knew, he had been taught, better put in a word or two too many than make it ambiguous the other end. There were forty-two groups.

He pushed the table away from the window and lifted the suitcase; with the key from his chain he unlocked it, praying all the time that nothing was broken from the journey. He opened the spares box, discovering with his trembling fingers the silk bag of crystals bound with green ribbon at the mouth. Loosening the ribbon, he shook the crystals on to the coarse blanket which covered the bed. Each was labelled in Johnson's handwriting, first the frequency and below it a single figure denoting the place where it came in the signal plan. He arranged them in line, pressing them on to the blanket so that they lay flat. The crystals were the easiest part. He tested the door against the armchair. The handle slipped in his palm. The chair provided no protection. In the war, he remembered, they had given him steel wedges. Returning to the suitcase he connected the transmitter and receiver to the power pack, plugged in the earphones and unscrewed the Morse key from the lid of the spares box. Then he saw it.

Mounted inside the suitcase lid was a peice of adhesive paper with half a dozen groups of letters and beside each its Morse equivalent; they were the international code for standard phrases, the one he could never remember.

When he saw those letters, drawn out in Jack's neat, post-office hand, tears of gratitude started to his eyes. He never told me, he thought, he never told me he'd done it. Jack was all right, after all. Jack, the Captain and young John; what a team to work for, he thought; a man could go through life and never meet a set of blokes like that. He steadied himself, pressing his hands sharply on the table. He was trembling a little, perhaps from the cold; his damp shirt clung to his shoulder-blades; but he was happy. He glanced at the chair in front of the door and thought; when I've got the headphones on I shan't hear them coming, the way the boy didn't hear me because of the wind.

Next he attached aerial and earth to their terminals, led the earth wire to the water pipe and fastened the two strands to the cleaned surface with tabs of adhesive plaster. Standing on the bed, he stretched the aerial across the ceiling in eight lengths, zig-zag as Johnson had instructed, fixing it as best he could to the curtain rail or plaster on either side. This done, he returned to the set and adjusted the waveband switch to the fourth position, because he knew that all the frequencies were in the three-megacycle range. He took from the bed the first crystal in the line, plugged it into the far left-hand corner of the set, and settled down to tune the transmitter, muttering gently as he performed each movement. Adjust crystal selector to 'fundamental all crystals', plug the coil; anode tuning and aerial matching controls to ten.

He hesitated, trying to remember what happened next. A block was forming in his mind. 'PA – don't you know what PA stands for?' He set the meter switch to three to read the Power Amplifier grid current . . . TSR switch to T for tuning. It was coming back to him. Meter switch to six to ascertain total current . . . anode tuning for minimum reading.

Now he turned the TSR switch to S for send, pressed the key briefly, took a reading, manipulated the aerial matching control so that the meter reading rose slightly; hastily readjusted the anode tuning. He repeated the procedure until to his profound relief he saw the finger dip against the white background of the kidney-shaped dial and knew that the transmitter and aerial were correctly tuned, and that he could talk to John and Jack.

He sat back with a grunt of satisfaction, lit a cigarette, wished it were an English one because if they came in now they wouldn't have to bother about the brand of cigarette he was smoking. He looked at his watch, turning the winder until it was stiff, terrified lest it run down; it was matched with Avery's and in a simple way this gave him comfort. Like divided lovers, they were looking at the same star.

He had killed that boy.

Three minutes to schedule. He unscrewed the Morse key from the spares box because he couldn't manage it properly while it was on that lid. Jack had said it was all right; he said it didn't matter. He had to hold the key base with his left hand so that it didn't slide about, but Jack said every operator had his quirks. He was sure it was smaller than the one they gave him in the war; he was sure of it. Traces of french chalk clung to the lever. He drew in his elbows and straightened his back. The third finger of his right hand crooked over the key. JAJ's my first call sign, he thought, Johnson's my name, they call me Jack, that's easy enough to remember. JA, John Avery; JJ, Jack Johnson. Then he was tapping it out. A dot and three dashes, dot dash, a dot and three dashes, and he kept thinking: it's like the house in Holland, but there's no one with me.

Say it twice, Fred, then get off the air. He switched over to receive, pushed the sheet of paper farther towards the middle of the table and suddenly realized he had nothing to write with when Jack came through.

He stood up and looked around for his notebook and pencil, the sweat breaking out on his back. They were nowhere to be seen. Dropping hastily to his hands and knees he felt in the thick dust under the bed, found the pencil, groped vainly for his notebook. As he was getting up he heard a crackle from the earphones. He ran to the table, pressed one phone to his ear, at the same time trying to hold still the sheet of paper so that he could write in a corner of it beside his own message.

'QSA3: hearing you well enough,' that's all they were saying. 'Steady, boy, steady,' he muttered. He settled into the chair, switched to transmit, looked at his own encoded message and tapped out four-two because there were forty-two groups. His hand was coated with dust and sweat, his right arm ached, perhaps from carrying the suitcase. Or struggling with the boy.

You've got all the time in the world, Johnson had said. We'll be listening: you're not passing an exam. He took his handkerchief from his pocket and wiped away the grime from his hands. He was terribly tired; the tiredness was like a physical despair, like the moment of guilt before making love. Groups of four letters, Johnson had said, think of four-letter words, eh, Fred. You don't need to do it all at once, Fred, have a little stop in the middle if you like; two and a half minutes on the first frequency, two and a half on the second, that's the way we go; Mrs Hartbeck will wait, I'm sure. With his pencil he drew a heavy line under the ninth letter because that was where the safety device came. That was something he dared think of only in passing.

He put his face in his hands, summoning the last of his concentration, then reached for the key and began tapping. Keep the hand loose, first and second fingers on top of the key, thumb beneath the edge, no putting the wrist on the table, Fred, breathe regular, Fred, you'll find it helps you to relax.

God, why were his hands so slow? Once he took his fingers from the key and stared impotently at his open palm; once he ran his left hand across his forehead to keep the sweat from his eyes, and he felt the key drifting across the table. His wrist was too stiff: the hand he killed the boy with. All the time he was saying it over to himself – dot, dot, dash, then a K, he always knew that one, a dot between two dashes – his lips were spelling out the letters, but his hand wouldn't follow, it was a kind of stammer that got worse the more he spoke, and always the boy in his mind, only the boy. Perhaps he was quicker than he thought. He lost all notion of time; the sweat was running into his eyes, he couldn't stop it any more. He kept mouthing the dots and dashes, and he

knew that Johnson would be angry because he shouldn't be thinking in dots and dashes at all but musically, de-dah, dah, the way
the professionals did, but Johnson had not killed the boy. The
pounding of his heart outran the weary tapping of the key; his
hand seemed to grow heavier and still he went on signalling
because it was the only thing left to do, the only thing to hold on
to while his body gave way. He was waiting for them now,
wishing they'd come – take me, take it all – longing for the footsteps. Give us your hand, John; give us a hand.

When at last he had finished, he went back to the bed. Almost
with detachment he caught sight of the line of crystals on the
blanket, untouched, still and ready, dressed by the left and numbered; flat on their backs, like dead sentries.

Avery looked at his watch. It was quarter past ten. 'He should
come on in five minutes,' he said.

Leclerc announced suddenly: 'That was Gorton on the telephone. He's received a telegram from the Ministry. They have
some news for us apparently. They're sending out a courier.'

'What could that be?' Avery asked.

'I expect it's the Hungarian thing. Fielden's report. I may have
to go back to London.' A satisfied smile. 'But I think you people
can get along without me.'

Johnson was wearing earphones, sitting forward on a high-
backed wooden chair carried up from the kitchen. The dark green
receiver hummed gently from the mains transformer; the tuning
dial, illuminated from within, glowed palely in the half light of
the attic.

Haldane and Avery sat uncomfortably on a bench. Johnson had
a pad and pencil in front of him. He lifted the phones above his
ears and said to Leclerc who stood beside him, 'I shall take him
straight through the routine, sir; I'll do my best to tell you what's
going on. I'm recording, too, mind, for safety's sake.'

'I understand.'

They waited in silence. Suddenly – it was their moment of utter
magic – Johnson had sat bolt upright, nodded sharply to them,
switched on the tape recorder. He smiled, quickly turned to transmission and was tapping. 'Come in, Fred,' he said out loud. 'Hearing you nicely.'

'He's made it!' Leclerc hissed. 'He's on target now!' His eyes
were bright with excitement. 'Do you hear that, John? Do you
hear?'

'Shall we be quiet?' Haldane suggested.

'Here he comes,' Johnson said. His voice was level, controlled. 'Forty-two groups.'

'Forty-two!' Leclerc repeated.

Johnson's body was motionless, his head inclined a little to one side, his whole concentration given to the earphones, his face impassive in the pale light.

'I'd like silence now, please.'

For perhaps two minutes his careful hand moved briskly across the pad. Now and then he muttered inaudibly, whispered a letter or shook his head, until the message seemed to come more slowly, his pencil pausing while he listened, until it was tracing out each letter singly with agonizing care. He glanced at the clock.

'Come on, Fred,' he urged. 'Come on, change over, that's nearly three minutes.' But still the message was coming through, letter by letter, and Johnson's simple face assumed an expression of alarm.

'What's going on?' Leclerc demanded. 'Why hasn't he changed his frequency?'

But Johnson only said, 'Get off the air, for Christ's sake, Fred, get off the air.'

Leclerc touched him impatiently on the arm. Johnson raised one earphone.

'Why's he not changed frequency? Why's he still talking?'

'He must have forgotten! He never forgot on training. I *know* he's slow, but Christ!' He was still writing automatically. 'Five minutes,' he muttered. 'Five bloody minutes. Change the bloody crystal!'

'Can't you tell him?' Leclerc cried.

'Of course I can't. How can I? He can't receive and send at the same time!'

They sat or stood in dreadful fascination. Johnson had turned to them, his voice beseeching. 'I told him; if I told him once I told him a dozen times. It's bloody suicide, what he's doing!' He looked at his watch. 'He's been on damn near six minutes. Bloody, bloody, *bloody* fool.'

'What will they do?' said Haldane.

'If they pick up a signal? Call in another station. Take a fix, then it's simple trigonometry when he's on this long.' He banged his open hands helplessly on the table, indicated the set as if it were an affront. 'A kid could do it. Do it with a pair of compasses. Christ Almighty! Come on, Fred, for Jesus' sake, come on!' He wrote down a handful of letters then threw his pencil aside. 'It's on tape, anyway,' he said.

Leclerc turned to Haldane. 'Surely there's something we can do!'

'Be quiet,' Haldane said.

The message stopped. Johnson tapped an acknowledgement, fast, a stab of hatred. He wound back the tape recorder and began transcribing. Putting the coding sheet in front of him he worked without interruption for perhaps quarter of an hour, occasionally making simple sums on the rough paper at his elbow. No one spoke. When he had finished he stood up, a half-forgotten gesture of respect. 'Message reads: Area Kalkstadt closed three days mid -November when fifty unidentified Soviet troops seen in town. No special equipment. Rumours of Soviet manoeuvres farther north. Troops believed moved to Rostock. Fritsche not repeat not known Kalkstadt railway station. No road check on Kalkstadt road.' He tossed the paper on to the desk. 'There are fifteen groups after that which I can't unbutton. I think he's muddled his coding.'

The Vopo sergeant in Rostock picked up the telephone; he was an elderly man, greying and thoughtful. He listened for a moment then began dialling on another line. 'It must be a child,' he said, still dialling. 'What frequency did you say?' He put the other telephone to his ear and spoke into it fast, repeating the frequency three times. He walked into the adjoining hut. 'Witmar will be through in a minute,' he said. 'They're taking a fix. Are you still hearing him?' The corporal nodded. The sergeant held a spare headphone to his ear.

'It couldn't be an amateur,' he muttered. 'Breaking the regulations. But what is it? No agent in his right mind would put out a signal like that. What are the neighbouring frequencies? Military or civilian?'

'It's near the military. Very near.'

'That's odd,' the sergeant said. 'That would fit, wouldn't it? That's what they did in the war.'

The corporal was staring at the tapes slowly revolving on their spindles. 'He's still transmitting. Groups of four.'

'Four?' The sergeant was searching in his memory for something that had happened long ago.

'Let me hear again. Listen, listen to the fool! He's as slow as a child.'

The sound struck some chord in his memory – the slurred gaps, the dots so short as to be little more than clicks. He could swear he knew that hand . . . from the war, in Norway . . . but not so slow: nothing had ever been as slow as this. Not Norway . . .

France. Perhaps it was only imagination. Yes, it was imagination.

'Or an old man,' the corporal said.

The telephone rang. The sergeant listened for a moment, then ran, ran as fast as he could, through the hut to the officers' mess across the tarmac path.

The Russian captain was drinking beer; his jacket was slung over the back of his chair and he looked very bored.

'You wanted something, Sergeant?' He affected the languid style.

'He's come. The man they told us about. The one who killed the boy.'

The Captain put down his beer quickly.

'You heard him?'

'We've taken a fix. With Witmar. Groups of four. A slow hand. Area Kalkstadt. Close to one of our own frequencies. Sommer recorded the transmission.'

'Christ,' he said quietly. The sergeant frowned.

'What's he looking for? Why should they send him here?' the sergeant asked.

The Captain was buttoning his jacket. 'Ask them in Leipzig. Perhaps they know that too.'

Chapter 21

It was very late.

The fire in Control's grate was burning nicely, but he poked at it with effeminate discontent. He hated working at night.

'They want you at the Ministry,' he said irritably. 'Now, of all hours. It really is too bad. Why does everyone get so *agitato* on a Thursday? It will *ruin* the week-end.' He put down the poker and returned to his desk. 'They're in a dreadful state. Some idiot talking about ripples in a pond. It's extraordinary what the night does to people. I do *detest* the telephone.' There were several in front of him.

Smiley offered him a cigarette and he took one without looking at it, as if he could not be held responsible for the actions of his limbs.

'What Ministry?' Smiley asked.

'Leclerc's. Have you *any* idea what's going on?'

Smiley said, 'Yes. Haven't you?'

'Leclerc's so *vulgar*. I admit, I find him vulgar. He thinks we compete. What on earth would *I* do with his dreadful militia? Scouring Europe for mobile laundries. He thinks I want to gobble him up.'

'Well, don't you? Why *did* we cancel that passport?'

'What a *silly* man. A silly, vulgar man. However did Haldane fall for it?'

'He had a conscience once. He's like all of us. He's learnt to live with it.'

'Oh dear. Is that a dig at me?'

'What does the Ministry want?' Smiley asked sharply.

Control held up some papers, flapping them. 'You've seen these from Berlin?'

'They came in an hour ago. The Americans have taken a fix. Groups of four; a primitive letter code. They say it comes from the Kalkstadt area.'

'Where on *earth's* that?'

'South of Rostock. The message ran six minutes on the same frequency. They said it sounded like an amateur on a first run through. One of the old wartime sets: they wanted to know if it was ours.'

'And you replied?' Control asked quickly.

'I said no.'

'So I should hope. Good Lord.'

'You don't seem very concerned,' Smiley said.

Control seemed to remember something from long ago. 'I hear Leclerc's in Lübeck. Now *there's* a pretty town. I adore Lübeck. The Ministry wants you immediately. I said you'd go. Some meeting.' He added in apparent earnest, 'You must, George. We've been the most awful fools. It's in every East German newspaper; they're screaming about peace conferences and sabotage.' He prodded at a telephone. 'So is the Ministry. God, how I loathe Civil Servants.'

Smiley watched him with scepticism. 'We could have stopped them,' he said. 'We knew enough.'

'Of course we could,' Control said blandly. 'D'you know why we didn't? Plain, idiot Christian charity. We let them have their war game. You'd better go now. And Smiley . . .'

'Yes?'

'Be gentle.' And in his silly voice: 'I do envy them Lübeck, all the same. There's that restaurant, isn't there; what do they call it? Where Thomas Mann used to eat. So interesting.'

'He never did,' Smiley said. 'The place you're thinking of was bombed.'

Smiley still did not go. 'I wonder,' he said. 'You'll never tell me, will you? I just wonder.' He was not looking at Control.

'My dear George, what *has* come over you?'

'We handed it to them. The passport that was cancelled . . . a courier service they never needed . . . a clapped-out wireless set . . . papers, frontier reports . . . who told Berlin to listen for him? Who told them what frequencies? We even gave Leclerc the crystals, didn't we? Was that just Christian charity too? Plain, idiot Christian charity?'

Control was shocked.

'What *are* you suggesting? How *very* distasteful. Who ever would do a thing like that?'

Smiley was putting on his coat.

'Goodnight, George,' Control said; and fiercely, as if he were tired of sensibility: 'Run along. And preserve the difference between us: your country needs you. It's not *my* fault they've taken so long to die.'

The dawn came and Leiser had not slept. He wanted to wash but dared not go into the corridor. He dared not move. If they were looking for him, he knew he must leave normally, not bolt from the hostel before the morning came. Never run, they used to say: walk like the crowd. He could go at six: that was late enough. He rubbed his chin against the back of his hand: it was sharp and rough, marking the brown skin.

He was hungry and no longer knew what to do, but he would not run.

He half turned on the bed, pulled the knife from inside the waistband of his trousers and held it before his eyes. He was shivering. He could feel across his brow the unnatural heat of incipient fever. He looked at the knife, and remembered the clean, friendly way they had talked: thumb on top, blade parallel to the ground, forearm stiff. 'Go away,' the old man had said. 'You are either good or bad and both are dangerous.' How should he hold the knife when people spoke to him like that? The way he held it for the boy?

It was six o'clock. He stood up. His legs were heavy and stiff. His shoulders still ached from carrying the rucksack. His clothes, he noticed, smelt of pine and leaf mould. He picked the half-dried mud from his trousers and put on his second pair of shoes.

He went downstairs, looking for someone to pay, the new shoes squeaking on the wooden steps. There was an old woman in a white overall sorting lentils into a bowl, talking to a cat.

'What do I owe?'

'You fill in the form,' she said sourly. 'That's the first thing you owe. You should have done it when you came.'

'I'm sorry.'

She rounded on him, muttering but not daring to raise her voice. 'Don't you know it's forbidden, staying in a town and not reporting your presence to the police?' She looked at his new shoes. 'Or are you so rich that you think you need not trouble?'

'I'm sorry,' Leiser said again. 'Give me the form and I'll sign it now. I'm not rich.'

The woman fell silent, picking studiously among the lentils.

'Where do you come from?' she asked.

'East,' said Leiser. He meant south, from Magdeburg, or west from Wilmsdorf.

'You should have reported last night. It's too late now.'

'What do I pay?'

'You can't,' the woman replied. 'Never mind. You haven't filled in the form. What will you say if they catch you?'

'I'll say I slept with a girl.'

'It's snowing outside,' the woman said. 'Mind your nice shoes.'

Grains of hard snow drifted forlornly in the wind, collecting in the cracks between the black cobbles, lingering on the stucco of the houses. A drab, useless snow, dwindling where it fell.

He crossed the Friedensplatz and saw a new, yellow building, six or seven storeys high, standing on a patch of waste land beside a new estate. There was washing hanging on the balconies, touched with snow. The staircase smelt of food and Russian petrol. The flat was on the third floor. He could hear a child crying and a wireless playing. For a moment he thought he should turn and go away, because he was dangerous for them. He pressed the bell twice, as the girl had told him. She opened the door; she was half asleep. She had put on her mackintosh over the cotton nightdress and she held it at the neck because of the freezing cold. When she saw him she hesitated, not knowing what to do, as if he had brought bad news. He said nothing, just stood there with the suitcase swinging gently at his side. She beckoned with her head; he followed her across the corridor to her room, put the suitcase and rucksack in the corner. There were travel posters on the walls, pictures of desert, palm trees and the moon over a tropical sea. They got into bed and she covered him with her heavy body, trembling a little because she was afraid.

'I want to sleep,' he said. 'Let me sleep first.'

The Russian captain said, 'He stole a motorbike at Wilmsdorf and asked for Fritsche at the station. What will he do now?'

'He'll have another schedule. Tonight,' the sergeant replied. 'If he's got anything to say.'

'At the same time?'

'Of course not. Nor the same frequency. Nor from the same place. He may go to Witmar or Langdorn or Wolken; he may even go to Rostock. Or he may stay in town but go to another house. Or he may not send at all.'

'House? Who would harbour a spy?'

The sergeant shrugged as if to say he might himself. Stung, the Captain asked, 'How do you know he's sending from a house? Why not a wood or a field? How can you be so sure?'

'It's a very strong signal. A powerful set. He couldn't get a signal like that from a battery, not a battery you could carry around alone. He's using the mains.'

'Put a cordon round the town,' the Captain said. 'Search every house.'

'We want him alive.' The sergeant was looking at his hands. 'You want him alive.'

'Then tell me what we should do?' the Captain insisted.

'Make sure he transmits. That's the first thing. And make him stay in town. That is the second.'

'Well?'

'We would have to act quickly,' the sergeant observed.

'Well?'

'Bring some troops into town. Anything you can find. As soon as possible. Armour, infantry, it doesn't matter. Create some movement. Make him pay attention. But be quick!'

'I'll go soon,' Leiser said. 'Don't let me stay. Give me coffee and I'll go.'

'Coffee?'

'I've got money,' Leiser said, as if it were the only thing he had. 'Here.' He climbed out of bed, fetched the wallet from his jacket and drew a hundred-mark note from the wad.

Keep it.'

She took the wallet and with a little laugh emptied it out on the bed. She had a ponderous, kittenish way which was not quite sane; and the quick instinct of an illiterate. He watched her indifferently, running his fingers along the line of her naked shoulder. She held up a photograph of a woman; a blonde, round head.

'Who is she? What is her name?'

'She doesn't exist,' he said.

She found the letters and read one aloud, laughing at the affectionate passages. 'Who is she?' she kept taunting him. 'Who is she?'

'I tell you, she doesn't exist.'

'Then I can tear them up?' She held a letter before him with both hands, teasing him, waiting for him to protest. Leiser said nothing. She made a little tear, still watching him, then tore it completely, and a second and a third.

She found a picture of a child, a girl in spectacles, eight or nine years old perhaps, and again she asked, 'Who is it? Is it your child? Does *she* exist?'

'Nobody. Nobody's kid. Just a photograph.' She tore that too, scattering the pieces dramatically over the bed, then fell on him, kissing him on the face and neck. 'Who are you? What is your name?'

He wanted to tell her when she pushed him away.

'No!' she cried. 'No!' She lowered her voice. 'I want you with nothing. Alone from it all. You and me alone. We'll make our own names, our own rules. Nobody, no one at all, no father, no mother. We'll print our own newspapers, passes, ration cards; make our own people.' She was whispering, her eyes shining.

'You're a spy,' she said, her lips in his ear. 'A secret agent. You've got a gun.'

'A knife is quieter,' he said. She laughed, on and on, until she noticed the bruises on his shoulders. She touched them curiously, with respect, as a child might touch a dead thing.

She went out carrying a shopping basket, still clutching the mackintosh at her neck. Leiser dressed, shaving in cold water, staring at his lined face in the distorted mirror above the basin. When she returned it was nearly midday and she looked worried.

'The town's full of soldiers. And Army trucks. What do they want here?'

'Perhaps they are looking for someone.'

'They are just sitting about, drinking.'

'What kind of soldiers?'

'I don't know what kind. Russian. How can I tell?'

He went to the door. 'I'll come back in an hour.'

She said, 'You're trying to get away from me.' She held his arm, looking up at him, wanting to make a scene.

'I'll come back. Maybe not till later. Maybe this evening. But if I do . . .'

'Yes?'

'It will be dangerous. I shall have to . . . do something here. Something dangerous.'

She kissed him, a light, silly kiss. 'I like danger,' she said.

'Four hours,' Johnson said. 'If he's still alive.'

'Of course he's alive,' Avery said angrily. 'Why do you talk like that?'

Haldane interrupted. 'Don't be an ass, Avery. It's a technical term. Dead or live agents. It has nothing to do with his physical condition.'

Leclerc was drumming his fingers lightly on the table.

'He'll be all right,' he said. 'Fred's a hard man to kill. He's an old hand.' The daylight had revived him apparently. He glanced at his watch. 'What the devil's happened to that courier, I wonder.'

Leiser blinked at the soldiers like a man emerging from the dark. They filled the cafés, gazed into shop windows, looked at the girls. Trucks were parked in the square, their wheels thick with red mud, a thin surface of snow on their bonnets. He counted them and there were nine. Some had heavy couplings at the rear for pulling trailers; some a line of Cyrillic script on their battered doors, or the imprint of unit insignia and a number. He noted the emblems of the drivers' uniforms, the colour of their shoulder-boards; they came, he realized, from a variety of units.

Walking back to the main street he pushed his way into a café and ordered a drink. Half a dozen soldiers sat disconsolately at a table sharing three bottles of beer. Leiser grinned at them; it was like the encouragement of a tired whore. He lifted his fist in a Soviet salute and they watched him as if he were mad. He left his drink and made his way back to the square; a group of children had gathered round the trucks and the drivers kept telling them to go away.

He made a tour of the town, went into a dozen cafés, but no one would talk to him because he was a stranger. Everywhere the soldiers sat or stood in groups, aggrieved and bewildered, as if they had been roused to no purpose.

He ate some sausage and drank a Steinhäger, walked to the station to see if anything was going on. The same man was there, watching him, this time without suspicion, from behind his little window; and somehow Leiser knew, though it made no difference, that the man had told the police.

Returning from the station, he passed a cinema. A group of girls had gathered round the photographs and he stood with them pretending to look. Then the noise came, a metallic, irregular drone, filling the street with the piping, rattling of engines, metal and war. He drew back into the cover of the foyer, saw the girls turn and the ticket-seller stand up in her box. An old man crossed himself; he had lost one eye, and wore his hat at an angle. The tanks rolled through the town; they carried troops with rifles. The gun barrels were too long, marked white with snow. He watched them pass, then made his way across the square, quickly.

She smiled as he came in; he was out of breath.

'What are they doing?' she asked. She caught sight of his face. 'You're afraid,' she whispered, but he shook his head. 'You're afraid,' she repeated.

'I killed the boy,' he said.

He went to the basin, examined his face with the great care of a man under sentence. She followed him, clasped him round the chest, pressing herself against his back. He turned and seized her, wild, held her without skill, forced her across the room. She fought him with the rage of a daughter, calling some name, hating someone, cursing him, taking him, the world burning and only they alive; they were weeping, laughing together, falling, clumsy lovers clumsily triumphant, recognizing nothing but each himself, each for that moment completing lives half-lived, and for that moment the whole damned dark forgotten.

Johnson leant out of the window and gently drew on the aerial to make sure it was still fast, then began looking over his receiver like a racing driver before the start, needlessly touching terminals and adjusting dials. Leclerc watched him admiringly.

'Johnson, that was nobly done last time. Nobly done. We owe you a vote of thanks.' Leclerc's face was shiny, as if he had only recently shaved. He looked oddly fragile in the pale light. 'I propose to hear one more schedule and get back to London.' He laughed. 'We've work to do, you know. This isn't the season for continental holidays.'

Johnson might not have heard. He held up his hand. 'Thirty minutes,' he said. 'I shall be asking you for a little hush soon, gentlemen.' He was like a conjurer at a children's party. 'Fred's a devil for punctuality,' he observed loudly.

Leclerc addressed himself to Avery. 'You're one of those lucky people, John, who have seen action in peacetime.' He seemed anxious to talk.

'Yes. I'm very grateful.'

'You don't have to be. You've done a good job, and we recognize that. There's no question of *gratitude*. You've achieved something very rare in our work; I wonder if you know what it is?'

Avery said he did not.

'You've induced an agent to *like* you. In the ordinary way – Adrian will bear me out – the relationship between an agent and his controllers is clouded with suspicion. He resents them, that's the first thing, for not doing the job themselves. He suspects them of ulterior motives, ineptitude, duplicity. But we're not the Circus, John: that's not the way we do things.'

Avery nodded. 'No, quite.'

'You've done something else, you and Adrian. I would like to feel that if a similar need arose in the future we could use the same technique, the same facilities, the same *expertise* – that means the Avery–Haldane combination. What I'm trying to say is' – Leclerc raised one hand and with his forefinger and thumb lightly touched the bridge of his nose in an unusual gesture of English diffidence – 'the experience you've made is to our mutual advantage. Thank you.'

Haldane moved to the stove and began warming his hands, rubbing them gently as if he were separating wheat.

'That Budapest thing,' Leclerc continued, raising his voice, partly in enthusiasm and partly perhaps to dispel the atmosphere of intimacy which suddenly threatened them, 'it's a complete reorganization. Nothing less. They're moving their armour to the border, d'you see. The Ministry is talking about forward strategy. They're really most interested.'

Avery said, 'More interested than in the Mayfly area?'

'No, no,' Leclerc protested lightly. 'It's all part of the same complex – they think very big over there, you know – a move here and a move there – it all has to be pieced together.'

'Of course,' Avery said gently. 'We can't see it ourselves, can we? We can't see the whole picture.' He was trying to make it better for Leclerc. 'We haven't the perspective.'

'When we get back to London,' Leclerc proposed, 'you must come and dine with me, John: you and your wife; both come. I've been meaning to suggest it for some time. We'll go to my club. They do a rather good dinner in the Ladies' Room; your wife would enjoy it.'

'You mentioned it. I asked Sarah. We'd love to. My mother-in-law's with us just now. She could baby-sit.'

'How nice. Don't forget.'

'We're looking forward to it.'

'Am I not invited?' Haldane asked coyly.

'Why, of course, Adrian. Then we shall be four. Excellent.' His voice changed. 'Incidentally, the landlords have complained about the house in Oxford. They say we left it in a poor state.'

'Poor state?' Haldane echoed angrily.

'It appears we have been overloading the electrical circuit. Parts of it are quite burnt out. I told Woodford to cope with it.'

'We should have our own place,' said Avery. 'Then we wouldn't have to worry.'

'I agree. I spoke to the Minister about it. A training centre is what we need. He was enthusiastic. He's keen on this kind of thing, now, you know. They have a new phrase for it over there. They are speaking of ICO's. Immediate Clarification Operations.

He suggests we find a place and take it for six months. He proposes to speak to the Treasury about a lease.'

'That's terrific,' Avery said.

'It could be very useful. We must be sure not to abuse our trust.'

'Of course.'

There was a draught, followed by the sound of someone cautiously ascending the stairs. A figure appeared in the attic doorway. He wore an expensive overcoat of brown tweed, a little too long in the sleeve. It was Smiley.

Chapter 22

Smiley peered round the room, at Johnson, now in earphones, busy with the controls of his set, at Avery staring over Haldane's shoulder at the signal plan, at Leclerc, who stood like a soldier, who alone had noticed him, whose face, though turned to him, was empty and far away.

'What do you want here?' Leclerc said at last. 'What do you want with me?'

'I'm sorry. I was sent.'

'So were we all.' Haldane said, not moving.

A note of warning entered Leclerc's voice. 'This is my operation, Smiley. We've no room for your people here.'

There was nothing in Smiley's face but compassion, nothing in his voice but that dreadful patience with which we speak to the insane.

'It wasn't Control who sent me,' he said. 'It was the Ministry. They asked for me, you see, and Control let me go. The Ministry laid on a plane.'

'Why?' Haldane inquired. He seemed almost amused.

One by one they stirred, waking from a single dream. Johnson laid his earphones carefully on the table.

'Well?' Leclerc asked. 'Why did they send you?'

'They called me round last night.' He managed to indicate that he was as bewildered as they. 'I had to admire the operation, the way you'd conducted it; you and Haldane. All done from nothing. They showed me the files. Scrupulously kept . . . Library Copy, Operational Copy, sealed minutes: just like in the war. I congratulate you . . . I really do.'

'They showed you the files? *Our* files?' Leclerc repeated. 'That's a breach of security: interconsciousness between Departments. You've committed an offence, Smiley. They must be mad! Adrian, do you hear what Smiley has told me?'

Smiley said, 'Is there a schedule tonight, Johnson?'

'Yes, sir. Twenty-one hundred.'

'I was surprised, Adrian, that you felt the indicators were strong enough for such a *big* operation.'

'Haldane was not responsible,' Leclerc said crisply. 'The decision was a collective one; ourselves on the one side, the Ministry on the other.' His voice changed key. 'When the schedule is finished I shall want to know, Smiley, I have a right to know, how you came to see those files.' It was his committee voice, powerful and fluent; for the first time it had the ring of dignity.

Smiley moved towards the centre of the room. 'Something's happened; something you couldn't know about. Leiser killed a man on the border. Killed him with a knife as he went over, two miles from here, at the crossing point.'

Haldane said, 'That's absurd. It needn't be Leiser. It could have been a refugee coming west. It could have been anyone.'

'They found tracks leading east. Traces of blood in the hut by the lake. It's in all the East German papers. They've been putting it over the wireless since midday yesterday . . .'

Leclerc cried, 'I don't believe it. I don't believe he did it. It's some trick of Control's.'

'No,' Smiley replied gently. 'You've got to believe me. It's true.'

'They killed Taylor,' Leclerc said. 'Have you forgotten that?'

'No, of course not. But we shall never know, shall we? How he died, I mean . . . whether he was murdered . . .' Hurriedly he continued, 'Your Ministry informed the Foreign Office yesterday afternoon. The Germans are bound to catch him, you see; we have to assume that. His transmissions are slow . . . very slow. Every policeman, every soldier is after him. They want him alive. We think they're going to stage a show trial, extract a public confession, display the equipment. It could be very embarrassing. You don't have to be a politician to sympathize with the Minister. So there's the question of what to do.'

Leclerc said, 'Johnson, keep an eye on the clock.' Johnson put his earphones on again, but without conviction.

Smiley appeared to want someone else to speak, but no one did, so he repeated ponderously, 'It's a question of what to do. As I say, we're not politicians, but one can see the dangers. A party of Englishmen in a farmhouse two miles from where the body was found, posing as academics, stores from the Naafi and a house full of radio equipment. You see what I mean? Making your transmissions,' he went on, 'on a single frequency . . . the frequency

Leiser receives on . . . There could be a very big scandal indeed. One can imagine even the West Germans getting awfully angry.'

Haldane spoke first again: 'What are you trying to say?'

'There's a military plane waiting at Hamburg. You fly in two hours; all of you. A truck will collect the equipment. You're to leave nothing behind, not even a pin. Those are my instructions.'

Leclerc said, 'What about the target? Have they forgotten why we're here? They're asking a lot, you know, Smiley: a great lot.'

'Yes, the target,' Smiley conceded. 'We'll have a conference in London. Perhaps we could do a joint operation.'

'It's a military target. I shall want my Ministry represented. No monolith; it's a policy decision, you know.'

'Of course. And it'll be your show.'

'I suggest the product go out under our joint title: my Ministry could retain autonomy in the matter of distribution. I imagine that would meet their more obvious objections. How about your people?'

'Yes, I think Control would accept that.'

Leclerc said casually, everyone watching, 'And the schedule? Who takes care of that? We've an agent in the field, you know.' It was only a small point.

'He'll have to manage by himself.'

'The war rules.' Leclerc spoke proudly. 'We play the war rules. He knew that. He was well trained.' He seemed reconciled; the thing was dismissed.

Avery spoke for the first time. 'You can't leave him out there alone.' His voice was flat.

Leclerc intervened: 'You know Avery, my aide?' This time no one came to his rescue. Smiley, ignoring him, observed, 'The man's probably been caught already. It's only a matter of hours.'

'You're leaving him there to die!' Avery was gathering courage.

'We're disowning him. It's never a pretty process. He's as good as caught already, don't you see?'

'You can't do it,' he shouted. 'You can't just leave him there for some squalid diplomatic reason!'

Now Haldane swung round on Avery, furious. 'You of all people should not complain! You wanted a faith, didn't you? You wanted an eleventh Commandment that would match your rare soul!' He indicated Smiley and Leclerc. 'Well, here you have it: here is the law you were looking for. Congratulate yourself; you found it. We sent him because we needed to; we abandon him because we must. That is the discipline you admired.' He turned to Smiley. 'You too: I find you contemptible. You shoot us, then

- 216 -

preach to the dying. Go away. We're technicians, not poets. Go away!'

Smiley said, 'Yes. You're a very good technician, Adrian. There's no pain in you any more. You've made technique a way of life . . . like a whore . . . technique replacing love.' He hesitated. 'Little flags . . . the old war piping in the new. There was all that, wasn't there? And then the man . . . he must have been heady wine. Comfort yourself, Adrian, you weren't fit.'

He straightened his back, making a statement. 'A British-naturalized Pole with a criminal record escapes across the border to East Germany. There is no extradition treaty. The Germans will say he is a spy and produce the equipment; we shall say they planted it and point out that it's twenty-five years old. I understand he put out a cover story that he was attending a course in Coventry. That is easily disproved: there is no such course. The conclusion is that he proposed to flee the country; and we shall imply that he owed money. He was keeping some young girl, you know; she worked in a bank. That ties in quite nicely. I mean with the criminal record, since we have to make one up . . .' He nodded to himself. 'As I say, it's not an attractive process. By then we shall all be in London.'

'And he'll be transmitting,' Avery said, 'and no one will listen.'

'To the contrary,' Smiley retorted bitterly. 'They'll be listening.'

Haldane asked: 'Control too, no doubt. Isn't that right?'

'Stop!' Avery shouted suddenly. 'Stop, for God's sake! If anything matters, if anything is real, we've got to hear him now! For the sake of . . .'

'Well?' Haldane inquired with a sneer.

'Love. Yes, love! Not yours, Haldane, mine. Smiley's right! You made me do it for you, made me love him! It wasn't in you any more! I brought him to you, I kept him in your house, made him dance to the music of your bloody war! I piped for him, but there's no breath in me now. He's Peter Pan's last victim, Haldane, the last one, the last love; the last music gone.'

Haldane was looking at Smiley: 'My congratulations to Control,' he said. 'Thank him, will you? Thank him for the help, the *technical* help, Smiley; for the encouragement, thank him for the rope. For the kind words too: for lending you to bring the flowers. So nicely done.'

But Leclerc seemed impressed by the neatness of it.

'Let's not be hard on Smiley, Adrian. He's only doing his job. We must all get back to London. There's the Fielden report . . .

I'd like to show you that, Smiley. Troop dispositions in Hungary: something new.'

'And I'd like to see it,' Smiley replied politely.

'He's right, you know, Avery,' Leclerc repeated. His voice was quite eager. 'Be a soldier. Fortunes of war; keep to the rules! We play the war rules in this game. Smiley, I owe you an apology. And Control too, I fear. I had thought the old rivalry was awake. I'm wrong.' He inclined his head. 'You must dine with me in London. My club is not your mark I know, but it's quiet there; a good set. Very good. Haldane must come. Adrian, I invite you!'

Avery had buried his face in his hands.

'There's something else I want to discuss with you, Adrian – Smiley, you won't mind this I'm sure, you're practically one of the family – the question of Registry. The system of library files is really out of date. Bruce was on to me about it just before I left. Poor Miss Courtney can hardly keep pace. I fear the answer is more copies . . . top copy to the case officer, carbons for information. There's a new machine on the market, cheap photostats, threepence halfpenny a copy, that seems quite reasonable in these dog days . . . I must speak to the people about it . . . the Ministry . . . they know a good thing when they see one. Perhaps—' he broke off. 'Johnson, I could wish you made less noise, we're still operational, you know.' He spoke like a man intent upon appearances, conscious of tradition.

Johnson had gone to the window. Leaning on the sill he reached outside and with his customary precision began winding in the aerial. He held a spool in his left hand like a bobbin. As he gathered in the wire he gently turned it as an old woman spins her thread. Avery was sobbing like a child. No one heeded him.

Chapter 23

The green van moved slowly down the road, crossed the Station Square where the empty fountain stood. On its roof the small loop aerial turned this way and that like a hand feeling for the wind. Behind it, well back, were two trucks. The snow was settling at last. They drove on sidelights, twenty yards apart, following each other's tyre marks.

The Captain sat in the back of the van with a microphone for speaking to the driver, and beside him the sergeant, lost in private memories. The corporal crouched at his receiver, his hand constantly turning the dial as he watched the line tremble in the small screen.

'The transmission's stopped,' he said suddenly.

'How many groups have you recorded?' the sergeant asked.

'A dozen. The call sign over and over again, then part of a message. I don't think he's getting any reply.'

'Five letters or four?'

'Still four.'

'Did he sign off?'

'No.'

'What frequency was he using?'

'Three six five zero.'

'Keep scanning across it. Two hundred either side.'

'There's nothing there.'

'Keep searching,' he said sharply. 'Right across the band. He's changed the crystal. He'll take a few minutes to tune up.'

The operator began spinning the large dial, slowly, watching the eye of green light in the centre of the set which opened and closed as he crossed one station after another. 'Here he is. Three eight seven zero. Different call sign but the same handwriting. Quicker than yesterday; better.'

The tape recorder wound monotonously at his elbow. 'He's working on alternating crystals,' the sergeant said. 'Like they did in the war. It's the same trick.' He was embarrassed, an elderly man confronted with his past.

The corporal slowly raised his head. 'This is it,' he said. 'Zero. We're right on top of him.'

Quietly the two men dismounted from the van. 'Wait here,' the sergeant told the corporal. 'Keep listening. If the signal breaks, even for a moment, tell the driver to flash the headlights, do you understand?'

'I'll tell him.' The corporal looked frightened.

'If it stops altogether, keep searching and let me know.'

'Pay attention,' the Captain warned as he dismounted. The sergeant was waiting impatiently; behind him, a tall building standing on waste land.

In the distance, half hidden in the falling snow, lay row after row of small houses. No sound came.

'What do they call this place?' the Captain asked.

'A block of flats; workers' flats. They haven't named it yet.'

'No, beyond.'

'Nothing. Follow me,' the sergeant said.

Pale lights shone in almost every window; six floors. Stone steps, thick with leaves, led to the cellar. The sergeant went first, shining his torch ahead of them on to the shoddy walls. The Captain nearly fell. The first room was large and airless, half of brick and half unrendered plaster. At the far end were two steel doors. On the ceiling a single bulb burned behind a wire cage. The sergeant's torch was still on; he shone it needlessly into the corners.

'What are you looking for?' the Captain asked.

The steel doors were locked.

'Find the janitor,' the sergeant ordered. 'Quickly.'

The Captain ran up the stairs and returned with an old man, unshaven, gently grumbling; he held a bunch of long keys on a chain. Some were rusty.

'The switches,' said the sergeant. 'For the building. Where are they?'

The old man sorted through the keys. He pushed one into the lock and it would not fit, he tried another and a third.

'Quick, you fool,' the Captain shouted.

'Don't fuss him,' said the sergeant.

The door opened. They pushed into the corridor, their torches playing over the whitewash. The janitor was holding up a key, grinning. 'Always the last one,' he said. The sergeant found what he was looking for, hidden on the wall behind the door; a box with a glass front. The Captain put his hand to the main lever, had half pulled it when the other struck him roughly away.

'No! Go to the top of the stairs; tell me when the driver flashes his headlights.'

'Who's in charge here?' the Captain complained.

'Do as I ask.' He had opened the box and was tugging gently at the first fuse, blinking through his gold-rimmed spectacles; a benign man.

With diligent, surgical fingers the sergeant drew out the fuse, cautiously, as if he were expecting an electric shock, then immediately replaced it, his eyes turning towards the figure at the top of the steps; then a second and still the Captain said nothing. Outside the motionless soldiers watched the windows of the block, saw how floor by floor the lights went out, then quickly on again. The sergeant tried another and a fourth and this time he heard an excited cry from above him: 'The headlights! The headlights have gone out.'

'Quite! Go and ask the driver which floor. But *quietly*.'

'They'll never hear us in this wind,' the Captain said irritably, and a moment later: 'The driver says third floor. The third floor light went out and the transmission stopped at the same time. It's started again now.'

'Put the men round the building,' the sergeant said. 'And pick five men to come with us. He's on the third floor.'

Softly, like animals, the Vopos dismounted from the two trucks, their carbines held loosely in their hands, advancing in a ragged line, ploughing the thin snow, turning it to nothing; some to the foot of the building, some standing off, staring at the windows. A few wore helmets, and their square silhouette was redolent of the war. From here and there came a click as the first bullet was sprung gently into the breech; the sound rose to a faint hail and died away.

Leiser unhooked the aerial and wound it back on the reel, screwed the Morse key into the lid, replaced the earphones in the spares box and folded the silk cloth into the handle of the razor.

'Twenty years,' he protested, holding up the razor, 'and they still haven't found a better place.'

'Why do you do it?'

She was sitting contentedly on the bed in her nightdress, wrapped in the mackintosh as if it gave her company.

'Who do you talk to?' she asked again.

'No one. No one heard.'

'Why do you do it, then?'

He had to say something, so he said, 'For peace.'

He put on his jacket, went to the window and peered outside. Snow lay on the houses. The wind blew angrily across them. He glanced into the courtyard below, where the silhouettes were waiting.

'Whose peace?' she asked.

'The light went out, didn't it, while I was working the set?'

'Did it?'

'A short break, a second or two, like a power cut?'

'Yes.'

'Put it out again now.' He was very still. 'Put the light out.'

'Why?'

'I like to look at the snow.'

She put the light out and he drew the threadbare curtains. Outside the snow reflected a pale glow into the sky. They were in half darkness.

'You said we'd love now,' she complained.

'Listen; what's your name?'

He heard the rustle of raincoat.

'What is it?' His voice was rough.

'Anna.'

'Listen, Anna.' He went to the bed. 'I want to marry you,' he said. 'When I met you, in that inn, when I saw you sitting there, listening to the records, I fell in love with you, do you understand? I'm an engineer from Magdeburg, that's what I said. Are you listening?'

He seized her arms and shook her. His voice was urgent.

'Take me away,' she said.

'That's right! I said I'd make love to you, take you away to all the places you dreamed of, do you understand?' He pointed to the posters on the wall. 'To islands, sunny places—'

'Why?' she whispered.

'I brought you back here. You thought it was to make love, but I drew this knife and threatened you. I said if you made a sound, I'd kill you with the knife, like I – I told you I'd killed the boy and I'd kill you.'

'Why?'

'I had to use the wireless. I needed a house, see? Somewhere to work the wireless. I'd nowhere to go. So I picked you up and used you. Listen: if they ask you, that's what you must say.'

She laughed. She was afraid. She lay back uncertainly on her bed, inviting him to take her, as if that were what he wanted.

'If they ask, remember what I said.'

'Make me happy. I love you.'

She put out her arms and pulled his head towards her. Her lips were cold and damp, too thin against her sharp teeth. He drew away but she still held him. He strained his ears for any sound above the wind, but there was none.

'Let's talk a bit,' he said. 'Are you lonely, Anna? Who've you got?'

'What do you mean?'

'Parents, boy friend. Anyone.'

She shook her head in the darkness. 'Just you.'

'Listen; here, let's button your coat up. I like to talk first. I'll tell you about London. You want to hear about London, I'll bet. I went for a walk, once, it was raining and there was this man by the river, drawing on the pavement in the rain. Fancy that! Drawing with chalk in the rain, and the rain just washing it away.'

'Come now. Come.'

'Do you know what he was drawing? Just dogs, cottages and that. And the people, Anna – listen to this! – standing in the rain, watching him.'

'I want you. Hold me. I'm frightened.'

'Listen! D'you know why I went for a walk: they wanted me to make love to a girl. They sent me to London and I went for this walk instead.'

He could make her out as she watched him, judging him according to some instinct he did not understand.

'Are you alone too?'

'Yes.'

'Why did you come?'

'They're crazy people, the English! That old fellow by the river: they think the Thames is the biggest river in the world, you know that? And it's nothing! Just a little brown stream, you could nearly jump across it some places!'

'What's that noise?' she said suddenly. 'I know that noise! It was a gun; the cocking of a gun!'

He held her tightly to stop her trembling.

'It was just a door,' he said, 'the latch of a door. This place is made of paper. How could you hear anything in such a wind?'

There was a footfall in the corridor. She struck at him in terror, the raincoat swinging round her. As they came in he was standing away from her, the knife at her throat, his thumb uppermost, the blade parallel to the ground. His back was very straight and his small face was turned to her, empty, held by some private discipline, a man once more intent upon appearances, conscious of tradition.

The farmhouse lay in darkness, blind and not hearing, motionless against the swaying larches and the running sky.

They had left a shutter open and it banged slowly without rhythm, according to the strength of the storm. Snow gathered like ash and was dispersed. They had gone, leaving nothing behind but tyre tracks in the hardening mud, a twist of wire, and the sleepless tapping of the north wind.